Blue Water
White Sand

Blue Water White Sand

By

Joy Hewett

Silk Hope Press
Pittsboro, NC 27312

Cover design by Shelia Rudesill
Format by Bud Rudesill

Library of Congress
Publisher's Cataloging-in-Publication data
Names: Hewett, Joy, author.
Title: Blue water white sand / by Joy Hewett.
Description: Pittsboro, NC: Silk Hope Press, 2017.
Identifiers: ISBN 978-0-692-85155-5
Subjects: LCSH Buried treasure--Fiction. | Family--Fiction. |
Friendship--Fiction. | Middle-aged women--Fiction. | Interpersonal
relations--Fiction. | Spirituality--Fiction. | Key West (Fla.)--Fiction. | Fort
Fisher (N.C.)--History--Civil War, 1861-1865—Fiction. | BISAC FICTION /
Contemporary Women. | FAMILY & RELATIONSHIPS / Friendship.
Classification: LCC PS3608.E94 B58 2017 | DDC 813.6--dc23

To my mother, Kathleen P. Hewett, whose love, courage, and creativity were always both inspiring and reassuring.

Chapter 1

When Sandy Perkins picked up the phone that June morning, the soft Southern voice of her long-time friend greeted her with news that took her by surprise. Glad as she was to hear her friend's voice, warm and sweet as molasses, Debra Bishop's message disturbed Sandy. She was even more surprised by the next phone call from North Carolina an hour later. Maybe that wasn't fair to say. The first message shocked her, the second puzzled her. Still, the tranquility of her quiet morning with her first cup of coffee shattered into fragments of broken thoughts and shards of memories, a patchwork of gold, jade, multicolored images scattered across her mind.

So Dave Burns was dead. Someone probably killed the jerk. Absorbing the news from Debra's recent phone call about the death of her friend's ex-husband, Sandy sipped her hot black coffee in the early morning light and stared out beyond the bougainvillea surrounding her lanai. Fuchsia blossoms, like little paper lanterns dangling from the latticework of green leaves, framed her view of Diamond Head beyond the fence and trees. Cardinals chirped and zebra doves cooed around her feeder at the back of the yard. Her thoughts were not on the beauty around her but on the message from Debra's daughter, now a thirty-year-old with children of her own, that had come next. Melody said they needed her in Key West for the memorial service, for a man Sandy hadn't seen in twenty-five years. Strange. After offering condolences, Sandy had said let her think about it, a stalling tactic without commitment, but now she found herself actually considering joining them. She was a self-employed cartographer and artist; she couldn't just drop everything at a moment's notice, but was there time now between projects with a little wiggle room?

That first phone call, from Debra, to tell her news of Dave Burns' sudden death, had taken her back—what, twenty-nine years? How could it be that long ago? The two women had spoken briefly of those early days of their friendship, when Dave had played a part in their lives. Then Debra had provided the few details she had about his death before she hung up. Sandy had not asked how her friend felt; she knew. She heard it in her voice. And she also knew Debra would not want to talk about that mother lode of mixed emotions.

That unexpected phone call carried Sandy back to Roatilla, a Caribbean island off the coast of Honduras, and the treasure hunting outfit she had joined as a young woman. After her first experiences with archeology as a college student had ended in 1970, along with a love affair, she had wanted to see the world, and archeology provided an interesting way to do it. Back then, expedition leader Dave Burns had given her an opportunity to catalogue finds, draw whatever lay on the bottom of the ocean floor, and the opportunity of a lifetime to dive in those clear turquoise waters of the Caribbean.

When she had first met with the mastermind of the treasure hunting operation in Florida, she thought her experience with archeology would be valued. Now at fifty-two, she knew her biggest asset at the time, though, had probably been simply that she was an eager young woman with scuba diving skills who wanted to join the expedition, not her art or archeology background. Being an enthusiastic, relatively attractive twenty-three-year-old had not hurt. It could open doors back then that she did not even realize might otherwise be closed. Sandy remembered how glad she had been to leave Florida and join the diving expedition where she had lived for six months. She had met Dave's young wife all those years ago living on the tiny bay island of the expedition's headquarters.

Sandy took another sip of coffee and listened to slack key guitar music on her stereo. She ran a hand through her short dark hair and watched doves pecking the ground below the whirr of red wings around the feeder. Memories of Roatilla and Dave's schemes that had resulted in the mutiny of his crew on the mainland and thoughts of his abuse of his wife Debra flooded her mind.

The phone rang again. Debra, saying she knew Melody had called Sandy, urged her to meet them in Key West for the memorial service. "I'll go if you'll go," Debra said. Sandy wondered aloud about why they needed to go. And then Debra sounded sad, but firm, when she insisted Sandy must join them for the memorial service, something about the will being read and Sandy having to be there, too.

Why? She had been only a year out of college when she had flown over to the island from La Ceiba with one of Dave's operation leaders, Stan, and his wife, Carrie. Decades ago. Since the mid-70s, she hadn't had anything to do with that big scheming organizer of those dreams for sale that so many men had bought into by the time she left Roatilla in 1971. Why was she being dragged into Dave's final service now in 2000? She had to admit she was curious.

What had happened to that jade figurine she had found among the coral encrusted clusters she had discovered, the gold doubloons she had thought she'd sighted in the shallow waters near the inlet that time she and Dave were down on the dive site together? They had disappeared before she could catalogue them. Dave had insisted she was trying to cause trouble, making up that glint of gold to try to create unnecessary drama. More distraction for the men already growing increasingly disgruntled with life on the island and the lack of any of the treasure they had been promised when they invested in the expedition.

###

The image of the jade goddess in the white sand that had been stirred by her fins first appeared when she pulled the green object from worm eaten wood forty feet below the surface of the dive site. At that first feel of the jade and its smooth curves in her fingers, a strong electrifying thrill ran through her. The jade, with clumps of wood and rusted metal, gold glints in its crevices, had been outside the grid she was drawing near a large brain coral beyond sea fans waving with the current. Only Dave and she had been left down there at the end of the team's dive. She had held on to the jade figure as he swam over, leaving the dredge to investigate. While silver crescents of air from their tanks rose around them, she caught a glimpse through her mask of his bulky body and his vigorous pointing for her to go up. So she did. Through the swirl of sand as she rose from the ocean floor, she had seen him stuffing the clumps into a dive bag.

###

Making a decision to go to Key West interrupted Sandy's memories of her treasure hunting days and the moment she had found that jade. Since she worked from home, she could take some time off and she needed a vacation. She hadn't seen her friends for several years; now, in the year 2000, after steady progress establishing her business throughout the '90s, she had the flexibility to leave for a couple of weeks. She had her contracts for doing art for the state firmly in place. She had just finished her latest project for state tourism brochures; even the proofs for the Sandwich Islands drawings had been approved and these were off to the printer, her part in the project complete. Her bookkeeper was due to update her books that afternoon. She had no other commitments for the week except to deliver the painting she was finishing for the Waikiki gallery that sold her work

Once she decided to go, the need to act, to call the airport in Honolulu and to make other arrangements, set her in action and took her away from memories and speculation. Sandy made her reservations, packed, and as an afterthought added her old Guatemalan shawl to her suitcase, then entered the studio where her unframed paintings were stacked in a corner. Her easel partially blocked the sliding glass doors to her lanai. Standing in front of her latest painting, still sitting on the easel, she admired the way the cool blue tints she had added to the shadows made the light on creamy plumeria blossoms pop in contrast. She knew the gallery could sell this painting quickly. She had gone commercial, painting for tourists, something she thought she would never do. But it supplemented her income, and she liked the cushion of stability. Where had the risk-taking young woman she once had been gone?

The conversations with Debra had unsettled her. She had more questions than answers. Even their conversation that afternoon, after she could tell Debra what flight she would be on, left her wondering. Debra alluded to the Pandora's box she might be opening, the only reference to what must be going through her friend's mind about their journey. Sandy could see a small crack in her own composure opening up with the questions the news had stirred, a fissure in the composition of her carefully crafted life.

But still, it was a good time to go. Her clothes for the two weeks in Key West were packed. The woman who rented the studio apartment beside the garage would water her orchids and other house plants. She didn't have to start working on another project right away, so she was free.

By the time Sandy went to bed, she and Debra had exchanged more phone calls that day than when they had shared the new millennium's arrival six months before. Then they had watched the historic event on TV together from their different time zones, with Peter Jennings officiating their New Year's celebration around the world. Still, telephone calls weren't the same as in person visits.

Before leaving her house the next day, Sandy checked to make sure she hadn't forgotten anything, and surveyed her art studio-living room and the lanai beyond one last time. She had her finger on the pulse of her life, her business, but would everything still be moving smoothly when she returned? She knew too well how life could change in a moment. She dismissed the thought, just that temporary discomfort of departure, and closed the door. The kiss of the trade winds in these islands she called home, the spirit of Pele, the volcano goddess who infused the beauty of the islands with her fire, these would remain. These would be here when she returned and soon she would see old friends. She would focus on that. Leaving behind the mundane workaday world that kept her busy and her mind occupied would be a much-needed break.

Two rainbows in the afternoon sky cheered her as she drove through traffic. Then Moe Keale's song on the car radio reached right into her heartstrings, his soothing Hawaiian voice calming her. She reached the Honolulu Airport in good time to catch her mainland flight. Leaving behind the fragrance of plumeria wafting on the trade winds, she boarded her plane wondering about what would unfold when she reached her destination. Once the plane lifted off into the sky, she watched its shadow cross the multi-colored waters of Waikiki. The silhouette of Diamond Head disappearing, she studied the turquoise, teals and cobalt blues of the Pacific below her and enjoyed the clouds with their myriad billowing shapes.

Finally, Sandy turned her attention to the passengers leaving Oahu along with her. The young woman with brown and blonde streaked hair sitting beside her was crying. She wiped her eyes and caught Sandy's eye. Sandy rummaged through her travel bag and offered her a Kleenex.

"My fiancé…we just got engaged," she offered. "I've been out here with him seven weeks and it's so hard to leave him."

"How long before you see him again?" Sandy asked, and then regretted asking. The girl was tearing up again. She tried to find a way to distract her. "When's the wedding?"

"We haven't set the date. I won't see him again until Christmas," the young woman answered.

"Where is he located?"

"He's out at Schofield."

"Did you get to the North Shore much?"

They talked briefly about the big waves, the surfers that flocked there in winter, but nothing stopped the tears, not the snacks the flight attendant provided nor the beverages she offered.

"Where do you live?" the girl finally asked.

Sandy told her about living near Waikiki, about renting a house she could never afford to buy. She could walk down to Kapi'olani Park and swim at Sans Souci, a sweet little beach not far from the towering image of the iconic Diamond Head, Le'ahi to those who knew and loved her. Determined to take the girl's mind off her sorrows, Sandy talked on about her art and cartography. She explained how she'd parlayed a drawing job for the Bishop Museum, where she had worked when she first arrived in the islands, into a small business. The girl was still looking mighty sad. Sandy couldn't think of anything comforting to say. She tried talking about her own early days on archeology digs, in both England and Crete, where she had met her first big love. That affair had been during her first summer in archeology before her last year in college. She mentioned briefly her second dig at Winchester where she had realized scraping the ground with a trowel, a quarter of an inch at a time, was not for her. It was her offer to draw the finds at the site as they uncovered a medieval village that had provided a new avenue for her talents. She did not normally share any of her life story with strangers. All these details, and still the young girl in the seat beside her seemed distraught.

Sandy tried humor. "You know the song, 'Winchester Cathedral, you're bringing me down'," she crooned off key and got a smile, but still the tears. The girl didn't know the song, but she seemed to find Sandy's singing amusing. The girl was still sniffling an hour into their flight.

Ah, young love. When had she last felt sad about leaving a man? She had to think. She had long since decided that if a man made you cry, he wasn't worth it. That would rule out most men she could care enough about to work up some tears. It hadn't stopped her from trying a few too many times, giving the few she cared enough about one too many chances, until she came upon that brilliant deduction. Or ran out of men she would want to cry about. There was one who'd broken her heart and led her to travel five thousand miles to put some distance from the strings that tied her heart to him. But that was more than fifteen years past. And there had also been Paul, the young student she backpacked with in Europe, the boy she had loved so much until he left her for Mexico. With that broken heart, she'd stayed in bed and moped about in her mother's house for weeks until her mother made her take scuba diving to get her out of the house and meet some people. There were only three men that had left her longing for more and feeling lost without them. Had she walked away from too many good men? Half a dozen in Hawaii alone she had left behind. Had she been too unwilling to settle for less than total adoration she felt was true love? She ran back over some of her affairs from the decades behind her. Same story. The red-eye special gave way too much time for rumination.

What ever happened to Bill? She was heading east, to memories of her youth on an island off Honduras where her sense of adventure had landed her among treasure hunters and men either seeking a gamble on a fortune or running from a life they wanted to leave behind. Bill had been in the latter group, a thirty-three year old leaving a dismal divorce and three children behind. Their romance had lasted until the chain of events that led to the expedition's ending on the island and everyone going their separate ways. Bill had even stayed with her that Christmas, broke and looking for work, before he settled in St. Pete and she broke it off.

She still remembered their sail around the island of Roatilla to a cove on the east side where they had anchored; she recalled how parrots squawked and rustled in the jungle vegetation, settling in with the sunset. Memories of that sail filled her mind as though she were there once more.

###

The boat gently rocked as she and Bill clung to the anchor rope in the water. Bill grinned at her, his black hair dripping and his brown eyes merry, lashes beaded with salt water. He slipped a hand around her waist. They buoyantly floated together and apart, his firm hold bringing her towards him; he kissed her, the salty taste of seawater and the tender touch of his lips before the next undulating wave pulled them apart again.

She let go of the line and took the few strokes to the ladder in back of the boat. She felt her slender body moving up the rungs, the pull of her weight on her arms as she lifted herself to the top and sprawled over the edge of the boat when the boat rocked with a wave. No grace in that move. And Bill was right behind her, the ladder knocking against the side of the twenty-eight foot yacht. She slipped a towel around her shoulders and sat down. Bill rocked the boat, hoisting himself over with more control than she had managed. She made room for him beside her on the teak slats of the seat running along the cockpit. The sunset lit the sky above them, billowing cumulus masses of red and gold. Bill's lopsided grin lingered a few moments before he spoke.

"Red sky at night, sailor's delight. Red sky in morning, sailors take warning."

Sandy rubbed the towel through her long hair and watched rays of gold shoot above the palms from the west. The waves out at sea moved with varying light flecks beyond their calm cove.

"Another beautiful day in paradise. This is so cool. Look at all those colors on the water," she observed.

A raucous disturbance of parrots screeching had quieted down as they settled into their evening roosts. The lulling sound of ocean waves rolled on into the twilight.

"Maybe Carrie and Stan would like to go sailing next time we take the boat out," Sandy said, thinking of the couple who had brought her down to Honduras with them.

The lingering light flickered on Bill's face and he frowned. "We'll have to see; Patrick may have said I could sleep on his boat while he's gone, but I don't know how many joyrides he expected me to take. Besides, Stan's all work and no play. He wants to go back to LA, and the sooner he gets done here, the sooner he gets back."

"That's true. He can be a little grouchy, but I like Carrie a lot; she could use something to do off the island. I think she's getting a little bored."

"We'll see. Dave's coming back next week so it may be a while before we can take this baby out again."

Bill got up and balanced himself, heading to the wooden door, lifting it up, and sliding into the dark cabin. He brought back saltines and they sat enjoying a few crackers as the last light of pinks, golds, and reds faded.

###

Sandy's memories of that evening on the sailboat were interrupted by her airline neighbor passenger asking where she was heading. She had finally stopped crying Sandy realized.

"Oh, I'm catching a flight to Miami after Dallas-Fort Worth. Destination Key West. I'm headed to a memorial service."

"Oh, I'm sorry," the young woman remarked. "Was it someone in your family?"

"No. He was my friend's ex. It's been a long time since I saw him. We weren't close, but my friend needs me and I haven't seen her, or her daughter, in a few years, so it will be good to catch up."

"Well, that'll be nice, then," the young woman said.

"I hope so," Sandy said and looked out the window at clouds below in the late afternoon sky. "I certainly hope so."

Sandy changed planes in Dallas-Fort Worth and had another window seat. The plane droned on above the clouds and the earth shrank below them—houses and farmland a patchwork pattern of colors and tiny ribbons of roads.

It was easy for her to fancy that the distance covered so fast came as a result of the size of the plane relative to the tiny size of the earth below. Easy to cover an inch from her window view as it appeared below them while they in the plane seemed to stay steady in space and the same size—the clouds and earth what moved, tiny increments below. Who was to say it wasn't so? she pondered. Why did reality have to apply to a logic of physics that said she was the same size as the tiny people below in those tiny cars? Maybe she and her plane mates were the center of the universe they inhabited, not the tiny dots in a vast universe the evening stars would remind her of when the sun set behind them. The red-eye special always brought her these flights of fancy. Free from her usual focus on work, her art, her activities, she let herself speculate on things she did not have time for in her day-to-day life.

Sandy's thoughts drifted back through the memories of Roatilla, the jade goddess, the gold doubloons and that vase she had buried for a scene in the cinematographer's footage. What was a jade piece doing in the wreckage? A relic of Mayan culture or some other native tribe that had inhabited those coastal regions? Where was it now?

Both memory and reflection occupied her during the hours the plane droned on through time zones. Her thoughts drifted through the clouds of memories. Somewhere buried in her past were the answers to the questions about her own choices, she felt certain, since surely her brain still stored all the facts linked to a certain truth, if only she could get there.

Chapter 2

Debra Bishop woke from dreams as if wrapped in cotton, soft, surprisingly sweet. Her eyes opened to a wet nose and Rosy grinning at her, starting to lick her face.

"Sweet girl," she said and reached out to pet the soft fur of her golden retriever. She pulled the closest ear before the dog turned, waving her tail like a happy flag, and headed for the door. Tinkerbell, purring beside her, uncurled herself and stretched.

Rosy was back licking Debra before she could even look at her clock. Light streamed through the curtains of the east window, dappled the floor and dog with moving shadows of oak leaves. She'd been having these sweet dreams, Dave coming to her in dreams wrapped in tenderness she didn't understand. This was at least the third dream of her ex-husband in two days. She hadn't thought of Dave much in years, an occasional comment from her daughter Melody about the only time her mind strayed that way. Their marriage ended twenty-five years ago. A lot of water had passed under that bridge since. She awoke from these dreams with a feeling of sweetness towards him certainly not typical of her waking memories of him or their last encounters. She was just waking from this last dream when her dog woke her and the phone started ringing downstairs.

She grabbed her robe off the hook and pulled it on as she and Rosy took the bare oak stairs down and entered the kitchen.

"Mama, Daddy's dead," Melody was saying when she picked up.

"Oh, sweetheart… what happened?"

"They found him in the water. In his boat. I heard from Liz last night. It was too late to call you. He was floating in the boat."

"Floating?"

"The boat was floating."

"Was it a heart attack?"

"Isn't that awful? Alone in the water," Melody continued without answering her question.

"I'm sorry, honey," Debra thought to say. And she was. Even though he had not been part of her life for years, she knew her daughter had grown to love him during her teen years. And supposedly there had been a great change in him the last decade or so. He had stopped drinking.

"Liz says…"

Liz was the third wife, she knew that, and had apparently gotten a version of Dave Debra had only glimpsed in tender moments of their first year together, out in California, before he became consumed with Oceanic Expeditions.

"Mama?" Melody was trying to get her attention.

"Sorry. What, darling?"

The dog was sitting at her feet. It was a cordless phone and she didn't have to stand there in one spot looking out the kitchen window like a zombie. She opened the back door to let Rosy out. Tinkerbell strolled across the kitchen floor, her tail high in the air, and stepped out, too. Melody was saying the flight was tomorrow; the kids would be with Jeff. She realized Melody was expecting her to go down to Florida with her.

"I can't just take off in the middle of a project, and the library…. Mel, this is so weird, I have been having these dreams. Your Dad coming to me in these sweet dreams. Don't you think that's odd?"

"Mama, focus," Melody said impatiently.

Debra knew her daughter had low tolerance for her mother's scatterbrained ways. Debra took on her mother-in-charge voice. "All right, darling, you want me to go, but why?"

"Liz insists. Something about the estate. Something about his will. But most important, Mama, I want you there with me. Please don't make me do this alone. All those disgusting Carsons will be there."

Mel continued without pausing, "And Jeff has that workshop with the Mustang Association already scheduled. It's a bad time for me to leave, but at least he's got Janie, that college girl, to help with the kids."

"Oh, darling, let me see what I can do. Let me think about it. There's your grandfather and Grams to make arrangements for. I'll call you back in an hour, okay?"

Her tortoise shell cat was mewing at the door and her golden retriever wanted back in. The coffee had to be made. Melody was pretty self-sufficient and liked to be in charge. But she sounded like the little girl Debra had raised alone from the age of four. Debra had been her dearest love until she entered teendom and stopped admitting to needing a mommy to confide in.

It was a call Debra couldn't resist.

She was still dazed by the coincidence, or whatever it was, that the man she'd left in the Virgin Islands after five years of following him from pillar to post, as her own mother would say, from California to Florida to Honduras to the Virgin Islands, the man she rarely thought about had come back to visit her, of all people, on his way to purgatory or heaven or hell. He'd stopped by to say good-bye or hello. Had he come before he died? After he died? Was it her own sixth sense? These mysteries couldn't be answered, but it was spooky, no doubt about that. But why the sweetness? The very tenderness of it was what surprised her so much from those dreams. She'd never had sweet dreams of him in all the years he'd been long gone from her life. No Patsy Cline moments for her. And she wouldn't go there now.

She made coffee and put the animal bowls out. She'd been too glad to be free of him, too disgusted and angry to be anything but relieved when Sandy had first taken her and Melody in all those years ago when she had no one else to turn to, her pride not letting her call her parents, whom she'd treated so badly in her own younger days.

Thank goodness Mel had not been the wayward teen she herself had been. When she and her cousin's friend had run off for San Francisco, she with flowers in her hair and bells on her toes, so to speak, a wayward flower child on the streets of San Francisco with a long-haired draft dodger, she had caused her own parents so much anguish and worry. Melody lived in the same county here in North Carolina, at least, Debra was thinking as she poured dry food for her dog and cat and headed to the hen house to let the ladies out.

By the time she had thrown out sunflower seeds to the six hens, closed the gate to the hen yard, and come back to the kitchen, she still could not make up her mind. She knew two people at the library who could use the extra work and would take her part-time hours. If their schedules didn't work out, she could call the woman who had retired recently, ask her. Then there were half-dry pottery bowls she would have to wait until she returned to fire. That would put her in a bind getting them glazed in time for the friend of a friend who wanted them for a wedding gift. When was that wedding anyway? Then her folks. Her animals. Too many details. What a hassle. She still had a shift at the library that afternoon she would need to do, too; it was too short notice to call in.

Still, time with her daughter was a precious commodity these days, and she knew she should take what she could get when she could get it. A road trip with her daughter? Or, technically, a plane trip?—that could be a blessing or a curse. Even if she did not want to go to Florida. Was still too blown away by Dave's sudden appearance in her life again. Or his leaving. Appearing and disappearing like a soap bubble bursting. That prism glistening on its surface before the bubble burst, stinging the eyes. It had left her so...tired. Discombobulated. Disconcerted, the proper word. But Mel sounded so sad.

The fresh smell of brewed coffee, Rosy's big grin and wagging tail, Tinkerbell rubbing against her leg, she was greeted with the familiar comforts of her morning routine. Was she ready to swap out this peaceful home life for a trip to the Keys and who knows what mess that ex-husband had left behind?

Chapter 3

Above the gravity of earth, Sandy Perkins could second guess herself. Would she have declared the jade figurine if it hadn't been stolen first? Would she have catalogued it with the other finds? Had she missed out on love when it was offered, or was there a wise woman inside, her inner wisdom, that had chosen the best course for her life as an independent, self-sufficient woman? Was the trade-off worth it?

From second-guessing herself to pondering questions this trip to Key West had roused, Sandy's mind roamed on. Who had taken that jade piece stashed under her bunk before she could discuss it with Dave? What more did it say about the Spanish galleon debris field they might have uncovered? Or had that figurine been part of some other journey into open water from some other vessel? Sandy's thoughts went back to that dive where she discovered the jade goddess. In her mind's eye, she pictured those moments after she put her hand on the jade.

###

Dave had pointed up, indicating she should surface, as she looked up through sunlit water to the rocking bottom of the small motor boat anchored near the platform of the air pump dredge. Sandy held on to the jade figure and her clipboard. She kicked her fins and rose with her air bubbles towards the surface. Looking back, she had a glimpse of Dave stuffing hefty clumps into the dive bag as butterfly fish drifted by. She heard the drone of another motor in the water; and then she broke the surface, with her clipboard hiding the figurine from the two men above. She treaded water with her fins' slow moves below her and her tank bobbing against her back. She wasn't ready to let this discovery go until she'd had an opportunity to examine it, detail its features. She wasn't ready to share it with anyone. Bill's hand reached for the tank as she freed herself awkwardly. He offered to take her weigh belt and clipboard but she shook her head and held on to those in the water.

"Hand me the dive bag, first," she said.

Bill gave her a quizzical look, his brown eyes below his tanned, lined forehead focusing on her face.

"What's up? Where's Dave?"

"He's coming," Sandy said and reached for the canvas bag. She maneuvered her clipboard and underwater pen, its cord wrapped around the figurine, into the throat of the bag and handed it up. Bill grabbed her tank and hoisted the metal cylinder over the side of the boat. She was often bringing bits of coral up to decorate her spare room, so Bill wouldn't think much of her having something stuffed in the bag.

Grabbing the metal ladder, she pulled herself up from the water, glad her strong arms could hold her weight steady until her foot found a perch on the metal rung. She lifted one leg over the back of the boat and slipped aboard. Bill's attention was already turned to the boat slowing to a stop beside them. Rolf, another expedition member who had come out with them, grabbed the edge of the other boat and the small clunk of their contact was minimized. Sandy saw a semi-bald man, maybe in his early forties or late thirties, grinning at them from the side of the other boat. It was easy to stash the bag with her fins and snorkel as everyone else's attention focused on Hal Greenberg, the big investor who had been scheduled to arrive that day.

He introduced himself, even though the three already knew who he was. When Sandy spoke, he was staring at her breasts and didn't bother to divert his eyes. She felt exposed and pulled her long wet hair across her shoulder, her elbow meant to block the view. Hal cut his eyes from her bikini to Bill and asked about Dave.

Just then, in a flurry of bubbles and motion, Dave broke the surface and Bill grabbed his tank. When he climbed aboard, he did not have the bag with him. He shot a quick look at Sandy and shook his head, a brief jerk to the side so fast no one else would notice.

"You caught the Cessna this morning?—it's usually later in the day. How was your flight?" Dave directed the conversation toward Hal, who held onto their rocking boat.

"A little cash can be persuasive," Hal replied. "The pilot was glad to bring me early when I waved a fifty at him."

Dave positioned himself to balance while he unzipped his neoprene wet suit. His hairy chest and belly exposed, Sandy turned away to the lean man at her side. Dave's bulky body contrasted distinctly with the trim build of Bill, the one man she had become close to among these divers. But beneath Dave's extra layer of flesh, a compactly muscled man exuded confidence and decisive power.

"I want to go down and see the layout," Hal said.

"We're heading in for lunch," Dave said. "We've used up the air. Tanks have to be filled in the morning. We'll go out tomorrow. Let's get you set up first."

Bill had a suspicious look on his face. His bushy black mustache curved above a fading smile. His wiry physique defined itself against the cumulus clouds behind him. He balanced the tanks and put the gear together behind the driver's seat. He glanced at Sandy and she looked directly into his eyes. A message passed between them as he stood back up. He said nothing. Rolf hadn't heard the conversation when he pulled up the anchor from the front of the boat, or he would have said 'we have plenty of air' in that thick German accent of his.

Both boats headed back to the bay. The expedition pier's rickety wooden boards swayed against their hands preventing the crunch of each boat as they docked. Sandy and Rolf sprang off to grab the ropes and secure the boats to the metal cleats. Already drunk, one of the island's colorful characters, Isaiah, sat on the dock box by the outhouse, holding his machete and muttering loudly, then sputtering shouts and curses. They hauled the wet gear past him to the storage shed where the generator and air filling station were housed. Sandy carried her mask and snorkel, fins, and bag up to the freshwater drum, rinsed them, and headed up the trail towards the dirt road and the main house.

The cook was complaining in the kitchen house, a few doors down the street from their headquarters. Sandy could hear her through the open window before she reached the sunbaked street. A couple of guests sat on the covered porch of the Bahia Bar and watched as the divers walked up the dirt path to the main street, shirts on as required by the sheriff of the little island town. Too many bare-chested gringoes walking the main street offended the sensibilities of the church-going islanders, descendants of the buccaneer Blackbeard, who was supposed to have brought the Queen Anne's Revenge down through the clusters of islands off the coast of Central America before he sank her on the shoals of North Carolina. He and his pirates left more than silver coins and gold chains among the island women, legend had it.

When Sandy got to the main house, Carrie was on the porch where a green parrot sat chattering on his swing. She was a tall, elegant woman who had come down with her husband to bring the glass-bottomed boat and other equipment from the States. Carrie had befriended her in Florida when Sandy joined the expedition and on the long drive through Mexico and Guatemala when Stan resented

Sandy as the extra passenger who couldn't drive stick shift. Now Carrie wasn't smiling.

As Sandy came up the steps, Carrie spoke. "Hal wants your room, Sandy."

Her hand on the railing of the steps, Sandy looked up at Carrie and her folded arms. "Really?"

"You'll have to move to the house up the hill."

"With the guys?" A shot of anger hit her nerves as she took the steps and faced the brunette.

"Hal and his money," Carrie fumed. "Or his daddy's money."

Sandy bit her lip. What stuff she had could be packed after lunch, no problem, but having to leave what felt like the safety of the main house and its activity, where they catalogued finds, and developed the pictures in the darkroom, was a pisser. It felt like a demotion of sorts, though she'd never had any status. She hadn't invested in this expensive venture, mostly an expensive vacation the men grumbled. Nevertheless, Hal throwing his weight around, claiming partnership due to his providing a third of the money invested to fund the island operations and the Navy boat being retrofitted in dry dock in Jacksonville, was unsettling. And she didn't want to go up the hill to the men's quarters, five rooms in a stilt house. But it would have to be done.

She saw Hal's suitcase and gear in the front room, next to the coral encrusted anchor and some old cannonballs, also encrusted in white bleached coral and barnacles. She opened the door to her room, an Indian print bedspread on the metal frame bed, fish netting on the window studded with dried starfish. She stashed her fins and snorkel gear, the finds bag with the jade figurine she wasn't sure what to do with now. Dave couldn't be trusted. That was confirmed by his handling of the clusters at the dive site, hidden without telling anyone, nor would she trust Hal any further than she could throw him. She tucked the goddess between the shorts and shirts in her suitcase and grabbed her cutoffs and a clean top to put on after her shower. She would double-check Carrie's pronouncement about a room change at lunch first and then move up hill in the afternoon.

"I'm sorry, Sandy," Carrie said when she came out. "I certainly don't want to look at Hal first thing in the morning, every day. Will you be all right?"

"Sure," she answered. "The guys won't mind, and there's only four of them up there anyhow." Being in the house with Carrie somehow made her feel safer, but she slept on the sailboat with Bill most nights.

"Dave should have made arrangements for another house for him. Debra and the baby are due next week. I guess he didn't want Hal at the hotel with them. Too close for comfort."

"Was this Dave's doing? Or did Hal come up with this on his own?" Sandy wondered aloud. "It's all right, Carrie. Nobody stays up there anyway except to sleep. The books are here and it's our main hangout. So I'll be down here when we're not diving…"

But it was the only house with a shower attached, Sandy thought, but didn't say. She wondered what it would be like when Dave's wife arrived from California. This wasn't the ideal place for a toddler, but it would be interesting to see how Dave and his wife interacted. Dave had only been here three weeks himself and he added a tension the lazy days of diving and spearfishing off the reefs lacked when the head honchos weren't down here on the island.

During lunch in the kitchen house, she confirmed the move to the hill house. After lunch, Sandy and Bill took the short walk down the dirt street to the main house. With a private moment, she decided to tell him about Dave's find.

"You know, when I came up this morning," she began, "I had found some coral-encrusted clumps and I saw a couple of round things break off when I accidentally hit it when I moved the hose. I think there was gold, or what glittered like gold. I think Dave hid it."

"For real?" Bill turned serious, looking at her intently.

"Dave didn't bring it up. Or mention it."

Bill frowned, his usually merry eyes when he looked at her now having a hard glint. "Are they still down there?"

"I presume so," Sandy said. "He put them in the dive bag. He didn't bring that up."

"Interesting. Which quadrant was that?"

"Over on the west side—south-west quadrant—but out of where I was drawing. Near some brain coral."

She could picture the purple and yellow sea fans waving in the slight current, the convoluted curves of the brain coral and the clumps the same sand color.

"Are you going to ask Dave about it?" Sandy asked.

"I don't know yet. We're diving tomorrow. Maybe I'll check around down there. I thought there was something fishy when Dave told Hal we needed to fill the tanks. I just filled eight and we only took four out."

"If he lies about this..." Sandy dropped off in thought. That was precisely why she hadn't wanted to invest money when she read the ad in back of the dive magazine for divers wanted for work on the treasure hunting expedition. How would anyone know when or how much or what treasure was discovered? Besides, she didn't have three thousand to her name. Naive as she was, she'd expected to be paid, fresh off an archeology dig with experience drawing on the grid system; not so naive that she hadn't wondered then, with the magazine ad in the dive shop, how could one tell if treasure had been found? She wouldn't know, that's for sure. But this morning had surprised her.

"Maybe I'll take the boat out this afternoon," Bill muttered.

"Wouldn't Hal want to go?"

"Not if I'm going spearfishing."

"Dave would know."

Bill didn't say anything, and Sandy headed back to her room to move her things. Kneeling by her bed, she pulled the suitcase out and held the jade figurine before her, feeling the smooth coolness of the jade, studying the details of the goddess, no longer than her hand from the base of her palm to the tip of her middle finger. A sense of wonder filled her, staring at the detailed carved face, the closed eyes and protruding lips, the curves of the deep green woman in her hands. Its translucence of light when held towards the window hinted at in the uniformity of color. Jadeite, she had learned from a quick glance at a rock and mineral book on one of the shelves, was different from the jade the Chinese prized.

She heard Hal's voice at her door and shoved the figure back between her clothes and closed the suitcase, then pulled the sheets off the bed.

"Moving out now," she said as she folded the sheets and put the few knickknacks in the extra netted dive bag she had with her, without turning around.

"I want to get set up this afternoon and take a nap," Hal said.

"It's yours," Sandy said, jerking the netting down from the window without taking the starfish off. One fell on the floor and she put it on top of her bundles and carried them out the door, turning sideways away from Hal who barely moved out of the way to let her pass. His grin irritated her and she didn't look at him beyond the brief glimpse to negotiate her way out to the main room when she slid by him in the doorway.

She had settled into the spare room in the men's housing. During the wet season that followed that summer, with mildewy sheets and damp towels that never seemed quite dry, she had spent little time in the yellow shack up the hill. Debra, Dave's wife, had arrived not long after she moved up there.

Chapter 4

It was when she found herself dangling upside down from a second-story window, held from landing on her head by an angry married man, that Debra decided this was not the life for her. The stoners in the room behind him did nothing to help. As the blood rushed to her head and her long hair swayed in the movement of her struggle to get her arms to the window ledge, Debra vowed to leave San Francisco. Her lover was holding her legs tightly, so she did not quite think she would fall to her death, but the fact her life depended entirely on a twenty-eight-year-old holding her nineteen-year-old self up from meeting her time to die was clear evidence that her karma wasn't moving in the right direction.

"You called my wife, you dumb fuck," he was hissing. "You bitch."

That was no way to treat a lady.

"Please, Richard," she pleaded, "let me up. I won't do it again."

"You're damned right you won't do it again," he said. He still gripped her legs but she knew she was getting heavy and he really might drop her.

She was scraped by the windowsill as he pulled her in, she helping once she could get her hands on the wall and then the window.

Debra looked at the flushed face of this bearded man with his angry eyes and pulled her tie-dyed shirt at her armpits back down towards her bell bottoms. Thank goodness she wasn't wearing her skirt. She didn't bother to say he'd given her the phone number. She didn't bother to say he told her they were separated. She wanted out. Out of this room. Out of this town. This wasn't the peace and love she'd expected when she left Georgia with her cousin's friend for Haight Ashbury. She may have found kindness on the streets and in the people who'd taken her in, but this was a plain old nasty situation she had gotten herself into, after her cousin's friend dumped her there and went north to Canada.

The acid-tripping couple on the mattress was kissing — or more — as the lyrics "Go ask Alice when she's ten feet tall..." drummed in her ears that were still pounding with blood. "White Rabbit" played on the stereo and Richard stood there in his leather vest and bell bottoms. Clenching and unclenching his fists.

"Go away, Richard," she managed to say and then moved as far away from the window as she could. She wrapped what dignity she could muster around her like a thin shawl. She was not going to cry in front of him. "Please."

"I wouldn't have let go," he said. "But you had no right. I told you I was living with her, not to call nights."

She didn't argue. Yes, she was lonely. And, yes, she had called at a time he had said not to. But he didn't say any wife still lived there. Who was the dumb fuck here? She managed to get Richard to leave with more promises that she'd never call again.

She sank into a beanbag chair folding around her and watched the candles flicker patterns on the walls and burn out before she fell asleep. She lay in the beanbag until dawn, when she could see where she was going, when she could gather her belongings in her knapsack and hitchhike out of town. This San Francisco flower child life was not for her.

And Debra did change her life then and there. She got a ride in a colorfully painted VW bus with some hippies who wanted to get out to the country, driving through Big Sur, to a commune somewhere. But she was striking out on her own, and did not stay with them.

What a space cadet I was, Debra thought ruefully from the perspective of a woman in her fifties. While she packed for this trip her own level-headed daughter had engineered, her memories haunted her. After the hippies had given her a ride down the coast, she had been picked up by a couple going to Tijuana who had stopped in Capistrano along the way. Her mother used to sing "When the Swallows Come back to Capistrano..." and Debra sent her a postcard from there, one of the many she posted over the six months she'd been gone. Had she really understood how much a mother could worry over a wayward daughter? Of course not. She had been as dim as a thirty watt bulb.

But she did manage to land on her feet, after hanging upside down in her window dangling episode, when she headed down the California coast. She found a waitressing job at a little café in Ventura. She found a room to rent and promised to pay as soon as her first check was cashed. She started taking yoga at the little seaside spot near the café and this brought her some comfort. She stopped smoking pot so she could breathe the prana the instructor said was there, so her brain could clear out and she didn't feel so fuzzy.

In this fertile valley between two rivers, she settled in. It was a few months into this new life, after a lonely Christmas, when she met Dave. He came into the café with another man who was wearing a suit, and he left a big tip. He smiled at her. He came by himself a few more times before he asked her out. She had asked around and knew Dave was single. She had checked. No ring, no white band on his tan finger where a ring had been. But she had asked someone who knew someone who worked at his dive shop and salvage business to confirm.

He was a businessman, of sorts, with big dreams. He had interesting plans to do with outfitting a boat and getting others to invest, along with treasure-hunting goals that sounded romantic. He might have been a little straight for her taste, but he was not an acid-tripping, pot smoking wanna-be hippie. He was a man with a neat apartment and no wife lurking anywhere. She felt safe. She felt protected with him. He might have been a businessman, but he wasn't part of the capitalist establishment.

Now, decades later, Debra recalled their first date as she finished packing her suitcase for the trip she did not want to take, lifting her cat Tinkerbell out to put a last minute sweater in the suitcase. For that first date, Dave had met her outside the café where she worked. He had offered to pick her up at her place, but she was not willing to share her address or share her own personal life with the woman who rented her a room.

"You look really nice," he said, smiling. He gave her a light hug, not too tight, but she could smell his manly clean odor and get a sense of warmth from being so close. His eyes seemed to soften looking at her. Her reflection in the café window showed her reddish brown hair swept past her bare shoulders and her new peasant blouse, from a local thrift shop, exposed a creamy neck. The early spring air, even for California's mild weather, felt hopeful, offering a hint of new life.

They walked down towards the waterfront. In the early March light before sunset, the waters sparkled along the harbor. Behind them, the slopes of hills leading to distant mountains gave a comforting snugness to this small coastal city and harbor village. She took in the light on palm trees and harbor, the steep slopes rising beyond the buildings, and this strong man beside her. A breeze off the ocean, fishing boats, and seafood restaurants added to the charm. Dave took her to a restaurant near the harbor, upscale by the standards of her café, but not too formal. Perfect. He opened doors for her and seated her like a gentleman would. Little candles glowed on the tables and white table cloths added ambiance to the dimly lit setting.

"Are you vegetarian?" he asked after the waiter brought the menus.

"In fits and spurts," she said, shaking her head no. "I just don't eat red meat."

"They have several good fish dishes," he pointed out.

She was touched by his attentiveness. His amber tinted brown eyes glowed warmly in the flickering candlelight. She hoped she looked pretty. After he ordered their dishes, he asked how long she had been in California and where she grew up. She told him simply that she had moved from Georgia less than a year before. He had not asked about her southern accent, a mark in his favor, since many had teased her or imitated her drawl, which annoyed her to no end. Annoyed the pea turkey out of her, as a matter of fact. She might as well bring up the accent herself and get it over. She told him her story of the inappropriate use of "y'all" someone had tried on her, how she had been greeted at a party by a girl saying "Hi, y'all" and when she looked around no one was behind her. She looked down, in the restaurant as she had then at that party, and said, "I'm not with child." He laughed. It pleased her to make him laugh.

But that night he did ask how a Southerner had ended up in Ventura.

"A couple who was heading for Tijuana dropped me off here," she said simply. "I liked the citrus groves and the old Spanish mission..."

"No, I mean, how did you get from Georgia to California. It's a long way for a young woman alone."

Young woman she noted. Not chick. Not Sugar Magnolia like that last creep called her. Not that she didn't like the Grateful Dead.

Where to start? With the stunning assassination of Martin Luther King, or the protest marches? She had decided she wanted no part of the system that waged war on innocent people far away and sent young men to die for no good reason, or a university that held her captive as a freshman girl locked in a dorm, curfew they called it. Or should she admit that one too many frat boys had barfed in front of her? She remembered the football culture had bored her silly. Vince Dooley rah rah. Drunk frat boy on a blind date throwing up bourbon after the game. These details she didn't share, but she did pick one of her many reasons for leaving Athens, where she had dropped out of the university the spring before, when her cousin had introduced her to a friend protesting the war in Vietnam and heading for California. He had a car and a tank of gas. That's all it took that early April day after Dr. King died.

Their food arrived and she had a moment to think in the flurry of plates slipped onto the table, the wine bottle opened and pinot grigio tasted before pouring. Should she include how she ended up in San Francisco alone after she didn't want to go north to Canada? She did not want to tell him about the postcard she had sent to her mother from Capistrano. She had been overwhelmed with homesickness then. She chose the middle ground, something not too heavy, while he waited for her response. Picking up her fork and pausing before she cut into her ahi, she spoke of her first demonstration for coed equality and described college life for a young woman living in the South in the late '60s.

"It felt like a prison," she said. "Girls were locked up before midnight in the dorms. Strict curfew. Once I forgot to sign out before I took the bus home and had to go to honor court. I had to stay in my dorm room on restriction.... Then PE—we weren't allowed to wear pants on campus without a raincoat."

At this Dave's eyebrows rose and he smiled. "I can picture you in a trench coat."

"It was hot. Over that gym outfit, I sweltered one too many times. I had these two classes back to back, down one hill and up another and I was always late for the second one, and wearing a coat to class."

"What did your parents think? Dropping out?"

"They weren't pleased," she understated. "My dad in particular. He had been a Marine. Rather strict. My mother was okay. I call her from time to time."

She changed the subject, didn't want to discuss her mother's pleas to come home. Or her father's anger that she'd run off with a long-haired war protester. He hadn't known he was a draft dodger, too.

"What about you? How did you avoid the draft, or did you go?"

"I enlisted in the Navy," he said. "It seemed the best way to stay out of combat duty in Vietnam."

"That was smart," she replied. "Many guys I knew were just in college to avoid being drafted."

Dave talked awhile about Navy duty, his love for the sea and travel, and she was entranced. She too wanted to travel, see the world. He had come to treasure hunting, she learned, through his early boyhood interest in the gold rush and the '49ers, his own childhood fun panning for gold. He told her pirates had lurked around this part of the California coast. When he told her about a pirate attack leaving the mission in tact that she had visited, San Buenaventura, after it was briefly evacuated in 1818 and the mission spared, she watched his face light up in the telling.

She told him, "I like to walk around the Spanish mission and its old fountain. I've gone there several times, soaking up all that long-time-ago feeling. Like everything's not moving so fast. There's history there. I was reminded of the architecture of St. Augustine in Florida where my family visited once."

Before she added how the oldness of those buildings had intrigued her, she made sure he was still interested. His eyes were on her; he was listening. "The fact the Spanish had built those structures in the 1500's, before the British colonized, amazed me. I like Ventura's old mission, and the Spanish architecture of California in general." She didn't mention the way the palm trees reminded her of pineapples on a stalk, realizing it made her sound silly, something she very much did not want to do. Surprised to learn that he was only twenty-six, she felt he had a presence that seemed older, more mature. She wanted to seem more grownup than she felt.

When she asked about his growing up in California, Dave told her he had lost his parents in a plane crash, and was raised by an aunt. He said it very matter-of-factly.

"California was a great place to grow up. Learned to surf and spent so much time in the water I could have been a fish. My aunt kept a loose rein. When we weren't at the beach, we were out roaming the foothills. We panned for gold, whenever we were near a stream," Dave said.

"We?"

"My brother and I," Dave said, then, taking a sip of wine, added, "He's dead. Killed in Vietnam."

"Oh, I'm so sorry," was all she said. He poured the last of the wine into their glasses.

Debra could tell he didn't want to talk about it, so she encouraged him to talk about the gold rush, the earlier days when the Spanish had explored for gold and silver. The serious expression in his eyes eased and his enthusiasm delighted her when he described Havana shipwrecks of Spanish galleons loaded with gold, how he already had investors to search off the bay islands of Honduras, Central America, and was in the process of purchasing a former Navy vessel to be retrofitted for diving for his treasure hunting expedition.

Their conversation spanned topics that were safer than their personal lives, far from politics or home sickness, far from death or despair. She peppered him with questions to keep him talking. He talked about the current lawsuit in Florida, a man named Mel Fisher, a treasure hunter whose finds drew the interest of the state, which wanted the profits of these hard working treasure hunters risking life and limb, just to turn it over to the state. How wrong that seemed. When he started talking about the difference between looting a sunken ship, and carefully preserving the finds by recording them, how these buried treasures would remain lost if not for the investment of outfitters willing to risk time and money to uncover them, he grew passionate, and then caught himself.

She told him she admired his responsible approach. "Even if archeologists might claim the divers on wrecks were destroying history, they were uncovering it, like you said. What might have remained lost for centuries more."

Details about wrecks off Havana, his own exploratory efforts off the coast of Central America, these tales stirred her imagination and took her away from her own unsorted life. With his description of the Spanish fleet leaving Havana in 1622 with gold bars and silver bullion, she could picture the Spanish shipments of gold and silver going overland through Panama or by boat travelling through the Caribbean before heading across the Atlantic. He made it come alive for her.

After dinner, they walked around awhile and she let him walk her home. He didn't try to come in. He kissed her gently on the lips at the door and her heart quickened. She loved being in his arms. But he pulled away, smiled, and asked, "Can I call you?"

She felt a bit let down. But he wanted to see her again. Maybe it was a good sign. Respect. Standing there at the door at the date's end, she didn't have paper or pen with her, nor he, so he made arrangements to stop by after her next shift so he could show her around the shop and his boat. He would take her out to the Channel Islands if she had free time and wanted to go. Of course she did. She would go anywhere he wanted to take her. Fool that she was, she would have followed him to the moon and back. The stars were already in her eyes.

And from there, the rest was history, as they say. A three month courtship, then they were married by a justice of the peace. No big white wedding. A photo sent to her parents. Her father still hadn't forgiven her for wasting his money for college and running off with a protester. Her mother did fly out for the birth of the baby ten months later. By then, Debra had realized Dave drank a lot. But he still had those big plans, maybe too many irons in the fire, Debra remembered as she stirred from reverie.

She lifted the cat out of her suitcase one last time, wiped off the cat hair, and closed the lid. She greeted her grown daughter at the back door of the farmhouse, ready to help her with her luggage for the trip to Key West.

Chapter 5

Melody was irritated by what her mother claimed was not dilly-dallying; irritated by her mother waiting until the last minute to announce her intention to go and then to get the grandparents set up with Etta, their former housekeeper, coming by every day while they were gone. Even the offer for Jeff to come or send the barn kids to feed her mother's critters was met with a waffling response until the last minute. She had the nerve to tell Mel "not to have a hissy fit". Still, Mel had to be thankful she was coming.

They were actually early arriving at the airport, with Debra's I-told-you-so expression irking Mel even more, so there wasn't much talking on their flight to Miami or through the car rental business.

On the long bridge through the Keys, Mel was surprised when her mother said, out of the blue, "Your daddy was a good dancer." Then she had added, "He asked me to slow dance on the beach the day we got married. We were barefoot."

Tears welled up in Mel's eyes; she bit her lip and kept driving. A quick glance towards the passenger's seat of the convertible revealed that her mother was looking out at the water whizzing by. Her mother had never offered up much in the way of details about her father or their relationship. And once Mel had her own relationship with him, after his second wife, that witch-wife, was gone, and Mel's new stepmom encouraged their connection, Debra kept her lips sealed. They never discussed him. Her mother let Mel form her own opinions, create her own memories of the man, which Mel had to respect. Not even much of a "hmmm" would come from her mother's pursed lips to let her know she was even listening if Mel said anything related to him. And now this, a tender moment revealed. It suddenly dawned on Mel maybe his death was having more of an emotional impact on her mother than she'd thought possible. She was stunned.

Big clouds on the horizon were underlit with the late light on the waters. Occasional islands of palms and palmettos and the salty sea smell of the air created a tropical feel that lightened the worries that weighed her down and would have induced a carefree feeling under other circumstances. Today it just mellowed Mel's tenseness.

She interrupted the silence. "You know, Mom, I never asked you much about him. I knew you didn't like to discuss him and I guess I was busy being a youngster. Too busy being a kid to ask questions."

"You have your own memories, Melody." Her mother turned, her thick auburn hair whipping and glinting in the late afternoon light. Her fifty-one-year-old mother's baby face belied her age. Always the upturned corners of her lips provided a perpetual smile. Thank goodness, she hadn't taken on her mother's tendency toward a little spare flesh. Even her father had been on the stout side, so she wasn't sure where her own trimness came from. Grams? Or her fastidious calories in, calories out mentality?

"I have no memories of him when I was really little, though. Y'all were together how long?"

Mel slowed for a car ahead getting ready to turn off the seven mile bridge onto a key.

"You were four when I left. You don't remember sitting in his lap with the bunny rabbit book?"

"I have a vague memory of a memory," Mel said, pressing on the gas pedal again. "With that flop-eared bunny I used to drag around. I still have that thing. I remember sort of being up against his chest, and me holding the bunny. Him, I guess, holding me and the book."

"That would have been at our place in the Virgin Islands," Debra said and turned away. "You were too young to remember Roatilla."

Mel remembered a rocking boat, her dad holding her too tightly as she tried to squirm away to see the fish.

"Dad loved the water. He always loved the water. He never talked about the expedition, even after I got to know him with Liz."

"It had some dark days, Mel," her mother said. "You say he was in good spirits last time you saw him?"

"Yes. You know, they found him near one of these keys, in his boat, floating in the water. He had a cut on back of his head. Not a deep gash or anything." She could picture him on the boat in the clear waters, the boat drifting around its anchor...white sands, clear turquoise water, a vast sky above, bright sun of midday.

"That's odd. Why would he be diving alone?" Debra raised her same question. "Or was he fishing? Is there an investigation, then?"

"I'm not sure, Mom. I'll get more details tonight. When I go over to Liz's."

"If he were fishing, that's one thing. But he never dove alone."

They rode in silence awhile, each woman following the winding path of her own thoughts.

"What time is Aunt Sandy arriving?"

"I think she'll get in before noon. She'll catch a flight out of Miami to that little airport for Key West. She'll be pretty pooped after that long flight from Honolulu." Debra continued, "I told her we could pick her up. Or I can."

"We can pick her up together. But we better call the airport first. See if it's on time. It'll be good to see her."

"Um hmm," Debra mused. "It is odd Liz said she needed to be there for the reading of the will. It's odd I am supposed to be there."

"I'll see what I can find out tonight. Liz was pretty tight lipped, but pretty insistent." Melody added, "After we get checked in at the Westwind, I'll call her."

"Let's find some good seafood for supper. I'm hungry already." Debra inhaled deeply. "All this fresh salt air whets the appetite."

"Sure, we can walk to the restaurant and stretch our legs."

They were passing Big Pine Key and it wouldn't be long now before they found the hotel and had the convertible parked. When she'd ordered a convertible, her mother had said, "That's my girl" in a tone that could go either way— praise or irony, take your pick.

Debra, as navigator, was folding the map for the last stretch of the journey to locate the streets for Key West. "These things are always so ornery," she muttered. "They never fold back like they were originally or even in the same creases. Almost as frustrating as untangling wire hangers in a closet too full of clothes."

"They're plastic now, Mom."

While her mother struggled with the map in the wind, wrangling it to submission, she wondered about the days ahead.

"I haven't seen Sandy since she came through in '96," Mel said. "That was four years ago. I was still pregnant with Leslie."

"I remember. We all went for a ride, and you got so mad we left you behind."

Mel made a face but said nothing. They had been right— a woman eight months pregnant might not do well on a horse, even one with a smooth gait at a walk, and nobody had wanted her going into early labor on the trail. Like that would have happened. Still, she thought they should have all gone for a walk instead of leaving her behind while they went riding. Mom and Aunt Sandy, who was really no blood kin, had a bond that went way back, and Sandy was a part of her childhood memories, from when they all lived together. The two were what Mel called "woo-woo" sisters when she was talking privately with Jeff. They even believed that two Georgia girls meeting on a tiny island off Central America was not a coincidence. And astrology—Aunt Sandy was big on that. Mel thought stars were for enjoying on a clear winter night with her husband after the horses were fed. Not studying for angles and trines and all that. Yet Sandy had nailed Mel's two kids' personalities pretty well, she had to admit, even on the day they were born. When Mel's own chart came up, Sandy just laughed and said, "Mum's the world, you non-believer." And that charming way she said it just made Mel forget she was being teased.

Chapter 6

Sandy couldn't believe she was sitting on her fanny on an airplane bound for a memorial service for a man she despised, and wondering who had murdered him. There were plenty who had reason back when she knew him, but who in his life now would want him dead that much? Her thoughts kept returning to those days of her early twenties down in the Caribbean. And she remembered her first encounters with his first wife, her friend, whom she would be seeing when this plane touched down. She still remembered the day had she met Debra like it was yesterday. That hot August afternoon.

Sandy and Bill had been kept busy sanding one of the wooden boats in the clear area by the pier. Houses clustered in the bay, on the west side of the island, were mostly hidden by the palms. Whenever the heat and mosquitoes became too insufferable, they took a break. Since there was no electricity except from six to ten at night, they saved the expedition generator for the air compressor. So this was a hand job, Bill liked to joke.

Sandy had not been back to the site all week, not since Hal and Dave had commandeered some of the dive equipment and taken the dive boat out four times. She was scheduled to plant a vase and a gold chain for the cinematographers who had arrived with Dave's wife the afternoon before. They would be filming at the site this afternoon.

"I'll be glad to be back in the water," she said as she leaned her body into the sanding to save her arms.

Bill looked up from the other side of the hull. Sweat beaded on his forehead. "I didn't try to get out this morning with Dave all over the equipment cleanup, so I still don't know..." his voice trailed off as one of the Swedish archeologists stopped by.

"Have you seen Dave's wife and their little girl yet?" Sandy made small talk to engage the tall blond standing there watching them work.

"Nej. No, have you?" the archeologist replied.

Sandy shook her head. "They didn't eat supper with the group last night, remember? And I went to bed early. Carrie and Stan ate at the hotel with them. I guess they were tired from the long flight."

"They should be on the boat this afternoon. It'll be quite a party," he said as he moved on to the pier.

By the time the two boats had anchored out near the site, it was early afternoon. Neither boat held the woman and child. Too much activity with camera equipment and divers to have a toddler on board, Dave had decided. So the wife stayed back. Another reason to be glad she was single and free, Sandy thought as she slipped below the surface and into the weightless world where she always felt like she was flying. Down into blue water, she waved her fins with smooth motions extending from the tops of her legs straight down to the ankles, all one powerful, fluid stroke from each leg propelling her. She glided away and began descending forty-five feet to the sea floor. Between elkhorn and fire coral, four-eye butterfly fish and striped sergeant fish darted in kaleidoscope colors. She looked back up through the clear azure water to a surface shimmering in sunlight. Near her, the cameraman with the underwater camera motioned towards the shallower water of the site. Dave had directed her to bring the glass vase back up after she buried it and it was filmed being "discovered". She gripped the coral-encrusted vase and swam towards the site.

A parrot fish crunched on coral, oblivious to their activity, and schools of other fish leisurely appeared and disappeared, camouflaged in the colorful background of their world. After she buried the vase, she tried to stay out of the way while Rolf pretended to search and find it. She still had plenty of air as the vase was uncovered and rediscovered, then buried again for a better angle by the diver filming Rolf underwater. When Sandy finally rose toward the surface with the vase in tow, she could see a second cameraman bobbing with the boat, his dark image on the undulating surface backlit by blue. Silver crescents of air rose faster than she did, wiggling large and small skyward. As she surfaced, to hand off the vase to the reaching arm above, she heard the cameraman curse.

"Damn, a woman in the shot. You just ruined it."

Macho. They believed only men divers belonged in their "manly" treasure hunt, she thought while his tirade continued. Men who believed they were invincible and went down too far in search of black coral, and then came back with a mild case of the bends, too manly to decompress midway. There was no decompression chamber on the island and they were taking risks with their lives she wouldn't. She didn't even dive more than once a day, in order to avoid calculating the time and depth limits needed to keep from getting nitrogen bubbles building up in her own blood. Better safe than sorry. She was too smart for machismo foolhardiness. And here was a jackass acting like women could not be part of an adventure like this. She treaded water while waiting a moment for him to calm down.

The cameraman was still raving when she climbed aboard the boat. This was the pudgy one who had told her, when they had been on the Navy boat in dry dock months back, that if she put a penny box beside her bed, she'd be the only one with any money at the end of the trip. Along with disgusting remarks like that, and comments about how women onboard ships were bad luck, she had also learned the expedition she had joined to go to the Caribbean might not be headed there after all. After it was retrofitted for diving, the boat was going to be diverted to Charleston instead of coming down here. This secret, the different plans for the Oceanic Rover, had made her decide to jump ship and head for the Caribbean with Carrie and Stan who were leaving Florida dry dock to drive to Honduras. And here she was diving in crystal clear waters, even if she had sexist assholes to contend with.

After she boarded the motorboat, she ignored the cameraman and found a seat. But her own anger cut like a knife, almost severing reason from common sense. She swallowed both her emotion and any retorts she wanted to make, and watched the men finish stowing the gear and pulling up the anchor without lifting a finger to help. She was still furious when they reached the dock and she headed back along the rickety pier to wash up.

When she glanced up, there was the wife, toddler in tow, watching them disembark.

Debra saw the young woman stand up and took a deep breath. Dave had told her the men liked Sandy's tits and ass, repeating their salty words verbatim, but no one had told Debra about the long slim arms and legs. The long bare waist. This girl had a gorgeous body, the young mother saw in a glance. Blue water, blue sky, and bikini-clad beauty.

Melody pulled at her hair and squirmed in Debra's arms. "Dow...Dow..." she commanded, and before she could set up a wail, Debra shifted her from one hip to the other and kissed her warm forehead, the sweet smell of baby filling her nostrils.

The other woman was coming down the pier at a fast and angry clip, skipping the missing boards as she pulled her shirt together, buttoning with one hand, carrying dripping mask and fins in the other.

"Hey," Debra managed to say as she jiggled her daughter in the bright sunshine.

Sandy looked up. Here the young woman from California stood in a purple Indian cotton top and neat khaki shorts, an odd combination, and a toddler in a floppy little hat squinting and reaching out towards Sandy with one of her little hands.

"Oh, hi. I'm Sandy. You must be Debra?"

Sunglasses covered the wife's eyes, but full lips with a curve at the corners were unexpectedly pretty, Sandy thought. She looked privileged and safe.

"Yes, we arrived last night—or yesterday. It seemed like night after the red-eye special."

Carrie was coming down the pier behind Debra. The second boat, carrying Stan, Dave, and one of the archeologists, was pulling up to the dock. The first crew was clinking and thumping down the boards toward them. Sandy didn't stay to talk.

"Friendly, that one," Debra observed to Carrie.

"She's really nice once you get to know her," Carrie said. "Sometimes the guys give her grief. Maybe that's what's going on. Here, let me take this sweet girl."

Debra handed her diapered darling off to Carrie, who cooed and carried on to Melody's delight. Too sweet, she thought, and realized she really meant it as she watched the tall dark-haired woman baby talk her child, who just a few minutes before had felt like a big weight, like an anchor mooring her to this man striding down the pier to greet her.

Dave smiled, put a heavy arm around her shoulders and pulled her to him. He introduced her to the crew standing there holding gear. His wetness was cool against her side. The sixteen-month-old in Carrie's arms reached out for him, fingers wiggling as though they could stretch out and touch him. That warm familiar feeling of love connected her to her man. She dismissed her disloyal thoughts of a moment before, when she had felt tethered by her commitments, as hormonal flux or travel weariness. Together, they walked back towards the island in the bright hot sun.

Before Sandy cleaned up, she headed to her room in the crew quarters for a fresh shirt. The jade figurine was still between the folds of her extra clothes in the suitcase. It was cool to the touch and somehow comforting to hold. She rubbed her fingers along the carved features of the serene little face. The irritation that had gripped her subsided. The wonder of touching the jade goddess replaced her disgruntled feeling. It somehow felt healing to hold this small ancient figurine in her palm. She had let the cameraman get to her. That was on her, she knew; she had to let it roll off.

Later, as the sun was sinking low, the mountains of Honduras, sometimes visible in the distance like a blue mirage, were cloud-covered with the brilliant golds and rosy reds that made her want to get her paints out. She headed for the pier, but saw Debra and Dave sitting out there to watch the sunset. So Dave had a tender side. Why should that surprise her? He wasn't always barking orders or being a gruff businessman. He had let her join the expedition without the three thousand dollar investment, an offer which could not be considered a business move, after her expectations of a paying job were squelched. Why had he let her come, with only the requirement of a plane ticket home? She would never know. She had not seen him crack a smile in all the weeks he'd been here, until she'd cast a backward glance at the pier this afternoon where he stood with Debra and his child.

Watching the last colors fading from the sunset, she stood a few minutes in the tranquil afterglow of dusk. The Bahia Bar lights were coming on, and music was pouring off the porch when she turned around. Walking from the shoreline in front of the hotel and back along the path, she stepped on the porch to the Rolling Stones and "I Can't Get No Satisfaction". One of the vacationing Peace Corps volunteers was tapping his feet and Marie, hotel owner, came out with her dishtowel and danced with it over her head. Sandy joined in with the lyrics of "I tried and I tried…but I can't get no…" and danced to its throbbing beat. How she loved dancing. When the song was over, she sat down with Bill, Dan, and Rolf who had just arrived on the porch bar and ordered cerveza. Dave, too, had come on the porch from the pier and was sitting nearby at the next table.

"Where's your wife?" one of the men asked.

"She'll be out here. Just went to the room. Checking on the baby."

The men began talking about the time Dan, one of the expedition divers, had been lost spearfishing and surrounded by sharks, whapping his spear in the water as they circled. It would have been all sheroo if the boat hadn't found him before dark. The tale wound down with a few jokes.

Debra slipped onto the porch, waited until the men had said their hellos, and told Dave the baby was asleep. Someone had put on The Beatles, but Sandy couldn't get Bill to dance, so she danced alone. When "Twist and Shout" started its glad refrain, Debra was up and on the floor, too, twisting away with gusto. She could almost reach the floor in corkscrew moves and she was surprisingly graceful, Sandy thought. Just then, she caught Sandy's eye, and in that moment their eyes met, merry with the delight of dancing; a spark of recognition for a kindred spirit leapt between them and they both smiled. Bonded by *joie de vivre*. Sandy danced with her characteristic fierce joy. Debra's smooth moves and swiveling hips kept the beat of the next song, until Dave stood up to claim her for his own in a slow dance, and Sandy sat back down, laughing.

Bill joked, "Shake it up, baby. Shake that booty."

"Eh, Bill, you better get her out on the floor yourself and hold on, or she'll fly off the porch next time," Rolf spoke up in his German accent.

The couple who owned the hotel was out on the floor, too, but it was Dave and Debra whom Sandy and the men watched. Their slow moves, in sync with such a gentle swaying, fascinated her. There was a tenderness that touched her unexpectedly and she almost liked Dave for a split second.

Chapter 7

Debra and her little girl were talking to the green parrot sidestepping along its bar swing and back, the baby reaching for the bird and saying, "Bir. Bir." Sandy came up the steps of the main house and approached them.

"His name is Pedro," Sandy said.

Debra, with her little one on her hip, turned and smiled. "She loves all animals. Big. Little. It doesn't matter. Fearless where dogs are concerned."

"There are some kittens under the kitchen house. The mother's pretty cautious, but I've been working on the kittens now they're big enough to be exploring. Trying to get them friendly. Get them adopted. The mother's a stray."

"We'll have to check them out," Debra said, "when they're tame enough not to scratch her." Addressing her daughter, she added, "Would you like to see some kitty-kitties, sweetheart?"

Then, seeming to realize this child would probably insist on now, she pointed at the parrot, "This is Pedro, sweetie. Pedro."

The toddler turned her attention to look up at her mother's face, her earnest eyes squinching at the bright sunlight behind her mother's head, then turning back to Pedro. She reached toward the parrot.

"Does he peck?" Debra asked.

"No, actually, he's pretty friendly."

Debra took her small daughter's chubby little fingers towards the feathers of the parrot's wing. He bobbed his head, but didn't offer to peck; he did bring his beak down towards their hands and gently nibbled with its tip. The child laughed.

"She's a cute kid," Sandy offered.

"Thanks," Debra said, kissing the curls on top of Melody's head. "She's my peach."

Sandy smiled. "Her name is Melody, right? I think that's what I heard. Pretty name."

"Dave calls her Mel sometimes. It'll probably stick."

Sandy glanced at Debra. She could not read her expression, turned as she was towards her daughter and the parrot. Melody's attention was glued to the bird.

Sandy excused herself to check on the darkroom to see if Bob were there to work in the lab. "See y'all later."

Dave and Hal were arguing over a map when she entered the main room and they didn't stop to acknowledge her. Hal, a full head taller than Dave, was growling that the archives in Seville had indicated that the 1612 ships leaving the coast of Guatemala and later wrecking would have been more than a hundred miles north of their current diving location. Even if one of the three boats shipwrecked on coral reefs had left a long debris trail as hurricanes and time spread the broken-up ship southward and scattered its contents across the seafloor, the bits of rusted metal and silver coins they had found so far probably did not belong to a wrecked vessel from the fleet, *Flota de Indias*. Though the fleet had been headed towards Havana, along the Spanish West Indies route, Dave insisted that the debris field could have extended this far south; the years of hurricanes and waves could spread wreckage thirty to fory miles after a shipwreck. In addition, the exact route could have changed no matter what ship manifests or letters Hal found may have said.

"It's just too costly to relocate now," Dave said.

Hal replied, "We need to send a group up there. The boat's almost out of dry dock. It could be down here in two months. Use my coordinates."

Sandy knew the retrofitted boat was not coming, so this meant Hal didn't?

"One hundred miles north—we'd be in the territorial waters of Belize. We'd have to deal with Belize, Hal." Dave's voice was rising. "There's no way I'm—"

"We don't have to set up permanently," Hal interjected.

The men continued arguing about the boat, paper work, and expenses, as though Sandy hadn't walked through the room. Sandy knocked on the darkroom door without interrupting the men ignoring her and entered. Bob, who was the official black-and-white photographer for the expedition, was not in the lab. Sandy didn't want to mix chemicals without him and she knew he'd poured out the stop bath. He was precise, and she was a little too free-handed with measuring to suit him. Magic instead of science. Not the way he ran the lab. The heat made guesswork of the development process, anyway, Sandy felt. Some of the work had to wait until the generator provided electricity, and it was too hot in the lab to develop midday, but she could take dry photos from the line and sort them for quality. Once she had the pictures stacked, there was little else to do. She closed the door behind her.

Carrie, brushing her hair as she came to her bedroom door, said, "We're going for cocomalts. Want to join us?"

"Sure," Sandy said. "I want to print some of the film we developed, but it has to wait until tonight, anyway. I'm done."

She walked into Carrie's room. Carrie rolled her eyes and motioned towards the men in the other room.

"They've been arguing all morning," she whispered.

Carrie was Sandy's pipeline of information about the ins and outs of some of the politics and behind-the-scenes goings on of the expedition, which seemed now to be on shaky ground. It had been Carrie's news from Stan that the Oceanic Rover, the ship they were retrofitting in Jacksonville, was going to Charleston's murky waters, not down to Roatilla's crystal clear seas as planned, that had been the deciding factor in Sandy's choice to leave with Stan and Carrie. She had joined them for the long haul through Mexico and Guatemala to bring supplies and a glass-bottomed boat to the port at La Ceiba and then ship them over to the island. Being privy to the secret that the ship wasn't joining the dive team on Roatilla, ahead of the crew, who still didn't know, made her decision easy. That and her misguided affair with one of the men on the ship, a man whom Carrie had disliked and warned against; but Sandy had gone ahead, being young and easily persuaded by his take-charge approach and good looks. She was such a sucker for good looks. She had been swept up in passion, and at that time thought she didn't have anything to lose. The affair was short-lived. But she had had to admit she had made a misstep with the twenty-seven-year-old with whom she'd had that affair. When she had wanted to end it, he became her enemy. It had been a good idea to head south instead of north to muddy waters. But this argument in the other room meant Hal didn't know the boat wasn't coming down to the Caribbean, or if he did, wanted to redirect operations.

"Hal spent all that money flying to Spain," Carrie interrupted her thoughts. "Now he wants to prove he's right and the money was worth it."

"And throw his weight around," Sandy added. Sandy had said nothing to anyone but Bill about Dave's and her discoveries, and nothing to anyone at all about the jadeite figurine that she couldn't part with. She couldn't afford to cross Dave. Besides, it wasn't her place to say anything. It could have been nothing worthwhile Dave hid. She felt a little guilty not sharing with Carrie, but she thought she should sit on her find and Dave's actions down there until she had a better idea what they meant. It was strange, though, that the two men didn't care whether she heard their argument.

Whispering in her room after she closed the door, Carrie told her Dave was worried about the costs, renting houses and running operations down here, especially now that the ship they had poured so much money into would not become the base of operations for the Caribbean. Carrie, who had known Debra in California before Carrie and Stan went east to help oversee the vessel being converted for treasure hunting, said Debra had confided she knew Dave was worried because he was drinking more and talking less. He had brushed it off when Debra asked, after a few remarks he'd made about how far in debt the boat had put them, even with new investors, and how little they'd found in almost two years on Roatilla. Apparently now more money was needed for Oceanic Rover before she would be seaworthy even if they had scrapped plans to bring her here.

"Don't say anything about the drinking," Carrie cautioned, "or let on you know about the money."

Sandy nodded.

"Let's get out of here," Carrie said.

The two left the room, passing the men standing over the table with the map. She and Carrie walked out on the porch to find Debra sitting on the swing, the child beside her. She looked uncomfortable, Sandy thought, but Debra smiled and stood up. The heat from the dirt street and no breeze made it stifling. The three women, with toddler in tow, walked the couple of blocks along the main street lined with ramshackle wooden houses to the cocomalt stand. They reached the little structure and the weathered old man who ran it, one of the shopkeepers who were so trusting that when Sandy didn't have enough change, they let her pay later. It was like the small town of her childhood back in Georgia. Behind him in the dark shadows, she could see the bright smile of a young black woman grinning at them as she prepared their drinks. A battery-operated radio was playing the music Sandy had come to love, Jimmy Cliff, the islanders' favorite and a Caribbean hero. The clipped island beat of this lively music cheered her.

There was no mention of the dispute Sandy had witnessed in the main house. Debra must have overheard it through the large open windows of the house. Though most arguments or discussions took place behind closed doors, obviously this disagreement didn't need to be confined, she supposed. Still, it surprised her.

Cocomalts finished, they walked back towards the shade near the pier, where a slight breeze stirred and Debra could put Melody down to play along the edge of the shallow water, palm fronds and bits of flotsam fascinating the small child, feet wet, stomping in the water. With the breeze, the mosquitoes were not so obnoxious. Still, Carrie swatted one that left a small splat of blood on her arm.

"I brought plenty of insect spray, even if I don't like all those chemicals," Debra said, "but these sand fleas are awful."

"I counted twenty-five bites on one leg the other day, from knee to ankle, and that didn't include my foot," Sandy said.

Debra offered them some spray from the big bag she was carrying. "I hope the baby doesn't get infected from scratching her bites…. But I wanted to see this place before—" Debra hesitated.

"Before?" Sandy prompted.

Debra turned to her, staring at Sandy's quizzical face, her green eyes, and seemed to improvise, "Before anything happened so I couldn't get down here…. We've still got the apartment in Jacksonville, but I'm back and forth from California. You know, we have a dive shop and salvage operation there."

She was diverting the conversation from anything concrete about the expedition.

"Well, Stan says we'll be down here through October at least. I'll be glad to get back to California myself," Carrie added conversationally, all of them avoiding discussion of the argument they'd heard. "Mosquitoes. Sand fleas. Heat. Grumpy men."

Sandy laughed. She recognized the need not to put Dave's wife in a spot by pinning her down. She described the incident on the boat when filming the vase and added, "Macho to the max. Some sexist pigs those cinematographers are."

"You've got that right," Debra added. "I had to fly down with those two. Crude remarks about the stewardesses like I wasn't even sitting next to them."

Carrie added stories from the six months she and Stan lived in Florida with the ship in dry dock. Sandy told about the engine room operator who was trying to help her find something to do on the boat that would make her a valuable crew member before she decided to jump ship and join the pair heading to Honduras. She gave up on the noisy engine room when the Vietnam vet, startled by every unexpected movement, but prone to clanging heavy metal hatches for effect, had jumped out from behind a door to scare her with a "ratatattat" machine gun imitation and said, "If I'd had a gun, you'd be dead now." Too weird. She left Bill out of the male-bashing conversation. He'd left a wife and three kids, she knew, but she didn't know if he was paying alimony while he was enjoying himself in the Caribbean. Maybe he was no hero. Still, he had been her friend, and her lover, and he had been kinder to her than the other guys. Being with a man here reduced tension with the other divers, she felt, since the only women here "belonged" to someone.

They eased into the comradery of the put-upon; then Sandy described the way the men wouldn't take the time to decompress and a few would end up with mild bends because they were trying to outman the other divers. From there they talked sharks. Sandy's fear of every shadow below when she was on the surface was augmented by the spearfishing tales where the guys described sand sharks of three to four feet in the water with them.

"I have managed not to see a shark in the water. Barracudas I have seen. They give me the creeps," Sandy said, moving her mouth the slow methodical way the barracudas did. The women laughed at her jutting lower jaw moving in imitation. "Standing still in the water eyeing me—I can feel them before I see them."

"Bad, bad, bad vibrations," Debra reframed the Beach Boys song. The baby, who had been absorbed by the little bits of wood she'd found and enjoyed tossing back at the sea, waddled up to her mother's knees and began dancing by bouncing up and down bending her knees.

"You have a Southern accent," Sandy finally said. "Where are you from?"

"Georgia," Debra replied, helping her little daughter dance. "Originally."

"Golly! Me, too!" Sandy said. And from there they identified their hometowns and wandered a little into life history; a move to a bigger city and then Florida for Sandy, Debra's parents still in the same town in Georgia where she had grown up. Discovering their mutual Georgia roots, the two women felt a bond established in those early days of their time together on the island.

That was the day, however, when Sandy returned to her little room in the men's quarters up the hill, the goddess she'd become so fond of, the jade goddess she had spent a few minutes examining for her Buddha-like serenity and exquisite curves whenever she opened her suitcase and pulled back the cutoffs and shorts; that was the afternoon, when she moved the clothes, nothing was there. Not anywhere in the suitcase. And nowhere in the room. The goddess was gone, and the only thing missing. A sense of loss consumed her, and instead of anger, a void beyond sadness, a feeling of emptiness. She felt betrayed, but by whom? She felt violated, but had no sure way to know whom to blame. It could be anyone. Dave. Hal if he had seen her like she suspected when she was packing up the week before. Some random person from the village. The incredible beauty of the little goddess, and the comfort she provided, was simply gone.

Chapter 8

Debra pulled away from the warmth of her husband's body, lifted his arm slung across her stomach, and slipped out of the bed. The baby would still be sleeping for a while, so this early morning time was hers. The only thing of her own she had held on to was her yoga practice, all else had been absorbed into her husband's world and now this child. She had devoted all her time and energy to Dave's world and this family they had created together. Falling in love with Dave had been easy, but she had been surprised by falling in love with her baby, how much love could well up when she held that newborn or had let the tiny baby suckle at her breast, a warmth and sweetness surrounding them, flooding her heart with tenderness. Now nearly a year and a half later, she missed that sweet bliss of nursing, but the deep love she felt looking at her child had not diminished.

She checked on Melody's sleeping form, her light lashes against her cheeks and her soft brown curls so sweet, before she dressed in the hotel room, pulled on her yoga pants and loose cotton top. The empty rum bottle Dave must have finished the night before sat on the table. A momentary sadness came over her, but she pushed it away like so many breadcrumbs on a tablecloth.

Slipping out the door and down the hall to the palm-fringed courtyard, she settled on a blanket at the end of the hotel pier. Dim predawn light shimmered on the water. She began her deep breathing exercises, before she moved into stretching and neck exercises, on into cat and cow, the fish and bridge postures and forward bends, the bow, the plow, warming up to the sun salutations after inverted V and tree poses. The ujjayi breath drew her into her own being, her own body, like the sound of the sea at peace, calm and continual, drawing her into that state of calm. She did not attempt the full lotus seating, her knees yelling at her if she did, but she sat up tall, spine erect as she finished with kapalabhati breathing, imagining prana shining through each cell of her body, healing and uplifting her. The drawing in of oxygen from the ocean, the soft rhythmic sounds of calm waves...she took this moment of quiet to enjoy looking out at the sunrise clouds now fading as the strong sun turned the early morning into day, and she would have to return to an active baby and a troubled husband, consumed with his concerns about money and putting out fires with the boat crew in Florida, frustrated by the slow communication, letters and sporadic telegraph service not quick enough to suit him.

As she picked up her blanket, she saw an old woman fishing with silver minnows at the end of the dock the expedition crew used, and there at the land end of that pier, she saw Sandy sketching, intent on her drawing. Sandy looked up from her pad and smiled at Debra, waved silently and resumed her quick pencil strokes. Sharing the brief tranquility of early morning before the hot sun bore into every inch of their bodies, its rays like hot fingers searching out every crevice in the wood on these piers, burning the paint on the dock boxes and scorching the roofs of the village houses.

The baby was crying when she got back to the room. Dave was dressing, shushing the baby with her loud piercing wails.

"Can you get her," he said in an irritated voice, "before she wakes the whole place?"

"Sure, honey," she said, knowing he was probably hung over and the brief honeymoon of their reunion was done. It didn't occur to her to tell him he should have picked Melody up, until she was changing the wet diaper and making Melody laugh at her facial expressions and silly sounds after he left the room. As much as she knew Dave loved them both, she also knew he was not going to change a wet diaper or think of this child's needs when there were more important matters on his mind he thought he should attend to.

The anxious feeling that knotted up in her stomach, like tangled cords on a window blind, started up again. She remembered to take a deep breath. She carried the freshly powdered baby out to see what was cooking for breakfast. She could smell bacon and the aroma of coffee. Dave had already finished and it was just she and the cook while Debra fed Melody. Marie, the hotel owner, came in the kitchen.

"You want me to hold the baby while you eat?" she offered. "My two boys don't let me cuddle them anymore and I'd be delighted to play with this little ladybug."

She took Melody from Debra's arms and started investigating the red dots of cartoon insects on the ladybug top with the easily distracted child.

Thank goodness she likes people, Debra thought. No one was a stranger to her daughter. She took her plate onto the porch. She saw Sandy walking up the path by the hotel bar-porch, sketch book under her arm. They spoke briefly through the foliage by the porch rail. Debra put her dish of food on the table.

"Yoga?" Sandy asked, nodding towards the pier.

Debra nodded. "It helps get me centered.... What were you drawing?"

Sandy showed her the pier with the old woman at the end fishing, and a quick sketch of herself in the tree pose at the end of the pier. With just a few strokes, Sandy had caught her, hands above her head, balanced on one leg, the other propped at an angle to her thigh, a wave or two to indicate the water and a few curves for clouds. And there was surprising grace in the figure before her in yoga pose. Debra was pleased with how graceful she looked.

"You're really good."

"Thanks," Sandy said, and with a teasing grin, added, "and this is what centers me."

"Can I see more?"

Sandy handed her the sketch pad over the railing and Debra turned the pages. "You've really got good perspective."

"A degree in art helps with technique," Sandy said, "and my mother is a fashion illustrator so I come by my interest naturally. Maybe the degree itself doesn't help, but some professors did; others not so much. It could squelch your talent if you took some of them too seriously."

"Isn't that the truth. Depends so much on the individual teacher."

"Learning how to work with materials, see different techniques applied—that was the most help," Sandy chatted on as Debra turned the pages. Then she noticed Sandy's green eyes divert from the sketchpad towards the street.

Sandy saw Bill on the main road pushing the wheelbarrow with a block of ice for the kitchen. Debra passed the sketchbook back to her and Sandy excused herself to catch up with Bill.

"Want to dive this morning?" Sandy asked him.

"Can't," he said, balancing the load as he walked and talked. "Hal changed up the air compressors and tanks. Dave's furious. May have gas mixed in–got to empty all the tanks."

"Really?"

"Carbon monoxide. Could be deadly. Want to take the glass bottom boat out instead?"

"Sure," she said. "Why'd Hal mess with the setup of the tanks?"

"Why does he do anything? Guy's an idiot."

Sandy followed him to the kitchen house where the local cook was fixing breakfast and several men were drinking coffee. Bill delivered the ice to the cook and helped put it in place in the icebox.

The tall black woman, who refused to heat water to wash dishes, claiming hot water gave her rheumatism, had her little helper washing and drying the cooking pots while she was ladling scrambled eggs on a platter.

"Smells good," Sandy said, joining them in the cook room, next to the dining area, and taking the platter out to the table. Eggs were forked quickly onto plates by guys stabbing at each other in jest. Sandy grabbed two cups of coffee; both she and Bill drank their coffee black, after milk was sometimes "iffy," either sour or none available. She sat down on the bench. Bill, carrying a platter of bacon, joined her. He jerked his hand back from the bacon as the same clowns jabbed their forks in that direction. They aimed for him and each other, not the bacon.

"Hey, hey—watch it now," he laughed.

They filled their plates and joined in the general conversation. Rolf and Dan were discussing the air tank situation and getting those cleared out. There was more than the usual grumbling about the expensive vacation this treasure hunting had turned out to be. And now they had to worry about diving with a lunatic.

Sandy and Bill cleared out quickly and headed for the storage area to get the glass bottom boat. Only so many could help with the tanks and they weren't needed. Neither of them wanted to be there with Dave, still cussing about the screw up, and Hal, who was standing around being useless and explaining himself, trying to minimize the problem. They could hear the two men from the storage shed while they lifted the ends of the boat and carried it to the pier. Sliding the small craft into the water, they got on board. Bill adjusted the engine. After a few false starts, the Evinrude purred into life.

Sandy tied the strings of her floppy hat under her chin and Bill, his shirt unbuttoned and fluttering in the breeze, squinted in the direction of the lagoon. Sandy could see fish gliding under the boat's clear bottom. A few minutes later, they were nearing the mangroves and puttering into the canals between the leggy roots. The little trees hid nurseries of reef fish, tiny minnows hiding in the shade. It was murky there, maybe not such a good place for the glass bottom of their boat, roots having a way of showing up suddenly. The visibility wasn't good and the mosquitoes were bad. Bill backed the boat out of a snarled area, and they puttered back in the clearer water along the edges.

Still mosquitoes swarmed out at the smell of human flesh.

"We shoulda brought bug spray," Bill grumbled.

"You know, Rachel Carson said our using pesticides, and DDT, stuff like that, is like killing a mosquito with a sledge hammer. Or something to that effect," she said. Teasing him in his misery as he swatted one then another of the vicious attack squad, she joked in song, "If I had a hammer, I'd hammer in the morning, I'd hammer in the evenin' all over this land. I'd hammer out skeeters; I'd hammer out freedom…"

She, too, was soon under attack and they moved out into the open ocean, towards the lagoon and away from the murky mangroves. As they floated along the edges of the lagoon, looking at the schools of fish darting under the boat and swimming nearby, teal shadows below them, Sandy was reminded of the green figurine she had uncovered and lost so suddenly.

"Do you think objects can have power?" she asked

"Like what?"

She didn't want to say and hedged a bit. "Or like places, like Findhorn they say has special energy—"

"Or the Bermuda Triangle?" Bill joked. "That's one you don't want to mess with."

"Always the joker," she replied, glad to move away from the real subject on her mind, that green goddess and its whereabouts, the feelings it had stirred while it was in her possession.

The night before, they had discussed the argument she had overheard between Hal and Dave in the main house. Sandy had wondered aloud why, if Dave had found find items near the site, he wouldn't tell Hal, to reinforce staying on Roatilla. Bill had thought there was more going on than that. And when they returned to the bay, they learned Dave was planning to head to the mainland, leaving with the camera crew in the Cessna that afternoon. The morning mail had come in and he had urgent business in Ventura.

"Wow, that was quick," Sandy said, wiping out the boat. "What about Debra?"

Bill shrugged. He pulled the engine up and locked it in place.

"She just got here. I doubt she wants to get back on a plane," Sandy added.

"I guess we'll see pretty soon."

They got the boat back in storage, checked on the progress with the tanks, which had been refilled, and headed for the main house.

Debra was bringing Melody in for a nap when she found Dave packing a duffle bag.

"What's up?"

"I got an offer on the dive shop. I'll be back in a week."

"Honey," Debra said. "What about us? We just got here."

She wished she hadn't said it from the look on his face. He looked stressed, but she saw also a simmering anger beneath the surface, like a pot left on high too long and about to boil over, or more like a grease fire you didn't want to lift the lid on, she decided.

"Look, Debra, I'll be in Ventura less than a week. And I can call Florida from there. Got a telegram this morning and I need to check in with Gene. Communication here is too slow. I'll be back soon. You just stay here, enjoy the water, keep an eye on things."

He had too many irons in the fire, she wanted to say. But he did not need to hear that now. Selling the dive shop was a good start. She had put Melody down to sit on the bed, but her toddler climbed off and headed for the bag on the floor where Dave was standing, pulling socks from the drawer and folding them.

"Here, let me help," she offered and stood back up.

"I'm just about done. I'm sorry about this, hon," he said, turning to look her in the eyes.

Was his lip trembling? Debra looked at him without saying anything.

"Hal's threatening to pull his money out, not put that other half of his investment in. I've got Stan on it. Maybe he can talk some sense into Hal. I'm too pissed to talk reason right now. Give him time to be big chief a few days without me. You turn on that Southern charm. Be nice to him. He'll calm down. Stan can make sure he doesn't pull another caper like this morning."

Squatting by the duffle bag, Melody was about to put a coin in her mouth and Debra reached over to take her hand. It looked like gold. She took it from the child and saw there were more coins along with these little gold inlaid teeth, or teeth rimmed in gold, in a small open bag.

"What's this?"

"Nothing. Some stuff I'm taking to be identified," he said, snatching the bag up. It almost knocked her over, his quick gesture as she was squatting with one arm around Melody, a hand on the coin.

"Here, let me have that," he said and roughly took it from her hand to thrust into the bag. He stuffed it in a pocket beneath the bottom lining of his duffle bag.

"Gosh, Dave," she said, carrying Melody to the makeshift crib. Melody had started to rumble, a cry about to erupt, but Debra had the floppy bunny she'd picked up in the airport doing a little dance for Melody and talking bunny talk. The child was distracted and flapping the big ears herself. Debra gave her another toy, a rubber duck, too big to swallow, and distracted her with two choices.

"Keep this to yourself, Debra. I don't want Hal to do anything, and he's too—just don't get him riled. Keep him happy thinking he's top dog around here 'til I get back. Seriously, don't say anything to anybody about this stuff."

She turned back towards him, the baby in the crib with the toys, pacified to play a while. Dave had his bag zipped and was putting his watch on his wrist.

She hugged him from behind, and he turned and held her, gave her a quick peck, and said, "I'll be back soon, darling. You relax, enjoy the island, and we'll go diving soon as I get back. We'll get someone to watch Mel, and I'll take you out. Just you and me."

He was already out of there, she could tell from the quick kiss and the placating words to dismiss her worries before she could even express them.

"I'll hang out with the girls," she said, to give him an easy exit. "You get the sale done and I'll see you next week."

She walked him out to the hotel door, where one of only two pickup trucks on the island was sitting, driver ready to carry the three plane passengers to the little coral runway at the end of the island. She saw the cinematographers hoofing it over to the truck with their gear. She turned away from them. Tweedledee and Tweedledum.

"See you soon, honey," she said and hugged him, wanting to hold on, but with his quick squeeze and another peck, he released her.

Chapter 9

When Sandy disembarked from the plane, to the fresh air tinged with the salty scent of the keys, she saw a tall slim woman and a shorter, middle-aged one with a big welcoming smile, her dear friends, waving from the building. Sandy felt exhausted from the overnight flight, but glad to be back on solid ground and breathing fresh air, and glad to see her greeting committee already waiting for her. Walking across the asphalt towards the terminal with its sign welcoming her to the Conch Republic, she took in Debra's big grin. Debra still looked composed, and as attractive as ever, Sandy thought. The two old friends hugged tightly and then Melody gave her a brief, friendly hug.

"Wow, I'm so glad to see y'all!"

"We were so excited to see you coming off that plane," Mel said. "Mom has been beside herself."

Debra grabbed her carry on. They walked toward baggage claim.

"You look lovely," Debra said, "even if I know you're bone tired."

"When Mom saw you, her first words were 'she's still as long and slender as a palm tree'."

"Really? I feel like a wilted piece of celery."

"You had such a youthful gait, striding across that tarmac; you looked like a girl. All I could think was 'drats, couldn't the woman at least age gracefully?'"

Mel shook her head. "Meaning?"

"Meaning, she's supposed to look older! Like the rest of us in our fifties!"

Sandy smiled. "The lines in my face are as graceful as it gets. And there are plenty! Did you think I'd age that much in four years?"

Debra just laughed. The three claimed baggage and loaded the trunk of the red convertible.

"Fine ride," Sandy commented as she got into the back seat and chatted on about flight weariness and airline food. Before Melody started the car, Debra smiled back at her, her bright hair gleaming in the sunlight, and Sandy added to Debra, "Your hair looks great."

"Thanks!" The thick auburn hair furled around Debra's shoulders and framed her face. Once the car pulled out of the parking lot and they headed down the road, the wind began whipping Sandy's own short locks in her face. Debra turned back around in the passenger seat. She reached back and patted Sandy's knee. "I'm so glad to see you. Four years are too long!"

"You got that right!" Melody added. "We miss you."

"I miss y'all, too. You need to come out–free place to stay in Paradise!"

"I've been out twice already, honey, that's all my budget allows for a while. I still remember sailing out of that yacht club, in what, Kaneohe? And the Academy of Arts, and so many gorgeous flowers! Waikiki at sunset and all that Hawaiian music. Remember we went to that hula festival? I have lots of fond memories." Debra turned to her daughter, added, "She took me to the Toilet Bowl. When she said it was a scenic spot, I had no clue! It turned out to be this giant blow hole, a geyser of ocean waves spraying up through the lava!"

"Yeah, I remember you telling me that story," Mel said, her eyes on the road.

"People get hurt trying to go down in that thing," Sandy contributed. "She also went with me to the Big Island and met Pele, our goddess of volcanoes, up at Halemaumau. You can really feel her energy on the Big Island."

Mel drove along the strip showing the beaches, the seaweed curving at the surf's edge, and did not respond. Debra looked back at Sandy and winked.

Sandy changed the subject. They chatted briefly about her long flight, and the hotel where they were staying, not broaching the more serious reasons for their reunion. Sandy talked about her life in the islands, the lawyer she'd stopped seeing months before, and her cartography business, adding, "I've really been busy getting my Sandwich Islands T-shirts distributed through the islands. I've got a deal on Kauai, too, for the art on their tourism brochures. Maybe on their world wide web site, too."

"That's great, Sandy," Debra said, holding her hair back from the whipping wind, when she turned again to smile at Sandy. "You are so brave to have your own business. You've always been brave. But I never imagined you'd be so business savvy."

"Well, I won't get rich, but it pays the rent. How about you? How's your pottery going? Your critters? Your folks?"

"Rosy's six and Tinkerbell's what—nine, now? I've got half a dozen hens. I have a broody hen, a Buff Orpington; she'll be done about the time we get back and she's already raised several chicks. She's a good mother."

"Mom's the stork," Mel added. "I don't know why she doesn't just get a rooster."

"I had one, another mouth to feed, but he just badgered them to death, horny fellow." Debra turned and whispered, "He nearly f—ed 'em to death. My system works. When she's been sitting three weeks, I just put a new tiny chick under her from the feed store, and she doesn't ask any questions. Doesn't ask why there's no cracked egg shell, just loves her new baby. Works every time."

"And your folks?"

"Grams is enjoying the apartment close to friends; Gramps—we stopped calling him Grumps when he had that stroke—has actually gotten sweeter. I never thought I'd live to see it."

"Mel, how about your young ones?"

"We're big on crawdads these days. Jack has discovered the crayfish living near the creek, ones that burrow on land. I didn't know there were different kinds. Leslie—she's almost four now, can you believe it? Just follows him around and carries the bucket. Jeff's got a mustang gathering at the farm, so that's been keeping us busy getting ready for that—that's for people who adopted wild horses; we've hosted the North Carolina group twice now. We have a roan, Blue, that we adopted. Great horse."

They chattered on until Mel asked if anyone was hungry.

After conch fritters and salads, Mel dropped them off at the Westwind. "I'm going over to see Liz," she informed them, then added, in response to Sandy's quizzical look, "Liz is Daddy's current wife. Or was.... When I get back, we're supposed to go to dinner at Dan's."

"Who's that?"

"That's Daddy's second wife's son. Daddy kept her boys in his life after they split up."

Sandy couldn't hide the surprise on her face. "The second wife. She's here?"

Only Debra was looking. She rolled her eyes like a teenager.

"Why—?" Sandy started to ask.

"She's attempting to be civil," Melody explained. "Not that it undoes years of being a total ass."

"She knows not to use the *B* word here." Debra winked.

Sandy waited until she'd gotten the key to her own room, changed, and she and Debra were at the pool, to ask the real question, the burning question: "Why the hell are we here?"

They sat in lounge chairs in a shady part of the pool area, both slathered in sunblock and sipping sweet tea. Debra shrugged and shook her head.

"Well, I came because Mel wouldn't have spoken to me for a month If I hadn't, and that wouldn't be so bad," Debra grinned, "but she could deny me access to my grandkids through eternity—or until they're teenagers and no fun to be around."

"Really, Debra," Sandy asked, her eyes turning serious. "Why us? Why me?"

Debra turned to look her square in the face. "It's something about Roatilla and Dave's will. There's something involving you, Liz said."

"That's weird. A will? Inheritance? You mean all that money he hid from you?" Sandy said, a tinge of anger creeping into her voice with the memory. "Or the things he stole from Honduras?"

"Allegedly stole," Debra corrected.

"You don't have to be loyal to him now," Sandy remarked.

"I'm being sarcastic, Sandy. Or ironic. I'm not sure which," she said, "But this certainly has dredged up some old memories."

"For me, too," Sandy added, feeling more sympathetic as she looked at Debra's sad expression. "Gosh, we were young then."

"No joke," Debra replied. "I'm okay with this age, being in good health and all, but how fast the time has passed.... I rummaged through some old pictures last night, even brought a couple down with me. I can't believe how young and good looking we all were—I look like a baby with a baby."

"How's Melody taking all this?"

"She's a trouper. She's a lot more resilient than I give her credit for sometimes," Debra said. "She's a lot better at taking care of herself than I was. I've learned a lot about looking out for my own needs watching her."

"It's that age group. Generation X. I worked with some apprentices at the museum when I worked part-time out there until my own business was doing well enough to quit the museum. Of course, they were young. But since then, some of the people I do business with from the mainland now are late twenties, early thirties. They march to the beat of their own drum."

"And by their own rules...not our rules," Debra added. "That does sound familiar."

"Question authority. That was our generation. They took our advice."

"I guess every generation thinks the younger generation is going to hell in a handbasket. I know my parents did."

After a pause, Sandy continued with her original line of questioning. "So Melody is handling his death okay? They were closer after this second wife was out of the picture, right?"

"I think the third one was the catalyst. For Melody and Dave. "

"They had fifteen years, I guess, on fairly good terms," Sandy mused.

Debra nodded, but only sipped her tea.

Sandy dove into the cool water of the deep end and Debra slipped in from the side of the pool. They swam a while without talking and eventually Debra got back out and sat in her chair. Sandy did laps, managing to avoid the two children playing with a ball near the shallow end, maneuvering around their splashing bodies, before she got back out. Standing there dripping wet and wiping down with a towel, Sandy saw the pensive expression on Debra's face

She finally spoke. "What's up, Debra? What ya thinking about?"

"Just about all this stuff happening, having to see Dave's wife—widow..." Debra replied haltingly. "I never met Liz, only have a vague impression of her from a picture Melody has in her house."

"And?" Sandy prodded, noticing how hesitant her friend was to open up. "What's she look like?"

Debra frowned. "Well, actually, the photo had Dave in it, too. I avoided it. It was one I chose not to examine carefully for glimmers of remorse or guilt on Dave's face, knowing it wouldn't be there, afraid to find he was happy looking after all the grief he had given me."

"Oh," Sandy said.

Debra took a sip of her tea. "It didn't seem fair. But life isn't fair."

"No, it isn't. I think you're right there...or else we don't see the big picture. "

"I long ago decided life is a series of lessons and if you didn't learn the first time, or pass the test on one, you spiraled back to a similar set up somewhere down the line. A cosmic joke."

Sandy looked at her. "Well, I think that may be true, too. The lesson thing. When I was flying here, all that time to think, trying to sort through some of my own questions...we grow, though, don't you think? We learn something about ourselves each time? If we recognize it's the same issue in a new guise?"

"My mind's been wandering back to whatever lessons I learned living with Dave, and I haven't got an answer yet." Then Debra's serious expression changed to a smile. "All this sounds so—"

"Profound?"

Sandy grinned at her.

Debra's smile widened. "Deep. Really deep.... Enough of this. What time is it?"

"Don't know. What time are you supposed to go to this second wife's son's house?"

"Us, dear; we're not leaving you home alone," Debra said. "I haven't seen you in four years, longest time since I've known you; we have to make use of what time we've got. Plus the more of us there, the less I'll have to talk to these people."

Sandy's argument against going was feeble—tired after a long flight, she needed recovery from the time zone change— and she quickly gave in because she was curious to see who these people were. Most of all, time with the closest she had to family was precious.

The late afternoon sun through palm fronds cast shadows across the patio and the water shimmered with reflected light. They took up their towels and belongings and left to find Mel and determine when to be ready. Melody was finishing a shower when they got back to their rooms. Sandy had time for a short nap before they were supposed to go.

Once they were cleaned up, dressed, and ready, Debra and Mel knocked on Sandy's door. She finished curling her short hair and put the curling iron down, brushed out her hair, grabbed her small purse, and admired how good they all looked. Debra wore a sundress with a shawl, while Sandy had chosen her raw silk pants and jacket with a pastel silk blouse. They were both prepared to be hot or cold. Melody was dolled up with silver bracelets, a silver hair clasp holding her thick sandy blonde hair back, even dangling earrings. Her dress was simple and she brought no wrap. Hot blooded, Sandy reflected.

"A fashion parade," Debra said as the three made their way along the uneven bricks to the car. Sandy smiled. Melody did not take the top down in deference to their hair and the occasion.

She drove them to the house where her stepbrother, Dan lived, the one who had been in the salvage business with Dave. Filling them in with a few background details, Mel explained that Nelson, the younger stepson who was around twenty-eight, and Dan, the older one at thirty-three, would be there along with Barbara, their mother who had lived in Miami with Dave before he moved operations to the Keys. Dan's wife and children, of course, would be at the house, too. Liz had not been invited, they had learned, but Melody said she would have been too broken up to want to come, anyway. She was taking this loss pretty hard. The memorial service in two days would be the first time the three wives would be in the same room together.

They passed the casual old houses of Key West, narrow driveways with beguiling entrances to a multitude of other worlds, hidden gardens suggested behind many, and tropical foliage crowding upward for light, crowding any open space in the variegated shade of palms, oaks, shrubs. Pre-dusk light filtered through the neighborhoods as Melody drove through the old part of town, and north towards Dredger's Key.

"We should go watch sunset one of these days we're free," Sandy said.

"It's quite a spectacle," Mel noted.

"Pina Colada on the beach suits me better," Debra said.

"Too sweet," Melody interjected.

"Margaritas," Sandy pronounced, almost in unison with Debra.

"Maybe we could get a bottle of Cuervo on the way home—or sometime tomorrow," Debra added.

"I make a mean Margarita."

"She's not kidding, Mel."

"I think I'll pass," Melody said.

Before they pulled into the drive of the modest looking house, the three women stopped chatting and planned their exit strategy. Together they walked to the house and Mel rang the bell.

Nelson, Dave's younger stepson, opened the door, drink in hand. The medium-built man with thinning hair led the three towards the back of the house, which opened to a surprisingly elegant back yard with small pool, a water fountain splashing in rhythmic constancy. Two small children were being wrapped in towels by a dark-haired woman. Dan, taller and more broad-shouldered than his brother, greeted them with a pleasant smile and a brief hug for Mel, and the older woman in a white wicker chair turned to stare. She gave them the once-over before she got up.

"You must be Debra," the woman in the black sheath spoke as she reached for Debra's hand. "You look like those pictures we had—the one or two old pictures David kept."

She oozed ownership. Like he was still hers. She seemed not to realize Dave had left her long ago.

Pausing, Debra finally took the offered hand but pulled back quickly. Sandy, seeing Debra's reluctance to extend her hand, moved toward the two women standing there on the patio. Before Sandy reached out to shake, she noticed the woman's polished, well-manicured nails, and the gold rings. As the woman began to introduce herself, Sandy felt her grasp, a bit cold.

"I'm Barbara," she said too sweetly. "You must be their friend Dan said was coming?"

"Would you like something to drink?" Dan asked before Sandy could respond.

All three accepted glasses of red wine from the Merlot and Pinot Noir bottles already open on the outside bar. Rum, bourbon, vodka were also being offered by Nelson, mixing himself another drink. They had agreed to stay sober, but not look stuffy, and Debra had told Sandy she knew her limit before her tongue might loosen, "like an old elastic waistband on worn out pantyhose, slip like hot butter on a skillet, or worse, pop like a cork ready to go in a champagne bottle." Sandy had laughed. She wasn't worried about her own loose tongue and didn't take long after introductions to ask this second wife, Barbara, a few questions. Sandy wanted to get the lowdown on this lady before dinner.

Number Two's thin, long nose and narrow lips contrasted with the softer features and upturning corners of Debra's full lips, Sandy observed. And Debra's eyes, even in these circumstances, had a kindness that the other woman's lacked. Dave had certainly done a one-eighty on wives, Sandy couldn't help but think.

"How did you and Dave meet?"

Barbara looked a little startled by Sandy's directness, interrupted while she was studying Debra's appearance and full figure, doing the annoying once-over Sandy had found so distasteful earlier. Mel was studying the collection of sea shells behind the bar, and looked up.

"Why, we met at a yacht club," Barbara said.

"Was that on Saint Thomas, or in Miami?" Sandy asked.

"We were living in Saint Thomas, weren't we, Mom?" Nelson offered. "We moved back and forth from Saint Johns to Saint Thomas. I was only three, so I hardly remember when he wasn't in our lives."

"Unlike my own daughter," Debra muttered behind her wine glass, so low only Sandy was close enough to hear her.

Barbara turned and directed her comment to Debra, "What's that?"

Just then, Dan's wife, Marge, walked out on the patio, "I'll set the kids in the den with cartoons. We should have a little adult time before they get restless. Dan, did you offer anyone appetizers?"

She looked at the faces around her, tension palpable. She picked up a tray from the counter. "I had to get Carly and Justin bathed and you were supposed to offer our guests those delightful crab cakes and the spinach dip I spent all afternoon laboring over."

"Yes, the trip to Publix and the bakery were quite grueling," Dan joked.

"Here, I'll be glad to help," Mel offered, grabbing the tray of hors d'oeuvres from her hostess.

"Thanks," Marge said and turned to the bar.

"I'll have a splash," Barbara said as Marge poured herself a glass of wine.

"So what were you doing in Saint Thomas?" Sandy zeroed in as she took a chair between Debra and the second wife.

She seemed reluctant to answer. "I was a cocktail waitress," she finally admitted.

Barbara sipped her wine, then looking at no one in general, added, "Dave was looking for investors, you know, the way he always did. I was getting divorced. He had approached several club members the year before, my husband included, and I remembered him. He took the children out in his boat a lot when we began—began seeing each other. When he decided to move to Miami, he took us with him. I wouldn't go unless we married. Dan, Brenda, and Nelson needed a father."

"Brenda?"

"My daughter. She was living with her father in Australia. She left after I married Nelson's father and I hoped we could all be one happy family again when we moved to Florida. I always hoped he'd adopt the boys, at least."

Well, her tongue was certainly getting loosened, Sandy thought. She figured Dave had gotten up with Barbara before his bed with Debra was cold.

"Mom always worried about that," Dan said, joining the group. "But here we are all grown up and doing fine."

"I don't know about that," Barbara said. "Money's tight and—"

"Mom, we're going to start making the shish kabobs. Are y'all getting hungry? Mel, want to come help us? We haven't had time to catch up," Dan interrupted, smiling at Mel, and moving back towards the sliding glass doors of the kitchen. "Have some more appetizers. It will be a little while."

"Let me finish this glass, and I'll be right in there," Mel said before he closed the doors.

The younger brother, whose light blond hair was already thinning on top, sat down momentarily with them on the patio. Nelson had his older brother's light blue eyes, but that was where the resemblance ended. He grabbed a couple of mini-crab cakes, and then got up to join the kitchen crowd.

When Barbara took the tray back to the kitchen to refill, Sandy leaned over, "Did you see her neck?"

"Must have had a face job."

"Tsk. Tsk. *Catteee*, you two!" Mel whispered before she stood up. "Behave, y'all." She left her wine glass on the bar and opened the glass doors.

Barbara returned from the kitchen to the two guests sitting together, put the tray on the table, sat down, and turned to Debra.

"So you're the one."

"The one what?" Debra asked.

"The one David used to dream about. He'd mumble your name in his sleep. I got used to it. At least he didn't use your name when we—"

She stopped and smiled. Her lips curled down, in what Sandy could only think was a smirk. Debra was still. Too still. She was looking down at her drink. Sandy couldn't read her expression.

"I've always wanted to meet you," the second wife said sweetly.

"You mean before or after he dodged alimony and child support?" Sandy interjected.

"And this applies to you how?" Barbara replied crisply, giving her a look Sandy knew the Hawaiians would call stink-eye.

The three were silent. The young adults in the kitchen were laughing and talking, spearing peppers and onions along with beef on skewers.

"Times were hard," the second wife said stiffly. "That's long past."

She got up to pour herself another glass of wine and sat down. "We have to focus on David's good points. For the sake of the children. We also have to consider who helped him out most when he needed it. After all, we helped him build up his fortune after those unpleasant days. The lawsuits and legal fees. And this salvage business didn't take off here until '92, after Hurricane Andrew. These last eight years were much more prosperous. Even if Dave and I had gone our separate ways, the boys were quite helpful to him. After the hurricane there was quite a lot of work. Dan practically ran the operation."

Dan, who was walking out with another bottle of Merlot to uncork and offer refills, overheard her last remark and said, "Oh, I wouldn't say that, Mom."

Nelson, coming out to grab more appetizers, stood beside his brother.

"Dad was a real enterprising guy. Quite smart," Dan said a little wistfully. "He knew his way around a boat. That's for sure. He could stabilize a wreck quicker than anyone around in the salvage boat business. The *Wishbone* on the coral reefs off Marathon—remember that, Nelson?"

Nelson added, "He might not have been in the best shape these last years, but he could certainly right a vessel and keep us out of harm's way quicker than any of the old sea salts or the young guys—"

Sandy prompted, "But wasn't he with Liz by then, even before Hurricane Andrew?"

The two brothers exchanged puzzled looks, and Nelson spoke up. "We worked with him from the '80s, even as youngsters. Dan liked the challenge when he was old enough to be a real help. I wasn't interested in the salvage end as much, more the finding end, looking for whatever could be uncovered. But Liz enjoyed having us around. She wasn't involved in his salvage business, if that's what you're getting at."

He gave Sandy a look that said to back off. She kept her gaze level, looking back at him. He looked away.

"Well, the boys certainly deserve the credit," Barbara said. "I don't think Liz and Dave would have been so comfortable without these men taking care of business. Without his sons helping."

Sandy cringed. It sounded so weird to have strangers claiming Mel's father as their own, taking credit for whatever success he might have had.

"Won't be long before we eat," Dan said. He lit the tiki torches and the candles on the tables. He and Nelson returned to the kitchen.

Through the glass doors, Sandy could see the four younger people finishing up with skewering vegetables and meat for shish kabobs. Marge had recruited the two children, given them their own bamboo sticks and let them thread mushrooms, peppers, onions and meat on theirs. Then she answered the phone. She stepped out to speak to her mother-in-law.

"The babysitter just called. Melody said the service Thursday starts at three, so we can pick you up at two thirty. If you would like to stay for refreshments, after, I can make plans with the babysitter. I told her I would call her this evening, but she just called and wants to know when we'll be done. Is that all right—to stay after the service?" Marge asked. "I need to call her back before it gets any later."

"We can all stay if Dan wishes," Barbara said, "but it would probably be a good idea to keep the babysitter awhile. We don't know how long it will all take. Say six, or make that seven?"

Marge looked a little nonplussed by the answer, but simply said, "I'll tell her seven."

"Well, Sandy," Barbara said, after Marge returned to the kitchen. "You've been asked to join the reading of the will. I don't remember Dave mentioning you before. My sons told me you and Debra are friends, and that you knew my ex-husband."

"I was on Roatilla. Part of the dive expedition down there."

"The Oceanic treasure hunters that went bust?"

"The very one. That's where I met Debra. When she and Mel joined us down there. Mel was just a baby."

"So you were part of that original expedition of treasure hunting," the black-sheathed woman said, taking a sip of wine, her angular features adding a sharpness to her remarks. Barbara then smiled and looked at Sandy. "Hunting and finding golden doubloons and pieces of eight. Then you certainly understand how these young men deserve their share of Dave's fortune."

"Fortune?"

"He said the treasure hunting was his big dream, and he said they found gold. He always said the funds ran out. Not enough investors, too many expenses, I always thought there was more to it than that. He and Nelson did a little searching on their own. Florida takes twenty-five percent right off the top of anything you find. How was it down there? Did you have to report finds?"

"You know, I don't know that much about that end of things," Sandy said. "He had archeologists. We catalogued some of what we found—"

"Some?" Barbara perked up. "Like what?"

"Oh, I don't know," Sandy hedged. "Cannon balls, a few silver chains...certainly no golden doubloons. It's been a lifetime ago. I was just enjoying wonderful diving in clear blue waters. It was a wonderland. Not like the reefs today. Visibility was clear as crystal."

"And you, Debra," Barbara said. "Did you dive?"

"I did some, Barbara," Debra replied. "I wasn't a strong swimmer, so I wasn't as comfortable in the water as this lady was."

Debra smiled at Sandy. It was the first time Sandy had heard her say anything in quite a while.

"And did you ever find any valuables down there?" Barbara asked.

"Me?" Debra laughed. "Diving for Spanish galleons and hunting for gold doubloons was Dave's idea of a good time, not mine."

"Well, treasure hunting sounds quite romantic," Barbara said. "And profitable. Look at Mel Fisher's success. Or that of his family."

"It was an adventure," Sandy said. "I can give Dave credit for that. It was quite an experience for a young woman bent on seeing the world."

"Yes. You can give Dave credit for that. He had such a flare for getting people behind his dreams."

"Or schemes," Sandy added. Before anyone spoke, Nelson came out with a platter of skewers for the grill. He put the platter down and opened the grill.

"My boys were always glad to get out there with him. And help when he needed it…even after we split up. Isn't that right, Nelson? Sweetie, how about another splash?"

Barbara took the bottle Nelson handed her, and before Debra could protest, half-filled her wine glass.

Sandy held out her wine glass for the finish of the bottle.

"Dave may not have legally adopted them, but these young men certainly earned their share of his business. Don't you think so, Debra?"

Debra, who was swirling the wine around in the glass watching the light from the torches play across the moving surface, turned. "What? I missed what you said."

"I was saying the boys should enjoy the fruits of their labor. After all, they spent more years with David than your daughter did."

"What are you getting at?" Sandy asked, since Debra was just staring through the candlelight at the second wife, like a deer caught in the headlights.

"We wouldn't want to have to contest the will. I'm sure we can sort this out amicably, without getting the courts involved."

Sandy noticed she stumbled on the word "amicably" and the splash of wine was already gone.

"We don't even know what's in the will," Debra spoke up.

"You might be jumping the gun," Sandy added. She saw where this woman was going with the business angle, inheritance and all that. No telling how Dave had arranged that. Thinking about the legalities made her head swim.

"Well, in case there are any issues, we want to be clear on one thing," Barbara said and stood up. "These boys *will* get their inheritance. The money is coming to them. I'll see to that."

Sandy thought she'd said enough herself, and Debra seemed unwilling to get in a verbal confrontation though Sandy would have backed her up if she had. Barbara excused herself to go to the restroom before everyone came out of the kitchen and the group's activity centered around the grilling and eating of food, easy bantering by the younger set, and the three older women eating and occasionally contributing to a general conversation that no longer veered off into dangerous territory.

Once dessert was over, Sandy began to yawn and mention how tired she was. This was the cue.

Mel, who had been laughing at one of Dan's stories, not privy to this earlier conversation among the women at their end of the patio, picked up her part when she saw Sandy yawning. "Aunt Sandy, you've had a long day. We should get you home."

"Are you sure you'll be okay to drive?" Marge asked.

"I only had one glass of wine," Mel responded. "I'm fine to drive. It was good to see you again, Marge, and to get to know your two little ones a little bit."

Although Nelson had cast a few glances over to the three women around the glass-topped table, Marge seemed oblivious to the verbal skirmish and the tension among the quiet women.

"What's with you two?" Mel asked after she pulled away from the house.

"That woman, Barbara, threw down the gauntlet," Debra said. "She seems to think Dave is leaving you a big inheritance or something. She plans to contest it."

"What?" Mel said, putting on the brakes.

"Drive," Sandy directed from the back. "We'll fill you in as we go. You just have to promise to keep your eyes on the road. I think Barbara was drunk. She had a glass when we got there. And all those splashes. I was watching and she had to have at least four or maybe five glasses."

"What did she want? Testing the waters?" Mel asked. "To see if you knew anything? Knew anything about the will? What?"

"Or try to make sure the current wife doesn't get the business?" Sandy asked. "I was confused. Why didn't you speak up, Debra?"

"Lie down with dogs, get up with fleas."

"Good point. Or like I heard in Hawaii, we have two eyes, two ears, one mouth, so use them proportionately," Sandy added. "Smart. She meant to get us on her side, I think. But her fangs came out too soon."

"Lord, we don't need this," Debra said.

"Maybe she wants you to settle without contesting the will," Sandy suggested.

Turning towards her daughter, Debra said, "He owes you plenty, Mel, for all those years you had to do without."

"Well, I may have been without a father for a while," Mel said hesitantly, "but I wasn't without love or a roof over my head."

"It's too early to be fighting over the carcass like jackals," Debra blurted out, shocking them all. "Oh, I'm sorry, sweetheart. That was a bit graphic."

"It's okay. But do you know anything specific?" Mel asked.

"No, do you?" Debra asked. "About any of this?"

"Well, I did ask about the boat and the circumstances of Dad's sudden death."

"That sounds dramatic," Sandy said, ready to change the topic of wills for the time being, but plenty curious about what the next days would bring.

"There was evidence someone else had been on the boat. Dad wasn't drinking. I'm sure of that."

"Was there an autopsy?"

"No results yet; they think it was accidental. Fell. Hit his head. Someone saw the boat and called the coast guard."

"What do you think of these guys?" Sandy asked.

"Dan always seems up and up to me," Mel said, "but Nelson, I'm not sure about him. I know Daddy relied on Dan. They were in the salvage business more than sixteen years. Since he was a teen. As long as I've known him. I haven't seen him, either of them, much since…since I got married. Even before that. College and all…"

They drove in the dark in silence a few minutes. Finally, Mel spoke.

"I liked Marge," Melody said. "She seemed real genuine, down to earth."

"Your ex-step-sister-in-law. Or step-ex. That's quite a handle," Sandy commented.

Car lights and shadows played across the two women in the front seat. No one responded to her attempt at light heartedness. They were all tired, she especially, after the long day.

After they reached their hotel, Mel let them out, and went to park the car.

Under the lights flickering through the palms as a night breeze moved through the fronds, Sandy said, "I've been thinking a lot about our days on Roatilla. Ever since you called, Debra."

"Me, too. I had put Dave behind me so long ago. And now all this. It's like opening your closet and finding clothes you haven't worn since high school that don't fit." Debra paused. "Or riding down a country road minding your own business and a sinkhole opens up and swallows you."

"Wow, a sinkhole? That bad? I remember when Dave left Roatilla, and you were left down there with us," Sandy continued. "And Mel was so little. You seemed so vulnerable.... You still do."

"Now Mel's older than we were then," Debra said.

"When I first met you, I thought you were some privileged sort, but my impression changed so quickly."

Before Debra could respond, Mel was walking up to them. She had parked the car and joined the two women standing at the door to Sandy's room before they said good night. The soft island breeze blew through the dark night air, like dreams that pass in the night and then are gone. And the memories that drift into those dreams, pass through the chambers of the heart, leave the dreamer stirred, but unaware of why, when the breeze that blew them is gone.

Chapter 10

When Sandy and Debra had first become friends back in the early '70s, Roatilla was a sleepy little island. While the villagers passed their days in the hot somnolence of that summer, the treasure hunters spent theirs in the cool blue waters of the Caribbean. A week had gone by and Dave had still not returned to the island. Debra had put on a brave face in the disappointment of his absence, but it was starting to slip, Carrie noted to Sandy. Debra had begun to look worried, but she did not talk about it, and they didn't ask.

As the second week came and went, the three women spent some of their afternoons at the main house, reading while Mel was napping, or down by the water, even swimming while one or the other watched the baby, but visibility was poor in the cove where the village spread along its shore, and Debra didn't want to go out in the boat without Dave.

Sandy dove with Bill and Rolf and some of the other men. She avoided dives with Hal by checking first to find who was going out. She had been surprised to learn the dredge had been moved, that first morning after Dave left for California, to another section near the lagoon. Stan had been in charge of the move and Hal was indifferent to these locations, grumbling still that they would need to move north to find the routes of the Spanish fleets laden with goods from their ports in their new world empire, gold and silver treasure looted from the Aztec, Incas, and Maya they had conquered. Yet Hal seemed somewhat smug at times. Sandy was also nonplussed to discover the last two grid drawings she'd done were not in the catalogue drawer. She was pretty sure Hal didn't know about the grid drawings that were missing. She said nothing.

After diving mornings, Sandy spent her afternoons with Bill or the women. Bill and some of the men would dive in the afternoon and bring in fish they caught, but Sandy only dove once a day. During those morning dives, Sandy continued to sketch everything laid out on the ocean floor after the air lift hose had made a run across the area, lifting sand and mud up to where the guys picked out bits of coral and anything of interest from the screen at the other end on the platform, but nothing significant appeared.

Carrie and Sandy talked, both wondering where all this was headed, since no word from Dave came for a week, and then another week. Stan seemed to be in the dark, too, and, except for making sure Hal was contained, continued day-to-day operations as before. On the day a letter finally arrived for Debra, she told them he'd finished the deal with the dive shop and had gone to check on the boat in Florida. What remained unsaid was their knowledge that the boat being retrofitted for their diving operation was going to Charleston, not Roatilla, and there was an entire crew in Jacksonville unaware of the change of plans. Or so they thought.

Letter in hand, Debra passed off the sale as being needed so Dave could focus on Oceanic Expeditions and then settled into a chair in the main room and stuck her nose in her book. The boat arriving with mail and supplies for the island had finally delivered word from her husband, but too much remained in limbo. Debra put the letter in the book she was reading, checked on her daughter asleep on Carrie's bed, returned to the main room, and said she needed to get some supplies from the hotel, milk for Melody when she woke up. Sandy thought she looked like she wanted to cry, but Debra was keeping her chin up and her eyes down.

After Debra had gone over to the hotel, with sharing just the basic facts about selling the shop, and saying Dave wanted to focus on Oceanic Expeditions, Carrie told Sandy, "They're cash-strapped. Maybe she knows how much or maybe she doesn't. Still, it has to be a disappointment he's going to be gone longer than she expected."

They were both reading when Debra returned to the house. The afternoon was hot and muggy. As a diversion, to pass the time and get Debra's mind off worrying about her husband's return, Carrie brought out the tarot cards and her astrology book of the sun signs. Carrie, a Cancer, said the description fit her. She asked Debra what her sign was.

"I'm Taurus," Debra answered, looking up from her book.

"Oh, my moon is in Taurus," Sandy said. "My mother's, too. It's exalted there. Taurus is ruled by Venus. Love of beauty, music, arts..."

"I thought it was Ferdinand the bull, sniffing the flowers in the pasture. Pastoral nature," Debra said.

Sandy smiled. "That, too. Earthy."

"Peace loving," Carrie added.

"Unless we see red?" Debra asked.

"I can see that," Carrie said. "But so far, we haven't encountered that side of you."

Next, Carrie picked up her tarot cards. Sandy shuffled the deck a few times, and Carrie laid out the cards with their medieval-looking characters and symbols, pentacles, swords, wands, and cups, arranged in two long lines, with cards across in a horizontal line. Similar to the astrological air, water, fire, and earth signs with which Sandy was already familiar, the symbols on the cards fascinated her. Sandy's reading take-away was she had suffered in her life but had strength to overcome difficulties, and a man whose interest was philosophy would come into her life. But when Carrie read Debra's cards, the young mother was disturbed by the looks of the cards: a fool, a hanged man, and a tower with flames among the images…and someone falling from that tower.

Carrie put the cards away. The women went back to reading. Sandy had finished *The Lost Continent of Mu* and offered it to Debra for whenever she finished *The Sun Also Rises*, but the underwater continent of Lemuria in the Pacific didn't appeal to Debra. Debra gave her a copy of *Electric Kool-Aid Acid Test* she had in her big baby bag. Carrie herself had recently finished the copy of *The Sun Also Rises*, which Sandy had read the year before when she travelled in Spain with the love of her young life, and Carrie was curious what Debra would think of it. Debra, almost finished with the book, agreed with the two women that Hemingway was sexist. The three discussed his portrayal of how Brett having an affair with the matador interfered with his beautiful art, a woman bringing him down, Sandy complained; but they agreed Hemingway's depictions of Spain were so detailed, they could all say they felt they'd been there. Sandy pointed out she herself actually had been.

"I saw El Cordobés fight when I was in Spain," Sandy reminisced. "He was a national hero; the Moonlight Fighter they called him. When he was young, he sneaked out and fought young bulls in the pasture, which was a no-no. The bulls had an advantage when they got in the ring…. I was reading *Or I'll Dress You in Mourning*, at the time. It was about his life. Everyone passed around novels set in the particular country we were travelling in, so it gave interesting insights, always added to the experience. That book we were reading before I actually watched my one and only bullfight. Paul wanted to see El Cordobés, so we went. The bull jumped the barrier into the crowd, which I thought showed great boldness on the bull's part, but the Spanish jeered. They considered it too small for El Cordobés."

"You've had some interesting experiences. You're quite an adventurer," Debra said.

"I love travel. So many worlds out there. It's all so amazing. When I read *On the Road* by Jack Kerouac, I wanted to be like the guys, on the road having all the adventures, not stuck on the East Coast or the West Coast waiting for the guys to get home and washing their clothes like their women did."

Debra got a funny look on her face at the exact moment Sandy realized what had popped out of her mouth. "Oh, I'm sorry. Marriage works for some, I just don't see it as an option for me. Or not any time before I've had all the fun I can." She looked at Debra. "Am I making this worse?"

Carrie said, "When you get your foot out of your mouth, you might help decide how we can convince Debra to go snorkeling with us."

"Or tell us how you met that guy you travelled with — Paul?" Debra suggested. Then she added, "When you were on the road with the guys?"

Sandy looked quickly at Debra, who was smiling, though her smile appeared a bit sardonic. Debra winked at her.

"Okay, you're mocking me," Sandy said, "so we're even."

"Let's go snorkeling," Carrie repeated.

"We could take Melody," Sandy offered, unsure of her footing and eager to change the conversation.

Almost on cue, the baby starting to wake up could be heard with her early coos. Debra headed for the room before she started to cry.

"Naptime's over."

Diaper changed and the bottle finished, Debra brought the child out and put her on her lap.

"We could take turns, maybe, keeping her entertained," Sandy suggested.

"She gets restless pretty quickly without Debra in sight. It might be hard to really enjoy the water. Do you think Marie would watch her, Debra?" Carrie asked. "If we go this afternoon?"

"I don't want her out in a boat without Dave or me..."

The baby wriggled from her mother's lap; Melody was quickly absorbed in trying to pull the books off the shelf, and Debra was putting them back, making a game. Once the toddler started trying to put them back herself, Debra sat on the porch swing watching her through the window. Debra, kicking the swing back and forth, one foot pushing off the porch boards as the chains creaked, looked down the hot dirt street, where the school kids could be heard speaking Spanish in the little building beside the hotel. The parrot chattered on his perch. "Well, it's not getting any cooler today. And Marie might do it; I could pay her."

"Oh, Debra, you'd enjoy the reef so much. The fish are so outasight," Sandy said and stood up from the rocking chair. "Let me go see if we can get Bill to take us out."

Sandy put her book in the chair and headed down the steps. She was glad to get out of a sticky situation, her "think before you speak" lesson still smarting. How could she be so careless? The role of wife was one that didn't suit her; the women in the kitchen while the men watched the game was one image that stuck with her from going home with friends during college. The role of housekeeper or child tender while the man expected a clean house and good meal and got to have a full life outside the home was totally unappealing to her. Women were stuck with all the housework and the men had all the fun, she thought, but if you loved someone, like she had once loved Paul, maybe it worked. For Debra, for Carrie, having a man in their lives had meant this adventure for them. They wouldn't be down here without their men. For her, it was simpler to go it alone. Or was it? Tweedledee and Tweedledum, as Debra had dubbed the cameramen who'd left with Dave two weeks before, had reminded her how complicated and unpleasant navigating the world as a single woman could be. Having a man cushioned you from some of the complications or harassment, she saw, but it created other problems.

Bill was half asleep on the sailboat when she reached the dock to find him.

"Hey, good lookin'," he murmured as he squinted up at her peering down from the deck of the boat, the bow hatch raised and sunlight behind her. "Come join me."

"How 'bout we go out snorkeling this afternoon? Would you consider taking Debra out with us? Snorkel, maybe, one of the shallow reefs? I think Carrie wants to go, too."

"Both boats aren't out?"

"No, one's still here. Debra really needs to get in the water. Cheer her up."

"What about the baby? We take her, too?" He sounded skeptical.

"Maybe," she said, slipping down the opening into the cabin bed without stepping on Bill.

"Golly, it's hot in here." She leaned over to kiss him as he made room for her.

"We could make it hotter," he smiled and kissed her harder. "What time are you talking about going?"

The bristles of his mustache tickled her lip and cheek as he rubbed it across her face.

"Now. You game?"

He leaned up on an elbow. His dark brown eyes still looked drowsy. He yawned.

"Don't do that," she said, "or I'll get sleepy, too. Let's do this."

"Lemme change and I'll be up in a minute," he said.

She crawled out of the bed and stabilized herself to head out to the cockpit and back up on the sunbaked pier. "Hot, ouch," she said, slipping into the flip flops she'd abandoned when she climbed aboard.

"What's that?" he asked below.

"It's cooking out here," she said. "It will be good to get wet."

Marie had agreed to watch Melody and keep her entertained at the hotel. Snorkels, masks, and fins in tow, the three women padded down to the pier where Bill was messing with the motor and putting life jackets down on the sun baked seats. "Anybody else want to come?"

"Nah," Sandy said.

"Stan wants to take a nap. He went out this morning," Carrie said.

"Hal and the ones who went out after lunch aren't back yet," Sandy added.

Squinting in the bright sunshine, she pulled her sunglasses from her pocket, put them on, and grabbed the line attached to the cleat to pull the boat closer to her perch on the pier. Bill gave the two other women a hand, and Sandy unwrapped the ropes that moored the boat to the pier. Bill held the cleat to steady the boat as she boarded. They were off, headed north a few miles away to the shallow reefs lying twenty feet below the surface. Bill cut the engine and Carrie dropped the anchor. Without Melody aboard, the four could all snorkel at the same time. Debra and Carrie climbed down the ladder and splashed into the water.

"Oh, this feels delicious," Debra said, treading water and spending some time spitting into her mask to keep it from fogging, and then adjusting it for a tight fit. With Debra's first clear glimpse below, Sandy could hear a gurgle through the mouthpiece and Debra's face was back up. Moving the snorkel, she had a big smile that almost broke Sandy's heart. The girl had not had a chance to explore this underwater world since she had been on the island.

"Far out! This is wonderful! So many colors, like one of those kaleidoscopes you twist!" Debra took a big gulp of air. She was gone. The next time Sandy saw her, she was diving down, bubbles trailing from her air piece as she headed closer to the four-eye butterfly fish below, and then her snorkel appeared again over the array of sea fans and coral where multi-colored schools of fish passed close to the seafloor.

When Sandy slipped below the surface into the watery world below, Bill was motioning toward a starfish, and she saw spiny sea urchins hidden in the crevices of the coral before they surfaced again for air. She could not hold her breath for long and it was close up to the action below she most enjoyed.

"Not the same as diving," Sandy said to Bill as they held onto the ladder.

Carrie and Debra were back down, coming up for air and snorkeling along the surface, their faces down in the water until something caught their eyes. A kick of fins along the waterline and one or the other was back down. The afternoon was a success. Debra's mood was lifted.

"What fun! Thanks, y'all," Debra said after she pulled her mask off once she was back on the boat. Her nose was stuffed and red marks rimmed her cheeks and forehead, but she looked happy. She practically twinkled.

It was like seeing the sunshine after a very cloudy day, Sandy thought.

"I wanted to bring a conch back for Melody, but I guess it would die."

"It would stink like those starfish Sandy brought up," Bill pointed out.

"How long can they be out of the water?" Debra asked. "The conchs?

Sandy and Bill looked at each other, and neither had an answer. Carrie shrugged and guessed a few hours.

"I took some leopard snails once when we were diving near the caves," Sandy said, "and once they pulled in the spotted film or whatever that covered them, they were dull. Some of these animals look better underwater than dried up."

The four chattered on while the boat headed back to the cove, until they disembarked at the pier. The late afternoon masses of cumulus clouds, as if lit up from within, spread across the horizon of water.

"When Dave gets back, I want to dive," Debra said to Carrie while they gathered their gear and carried it back towards shore.

Behind them, Bill glanced at Sandy.

"What's taking him so long to get back?" he asked quietly after the two women were out of earshot ahead, dunking their masks in the freshwater barrel and babbling on about the sea life.

"He went back to Jacksonville you know."

"Yeah, but I'd think we'd hear something by now. Maybe Stan's heard something."

"If he has, he isn't telling."

"By, y'all," Debra called and waved before she headed up the path to the hotel, and Carrie turned right towards the main house.

Bill and Sandy lingered on the pier.

"Hal's pretty dissatisfied," Bill said. "He seems fed up with the location, thinks we're wasting time here."

"We should ask Dave what he's found so far when he gets back," Sandy said, "besides cannon balls and rusted metal."

"We could go out again tomorrow, to that other site near the inlet," Bill said. "I never found where he might have stashed anything."

"Oh, I'm sure he already brought up what he found. You know, I wonder why there wasn't more."

"It could have been a fluke…something those buccaneers had, loot of theirs, rather than from a galleon."

"Pirates' booty?" Sandy speculated. "That's possible."

"We don't know what the Indians had here before the Spaniards took them for slaves. There could be finds in some of the caves the locals talk about."

She and Bill had gotten a copy of the island's history written by one of the family members of the first white people to settle here. The descendants of those early settlers and a small black population were the local inhabitants now. Bill kept the book that the island school teacher had given them after they read parts that interested them both. He had said he wanted to get his own sailboat someday and write articles about the islands. Her curiosity about the early days somewhat satisfied, Sandy had left the mysteries about the early island natives to speculation. The legend of the round well, where expedition members drew water, said anyone drinking from it would always return, and that had appealed to her. Planters of bananas and coconut held less interest for her youthful imagination.

"So you think it's a fluke? We should be farther north like Hal says?" Sandy asked.

Bill shrugged, his classic response, and hesitated. "Did you think those were gold doubloons? Did you see anything else?"

"I couldn't tell," she said. "I went right up."

Evading a direct answer, Sandy pushed her sunglasses back up where they had slipped down her nose. She had kept her secret about the figurine; it might have cost her ever knowing where it went, but she wasn't changing course now.

"Well, if we don't find something soon, I don't see how we can continue indefinitely."

"You know the boat's not coming down. I already told you that," she said, trying to assuage her feeling of guilt for keeping one secret by having told him another.

"Yeah. I don't think any of the guys really believe it will come down here. Dave's just blowing hot air."

"You mean just our guys? Or all the guys? The ones in dry dock up there?"

"Our guys," Bill said.

"They should have already finished getting her seaworthy. The Oceanic Rover was not that far from finished when I came down months ago. And Dave said it only had a few inspections to go when he got here. The guys up there must be impatient to get out of port."

"Their money is already sunk into getting that boat afloat."

"So what do you think Hal will say when he finds out?"

"How can he not know is the question," Bill said. He buttoned his shirt and they walked up the pier to dip their masks and fins in fresh water. Neither spoke for a few minutes.

"Well, nobody talks to him," Sandy finally said. "They let him act smug and spoiled and Stan just diverts him with details about getting our boats re-equipped and the dredge's airlift redesigned for slower flow."

"The guy can't be that dumb."

As they reached the main street, Sandy saw a few of the boys taunting Isaiah with a large iguana they had captured. Fairly drunk, Isaiah was swinging his machete as the boys thrust the huge lizard toward him. Rusty and dull, the machete had seen its best days in the bush long ago, but Bill pointed out it could hurt someone.

"You boys leave him alone," Bill warned, "or I'll go get the sheriff."

The boys laughed and disappeared with the iguana between two houses, followed by several other small children running after them. Isaiah mumbled incoherently and stumbled onto the Bahia Bar steps, plopped down on one of the benches lining the porch.

"I've got some good pictures of him," Sandy said. "I printed a few. There are some of us. I forgot to tell you. After I shower, I'll get them. They were drying in the darkroom last night, so Bob may need the line if he hasn't already moved them."

Sandy went up to get her shampoo and change of clothes before she headed for the main house, where a fifty-gallon drum of lukewarm water awaited her off the back of the house. She would not miss cold showers, she knew that. Once she was dressed, she went into the darkroom where the smell of chemicals assaulted her nose. In the dim light where the black tarp had been raised, she found the pictures she was looking for.

From the darkroom, she heard Stan's voice.

"The telegram said Dave will be back tomorrow, Hal. Save this for him."

"I told him before he left I was thinking about not investing more than what he already got."

"Wait to decide until you talk to Dave. We can work this out."

"I've already put up more than I'll get back. We both know that."

"Your trip to Seville, that cost a pretty penny. There are legal implications," Stan said, his voice sounding irritated, "you may want to consider."

"The desalination equipment, the $21,000 for the magnetometer—this outfit is hemorrhaging money. And nothing to show for it."

Sandy didn't move, didn't want to be discovered in the darkroom listening to this argument. And she certainly couldn't walk out now. So she waited. Eventually she heard footsteps out on the porch leaving. Only one pair of feet, she thought. Patience was not one of her virtues, but she waited until she heard a door shut and more steps before she cracked the door. No one in sight.

Sandy slipped away quickly. She looked around before heading for the back door where the shower stall stood on the porch landing and then down the old rickety steps no one used except to bring up water for the drum. She would not make a good sneak thief she thought, slipping down the stairs, her heart pounding. She headed the back way towards a path to the main street. Any thought of searching for the jade goddess in Hal's room was out of the question. But the thought had entered her head. Still, she didn't know who had taken it. Dave could have it for all she knew. But sneaking around wasn't for her. Too scary, wrong feeling.

She would tell Bill about the argument, she thought, and she went to find him. There would have been no need to tell him Dave was coming back, though, because that evening Debra came on the porch at the Bahia Bar all smiles and everyone knew. Sandy had told Bill the whole story by then, so the news of Dave's return was old by evening.

"You'll see your old man tomorrow," Stan said when he and Carrie made room for Debra at their table. Debra had already taken Mel to the room for the evening, so she sat out on the porch until the electricity, which ran from six to ten at night, ended, the lights dimmed, and The Moody Blues ground slowly to a halt. Some stayed in the dim shadows talking and finishing their beers. Bill and Sandy, who had been sitting at a table with Rolf, walked out to the boat. The stars twinkled red and blue in the deep black of the night sky. The phosphorescence shimmered on the moving water and added magic to the evening.

"We're taking the sailboat out tomorrow to the key. I told you the guys want to work on the desalination unit. Want to come?" Bill asked and, of course, she did.

"That's ironic," she pointed out, "since Hal was just complaining about the cost and the thing's just rusting away."

"Yep. The whole Oceanic Expedition is one big irony."

"What do you mean?"

"I was getting away from a woman and making my fortune. Instead, the only treasure I've found was another woman," he said and gave her a squeeze. She wasn't quite sure how to take it, but she didn't ask.

He continued with a tinge of bitterness, "All these adventurers who joined this venture were gamblers. At least with a game of dice you have a chance of winning."

Quietly, she followed him to the sailboat gently rocking in the bay.

Chapter 11

Air mail letters could take six days to arrive and Dave's letter had come the same day Debra learned from his telegram he would be back. He'd sold the dive shop for less than they'd wanted, lost money on it. Debra was starting to worry about finances herself, but she had faith in Dave; he could handle the money and she wouldn't have to worry. Knowing her man was coming back, she felt a little tingle of excitement that next morning on the pier while she and Carrie watched with Mel as the group on the sailboat headed out. The plane should be in that afternoon.

Little Mel was somber and Debra thought that showing her the kittens Sandy had been feeding scraps under the kitchen house might perk her up. Sandy had said they were friendly enough now to pet and they would purr. That was one of the things about life with Dave. No animals. She'd like to settle down so pets weren't a problem. She brushed that disloyal grievance away and focused on the fact Dave would be holding her soon, all her loneliness erased in his warm embrace. Dave had mentioned trouble with the boat, which had delayed his return, but not enough detail for her to be certain about what was going on there.

An hour or so before sunset, the truck pulled up to the hotel and Dave got out, looking tired and frazzled, but as soon as she saw him and headed towards him, he broke into a big smile, then gave her that long and warm kiss she had been waiting for. He took his bags into their room, picked Mel up from her crib, and gave her several kisses as she laughed.

"She hasn't forgotten me," he said. "I feel like I've been gone forever."

"We missed you, honey," Debra said. "Three weeks you were down here before I got here, two weeks you gone—"

It was starting to sound like a complaint, so she quit.

"Things have gotten complicated, Debra," he said, holding Mel and her floppy bunny. "Did you get my letter?"

"It arrived yesterday," she replied.

"I was in Jacksonville all this week—broke the news they're going to Charleston first, not coming down here before December. The film crew won't be back here until after the rainy season for the segment out of the water."

Debra watched his face. From his cheerful smile to this scowl, his face revealed more to her than he usually showed others. She knew he allowed his face to show some of his true feelings with her.

"But we may negotiate the Charleston angle," he continued. "There are some seriously pissed investors who counted on being down here on the boat. And Hal has sent mail up there about his research. If I want the film finished by spring, we'll have to hustle. I'm not sure there's any money for it if we don't get more cash flow. I told you I didn't get as much for the shop as we'd hoped, right?"

She nodded and took the squirming toddler from him.

"The boat could make the trip to Charleston quicker than down here before we finish outfitting her, just got to get inspections completed. Gene set me up to meet a couple of investors in LA, but it fell through."

"So the Charleston trip, that's the War Between the States blockade runner you looked into last spring?" she asked.

"Different vessel. We found another boat to work. I told them how valuables being shipped out before the Civil War could net more profit for us sooner. I left Dick in charge of convincing them it would be worthwhile. Gene even flew in. There were blockade runners sunk during the war, but this one we'd be diving on was a private ship. Some rich planters from the low country were shipping their silver and gold out..."

He seemed to be glad to talk about history for a while, the possibility of new treasure, and take his mind off the business end of his trip. And then they were making sweet love, there with Mel awake in her crib, an uncomfortable feeling for Debra, but she was soon swept away by the warmth of their connection, his hands and mouth all over her, the hunger and need welling in them both.

A knock at the door, in the afterglow of their lovemaking, brought their private time to an end.

There stood Hal, ready to talk.

Debra was dressed by the time Dave opened the door, but it was obvious what they'd been doing and she turned away from the leer on the tall half-bald man's face and picked up her child. Dave and Hal were gone awhile, enough time for Debra to take Melody out on the porch where the last colors of sunset were fading from the sky, leaving the waters to their dark shadows. The ceaseless waves murmured. She could see Sandy and Bill who had come in earlier that day from their sail to the small key where they had taken several men to work on the desalination unit. The two dark forms were leaving the end of the pier to board the boat gently rocking at the dock. They'd probably been watching the sunset, Debra thought.

She recalled their return that afternoon. She and Carrie had been on the porch when Sandy, Bill and Stan came in from the key with the other men who went out.

"How was it?" Carrie had asked.

"The key is small, full of palm trees and coconuts," Sandy answered first.

"The desalination unit is getting rusty," Stan said, "but we worked on it a couple hours."

"Pete and Stan are pretty handy with tools. Mechanical prowess. I checked out the wiring," Bill added. "Electrical engineering not needed today."

"We snorkeled," Sandy said. "And had a land crab race. Mine won."

"Did not," Bill disagreed. "Mine went sideways faster than yours or Pete's."

"But not to the finish line," Sandy added and poked him in the ribs.

Their easy way with each other Debra almost envied. But she knew Sandy was just marking time. She could tell from little things Sandy did or said her heart was not in it. Their affair was a fun lark for her, Debra thought, and she couldn't read Bill. Having a twenty-three-year-old girlfriend on a treasure hunting trip might be a feather in his cap, but where was his family? Debra knew from conversations with Carrie and Sandy on those hot afternoons on the porch that he was divorced, that he had three children with an ex-wife. Still, he was a kind-natured guy and fun-loving. He was taking care of another man's boat until he got back from the States, and he kept Sandy occupied. It wasn't really any of Debra's business. They were having fun. An escape to a Caribbean island was a romantic interlude for them.

Debra, holding her daughter to watch the twilight move in, had other concerns to think about besides her new friend's dalliance. New friend, she realized; she had just considered Sandy a friend. It was true. She would miss her easy laugh and irreverent attitude when they left. How soon would that be? Debra was reminded of the tower card Carrie had uncovered in her Tarot reading, someone falling upside down from what looked like the tower of Babel, struck by lightning. Debra had been alarmed—horrified, really; she hadn't wanted to go near the cards after that. Some stones were better left unturned, she thought. If there were trouble ahead, there was no reason to cross that bridge until she came to it.

And the bridge was there before she knew it. Dave was angry and fuming when he came out on the porch. He ordered rum and coke and told her he would talk later, not on the porch. A pair of Peace Corp volunteers played checkers in the temporary light on the Bahia Bar porch. Neil Young drowned out the soft sound of the sea. Dave twirled the ice in his glass and sat silent. She knew the talk he'd had with Hal must have been serious, somehow threatening. Dave's mood was dark and she left him to put the baby down. She sat a moment on the bed in the dark, waiting for Melody to fall asleep in her crib, waiting to cross that bridge to change that lay before them.

Chapter 12

By morning, word had spread among the expedition's island group that Hal and Dave had had a blowout. The details were murky, but something was afoot. Sandy and Bill had walked up to the well to get water after breakfast, slapping mosquitoes which infested the spot and swarmed around their legs, hurrying to get buckets filled and poured into the big container and wheel it back to the kitchen house. The summer heat had not taken over the morning yet, and the sleepy village had its few early morning stirrings of activity. The cocomalt stand was closed as they passed by and wouldn't be opening until noon. The grocer smiled from the dim light inside his store and raised a hand to greet them through the open doors. Avocados and saltines, canned goods and mangoes mixed on the small shelves and in the bins of the little wooden structure with its window shudders' peeling paint. A small mixed breed dog nosed around the cans outside.

"Can Hal really pull out funds, you think?" Sandy had asked Bill once they were alone on their water-carting chore.

"He became a partner, he said. I'm not sure it's true, but I doubt he can get back the money he's put down already. Even if he sues. We gambled on an adventure. I don't think the courts would even consider our investments to have a guaranteed return. Nobody would. Not even us bozos who did it."

"Well, I certainly wondered myself when I read the ad for divers wanted, how anybody would know if anything of value was found...but I didn't have three thousand dollars to plunk down anyway."

"It was a risk worth taking for me," Bill said. "I think most of the guys down here were looking for an adventure. I don't know how many up in Florida actually expected to strike it rich. But if we did find treasure, lots of it, it could be a game changer for us all."

"But with Hal, why is that such a big deal?" Sandy returned to her big concern.

"He's got a lot more promised to invest. Or so he says. This outfit is leaking money—or maybe I should say gushing. What do you think it takes to retrofit a Navy boat for diving? Tens of thousands? Couple hundred for this whole operation?"

"Maybe, if Hal knew there was something worth exploring here, instead of moving the Roatilla outfit north..." Sandy mused aloud.

"Or ending life as we know it on Roatilla if he doesn't get his way," Bill added. "I think treasure-hunting operations would go on the boat. That would cut costs. Now everyone knows the Ocean Rover's not coming down, at least not before hurricane season ends and the rainy season is over."

"Finding out the boat's not coming may be what set Hal off. Who knows."

Sandy's attachment to the island, to this adventure in her life, was tempered with the knowledge she would need a job, need money, before too long. She just didn't want to give it up. The romance of the Caribbean.

"Don't look so serious," Bill said, stopping the wheelbarrow and giving her a hug. "Live for today. Let's go diving if there's room in the boat."

"Unless Hal's on it," Sandy said, unwrapping her arms from around Bill and smiling up at him. "Then what?"

"I could take your mind off things," he grinned, tousled her hair, and leaned down to pick up the wheelbarrow handles.

Hal did go out diving with the crew in the morning, and Dave was taking Debra out for a dive in the afternoon. Carrie had offered to take Melody for a few hours, naptime and beyond. Sandy saw an opportunity to talk to Dave before he took the boat out with Debra. Maybe if Hal knew Dave had found something…gold doubloons could change things. If Hal knew, and there was a reason to stay, perhaps they could all stay here longer.

She went up to the main house after Bill decided to work on the head in the sailboat. She saw one of the archeologists leaving as she walked up the steps. Dave was alone, looking at the finds catalogue documents when she walked in. She chit-chatted a bit, offering a welcome back, before she dove in.

"There's talk Hal is insisting on moving the search north, Dave," she said, standing by the table where he sat. He stood up abruptly. He closed the catalogue folder.

"Don't believe everything you hear," he said looking over at her and waiting. She was nervous and it showed. Speaking up was not something she'd learned in school. Speaking up to this man was not comfortable for her, but she felt she must. Now that he was standing, she felt even more intimidated, but she plunged on.

"You know, finding gold doubloons could change the game here. If Hal knew…if there's a reason to stay here… Remember that day Hal arrived? I saw some heavy clumps near the site, remember? What about that? Why didn't you bring that cluster up? Wasn't there gold? It looked…if Hal knew…if there's a reason to stay…,"she blurted.

"What gold doubloons?"

"The ones when we were diving that day and you didn't come up with me. I wasn't sure…. I saw you stuffing the clusters we found…"

"You saw me moving debris, Sandy," Dave said, his eyes stony. "Don't make a big deal out of that."

"We could have a find, even if we haven't found the wreck site yet."

"We haven't found the skeleton of a ship, yet," he said, moving their talk to safer ground. "That's why we're still moving the airlift around. We'll find something soon."

"Did you move those grid drawings?"

"Are you trying to stir up trouble? You'd better know what you're talking about before you create problems you can't solve. The grid should match the catalogue. You may be the one holding out. I'll need anything you might have brought up."

"Did you take the jade piece?" she blurted out.

"What jade?"

He was scrambling, she could see in his eyes; even though his face and even tone did not change, his smooth, in-charge expression gave way with a brief flicker in his amber eyes. Even with her own nervousness, jumping from question to question, unsure of solid ground, she registered his momentary hesitation.

"I found a figurine."

"It's missing, this figure? You don't have it?"

"It disappeared. Out of my room." She couldn't read his expression. He was calculating or thinking.

"So you're the one who's been holding out here," he said. "If you try to tell the men there's gold, there's gold missing, you'll just make yourself a troublemaker with no proof. No evidence to back you up. We've got enough going on here without you making up lies. Don't make problems you can't handle. Maybe it's time you took that one-way ticket back. We're done here."

She felt stricken. She had pushed him too far. He stood in the light from the window, his hands clinched, unmoving. One side of his face was in shadow, the other side held light flecking the amber tints of one eye, and shining on his tan cheek. An uncomfortable silence between them, they stood a moment. Too close for comfort, Sandy turned and left.

After her blow-up with Dave, Sandy avoided him. She had felt uncomfortable around this businessman-treasure hunter before, but now her discomfort was tinged with distaste and wariness.

After that, an uneasiness that had permeated the entire group became palpable to her; the uneasiness of the next two weeks was only alleviated by Hal's departure. When Hal's bags were packed there had been another dustup. Hal was furious when he left; there had been yelling between Dave and him. Sandy had not taken her one-way ticket back yet, but she knew it was only a matter of time. Carrie told Sandy that Debra noticed the tension between them when she mentioned Sandy in front of Dave; he made comments Sandy was trouble, but he dismissed her questions about it. So she asked Carrie instead. "There are parts to Dave you don't see," was her enigmatic reply. So Debra didn't ask again. Whether from pride or fear of an answer she didn't want to hear, Debra dropped the subject. Carrie herself only knew Sandy and Dave had argued.

The rainy season was coming. A hurricane blew through Central America packing 170 mph winds in mid-September, but the island was not impacted by more than a few squalls that came through. Rough seas that came with the squalls battered the boats. Pete fell through into the water when a couple of loosened boards broke on the pier. With choppy waves banging boats against the piers, Bill moved the sailboat to anchor. Having to use a dingy to reach her, he chose to stay in his own bunk in the yellow house when the rains and rough water were too much. Sandy's own sheets stayed damp, the mildew of the tropical climate creeping along in dark spotty lines like the wallpaper in a short story she'd read in college about a woman being driven mad, trapped by her husband.

Without the privacy of the boat, her rendezvous with Bill were limited.

A feeling of futility seemed to grow among members of the group. Everyone knew that when September moved into October and the rainy season began in earnest, the seas would be getting colder, the waves wilder, the diving less frequent.

Patrick, the owner of the sailboat that they had enjoyed, was expected to be returning any day, but when Patrick actually flew in, his anticipated arrival was a surprise. He brought news from Florida. From what Sandy learned from Carrie, there had been a mutiny and the boat in Jacksonville and many of those already living on it had headed to Bimini. They'd left with some men's possessions on board, members who hadn't been aboard when they took off, and also dive equipment recently purchased by the expedition when Dave was last up there. A telegram from Dave's partner, Gene Sherman, had come on the same day that the sailboat owner, Patrick, arrived. Flying down was as fast as getting a telegram delivered.

The next day, after taking a package to mail in the morning, Dave headed for the mainland of Honduras in the afternoon. Debra was left to pack up whatever personal items of theirs remained. Dave was flying out of La Ceiba straight to the Bahamas. Debra had a few choices: stay in the bay islands a little longer, settle business up in California and head for Florida to wait in their apartment there, or just stay in California until Christmas. She had learned that Dave had not renewed their lease on the apartment in California. That, Debra admitted to Carrie and Sandy, had been a surprise. She would have to oversee the moving of what personal possessions they had in the furnished apartment there to Florida, or to a storage unit Dave had arranged while he was in California. He had been busy. She had until the end of December to get the California apartment squared away, and she was reluctant to go or to deal with it. Less than a week after Dave left for the Bahamas, however, she, too, was gone. Stan was left in charge on Roatilla. And, Sandy learned, they would be dismantling operations here, shipping or selling everything. To Carrie's relief, she and Stan would be gone before the New Year, driving their van and what it could haul back north. The remaining treasure hunters played cards or read on rainy days, but with the water cooler, diving decreased. Bill was getting restless and Sandy was getting bored. She knew it was time.

During that last week of Debra's stay, when they knew her departure was looming, the three women continued to pass the time together, playing cards and chess from time to time. That continued until the very end. The friendship between Sandy and Debra had grown. In those weeks Carrie, Sandy, and Debra were on the island together, they had shared almost daily their enjoyment of reading, shared books and discussed books. Sandy had learned the little bit of yoga Debra could show her between Melody's demands. Even after Sandy's confrontation with Dave, the women continued sharing cocomalts and perspectives on everything from college to Europe, California to the massacre at Kent State which had propelled Sandy to leave the States in 1970 for her second summer abroad. Sandy and Debra had been surprised by some of their similar views on America and the discordance between the "straight" or "square" world and the anti-establishment counterculture.

The bond had grown, and despite their different lifestyles, they shared a kindred spirit. Debra had even confided stories about her brief flower child days in San Francisco, and, though they avoided talking about Dave or the future of the expedition, Sandy opened up to Debra about Sandy's big romance, stories of Stonehenge at full moon, Winchester Cathedral bringing her down. On those cool days when the squalls came through and they were cooped up in the house or on the porch, their talking could range from the deaths of so many public figures: Bobby Kennedy, Jimmy Hendrix, Janice Joplin, Martin Luther King, to anecdotes about their island life.

The Saturday before Debra left, they'd taken up the invitation of one of the black islanders, Roy, to come to their club for dancing. Roy sometimes helped with mechanical work on the boats, and when the club was open he was always there for a good time. There was moonshine flowing. Everyone got soused, danced a lot, and had a good time. "The island's black population is a lot more fun that the white one," Sandy had told Debra. Their partying was rowdy and noisy. Debra danced with Roy and stayed until eleven, but when she wanted to leave, Carrie and Stan headed back with her. An hour later, Bill and Sandy walked back through town to their shack in the dark. The crew and locals partied on and complained of hangovers that next day.

The day before she left, Debra and Sandy discussed their imminent departures. Sandy said she would be going home to her mother in Orlando, like a fledgling bird back in the nest. Her several attempts to fly the nest, she told Debra, ended in "home sweet home" again. "I feel like Icarus, flying too close to the sun; down I go," Sandy lamented.

Debra added more cheerfully, "Or maybe a phoenix rising out of its own ashes." Then Debra looked at her and added seriously, "Be glad you have a home like that when you crash and burn."

Surprised by her tone, Sandy took in Debra's expression. A trace of sadness showed in Debra's eyes, but the corners of her full lips turned up briefly in a wry smile.

"My father and I are estranged," Debra admitted, "and my mother is so dependent on him...she doesn't..."

Her voice trailed off, and Sandy did not pursue the topic. She could tell the subject was painful. But Sandy knew Debra had Dave, with his take-charge attitude and abundance of confidence, and Melody, a family, so what need had she of her parents to go home to? Still, that estrangement would be tough.

A few days after Debra left, Sandy found herself riding in the old pickup truck to the little runway at the end of the island. Bill, wedged beside her on the torn seat, was quiet. The island driver talked about the exciting skirmish that he had witnessed between Hal and Dave two weeks earlier. They were grappling over a bag, the driver explained, and demonstrated with hand flourishes that scared them both when he took both hands off the wheel, the old truck weaving back and forth on the rutted road. Neither Sandy nor Bill thought to ask who had won the skirmish.

She had given Bill her mother's address; Bill would be heading to Florida before Christmas himself. He gave her a brief kiss and a long lingering hug. Her bags were loaded on the plane, her little wicker case holding a few souvenirs. She boarded the plane.

As the little Cessna trembled down the coral runway, Sandy looked back to see Bill waving before he got back in the pickup truck. Once airborne, she watched the greenish land diminish in the turquoise and deep blue waters. When the tiny island was lost to sight in the blue waters of the Caribbean, Sandy knew she would probably never return, but it would be there, drifting in her memories like the butterflies on the hill where she had ridden horseback earlier in the summer. The island, drifting back into her thoughts, would remain a little green dot in a vast blue sea, a sleepy village, a treasure-hunting adventure always to remember, she thought then, but as time marched forward with new memories to be made, the island receded into the back of her mind.

Chapter 13

Looking at the photographs Debra had brought to Key West stirred memories long left behind for Sandy. They had shared so much during those weeks in the islands. The black and white pictures she had given Debra before they left Roatilla were like looking at ghosts or someone else's life.

"You were right about the pictures. Look how pretty and young we were," she commented.

"Still are, honey," Debra insisted. "The pretty part, anyway."

Sandy held up a shot from the pier looking back towards the island, showing palm trees, old houses and wooden church spires beyond the zigzag line of planks and missing boards, the outhouse tilted over the water.

"Look at that raggedy dock where y'all used to get off the boats hauling your gear. Remember the reggae music when we went for cocomalts, and how the islanders loved Jimmy Cliff? That was before reggae was called that in the States, Bob Marley and all. And all the time we spent on that porch swapping stories?" Debra commented as Sandy picked up a few photographs and stared at pictures of their younger selves. "I still remember, right before we all left, your telling us about your first love, and how funny you were! You went into such detail!"

A shot of Debra and Dave, holding their little toddler with her head full of curls, the child reaching for his glasses, Sandy examined for a moment before picking up a picture of herself and Bill on the steps of the main house.

"Bill was just muscle and bone. Look at that smirky smile," Sandy said.

"He thought he was hot stuff with a pretty, young twenty-something by his side, I bet. All the men wanted you."

"He was the one nicest to me," Sandy commented. "Rolf, the German guy, was pretty nice, too, but Bill was the first one there to be...different; easier to talk to, smart."

"He really liked you."

"I thought about him on the plane when I was coming here. We had a lot of fun, but I think in the end I didn't respect him enough. But maybe I was too picky,"

"Maybe so. Maybe not enough, sometimes." Debra's eyes twinkled briefly as she spoke, the first time she had shown a lighter side since they had gone to dinner. Sandy handed her back the photograph. "Remember when you told us that Minotaur story and I looked up all that Greek mythology after that? And I thought Ariadne was probably a spider...." Debra was babbling on now, not mentioning the family portrait, a robust Dave in his late twenties, the young wife with a beautiful smile gazing into the camera. "And that guy who was your first love?"

Sandy sighed. "That was a lifetime ago."

The night had been eventful. Looking at pictures her first evening in the keys, Sandy realized she was too weary to talk any more. A few more photographs, and then she put them back in Debra's hands. Tired as she was, she had agreed to go to Debra's room to look at them when they had been saying goodnight. Debra had looked so forlorn on the ride home after encountering that second wife, Barbara, that Sandy hadn't had the heart to say no. But after Sandy left Debra's room at the inn, her mind dwelt on the pictures of those young twenty-somethings they had once been. She could still remember the little island with its main street where they had spent so much time when they weren't exploring the underwater world beyond its borders and the confines of land.

In the days after Dave left the island, before the impending end of their treasure-hunting adventures in the Caribbean, Sandy offered up a piece of her past as a token of good will to bridge any gap created by the tension of unspoken conflicts. Once she got started, details poured out like sand through an hourglass, trickling on and on.

They were sitting on the porch again. Debra was looking a little pensive. Carrie, of course, had started it with, "A while back you were going to tell us about that love of yours, the one you travelled to Spain with; now's as good a time as any, Sandy."   `

"I met him on Crete," Sandy said. "I thought he looked like a Greek god, all tan with curly brown hair bleached blond by the sun. A beard, so cool I thought back in those days, and the warmest brown eyes; oh, I could melt in those big warm eyes. I could lose myself looking at him."

"Sounds like you did," Carrie replied.

"Well, not at first," Sandy replied. "I was still a virgin. What a waste."

"You were still a virgin at twenty-one?" Debra chimed in, distracted from her thoughts and paying attention now.

Sandy nodded, then shook her head and pushed off on the swing before answering. "I was waiting for the right one. I was so proud, only someone special was going to get me; I was holding out. Or maybe it was all that Southern upbringing about good girls...but all that did was keep me from dating a lot of cute boys in college. Once they realized..."

"You don't seem to have any trouble in that department now," Debra joked.

"Back to this guy," Carrie said, "the one who got you so interested in archeology?"

Sandy looked out at the dirt street and old houses of Roatilla stretching in both directions from the main house porch. The chains holding the swing creaked in rhythm with the motion of her gliding back and forth. She hadn't talked about Paul, not to anyone, in nearly a year, except for a few final remarks about him to her mother. Then she had closed the book on him. That chapter of her life and her early romantic fantasies were behind her.

But these two women were interested. Sharing stories had been part of what they had done to pass the time on those muggy afternoons when they weren't immersed in the clear blue waters of the bay island before the rainy season began in earnest. So her story unfolded, partly in layers like peeling an onion and partly in chronological order, with Carrie listening from one of the porch chairs, and Debra's eyes on her, watching her talk, eating pineapple, and asking questions. After her fiasco about the role of married women and her choice to be "on the road" with the guys instead, Sandy felt compelled to offer something up about her own mistakes or shortcomings, but this telling turned into an unravelling of the threads holding the tapestry of her own buried past, tangled in knotted emotions she didn't want to relive. She revealed more than she had expected.

The first summer she had been in Europe on money she had saved from part-time jobs, Sandy had come to Crete with a college girlfriend, but her friend, Carol, had had to return to the U.S. Sandy had stayed on, enjoying the company of a small group of wandering hippies backpacking in Europe and the delightful waters of the Mediterranean and beautiful seas around the island for a few days, before planning to head

north to mainland Greece itself. She remembered clearly that
first sight of Paul. He had come down to the sea with some of
the archeology students from the Knossos dig. She had noticed
him picking his way along the rocks, treading carefully on the
uneven terrain, his bare shoulders gleaming in the afternoon
light. He had looked up and smiled at her, just coming out of
the water in her bikini, wet and laughing. She had felt a surge;
her first reaction had been the thought, "What a good-looking
guy!" followed by a feeling of expectancy, something akin to
hope. He had spoken then, just a "Hi." Hesitating a moment
before his friend said something, he headed down the rocks to
the water.

    She sat on her towel on the edge of the group of young
Americans she had met up with when Carol left, and watched
him in the water. He seemed so at ease in his body, so alert
and easy in his movements. None of the other young men in
this group, bearded or clean shaven, long-haired or short, had
appealed to her, but this guy did. As he came out of the water
in his cutoffs, she continued to watch him and his pal as they
dried off. When they approached her group beside the trail,
one of the New Yorkers spoke up. The short fellow with Paul
already knew this group and sat down.

    "Dude, you want a hit?" one of the stoned boys asked,
and Paul, as she learned he was called, squatted down and
took a long drag from the doobie circling the group. Sandy
moved over, so he sat beside her on her towel. He passed her
the joint and their fingers touched. She smiled at him. His
eyes, warm, brown, and cheerful, met hers while he exhaled.
She felt an electric charge, a spark with those knowing and
bright eyes on hers. The corners of his eyes crinkled when he
smiled. She loved the sparkle in his eyes when he laughed or
smiled at her. She learned he was with the archeology group
digging on the island; he was attending Stanford University
but taking his junior year abroad. He was a year behind her in
school. But it was the nearness of his shoulder and arm, the

warmth of his young vibrant body that she remembered most clearly from that first hour sitting on the edge of Crete with the young man who would become her first real love.

From there, they spent the rest of the summer together. She joined the archeology team, abandoning her plans for more travel. They spent their days scraping in the dirt for shards of pottery or bone, their free weekends swimming, and then, eventually, making love along the edges of the sea, in the moonlight or in the dark of night accompanied by the sound of water and distant laughter and music. She couldn't get enough of him. She was insatiable. The feel of his body on hers, the taste of his kisses, him inside her and their rhythmic movement together, young, tender and desiring, always desiring. She was in love with every part of him. His tanned arms, the sun-bleached hairs of his chest, the curve of his eyebrows, the shape of his toes, his strong hands and fingers on her body. She was in love with every inch of him.

###

Debra had laughed when she told them that, her easy laugh tinkling in the steamy Caribbean heat of September. Though she had spared them most of those details of lovemaking, she couldn't help recalling aloud her adoration of his young man's body. She could still remember the curve of his arm encircling her shoulders.

Sandy lifted out of her reverie, here in Key West, before she fell asleep, remembering way back beyond Roatilla, back beyond her senior year of college to that summer when she first fell in love. Her memories belonged to a different young woman who had fallen in love, a different girl from the woman she was today. And that love-struck girl was different from the one on Roatilla. If she could go back to that young woman in the photograph Debra had pulled out of her suitcase and shown her that evening in the inn, what would she say to herself, to that younger self standing on the steps with Bill, the young woman smiling in that short, short shift?

But that twenty-three-year-old in the photograph was not the same young woman who had loved Paul that summer of '69 when men landed on the moon and peace and love landed in the mud of Woodstock. That young woman with stars in her eyes would have followed him anywhere, if he had wanted her to. But being young and in love was not enough. Or maybe it was too much. It had been the too much, she realized now, that would have frightened a young man wanting to go to Mexico with his buddies, not settle with some intense young woman who couldn't get enough of him. After their two summers in Europe together, she had gone out to California to be with him in the fall, that last year he was in college at Stanford, and it had turned into a disaster. Her eagerness had not been tempered with caution, Sandy realized, regretting her strong-willed determination to see California, not to wait for him to come to her, working in Florida, but to forge ahead, despite the warning in his letter. He had left her for Mexico; she had left Palo Alto for her mother's house, wings clipped and broke. She never saw him again.

Even now, decades later, she felt the tinge of regret. But for what? That younger woman's poor choices or the love she had lost? Bad judgment, or that over eagerness, or her caring too much? What was regret anyway but a foolish feeling that one path was better than another, when actually one's mistakes made you the person you became? Lessons to be learned, as Debra had said earlier that day. Did we have a choice, or was destiny set in the design, leading us to where we were meant to be? she wondered, before she drifted off to sleep.

###

But that day on Roatilla, she had not told them the details of the ending to her love story and her later realization of her own impetuousness, except to say that Paul didn't want to be tied down and had broken her heart. She talked instead of the two summers they spent in Europe together. She described that first summer, on their days off from the dig site, drinking cheap red wine and sitting on cliffs with cream white rocks and blue, blue sea below, listening to his tales of the legends of Knossos, bullfighters in Spain, or even his humming of Grateful Dead tunes. She loved the minotaur story she remembered from a classical civilization class in high school where she had studied the *Iliad* and *Odyssey* and Homer, with Paul, on that '69-'70 dig at Knossos embellishing the myth of half-bull half-man and the prince from Athens forced to fight him. He told how Minos, the ruler of Crete, had kept a minotaur in a labyrinth; when the Athenian prince fell in love with the king's daughter Ariadne, she gave him a ball of twine or thread, so he could follow its trail back out of the maze to her after he'd killed the creature. Ariadne and the prince escaped from Crete together.

Somehow, Sandy's memories of Paul and their affair were spun into the web of ancient myths, interwoven with them, bigger than life, and even warmer than those sunlit days near the rocky shore where water lapped gently, and flute music wafted from the caves above. Or the hours spent excavating near the palace at Knossos, the center of Minoan culture and civilization, long ago abandoned at the end of their Bronze age. She followed the maze of memories back out to the reality of three women swapping tales to pass the time on another island far away from the Mediterranean or the Sea of Crete.

Then she followed the labyrinth of tangled thoughts and memories to that second summer, when she had signed up for an archeological dig in Winchester, England, thinking Paul would join her there, the chaos of those last days of college, with the invasion of Laos and the massacre of students at Kent State behind her. She had chosen not to go to Greece again, after the movie Z came out, not to support a fascist regime, with questions of America becoming a police state itself too prominent in her mind.

"I wanted to get away; I needed to get away, after they shot those students on campus, our national guard...," Sandy was telling Debra.

"And they'd already shot Martin Luther King and Bobby Kennedy," Debra added. "It was such a disturbing time."

"I took my savings and went that first summer of '69 to Europe with such a desire to see the world...then I was hooked on going back...and then the summer I graduated, worried about America, its values...others wondering like I did about America's becoming a police state, and our killing so many people in Vietnam...but that second summer, along with the turmoil in America, it was really all about being with Paul. I was fascinated by the idea of archeology...and the dig at Winchester gave me the experience drawing on the grid, and detailing a dig site, like I've been doing here...but getting out of the country was critical."

"You were really political," Debra commented as Sandy tried to explain her reasons for wanting to get out of the U.S., propelled by her desire to see Paul again. "I sort of left it behind when I dropped out of college."

"It was hard not to be," Sandy murmured, "with the protests on our campus, on so many campuses, the veterans coming back telling us the government was lying to us, but I suppose there were some who could remain apolitical. The evening news seemed so alien, so far removed from what we were experiencing. I felt the establishment was just one big lie."

"Yeah," Debra said, "I left Georgia before that part of the protests really got underway, the anti-war stuff.... My big protest was coed equality. We had all these stupid rules at Georgia about girls being in the dorm by curfew, freshmen girls not out at midnight ringing the bell when they won a game. We even had a sit-in at the administration building."

"Dropping out, that was political," Sandy said.

"Maybe," replied Debra, not sounding convinced.

The conversation shifted when Carrie was curious about the antiquated rules of the Southern university, surprised somehow that the California wife she knew now had been a coed in Georgia. It was the next day, when the three of them were on the porch of the Bahia Bar and the baby was napping, that Sandy returned to the subject of love. Debra had brought up Ariadne and wondered aloud if she'd turned into a spider, but Sandy thought that was Arachne, from another myth. Debra had found the *Bulfinch's Mythology* among the books in the expedition library and started talking about how every culture had legends and stories that made their history fascinating.

Debra had mentioned that Dave was also one of those fascinating story tellers who enthralled listeners, ones who could leave such a lasting impression on the listener, like Paul had for Sandy. It was one of the few personal references to Dave that came up, Sandy recalled. Comparing these two storytellers they had each loved had been another insight into their connection, hers and Debra's. Debra mentioned Dave's telling her about the awe Spaniards used to describe the golden cities of the Incas. Dave could weave a tale and mesmerize her with his embellished stories, just as Paul's fascination with classical civilization that first summer and the next summer the Spaniards and their culture had captivated Sandy. Even Paul's vivid description of the running of the bulls in Pamplona took on a life of its own in her imagination. They were spell binders, men who could weave stories with their enthusiasm and their intelligence and wrap these women in tales of long ago, the romance of ages long gone. They had entranced these women, their imaginations engaged by the spinning of tales. But Dave had carried his fascinating tales to a whole other level, one of deceit and deception, whether he did it consciously or not, or whether he believed his own stories he embellished, Sandy thought, though she had kept that thought to herself.

"So tell me about that second summer," Debra asked, "when you went to England. Did you meet him at the archeology site? What was it like after almost a year apart?"

"He had been sick in Italy, spent time in the infirmary," Sandy recalled. "I think by then he was losing interest in archeology—and he'd been doing a lot of drugs, cocaine, hashish, maybe some heroin, I wasn't sure. We met again at Stonehenge for the summer solstice."

###

Sandy had hitch-hiked to Scotland with some girls she'd met on her charter flight to London; when those girls had headed for Ireland, she and the South Africans who had given them all a ride in their van headed south. When the fellows let her out, right after she pulled her back pack onto her back and hooked it, she saw Paul first in the distance. She looked up and there he was: mustachioed, his beard gone, wearing a fringed leather jacket and leather hat. He and his buddy with the wire-rimmed glasses were talking to some young women, standing near the huge stones on the Salisbury Plain beyond a field of daisies. She stood there, wearing her cotton pants made of an Indian bedspread in lines of gold and orange and brown, feeling the coolness brush through the cotton, watching him before she called to him.

"Paul," she finally shouted, waving with her one free hand, her other tugging at the pack strap binding her shoulder. He waved back, and headed toward her.

"Far out! Outrageous!" he was saying. She leaned toward him, expecting a kiss, but he grabbed her head in his hands and simply smiled beneath the brim of his hat, and said, "So far out to see you!" adding in a Bogart voice at the end, "Here's lookin' at you kid."

Andy, Paul's friend, greeted her. Then they showed her where they were camped, Paul filling in details about the ritual to be performed the next morning at sunrise; the Druids, in their robes, would lead a full moon ceremony that night.

It was only after the long line of participants had walked single file along the hills in the misty moonlight to honor and celebrate the moon, its light bright upon their faces, that she and Paul had time to be alone in their zipped-together sleeping bags, the magic of their reunion realized in the touching and melding of bodies, fingers, lips. The next morning before sunrise, they rose and joined the crowd gathered near the huge grey pillars, where Druids in robes addressed the four directions and invoked whatever spirits were present to bless this longest day of the year. Sandy entwined her fingers in Paul's for that brief time of ritual as sunrise appeared through the boulders. Early morning dew still damp on the ground, the light gathering, she felt the holy cosmic energy, and, of course, surrounding the whole experience, the glow of her love as the sun melted the shadows of dawn and the sleepy crowd of participants drifted away. Sandy and Paul drifted away, too, hand in hand, back toward their campsite.

The circle outside the ritual center of the Druids, the moonlight ceremony walking quietly and reverently together in harmony, these were spiritual moments for Sandy heightened by her intense feeling of happiness and contentment at being in love and, for once, feeling included, with a sense of belonging, not feeling solo as her hitchhiking days had been, but joyfully united with someone who made her feel special.

At noon, when they left the Stonehenge summer solstice rites behind, they hitched to Winchester. Andy and Paul put her on the edge of the road with her thumb out and hid in the bushes until a driver in a small, beat up Citroen stopped. Then, when the two young men emerged with their packs, the Dutch driver laughed, saying it was an old trick, and let them all cram into the small vehicle with their gear. They laughed through the first two days in Winchester. She had most enjoyed the laughter, the fun that Paul created with his light-hearted way of viewing whatever was going on. He made amusement out of human calamities or foibles that might have disheartened or irked her.

But disappointment followed that special time at Stonehenge. Paul decided the dismal weather of England did not suit him; he longed for sunnier climes. The two argued briefly when she felt they had a duty to fulfill their commitment to the dig she had signed up for and he wanted to head for Spain where friends had a condo on the coast in Alicante. Her desire to learn what she could to determine if a career in archeology was right for her, if she should commit to grad school in this field instead of wander like a tumbleweed through dead-end jobs, and her love for Paul battled inside her and finally spilled out when he said he was leaving whether she came or not. Her pride hurt, she said she was staying. He and Andy left her at Winchester a few days after joining the dig; the drizzly grey days, the long hours scraping the ground with a trowel one quarter inch at a time, did not suit him. Giving her the address of his friends in Alicante where she could join him, Paul left and took his laughter with him.

The dig was rough; eight thirty to six was a really long time to carry buckets of dirt. Sandy's hands were soon rubbed raw. This place was a combination of slave labor and summer camp, Sandy decided, remembering the more laid-back atmosphere of the summer before, but she stayed. When Paul and Andy packed up, Sandy was punished for being late from tea break while saying good-by; she had to wash bones, but her punishment was a relief from the labor ordeal. Singing "Winchester Cathedral, you're bringing me down..." became less amusing as Sandy toiled on, first at one site, then another, before she got the courage to ask her supervisor if she could learn how to draw graphs of the site, to lay out area plans on paper as they excavated .

He made her take a drawing "test".

"I had to cross-hatch and make oyster shell symbols and draw straight lines. I guess I passed. I went out with a piece of graph paper and drew in all the flints, bits of clay, chalk, and so forth in a medieval kitchen, where a group was excavating a house with a medieval oven. I thought drawing plans would be an interesting job for six weeks; that way I could be connected with archeology without having to be an archeologist or one of the digger slaves," Sandy explained to Debra and Carrie sitting at the Bahia Bar a year after that dig. "It cheered me up considerably. Digging a medieval rubbish pit for eight hours a day in the mud was not too exciting after several days."

"Brooks Street was a city dump and the supervisors were too strict," she added. She recalled trying to catch up with one of the archeologists walking off with a bit of dirt of a different color from its surrounding area that she'd found, wanting to know what he was going to do with it. In his British accent, with his khaki outfit, the middle-aged man had explained that the pollen in the dirt would be carbon dated to identify how old it was. It galled her that she had to run after the archeologist to learn she had discovered a medieval rubbish pit, when she was working all day for them for free, and they considered the diggers too far below them to share information with them. What was she here for? she wondered miserably, while she missed Paul more and more.

The weather cleared after she changed sites to Wolvesey Palace. She could still remember being on St. Catherine's Hill at midnight with a group of new friends, watching the stars as the city lights went out. On their walk back from the hill, it felt like the whole quiet city was theirs; there was not a car, not a sound anywhere. During lunch hours, she often sat on the cathedral green with other diggers. She ate cherries, apples, and bread she'd bought in the stores, but her thoughts wandered to Paul constantly. She began to regret not leaving with him, even though developing her skills with drawing according to a grid system with coordinates marked on the metric system, meters rather than feet and inches, might give her access to the world of archeology she so admired, without having to go back to school. She could use her artistic ability, she hoped, to travel to foreign lands and dig sites, without having to be a worker bee, a slave, like she had found this British experience to be. And thus, Sandy explained as she wrapped up her experience at Winchester, she had parlayed those skills a year later to this diving expedition off the coast of Honduras.

She resumed the story of her love affair after more questions from her two friends. After she had decided to leave England and join Paul in Spain, they had eschewed the modern American scene in night clubs for rustic villages and bottles of wine with locals, absorbing the local culture of the remote coastal areas, seeing El Cordobés fight, the matador known as the famous midnight fighter for sneaking into pastures with young bulls at night that Paul had told her about, and swapping Hemingway paperbacks with other travelers along that southern coast of Spain where paella and sangria and the thick salty sea of the Mediterranean buoyed both her body and her spirits. Amused that the flip side of "Bridge Over Troubled Water," so popular in the States, was the jaunty "Celia" that the Spanish played, Sandy drank wine and swam in the sea with Paul. Their romantic summer ended when he had to return to California for his last year of school, and she landed back in the States with three dollars in her pocket and a job to find. She took temporary jobs until she earned enough money to go west, then joined Paul in his rented bungalow near the Stanford campus as soon as she could. Little did she know when she headed out that she would crash and burn, returning to her mother's home to gather her resources and mend her broken heart, eventually looking for another way to fly out of the country, one that wouldn't involve a broken heart—a heart carefully sealed off. Sandy found an adventure that would make life worthwhile after her despair finally lifted and her dark sorrow lightened with a treasure-hunting venture that wouldn't involve her heart's treasure.

Paul's mellow laidback approach and his pure delight in the local life, the real Spain, not the tourists' version, had been part of his charm for her, but there was no room for the responsibility of a relationship in his plans. Her wanting to live with him was not his idea of a good time; he was not ready to be committed to her or anyone. He did not want to be tied down. His fun-loving enthusiasm for exploring the cultures where he traveled had been part of his charm, but his enthusiasm for freedom to explore left no place for her.

Maybe part of her quest, even in the early '70s, was for a home of her own, to stop being a tumbleweed, but she was too busy moving on and putting miles between her and heartbreak to know that's what she really wanted. Maybe her next quest would lead her to a life where no one could take home out from under her, even if she had to carry it on her back like a snail, or a turtle. She was always in motion to find that still point of being, where love resides at the center.

Thinking back on those times, Sandy knew that being broke and scrambling were part of being young, and not something she would have the energy to do again in her fifties; but back then the end of the treasure-hunting expedition had just been part of her quest for the richness of experience, a quest where she would eventually open her heart again, with that same lust for life and love that had propelled her into Paul's arms.

Chapter 14

The shock of the Miami airport both Sandy and Debra recalled. After the slow motion of Roatilla, the rush of the airport was quite a wakeup call to the realities of leaving that little sleepy island behind. The winter of '71-'72 found them both in the midst of their changing lives. Sandy had found a job with the newly developing Disney World under construction in what had once been orange groves in Central Florida, the scent of orange blossoms bulldozed away and artificial trees erected with the smell of money. The artificiality of it had struck her sharply in those first weeks working there.

That visitors to the Magic Kingdom were amazed by an artificial tree near the magic shop where she worked and by the effort involved in creating each individual leaf on it struck Sandy with irony. After she had seen the panorama of fire coral and colorful fish that Mother Nature herself had provided, people impressed by what human construction could do seemed so lame to her. Yet she soon joined the set design crew, relieved from emerging from the employee tunnels into the commerce of Main Street and her little shop, to be with the artists and construction crew itself. She lasted long enough to earn enough money to move back to her college town of Tallahassee. But that year in Orlando, she still lived in her mother's house.

Once Debra arrived in the States, Melody in tow, she dealt with clearing out their apartment in California, hiring a cleaning crew to help, putting a few more items in storage before she shipped their clothes east, leaving the things in storage Dave had there, but taking few personal household items from their furnished apartment with them. Parting with some of Melody's little baby things was hard, but a small box in storage could hold her little booties and some baby outfits Debra wasn't ready to part with; if there were another baby, she might need them again. A couple of locked trunks in the back of the storage unit raised her curiosity, but she had too much to do before she headed east, tired but with high hopes, and she soon forgot about them. She put the last box Dave had mailed from the islands in the storage unit as he had directed, then closed the door on that chapter of her life when she pulled the rattling metal barrier of the unit down and locked it.

Being home with her mother, Sandy recalled, had been one of those sweet but temporary times in her early years right after college. She could still hear the wind chimes outside her mother's porch, the elegant look of the dining room table set with her mother's china for special occasions. Just the two of them—her mother's man friend not a husband yet, Sandy's own restlessness to move on part of that independence children of the sixties carried into their adult years. Just for a wistful moment or two, Sandy would wish she had stayed longer, that year after Roatilla, but she kept those thoughts at bay in the early mornings of her later years, before coffee kicked in and she was on her way into her day. She had been a young woman with things to prove, self-sufficiency among them, determined to strike out on her own, independent spirit that she was. Ah, the follies of youth, that quest for adventure and the next bright light down the road.

She and Debra and Carrie continued to correspond, exchanging Christmas cards and letters from time to time, detailing books read and chronicling life events. Reading those letters was how Sandy learned of the expedition's demise, the lawsuits and legal wranglings going on for years. While Dave tried to untangle his legal and financial connections to that original failed enterprise, he moved his salvage operations to the Virgin Islands shortly after Debra uprooted herself from California. Debra and her daughter left Florida abruptly to join her husband. Debra's notes put a perky tone on the moves, but from Carrie Sandy learned murky details of the venture's darker side of shady dealings. Sandy wondered about the sunny face put on those darker dealings Debra portrayed in her letters; did she really understand what was going on, or was she living in La La land with Dave's dreams crowding out reality? The world he created was exciting and he was always on the move, looking towards bigger and better ventures ahead; that power to make things happen could be intoxicating.

The storage unit remained in California, but the salvage business moved to the Virgin Islands after their few months on the East Coast. In their move to St. Thomas, another storage unit was filled and remained in Jacksonville. Left behind were more treasured baby items and the little bits of pottery she had collected in California and Florida; the earthiness of the clay bowls and vases had been comfortingly stabilizing for her, but they were too much trouble to move to the Virgin Islands. For this move, she kept the units' keys in a small jewelry box she did take among the few possessions they shipped. She was beginning to feel like a gypsy caravan. Later, Debra would remember those years as so many boxes marking passages.

Sandy, too, had been on the move the couple of years she had been out of college; the feeling of being a tumbleweed, light and easy to roll, was beginning to bother her. It was time to settle down; painting sets at Disney World was not a permanent career. Her mother, a fashion illustrator for Jordan Marsh, was fast and efficient in her role in an advertising department, but Sandy did not want that pressure, nor did she think she had the speed or resilience for the fast-paced marketing world. The advertising world was too conservative for her.

During that year in Orlando, she and Bill continued to write. She was dating a young man in the costumed character department. He dressed as Donald Duck and went out in the open parts of the park for public walks where little children with ice cream cones dropped them on his webbed feet or pulled at his wings. Waddling through parts of the park open to the public in that hot suit and wobbling that big head, he would walk back into the tunnels in relief, joining her for breaks to share the latest underworld gossip. Everybody knew that Snow White was pregnant. She was soon replaced by a newer, fairer fairy-tale girl. The command to smile at all the customers, referred to as "guests" and she as "their hostess," had driven Sandy from the magic shop to the set design studio. Going to Rock Springs, a nearby park, and floating down the stream in the tropical foliage was her consolation that spring and summer before she moved.

When Sandy went down to the Tampa Bay area to visit Bill, they went out in the water off St. Pete where dolphins delighted her, following their wake and sliding along beside the bow of Bill's friend's boat. Fun as it was being on the water again together, Sandy knew it was time to move on. The spark was gone and his lack of a plan annoyed her. Her mother said she was too easily bored, too hard to please. Her mother had liked Bill well enough when he came up for Christmas, jobless and jibless at that time, broke and too poor for more than a small Christmas present, but Sandy wanted more from a relationship with a man she would truly love; not money, she wasn't that materialistic, but something more that she couldn't put her finger on at the time. So she moved on, man-wise, and eventually they lost touch. By 2000, Sandy, in her fifties, couldn't even remember why Bill had settled in St. Pete. She did know he had finally found an electrical engineering job before they stopped corresponding, and she had been glad for him. Was she looking for Mr. Right or was she just moving on before they did, after that disaster of a love affair with a man too young to appreciate her?

Meanwhile, Debra kept house in Dave's and her small apartment in St. Thomas, high on a hill overlooking the bay, with the sound of roosters crowing and small children calling in the nearby streets; however, the attitudes of some locals, some of the poor, felt like hate she could cut with a knife it was so thick. The dark looks of some on the streets pierced her sense of security. The time two men followed her and her daughter several blocks until she took Mel into a small shop scared her; the times men loitering at a corner called out and she felt they taunted her had made her too uncomfortable to go out often without Dave after the first few months living there. Even without feeling threatened, when she just felt a sense of hostility from some locals, she didn't want her daughter growing up like that, where she was presumed rich and therefore resented. She could hear laughter and women calling their children, but she didn't venture out much alone. She knew Dave and Gene were forming a new company, and that Dave was talking to new investors. There were more shipwrecks, more treasure to be found. Dave's businesslike manner and detailed knowledge of the new wreck site they were exploring convinced several to join. Attracted by his smooth talking and detailed layout, more adventurers risked their money on a gamble for glory.

A new venture was launched. Dave was traveling a good bit. They moved to a nicer apartment, out of sight of the poor, in a more exclusive section. But she knew they were there, resenting rich people and their privileges; whether she imagined the resentment behind the smiles of some who served her in shops or restaurants, she knew class distinctions existed.

Some of living down there in the islands was fun, though. She liked to go out in the boats or fly over to St. John's, but to

Debra's dismay, Dave's drinking had increased. During long nights in marinas and yacht clubs wining and dining potential investors, Dave drank and schmoozed. She would beg off and go home before the night was over; Dave would come home smelling of alcohol and cigarette smoke. Mel turned four, and that spring Debra felt more lonely and disconnected than ever in her life. She had nowhere to turn, she felt. Her father, a former Marine, had retired from the service to North Carolina with her mother and had taken a job at the university one of his old cronies, a military buddy, had recommended. So she didn't even have a home town or high school friends to which she could have returned. Her mother came down to visit, but her father had never forgiven her for dropping out of school, running off to California, and marrying a man he considered a schemer. He'd never met Dave, but still, from what little information he had gleaned from his wife, he'd pieced together a picture he disapproved of. And Debra, too proud and stubborn to admit defeat or admit she was scared, stayed where she was, in a marriage to a man who chased these pipedreams like Peter Pan and the Lost Boys, who brought other treasure hunters into Never Never Land. And she was tired of playing Wendy. And afraid to leave. "Better the devil you know than one you don't," someone had told her.

Debra was growing increasingly troubled by the stories Dave seemed to be telling these investors, until she had to admit they weren't fibs nor even little white lies, but absolute, darn-out lies, and he was a con man. Carrie's words before she left Roatilla came back to haunt her. There was a side to him she hadn't known, but now, more and more, as she peered into the picture Dave painted for his clients, looked through that window, she caught a glimpse of a swindler she didn't like, a con man. And he drank. More and more. He never hurt Mel or her, but she never knew which man was coming home, the drunk or the con man or the sweet daddy of her daughter. Sometimes he didn't remember things he had said or done the night before when he was drunk. That scared her the most. Loyal to him, stubbornly clinging to the belief her love could…she wiped the dangerous thoughts away like suds on dishes, bubbles bursting with a sting of soap in her eye.

When he didn't come home one night in June, she had to drag little Mel along to look for him the next morning; she finally found him passed out on a motor boat he had bought. That terrifying experience brought her to her senses. That, and Gene's constant calling to tell her she had to sign papers for the new venture when it was incorporated, where Dave would be president she would be secretary—her name legally involved, though Gene kept saying it was a paper title only— made her know she had to get out. Where could she go? She would not be homeless on an island where she had no friends. And she turned to the only one close by in Florida, who she felt would take her in.

Debra called Sandy in Tallahassee that afternoon she found Dave on the boat, after leaving him to sober up at the marina, and was greeted with surprise, hesitancy, then a warm welcome to come on up as the idea sank in. We'll make room, Sandy assured her. The next week, while Dave and Gene were out at the yacht club, she packed four boxes of Mel's and her clothes and necessities, and then mailed them to Florida on her way to the airport. The taxi driver helped, and she tipped him well for it. She had taken money from Dave's wallet and cashed a large check at the bank, before he found the money missing or them gone. She bought one-way tickets with cash from another check she had written on their new business account. Sandy would be driving down to pick them up at the airport. She, Mel, and Mel's floppy bunny were on the plane and in the air before Dave came home that night.

Chapter 15

Mel left her mother sleeping in the dim light of the hotel room and went out to the courtyard. Bromeliads, philodendron, and spear shaped leaves all turned to the morning light filtering through the banyan trees and palms. There, having breakfast in a patch of sunlight, sat Aunt Sandy. Mel joined her.

"Morning, sunshine," Sandy greeted her.

"Morning to you, too," Mel said. "You're up early."

"I'm on Hawaii time—six hours earlier there. So we went to bed at what—eleven or twelve last night? That was five or six pm Hawaii time. I'm not adjusted yet; besides, I've always been an early riser. Where's your mom?"

"I left her snoozing in bed. Didn't even stir when I left. I'm usually up at six, kids and animals to be fed."

They chatted awhile about the farm and horses, then lapsed into silence. Sandy was looking through brochures and suggested a snorkeling boat trip for afternoon. Debra and Sandy could go out, Mel said, but she was going over to see Liz. The service was the next day; this was the one free day for the two ladies, Mel pointed out, and they could have the car.

"We'd have to go in when we drop you off," Sandy asked, "wouldn't we?"

After a brief discussion, they agreed that if Debra wanted to wander around Key West or go snorkeling, she and Sandy could get where they wanted to go on foot, and Mel would take the car. Mel was relieved. She knew her mother would put up resistance to dealing with another of her father's wives when she didn't have to; Aunt Sandy made avoiding that easy. In the quiet of early morning light dappling their table, they sat in easy silence. Mel went to get coffee.

The night before had been interesting for Mel, watching her mother and her friend at dinner with this second wife of her dad's. Mel had been secretly amused by Sandy's directness, what bits she'd heard, and entertained by the two stepbrothers she hadn't seen much since she'd gone off to college, married, had kids, only coming down to stay with Liz and Dave a few days at a time through the years after those summers in high school. A couple of visits with her children in tow had been too busy for extended family beyond her dad and his wife. But there had been a time, back when she first came down to see the father who had been absent from her life for over ten years, when she had spent many summer hours with the two. Even then, Dan had been a hard worker and Nelson a drifter, in and out of trouble. Her mind wandered to the night before.

She had been in the kitchen with Dan, his wife Marge, and Nelson, piercing those pieces of meat and mushrooms with skewers, adding color from platters of peppers and veggies cut into slices, when both she and Dan reached for the same pepper. Their hands touched. Mel looked then into his warm sunny face, freckles still dotting his nose and cheeks, light brown hair curling over his forehead. His bright blue eyes met hers, smiling, friendly, open. She looked away. No one had noticed. No one would. Certainly not Nelson, who was talking about the days when he and Dave used to search the islands, scouting for small treasures.

It was the famous treasure hunter Mel Fisher's turf; Dave had long since given up searching for wrecks to explore as a business venture. But he still liked to dive, poke around in the remains of old wrecks. Though the two boys' mother was no longer married to Dave, whose then new wife had straightened him out and made it possible for Mel to be reunited with her father, Nelson and Dan were still involved with their stepfather, one working for him, the other treasure hunting and spearfishing with him. When Nelson mentioned the storage unit where they kept their finds, Mel was trying to pay him close attention, let the affectionate interaction between Dan and his wife pass out of mind, drift out of her conscious attention. And that brief meeting of eyes and hands between her and Dan was certainly no threat to marriages long sealed in security.

"He had a lot more stored in that unit than our measly finds," Nelson said and stopped. He lifted a glass of whiskey to his lips, wiped the grin off his face. His eyes met Mel's and his expression flickered, then he grinned again, lifting his glass towards the table. "A toast to the man who brought us all together, who brought fun on the water and fun on the land."

"Here, here," Dan added, lifting his glass, then seeing that Mel had left her empty glass outside, asked, "Can I get you another glass of wine, or something stronger?"

"No, no, I'm driving. Water will do."

Marge turned and took a glass from a cabinet, little painted seashells lining the middle, filled it with water and ice, and handed Melody the glass. Then she poured a sip's worth of red wine from an open bottle on the counter into another glass, and smiled at Mel before she said, "You're not supposed to make a toast with water. Use this."

"Good catch," Dan said, smiling at his wife.

"That's right," Mel said taking the glass Marge handed her and setting her water down. "Thanks, I forgot. Bad luck or something?"

They toasted, Marge laughing as they all tried to clink glasses across outstretched arms. Then Mel resumed picking through the veggies and meat to skewer. She checked out the window on her mother and Sandy, knowing Barbara, the second wife, could be nasty when drunk, not knowing what to expect next from her, pondering what Barbara had let slip about her father dreaming about Mel's own mother.

Sandy interrupted her reverie at breakfast on the Westwind patio. "Mel. Melody," she was saying. "Earth to Mel."

"I was thinking about last night. Nelson and Dan toasting Dad when we were in the kitchen..."

"Dan seemed nice, but I got a bad vibe from the other one. Why are those two stepbrothers of yours so different looking?"

"Two different fathers," Mel said. "Dad was her fourth husband. The boys had different fathers; her daughter lived in Australia with the first husband, and I think she thought Dad would be the golden goose. The one to provide health insurance and whatever riches she seemed to think he had. Kept trying to get him to adopt the boys, from what I understood."

"He never did?"

"Nope," Mel said, sipping her coffee. "But he did keep them on as teens working with his salvage business."

"So how long were they actually married, Barbara and your dad?" Sandy asked. "I do remember something last night about wanting him to adopt, but it got rather muddled."

"About seven years, I think," Mel said. "He was married to Liz when I was fourteen. She's the one got him sober. And Liz is the one who encouraged him to try to reach me, reestablish contact."

"You like her a lot," Sandy observed.

"I do," Mel said. "I think you and Mom will, too."

"Debra's really sleeping late," Sandy noted. "We'll ask her if she wants to drop you off or walk around instead. I doubt she's going to want to deal with another wife today."

"Thanks for being a good sport about all this, Sandy," Mel said. "I know Mom loves having you here. And I do, too."

"Oh, Melody, you're my favorite girl, and you know your mother means the world to me. I'm glad to spend the time with you. It's just so odd I was requested to be here. Your dad didn't like me defending y'all back when he and Debra broke up. He blamed me for helping her leave."

"That's when we lived with you in Florida. I remember the paper dolls you used to make for me, and coloring books; you used to draw those Disney characters with me in them."

"Oh, I'd forgotten about those. Good memory you've got. I enjoyed entertaining you. You were a handful," Sandy laughed. "I was illustrating children's books back then. I got a gig with a couple of children's book authors from drawing for *Orlandoland* before I quit Disney World. Did you know I dated Donald Duck for a while? Before I moved to Tallahassee?"

Mel smiled at Sandy. "Daisy Duck wasn't jealous?"

"Didn't last that long...I worked on sets and I guess all those characters just popped up in the drawings you and I colored together. Your mom was struggling with working two jobs and raising you on her own."

"Seriously, though, I think Dad understood your helping. I think he knew he was a jerk. I remember him saying you were strong. I heard him say it to Liz. Mom never talked about any of that."

"Your mom was the strong one. He really gave your mom a hard time, Mel," Sandy said, looking her in the eye with that clear green gaze of hers. "He burned a lot of bridges. He had a lot of people mad at him with those treasure hunting deals."

Mel winced. "Yeah," she said. "Nelson used to say they were searching for sunken treasure. He was quite good at convincing people to buy what they brought up, making up stories about them. I think Nelson enjoyed watching him in operation with customers until he quit. He could be quite charming and convincing with buyers. Dan, I think, didn't want anything to do with that. The salvage business was what kept him jazzed. After Hurricane Andrew went through, they had plenty of work to do."

Sandy, Mel knew, was probably thinking con man still. No love lost there. She could see Sandy holding her tongue. Those green eyes in the morning light gazed at her; fine lines at the edges, those eyes looked like a world of thoughts were hidden behind them. Sandy still was an attractive woman, Mel realized. The few grey hairs at her temple, the fine lines along her eyes and mouth added character and definition. But she had seen that same "something 'bout to pop" look in her horse's eye before he nipped one of the other horses for getting too close and she had to slap him, Blue calculating both natural instinct and learned consequences—weighing between following his instinct and catching its swift punishment.

"I won't ask what you're thinking," Mel said.

"Good."

"Can I tell you something, Sandy? Promise you won't tell Mom?"

"Is it something she should know?" Sandy asked. "I don't like keeping secrets…"

"No. But don't tell her or anyone."

"Okay. Spill," Sandy said, her curiosity showing as she sat up and leaned closer.

"Dan and I had a fling when I was seventeen," Mel said. "The last summer I came down and stayed for any length of time."

"Your stepbrother?"

"Well, not really kin," Mel emphasized.

"Not really incest, not like 'I'm my own grandpa' and all that," Sandy teased. "So how old was he?"

"Three years older than me. Twenty. I'd had a crush on him all summer."

"Did your dad know?"

"No way."

"Well, is that awkward now?" Sandy asked. She studied Mel's face.

"Not really. I went off to college. We both married other people."

"Interesting," Sandy said. "Your expression is inscrutable. But you have such a lovely face."

"I've never told anybody."

"Well, thanks for the confidence in me. That will be a hard one to keep under wraps."

"Aunt Sandy, you promised."

"Did I?" Sandy said, with a smile twinkling in her eyes, the mischief-making look Mel found endearing, remembering a few pranks they'd pulled, a few secrets they'd kept when she was a girl.

But Mel wondered why she had spoken now. After all these years. A secret best buried with the summer of her first love, like one of the treasures her mom and Sandy used to bury at the beach when she was small, digging for dolls in little boxes, soon to be washed away by the waves coming ashore, the sands of time washing out and exposing the treasures she didn't uncover herself. Lord, I'm getting as poetical as my mother, Mel thought, and there her mother was, walking up to their table through a shaft of sunlight that brightened the top of her head momentarily.

"Hey, y'all," Debra said, looking well rested and healthy. "Jeff just called the room. He said he left two messages on your phone."

"Oh," Mel said. "I left it in the car last night after I talked to him. Is everything all right?"

"He said call him. But everything was fine. The kids sent their love. Rosy and Tinkerbell sent their love too, he said, when he fed them this morning, and they both say hello. That was a sweet touch."

"He's a sweet guy," Mel responded. "I better go check with him. He's got the Mustang Association already coming in. Lots of teens to help, but it was a bad time to leave."

She got up as her mother gave her a quick hug and a peck on the cheek before she headed to the coffee. Mel had gone to get the cell phone by the time Debra sat down.

"The man adores her. She's been luckier in love than we were, Sandy," Debra said.

"When I first moved to Hawaii, the preacher at Unity said luck is when preparation meets opportunity."

"She was definitely smarter with love. She wanted a man who would treat her good. And he does."

"She was practical. I was looking for a soul mate; I expected too much—or not enough," Sandy frowned.

"You didn't want to settle," Debra said, "I remember that."

"All or nothing...but I let hormones get in the way plenty of times," Sandy grinned.

"I think we wanted to give our hearts, you and I both. If we couldn't give all the love we had to give..."

Sandy looked at Debra and said, "Sometimes you are so profound."

Debra laughed and so did Sandy. It was an old joke between them. "I'm going to be ready for those margaritas come sundown if we keep this up, Sandy," Debra said and smiled back at her friend.

"Do you remember that first time we made margaritas together?"

"How could I forget? I had a hangover that wouldn't quit."

Sandy continued, "I added twice as much tequila as the recipe called for to that second batch, I think."

"It was the fresh lime I loved," Debra recalled.

"Well, we'd better get a move on if we're going to do anything productive before happy hour."

She reached over and squeezed Sandy's hand. "I'm so glad you're here, sweetie."

Sandy's green eyes were bright in the sunlight and shadow playing across her face.

"Me, too. It's so good to be with you again."

Debra smiled at her friend, any secrets behind her eyes well hidden in the warmth of a loving glance before she looked down.

Chapter 16

When Debra put down her suitcase in Sandy's house outside Tallahassee, and let go of her four-year-old's hand, the first thing she noticed were the oil paintings of Roatilla hanging on the wall of the small cinder block's living room. A sunset from the dock looking north along the shore of old houses, palms, the church; the second painting a watery view with fish below lavender tinted swirls on the surface. She burst into tears.

A frightened Melody, looking up at her mother's face, spoke up for the first time since their arrival, "Mommy? Are you hurt, Mommy?"

Sandy turned around and looked at them.

"Hey, Melody," Sandy said quickly, "your mommy's tired, sweet girl. Let's get her something to drink, okay?"

Debra tried to pull herself together as her little girl followed this new person to the kitchen. Then Melody was walking back slowly with water in a plastic glass. Thank goodness Melody had never been afraid of strangers; in their drive back from the airport, Sandy had kept up a stream of little stories about Mel as a baby when she knew her long ago. Mel had taken to her right away.

"Are y'all hungry?" Sandy asked. "I can fix us some sandwiches after you settle in. Melody, let's get you something to drink, too; would you like that?"

Melody had discovered the cat, somewhat cautious about these new people, standing at the bedroom door and flicking its tail. She followed the tabby cat that darted under the sofa.

"She's like a duck on a June bug," Debra sighed, watching her daughter try to touch the cat.

Sandy opened the door beside the bathroom into a small bare room with two windows, a mattress on the floor, nothing else.

"Lucky my roommate just moved out yesterday. Perfect timing. She left without paying her share of the electric bill or next month's rent, but at least we have the house to ourselves. Students. I've got some extra sheets. I didn't have time to do much but sweep and mop it. We can take the lamp from the living room," she chattered on while she opened a closet where a few sheets and towels were stacked on a shelf. Debra took the sheets Sandy handed her.

"I got my art supplies up off the floor; maybe I'd better put them in my room...," Sandy said, turning back to the living room. Her paints and easel were crowded in the corner by a window looking out on a Spanish moss-draped oak. The white sand and scrubby brush outside were dimly lit by late afternoon sun heading towards sunset. While Sandy moved the easel, Debra took the sheets to their new room.

So far, Debra had said little but "Thanks" and "I'm alright sweetheart." She put her suitcase in the bedroom and Mel's bunny on top of it. Sandy was still talking when Debra returned to the living room. She was only half listening. She knew she looked shell shocked. She found Mel squatting at the sofa, calling "kitty, kitty" while the cat's eyes peered out, turquoise gleaming in the darkness. She started to get down on all fours to join her daughter, and then thought better of it. "Mel, honey, let's let the kitty adjust to us first, okay? It will come out and see you soon, okay?"

Mel ignored her mother and kept squatting and calling, her little dress bunched up above her knees.

"What's its name, Sandy?" Debra asked.

Sandy, who was moving a lamp from its spot on the table, wrapping its cord around the base, replied, "That's Snookybookums. Snooky for short. She just showed up a few months ago, right after we moved in. Skinny as a rail with a flea collar too tight around her neck. I took it off, and no one put another on, so I figured she was lost or abandoned. She kept coming around for food and finally just moved in."

Efforts to get Mel to move away, give the cat some space, were met with rumblings of a tantrum. Debra, too drained herself to want to deal, let her be.

"As long as she's not pulling the cat's tail, we're good," Sandy said. Sandy tried asking Mel if she wanted to help put sheets on the new bed, but Mel was not distracted. She wanted the cat. The two women went back to getting the room in order. A cardboard box, with a cloth covering, served for a lamp stand. After the bed was made, Debra followed Sandy back into the living room.

When Sandy went to her art supplies in her own room, Debra, trailing behind, noticed Sandy's bed was missing its mattress and a foam pad was placed over the springs, where it had not been remade. She winced at the thought they'd taken Sandy's mattress. Sandy caught her eyes. "It's fine. We'll go to the thrift store tomorrow, and I've got a friend who'll sell us a mattress; I already asked. I just got this picture framed; if you want, we could put it over your bed."

Sandy picked up a framed painting with colorful dancing characters from beside the door.

"It's lovely, Sandy," Debra said, taking the framed painting and holding it out to look at it.

"I may switch from oil to acrylic. Less messy."

"Your colors are so—so lively. I love it."

"Jazz age impressionist inspiration," Sandy said. "Archibald Motley, bold colors, vivid light and dark. My Van Gogh stage is already done—makes me feel too wild painting like that. I have some more muted pieces, trying Monet's capturing of light, if you prefer."

"Oh, it's cheerful, Sandy," Debra said, "I'd love to have it in the room. Original art from an original artist, how great is that?"

"Thanks. We'll hang it tomorrow, then." Sandy seemed pleased to see Debra a little more animated, and by the time they'd eaten, Snooky the cat had come out on her own. Mel was allowed to pet her gently and the child was finally satisfied. The two women had not talked much, and only after Mel had been bathed and put to bed with her bunny, and was through asking about her Daddy, did they relax. There were issues to discuss, getting a car, a job, the *what next*, but Debra was glad to put them off. She'd done enough for one day. She'd gotten out safely and Dave had no idea where she was. It had been a long day.

"You want a drink? I think we should celebrate," Sandy said after the dishes were washed.

Debra watched her get out limes from the fridge, limeade from the freezer, her moves quick and deliberate.

"Sure," Debra said, wondering if she had a choice or if an answer was even needed.

"Margaritas. I've got this used bartender's guide and the back of the Triple Sec bottle has a recipe. We can improvise," she said, and smiled at Debra, a genuine smile. "I'm so glad you're here. I really am, Debra. I've been hoping for a year you'd leave him, but I was afraid to say much. You sounded so sad the last couple of times I talked to you on the phone. Your letters sounded sort of—sort of..."

"Bleak?" Debra contributed. "I tried, Sandy, I really tried to make it work."

"I know you did."

"He was getting back into the same thing as Oceanic Expeditions. All over again. All that trouble. When we went to the marina, and he'd want me to talk up the clients, clients he called them, even though I knew, I was starting to accept he was conning these men. I didn't want to admit it. I told myself he believed the stories he was telling, and maybe he did, but the details he embellished.... I tried to talk to him, but he wouldn't listen," she sighed. "But it was the drinking. I thought if I loved him enough, if I stuck by him long enough, we could turn things around—"

"You stuck it out longer than I would," Sandy said. "You were loyal, I'll give you that."

And blind to a fault, Debra thought, but didn't say. As Sandy scooped frozen limeade into the blender, Debra asked, "What can I do to help?"

"Juice these," Sandy said, plopping a half dozen limes on the table with a cutting board. Two rolled off the table and Debra caught them before they hit the floor.

"I've got an orange juicer thingie somewhere," Sandy continued, searching under the counter. "Aha."

Night sounds of frogs in the woods, or crickets, came through the screen window. Debra wasn't sure which was making the chorus. The fan blew across them as they worked together to make margaritas, liming the rims of two glasses and scrunching the upturned glasses in salt.

"Let's put on some music," Sandy said. "Will it wake Mel?"

"She sleeps like a log," Debra said. "Thank the Lord for small blessings. Bless her heart; she's had a long day. We both have."

The hot summer night was still, and the fan did little to help. They took their drinks out on the porch, a cement slab; Sandy pulled a rocking chair out of the living room, and put it beside a broken-down wicker chair, stuffed with pillows, already on the porch.

"You get the rocker," Sandy said, "unless you prefer falling through those cushions. There's a hole in the seat. I know where to sit."

"Angel from Montgomery" came on the local radio station. Sandy turned the radio in the window to face towards them sitting in the dark. They sipped their drinks as Bonnie Raitt's voice wafted out. They finished their first drinks and started on the second ones. Debra was starting to relax, the alcohol soothing her frayed nerves, wound so tight from her nonstop motion of the past two days.

"These are good," Debra said. "The limes make them a tad tart—tangy, not too sweet."

"Tart for tarts," Sandy joked. It fell flat.

Sandy offered her a toke from the small pipe she lit. The sweet grassy flavor as Debra inhaled, coughed, and passed it back, lingered in her mouth. They had been sitting in the dark awhile, easy in the quiet of the night sounds and low soft music barely audible above the frogs; the sound, Sandy told her, belonged to tree frogs and bullfrogs by a shallow pond not far away.

"I can't thank you enough, Sandy," Debra said.

"You are welcome," Sandy said. "I'm glad to see you and glad to help. And I mean that."

They brought out a couple of candles and set them on the edge of the porch; a full moon had finally risen above the oaks, lending a silvery glow to the tree tops and sandy yard. The warm orange flicker of candlelight lit their faces from below. Sandy's face had matured a little in these few years since Debra had seen her; she knew her own had thinned and was no longer that of the baby faced young bride in the bay islands, but had become the older face of a young mother in her mid-twenties.

Linda Ronstadt's sad lyrics on the radio and the tequila that relaxed her released floodgates of emotion she had kept pent up like one of those tightly-coiled jack-in-the-boxes Mel was fond of opening with a squeal and then cramming back in the box. She had not allowed herself to think of life without Dave. Just the getting away. Consumed with the impulse to flee, the instinct to move, not dwell on what it would mean. But now it hit.

Their first year on St. Thomas she had been with him almost exclusively, except his few trips to California or Florida, when he brought a few boxes from storage after he dealt with lawsuits. The legal wrangling continued. Then Gene Sherman had come down to the island and there were more trips. But she'd still had her husband most of the time when he wasn't working on organizing a new expedition, dealing with investors and legal issues, or traveling.

Their life together was over. And she missed him. Not the drunk Dave. But the one she saw enjoying their daughter; the charming one escorting her out for an evening, suave and funny; the one taking them out on the water in the boat; the one showing Melody the fishes of Trunk Bay when they went over to St. John's. The man with big dreams and never a dull moment. She had spent time cooking and doing yoga and waiting on Dave to come home and fill up the apartment with his presence and now he would no longer fill the bed beside her, no longer kiss the nape of her neck when she was stirring a new recipe on the stove, learning to cook a few dishes he liked.

She heard the hoot of an owl somewhere in the dark, sounding forlorn on the night air.

"Have you ever missed someone so much, the air went of the room without them? Made it a complete vacuum?"

"Yeah, I have," Sandy said. "Once upon a time. The guy I travelled with in Europe, Paul—I told you about him on Roatilla—I felt so empty without him, so alone I thought my lungs would collapse, my body would crush in on itself in the vacuum of his absence."

"Wow, that's pretty lonesome," Debra said. "That's all alone, all right."

"So alone and empty, the whippoorwill sounds cheerful."

"So alone and empty," Debra paused, "You are the only one on the planet."

"So alone and empty, all the soft cushions are replaced with hard boards," Sandy whispered moving the pillows of the wicker chair, "or sharp sticks."

"So alone, the world so empty, it's like bare feet on rocks."

"Huh?" Sandy turned. "Does that one work?"

"Well, yours was hard and soft. So lonesome, the world so empty, there's no sound left in the world, only silence. Trees don't bother to fall in the forest since no one will hear. Silence out to infinity."

"Wow, that's profound. Profound."

They began to laugh. Then Debra was laughing and crying at the same time. Linda Ronstadt's "Never Gonna Fall in Love" couldn't faze them after that.

"So empty, like a bird's nest after a snake's come through."

"So empty, no fishes swimming in the sea."

"It's crying-in-your-beer music," Sandy said, "and we're laughing."

"I think we're drunk. My head is starting to swim. That second blenderful, I think you made them stronger."

They prattled on, sitting out in the fresh night air, cooler now than the rooms inside. Debra was reluctant to go to bed, to wake to the morning ahead. Shabby chic was the way Sandy described her fabric-covered secondhand furniture, India print bedspreads covering faded or threadbare cushions, cinderblock and board shelves. It was a far cry, Debra thought, from the apartments in St. Thomas, California, and Florida; she had grown accustomed to luxuries, but she was familiar with poor, too, before Dave, or even funky, like Roatilla. Living like that again scared her, but it was the unknown ahead that frightened her most.

Sandy spoke through her reflections, her silence.

"I think what you did was smart," Sandy said. "And brave."

"I'm scared."

"I know. But you're safe. Mel's safe. You made it out and lived to tell," Sandy said as cheerfully as she could.

"I wasn't—we weren't—in any danger," Debra pointed out, softly.

"It's an expression, that's all. 'And lived to tell' is just an expression." She picked up their empty glasses and stood up, slipping on the stoop. "I am drunk. That tequila hits hard. Let's go to bed. I don't have to work tomorrow, but it's late. We'll get you set up tomorrow."

Debra reached for the screen handle from her rocking chair and, after a few swipes at it, held the door open for Sandy. She stood up, her head swimming, leaned over to blow out the candles burning low, and fell right over. On to the dirt and whatever plants she felt beneath her.

"Oh, dang it!"

"Are you all right?" Sandy said, coming back out.

Debra had rolled over and lay on her back, looking up through dark trees to the moonlit sky. "It's cool out here. Think I'll sleep here."

Sandy gave her a hand to pull her up and fell on her knees; then they both managed to get up, laughing. They wiped gritty sand off her hair and back, sand and leaves off Sandy's legs. Sandy had managed to hold on to both glasses with one hand without breaking them.

"So lonesome empty there's no ground to catch you and you keep falling, falling through the sky," Debra muttered. "To infinity and beyond."

"Profound. Truly profound. But Mother Earth caught you this time."

Gritty as she may be, dirty as she may be, Debra thought. They tried to step back on the porch arm in arm, holding each other upright.

Despite the hangover that had come with the next morning, the memory of that silly night lingered as one of those fond moments of youthful folly in the shambles of the wreck that had become her life.

Chapter 17

What had she gotten herself into? Sandy wondered. Debra and Mel had been living with her five months now, and north Florida autumn was in full swing, with winter not far behind. They were driving to her mother's house for Thanksgiving in a few hours, and Debra wasn't back yet. Sandy didn't mind babysitting the kid, though she could be a brat sometimes, but she hadn't bargained for such a depressed woman and the melodrama, yet here she was. She knew she was doing a good deed, but it interfered with her love life. Debra being a downer didn't help. Her mother said to give her time.

She checked out the window in the living room to make sure Mel was still playing with dolls in the sandy front yard. She was waiting on the pecans and cranberries for the Jell-O mold. There would be plenty to do when they got to Mama's, ambrosia and dressing to make, potatoes to peel…. She stepped out onto the stoop and down to the ground, walked over to where Melody was singing to the Ginny doll, Sandy's old doll her mother had brought down from the attic. Debra wouldn't let Mel play with Barbies. Too sexist. So it was a Ginny doll and two plastic babies from the thrift shop.

The four-year-old was giving the little hard plastic baby dolls dinner. She smiled up at Sandy. Sunlight played on her smooth little cheeks and her curls of light sandy brown. Her bright eyes, young and clear — what a cutie, Sandy thought.

"This one's not eating her peas. She's being bad," Mel said.

"Well, maybe not too bad," Sandy said. "Maybe she'd like them better with soup."

She picked up a dry live oak leaf from the sand, and then chose a last year's acorn cap from one of the live oak trees. She passed the cap to Melody. "Try this."

About then, they heard the car coming up the drive.

Melody hopped up, leaving the dolls in the dirt to skip along the car rolling to a stop. "Mommy!"

Debra got out, smiling, and picked her up, twirled her once and set her down. "You're getting heavy! I brought you something," she said. "Help me bring in that little bag."

They carried the goods into the house, setting the bags on the kitchen counter. Debra pulled a bag of cranberries out.

Melody was hopping up and down. "Where's mine? What'd you bring me?"

Sandy saw the bag of fresh cranberries and her heart sank. "Did you bring any canned ones?"

"I did," Debra said and took the cans out last. "Did you think I'd forget?"

Sandy didn't answer that one. *Not only forgetful.*

"I may be a space cadet, but I made a list this time."

"We've still got time for this Jell-O to set," Sandy said, taking the can of cranberries.

"You don't want to wait to make it down there? Will it travel okay?"

"Believe me, Mama will keep us busy tomorrow," Sandy said, measuring water and pouring it into a pan to boil. Debra still hadn't packed, so Sandy figured the Jell-O with its nuts and cranberries added would be set by the time they took off.

After Debra handed Melody the M&M's, a concession, since sugar was not too frequently doled out, they talked and moved around the kitchen. "I'm making fresh cranberry relish, if that's okay."

"Sure. You know, we may be pushing the vegetables too hard," Sandy said. "She was making the baby dolls eat them."

Debra smiled. Melody had gone back outside. The tabby cat had followed her.

"I met someone at the market," Debra said. "I think he was flirting with me."

"Really? That's good," Sandy said. "What'd he look like?"

"Not tall like you like 'em," Debra said, "but nice. A grad student I think. We were feeling up the avocados and started talking about not too hard, not too soft. Quite erotic."

"Vegetable love?" Sandy quipped. She was glad to see Debra making a joke. Her mood seemed lighter and she was smiling. A nice flirtation to remind her she was an attractive woman was a welcome sign. There's hope ahead, Sandy thought.

Debra had spent the first month barely moving beyond getting their room cheered up with a few odds and ends from a couple of yard sales, not looking for a job the first couple of weeks, just doing yoga and tending her daughter. She did cook, even a few island dishes, so that pleased Sandy who came home from campus usually tired. She had gotten a job at FSU's Museum of Fine Arts part-time, also a freelance gig illustrating a children's book, and worked a design class around her schedule. She was working on an exhibit with a few other students for spring, but she kept her art supplies put away and got those out at night, the materials moved into her room.

Debra didn't like the first two ratty cars they looked at in a low price range, and decided on a lease rental. She had to do some wrangling to get the lease, finally getting her mother to sign for it, even though the money came out of what Debra had taken with her from St. Thomas. Maybe it was a smart move, Sandy decided, since she herself thought "poor," a mindset that left her debt-free, and paid for her used car without car payments. But it also meant breakdowns and repair bills. Her first car, the one the boatyard guys had borrowed and broken its axle during her expedition days when the ship was in dry dock, was long gone. This Ford she had—Fix Or Repair Daily—fit the profile of poor but it was paid off. Good thing she was friends with a mechanic at a car service in town. Debra's car lease eased the ride situation.

The melodrama had begun, however, when Debra called her mother the second day after her escape, once the hangover from margarita night wore off, and learned that Dave had already called there. Her mother was upset; Debra was unsure whether to give her the number at Sandy's. She had said she'd call back. Sandy heard her tell her mother, "I left him a note 'I'm gone. Don't look for us. I'll be in touch.' He should have gotten the letter I mailed the same time." Kinda harsh, Sandy thought at the time.

When Debra got off the phone, she'd told Sandy, "My father said if he came looking for me, he'd shoot the bastard. My father never even met him. I haven't seen my dad in six years."

Then there had been threats from Dave. If she didn't come back, he could press charges. She could be guilty of embezzlement for writing that check she cashed before she left St. Thomas. Sandy and Debra weren't sure of the legality of that, since Debra had written checks before on business accounts, but had refused to sign any incorporation papers for the second venture startup. But the threats had come a couple months after his attempts to sweet talk her, plead with her, had failed.

He had found a couple of Sandy's letters, tracked her down at the university, found their home. First he'd begged and pleaded as Debra weakened and waffled. He said he wouldn't leave until she went with him. He cried. They called the sheriff. He wrote. He called. Sandy shuddered at the memories only a few months old. Debra had decided it might be best to go back, but Sandy sent her to a domestic abuse counselor where she said she saw the wheel of escalation for abusive situations. He'd never hit her, or her child. Broken some of her pottery, but never her. But she was cut off in St. Thomas from friends and family, and that was part of the cycle. After she agreed to meet him in town to talk, he'd shown up drunk, and that was it. They got a restraining order. Debra had never told her about agreeing to meet him in town, but Sandy had figured it out from things he'd said in his drunken rant one night on the phone. She never mentioned it to Debra. The woman was trying to deal as best she could, and after all, she, Sandy, was someone Debra had felt close enough, safe enough, to come to. That, in its own way, was flattering and endearing, despite the hassles.

When Debra tried to talk to Dave about signing a separation agreement and, later, divorce papers, that was the lowest. He refused to pay alimony or child support. Ever since he'd declared bankruptcy the first time in the U.S., he'd had no traceable funds within the States. Debra was left to fend for herself. Debra told Sandy she thought she could wait him out; he would eventually agree to a divorce. Since custody would be a battle she did not want to fight, and it would become one way to control her, she was still in legal limbo. She was sure if she gave him time he would let her go. Sandy wasn't so sure about that. No paperwork could be filed until Debra lived in Florida long enough to qualify as a resident, anyway.

It was hard not to get down, herself, with Debra in the doldrums, swinging from worrying about how Dave was doing and missing him, to being firm in her resolve. Sandy tried to stay away from giving too much advice, knowing it could backfire. That was hard, too. Debra wanted a listening ear, so Sandy let her talk through her back-and-forth swings between despair and determination. When he said he'd move back to the United States, chuck it all for her, Debra didn't believe him, fortunately. Once she had moved past her denial of his dishonesty and scheming during the years she had kept staying with him and took a hard look back at some of the deals, the wake of destruction left from deals that blew up, the men angry at losses and betrayal, the lawsuits and bankruptcy, she knew she couldn't go back. She couldn't live with the lies, she finally told Sandy. Then the threats made her dig in her heels. Debra told her any love she had felt, she locked up in a trunk somewhere and buried it. Then burned the map. She would not travel that road again.

The flare up of melodramatic moments animated her to act or do, but once those were done, Debra was back to being depressed. Not so depressed she couldn't move or get out of bed, but definitely not much fun. Sandy tried to get her to go to a couple of parties. No luck. This trip to her mother's home was Debra's first social venture besides getting a part-time job pricing and shelving books at a used book store a few hours a week, then becoming a clerk there a few days a week. During that time riding in with Sandy, before she got a car, dropping Mel off in daycare at a nearby neighbor's, she found a woman who took pity on her and would alternate with Sandy getting her home in the afternoons. She clerked a couple of evenings when Sandy could watch Melody, but that tied Sandy down. Nonetheless, it was working by bits and pieces. Finally Debra had her own temporary wheels with the lease agreement.

Sandy's mind wandered over the events of the past few months while she cleaned up the kitchen and Debra finished packing. After they packed the car and set off down the road a little later than Sandy liked that November day, taking Debra's rental, a nicer car than her own clunker, Debra explained to Melody again where they were headed. Debra took the first shift of driving.

Having told her how her mother moved them from Georgia to pursue a career in Florida as an artist, she knew Debra would like the gumption her mother had had to strike out on her own back in the sixties. She had been a role model for a single mother and an advocate for women's independence. Sandy told her, "Mama has the first issue of *Ms.* Magazine. She's a charter subscriber."

"I met your Mama. She has strong opinions. But no bra burner," Debra said.

"No," Sandy agreed, "We need ours too much."

They both smiled at that. "I'll be glad to see her again. She's a ball of fire. I wish my mother were more like that."

Sandy knew Debra's mother had married a Marine, one who still had "Simper Fi" on the bumper of any vehicle he owned; as a wife, Debra's mother had never worked a day outside the home in her entire adult life. Sandy, on the other hand, didn't remember when her mother didn't work. First she worked for the REA in Georgia, a clerk at Rural Electrical Administration. Then after completing a correspondence course in commercial art, she had collected her work and gathered her courage to apply for work as artist for a department store in the advertising department, then on to Florida for a more prestigious job as a fashion illustrator, leaving Sandy that last year of high school with her grandmother so that she could finish high school with her friends. Sandy hadn't talked much about her childhood with a widowed mother, but as they travelled, she opened up.

"How did you lose your daddy?" Debra asked as the miles whizzed by. "We've never talked about that. I know your mother was a widow."

"I was four, maybe five. Mel's age. It was snowing. It never snows in Georgia, maybe north Georgia, but never us. Mama and I had gone out and made a snow man. A little one. We'd just made snow crème when the call came. I remember it as clear as day. My mother's face. He'd been out hunting, was driving home when a car slid into his lane; he lost control.... All sheerow."

Sandy checked Melody, sleeping in the back seat, and then added, "Funny how a picture sticks in your mind. I can still see the little snowman, the snow ice in cups...my mother.... Then they brought his dogs home, a pointer and a setter. They were scratched up, but still at the scene..."

"Gosh, that must have been hard."

"Back then, they didn't do anything about children and grief. I wasn't allowed to come near my mother the rest of the day. Her mother stayed with her. I was sent over to a neighbor's. They medicated her. Mama said we did sleep together that night. I don't remember that. Just the exile to the neighbor's, then the abyss. The deep abyss of loss."

The somberness of the moment, Sandy realized, might not be what they needed. She lapsed into silence.

"I'm sorry, Sandy," Debra said. "That must have been rough...on both of you."

Sandy shrugged and looked out the window.

"Mel's doing pretty well without her dad," Debra mused. "I've tried to explain as best she'd understand. But first I told her her daddy and I didn't make each other happy anymore. Then she started asking if she made me happy. Like I'd leave her, too, so I changed tactics. I've told her mothers and fathers grow apart. She asked if she'd grow apart from me. I told her mommies and daughters don't have to grow apart, but.... She asked when she'd get to see her daddy again..."

"Mel's a pretty tough little kid," Sand offered. "Resilient."

"She asks questions I can't answer, but I try to be close to the truth as I can without upsetting her," Debra said.

"I think you're doing pretty well, all things considered," Sandy said. Debra shot her a quizzical look before she put her eyes back on the road ahead.

"I had a little brother; died before I was born," Debra said. "I don't think my father forgave me for living when he didn't. Or for not being a boy."

"Golly, Debra, that's tough."

"He's a hard-ass," Debra pronounced. She braked for a truck pulling into her lane too closely. She changed lanes, but cars behind her were crowding in the fast lane. "The only concession he made for my mother was letting her stay in

Albany while he deployed a few times. She had family in those parts. But that meant as a child I got to stay put."

"I was a Daddy's girl, myself," Sandy said. "I remember that. Have you tried to talk to your Dad?"

"Nope. He believes you make your bed, you lie in it."

"But you haven't tried—"

"No," Debra said a bit forcefully. "Not after he yelled on the phone when he found out I left school; he was cussing and I hung up."

Then she added, "After that he refused to talk, and I refused to ask to speak to him. Probably still mad I wasted the money for college from the fund they started for my brother."

"What does your mother say?"

"We don't talk about him anymore. She is totally dependent on him...like I was with Dave," she replied, adding the last as though it were a new thought.

"I haven't been supported by a man since I was a child," Sandy pondered aloud. "My mother has been on her own since Daddy died. She wouldn't bring a stepfather into the house when I was growing up, but now she's got Charles. You'll meet him this weekend. I guess I grew up seeing my mother work, her sisters go through several divorces and end up at our grandparents' off and on, and decided Mama's life looked better. Calmer. I always was determined to be...to be..."

"Independent? Self-sufficient?" Debra suggested for her.

"Yeah. Not depend on someone else like that. It hurts too much. Mama was and is a career woman. I'm doing that, too, somehow."

"We are our mother's daughters," Debra said, peering into the dimming light of dusk.

"Yeah, I used to believe we created our own destiny; you know, we were in charge of what our life becomes...but I'm afraid our upbringing has more to do with it than I like to admit."

"Well, I hope Melody will be all right."

She was concentrating on the road and did not look at Sandy. The setting sun was fading.

"Before we get into Orlando, I'll drive," Sandy offered.

"Great. I haven't driven much since I was a teen and a while in Florida when we were in Jacksonville. Rusty as a nail in a pail of water."

"Now it's getting dark, it'll be harder to see road signs."

They drove on in silence, with a little conversation from time to time filling the quiet. Debra turned into a gas station before they reached Orlando. They got gas and changed places. Melody slept on in the back seat, her bunny nestled in her arms. As Sandy looked back to turn around, she saw Mel, the small child asleep with a small blanket over her feet in the play of light and dark while the car moved under the station's lights.

"Look at that. She's so sweet looking."

"In her sleep," Debra said. "Sweet in her sleep."

"And a bouncing bunny awake. Just like my mother—she keeps on goin', movin' and a-shakin'. Mama will be so glad to see her."

Sandy's mother's house was in a cul-de-sac of old brick houses, screened porch in front barely visible in the dark. An outside light came on as they pulled into the driveway. Her mother came to the door all smiles. Sandy was so glad to see her, the little blue-eyed redhead in her mid-fifties perky and bright as ever. Her mother's twinkling blue eyes lit on the small girl with genuine warmth and delight. Mel had woken up and was feeling disoriented, rubbing her eyes and looking a bit peevish. Sandy's mother, Maureen, disarmed her quickly. They were soon having hot tea and supper. Melody was exploring, playing with Maureen's Persian cat and looking at knick-knacks she showed her. Debra and Sandy's mother had hit it off instantly the first time they met, so this visit was a warm reunion for them all.

Later, after dishes were done, Debra and Sandy were dancing in the den. They had pulled out Sandy's old album of *Hair*. The contagious music and enthusiastic lyrics were all it took to wake them up from the fog of travel. Mel, coming in with Maureen, looked in wonder at the cheerful version of her mother she hadn't seen in months, and then at Sandy, who took her little hands and soon had her twirling and spinning. Even Sandy's mama was doing the twist while Debra and Sandy were singing the words, "freaky, streaky—I love my hair" and tugging on their own hair and swishing Mel's curly locks and making her laugh at their silliness.

The next morning after breakfast, they were set to work cutting oranges, Melody helping with the peeling, even wanting to use the scissors for cutting the white pith of orange sections, which slowed the operation. Debra was overseeing Melody's careful but awkward use of big scissors. The turkey was in the oven. Sandy was helping with making the dressing; Mel was enlisted to squish the cornbread, egg, white bread mixture with celery and turkey drippings, making a face when she first put her hands in the bowl, but quickly getting into squeezing the mess through her fingers.

"Better than mud pies," Sandy said. "Eh, Mel?"

Mel smiled back at her. "Ooey, gooey!"

She squeezed the dressing mixture through her fingers and laughed. Maureen looked over and smiled at Mel, then Sandy. Sandy smiled back at her mother. Debra, too, looked up from peeling potatoes, smiled, and went back to the potatoes.

Her mother had set the dining room table already, getting help with the extra leaf of the table before putting the lace tablecloth over it. Baked potatoes were cut open, the contents smashed, the emptied baked skins loaded with cheese and potato, and set back in the oven. Sandy insisted on mashed potatoes as well. Chilled asparagus waited in its serving bowl.

The kitchen was a busy and cheerful place full of good aromas and movement.

"Debra's been showing me some yoga moves," Sandy was telling her mother. "I've got her starting the pottery class at the community center."

"She twisted my arm. But it fits my schedule."

"Admit it's a good Christmas present," Sandy teased. "Debra's been bringing home all these old paperback cookbooks, Mama. "

She checked on the progress of the dressing squishing, and added, "She's tried everything from sweet and sour lentils to tabouli."

"I'm fixing to start on *Diet for a Small Planet*," Debra said from her station at the kitchen table, watching Maureen add more pan drippings to Mel's bowl mixing. "Tabouli is great."

Soon the stuffing was in the oven and the broccoli was cut for steaming. They chattered on in warm comradery until the guests arrived and the feast was set on the table with china and crystal.

Charles, a grey-haired bridge engineer with a ready smile, was in charge of carving the turkey, and his youngest daughter, a few years younger than Sandy, was even pleasant. The girl, with a drug problem and boyfriends Charles distrusted, had a night life Sandy could have never kept up with. Fortunately for her mother, Sandy thought, Jane was living in Tampa and wouldn't be in the house when Charles and her mother moved in together next year. The wedding was set for spring, but it would be a small affair. Still, Sandy was happy to see her mother in love, her mother happy.

After the blessing, which made Sandy cringe with a father-god reference when she had decided to believe the creator would be female, Sandy looked around the table at all the pleasant, expectant faces as they passed bowls of asparagus, raw cranberry relish—remaining largely untouched—sweet potato soufflé, string beans, then the turkey and dressing, and filled plates laden with baked or mashed potatoes, cranberry salad. She was thankful, later so very thankful for a memory that in future years would comfort her, a memory she would hold up to remember comfort, and love, and nurturing in the candlelit glow of faces smiling at her, faces she loved surrounding her.

Chapter 18

The paint set Melody had gotten for her fifth birthday was scattered on the floor, brushes wet with paint and a few stray marks smeared on the floor, the circles of color in the paint box muddy pools of mixed shades. But where were Melody and Tisha, her little friend from Sunday school? Debra was too tired to get off the sofa where she had fallen asleep. Her shifts at the bookstore mornings and afternoons, her weekend nights waitressing were taking a toll. She forced herself off the couch.

"Melody. Mel, darlin'," she called. "Where are you, sweetheart?"

She heard scuffling in Sandy's room, but Sandy was with her boyfriend in the North Carolina mountains, off canoeing the Nantahala.

Barefooted, Debra padded over to the door to Sandy's room and opened it. There stood her little girl, paint smeared on her shirt, her friend's shirt, and, oh Lordie, Sandy's painting. She realized it was a portrait of Melody and her there on the easel. Both surprise at how sweet the portrait was and how well the likenesses matched them, and horror at red paint smudged on the arms and cheeks of her little girl's image in the painting—both emotions flooded Debra at the same time.

"What have you done?" she gasped. "Out, out, now, you little devil! Scoot! You know you're not supposed to be in here."

Mel, caught in the act, still holding the tube of vermillion and a brush, squeezed the tube in surprise and a red worm of oil paint splatted on the floor.

"We were painting," Mel answered defiantly. Standing next to her, the little brown-skinned girl, with big brown eyes wide, wiped her green fingers on her shirt, the same greens and reds that were smeared on the canvas. They haven't been here long, Debra thought, or there would be more damage. But it was oil, not easy to clean.

"Put the paint down, Mel," she ordered. Mel hesitated, and then stooped to put the tube on the floor. Tisha took a step towards the door. "Wait, don't leave. Don't touch anything. Let me clean y'all up first."

She grabbed one of the rags next to Sandy's easel, chose two jars in a box on the floor. The odors of turpentine and linseed oil permeated the air as she opened the jars, sniffed to choose one, and dabbed turpentine first on Mel's fingers, then down Tisha's shirt and fingers. The paint smeared on Tisha's shirt, but holding their hands out, the girls obediently let her wipe their fingers and hands clear of paint.

"It stinks," Melody whined. "Ow, you're hurting."

"We've got to get this off you before it dries. Now both of you go outside and rinse your hands at the spigot. No, wait for me and I'll help. Stay put."

Debra rubbed at the red blotches on the floor, unsure whether to try wiping the painting. Using another rag, she worked at the green and red on one of the faces on the canvas, smearing a bit; some of the fresh paint came off, since, thank goddess, the layers Sandy had applied had dried. The bumpy surface of thick layers of dried paint yielded some of the new colors. But enough held fast to notice.

"Oh, hell," Debra sputtered under her breath. "Damnation."

"Mama, you're not supposed to say bad words."

Debra scowled and bit her lip but said nothing. Once she had gotten what she could off, with only a pale smear remaining faintly, she scooted the two girls outside in front of her. The kitchen's screen door flapped shut behind them.

"Wait here," she said at the dripping faucet where a toad the color of mud hopped away and startled her. Barefooted, Debra stepped back into the muddy patch. "Tarnation!"

The girls giggled. The tension broke. Since Debra had not fussed at them anymore and her severe expression had lessened, *tarnation* seemed like a hilarious word to the two girls; the grown woman's muddy toes added to their delight. Mel headed after the toad.

"Leave the toady frog alone, Melody. Let's finish this first."

Mel stepped back from the toad and turned around. Her well-worn shirt still had a smear of oil paint that Debra let be.

"Rinse your hands, girls," Debra commanded. "We don't want turpentine stinging if it stays too long. I'm afraid your shirt is ruined, Tisha. I'll go get some soap."

Returning from the kitchen with dish soap, relieved now most of the mess was cleaned up, Debra smiled and said, "Y'all are as rascally as the raccoons in our trash cans."

She soaped up both girls and they were soon occupied making foamy bubbles along their arms and feet. She dabbed at the little girl's stained top.

"It's not coming off your shirt."

Tisha hadn't said a word. Her lip trembled. "My momma gonna be mad."

"We'll get you another shirt, honey," Debra said. "We'll take one of Mel's new ones, okay?"

"No, Mama," Melody started to cry.

"Mel, you've got to share. Stay out here and I'll bring something for you, Tisha."

Debra went back inside, jiggled open her chest of drawers, grabbed a cute Raggedy Ann and Andy shirt she'd recently bought Mel, and went back out for a quick switch, pulling the wet top off the child while being careful to keep any embedded paint from touching skin. The little girl meekly accepted the change and the two girls sat in folding chairs set out under an oak, swinging their legs. Debra brought out peanut butter crackers and lemonade.

"Are we in trouble?" Mel finally asked.

"I'm the one in trouble now," Debra pointed out. "I dropped the ball. But you knew better than to go in Aunt Sandy's room."

"But my paints were all brown."

"That's 'cause you smeared them. You have to rinse the brushes, I've told you that, before you add a new color. But your paints are water-based. The ones in Sandy's room are oil. Oil doesn't come out."

Debra was relieved when Tisha's mother came to pick up her daughter and simply shrugged when Debra explained what happened and handed her the stained shirt in a paper bag. She offered to buy another if the one she substituted didn't suit, but Ms. Williams looked up from where she sat in her car and shook her head. "No need. These young'uns are always up to something. There's always a mess to be had somewhere."

"She can keep the shirt," Debra said, but Ms. Williams had started the Plymouth and the motor was running. Ms. Williams was laid back, thank goddess, Debra thought, but she'd left without having any iced tea Debra had offered.

"My Raggedy Ann and Andy shirt—" Mel pouted as the Plymouth backed up and turned around.

"Tough, kid," Debra said. "That's a small price to pay. I should spank you."

But I'm too tired, Debra thought as they stood watching the car disappear beyond scrubby foliage and twisting trees. Mel looked up at her with an expression of doubt.

"Go see if you can find that toad. I'm going in to see if I missed any spots from your painting extravaganza."

Mel took her hand a moment, cool fingers curling around Debra's own warm ones. The five-year-old took a final sip from her lemonade before she handed the glass to her mother and scampered away to look for Toady.

Kneeling near the spigot, Mel looked back at her. "Thanks, Mommy. I'm sorry for making a mess."

Debra's heart melted.

Debra cleaned up the paints the girls were supposed to be using and put them away in the closet, on the wobbly book shelf she had salvaged from curbside in town where some college students had moved out and left broken chairs and trash. One man's trash, another man's treasure. Yeah, right, she thought. She still had her shift at the restaurant to get through and Blanche, the waitress she rode with, would come pick her and Mel up before long. Thank goddess Blanche had a teenage daughter who needed babysitting money and Debra could split costs with Blanche, since she had a couple younger ones the teen kept an eye on as well. She checked on Mel, making a mud village for the toad, before making herself a cup of coffee. She'd have a few minutes to drink it before she called Mel in for her bath. Sighing, she finished her coffee and drew a bath for her dirty daughter in the clawfoot tub.

The next day, Sandy was back before dark. Tom's beat-up pickup truck, with its cracked windshield and an Old Town canoe strapped atop and tied down in front and back, made a funny scene pulling into the yard. Like some prehistoric dinosaur with a big beak. A beautiful canoe, a crappy vehicle. A contradiction the two women had joked about. Debra could see through the front door screen as Sandy gave the bearded man a kiss and slid out her side of the truck. She grabbed her bag from the bed of the truck. Tom turned around and headed back out the drive. Offering a hand up laconically out the window, he waved before he disappeared behind the trees.

"He didn't want to come in?" Debra asked as she opened the door for Sandy, looking tired but happy, her long hair disheveled, half its brown strands pulled loose from a ponytail riding low on the back of her neck.

Sandy replied, "It was a long day. We've both gotta go back to work tomorrow."

She was heading for her room to dump her bag, and Debra caught her arm. "Wait. There's some bad news."

Sandy turned, her face anxious.

"Not that bad," Debra quickly added. "Mel got in your paints and…"

Sandy, her hand on the knob, looked startled and opened the door. "Where? What'd she do?" Sandy stood before the easel. "That was your birthday present. I just finished it before we left."

"I got the oil off the floor. It's just on, on Mel there…"

"Well, I can paint over it. Or you can get it that way as a reminder," Sandy said, her tone somewhere between irritated and disappointed. Debra stood behind her, couldn't see her face. "What happened? She knows not to come in here."

"I'm sorry, Sandy. I left them alone five minutes. That's all it took. I fell asleep for just a second on the couch. She had her friend over yesterday…"

"It's okay."

Debra couldn't decide if Sandy was being more gracious than need be or was actually madder than she showed. It was hard to tell. "It's a beautiful painting, Sandy." She didn't want to sound ingratiating but she couldn't help adding, "Your colors are so vivid. With a few strokes you caught light and shadow."

"Impressionism…and Archibald Motley, a jazz age artist, influenced this one, too, like the one in your room already. I'm trying to use an economy of strokes to build suggestions of detail," Sandy said, leaving her bag on the bed and coming back out. "You like it?"

"I love it," Debra said following her back out of the room.

"I gotta take a bath. We camped, and I haven't bathed since Thursday—except to get half dunked in ice cold water."

"Are you hungry? I made a casserole. We already ate."

"Where's Mel?" Sandy asked.

"In our room. She's afraid to come out. I told her she'd been bad. She thinks you'll be mad at her."

"Well, it's okay. She just needs to stay out of my stuff," Sandy said.

She wasn't making Debra feel any better. Ever since her lease on the rental ran out, and Debra had resorted to catching rides and borrowing Sandy's car to save money for her own vehicle, tension had built up. She had enough saved to buy a used car now; she'd finally found one, a rat trap as bad as Sandy's. She'd get the title signed over Monday and have her own wheels. Money her mother sent for her birthday had sped up the process.

"I'm getting a car tomorrow," Debra said, watching Sandy spoon out tuna casserole from the dish on the stove and sit down with a beer.

Sandy looked up, "Good. It's about time."

Debra flinched but said nothing. She's madder than a wet hen, Debra thought.

"How was your trip?"

She got a glass of water and sat down at the table with Sandy. Between swallowing mouthfuls and swigging on her beer, Sandy detailed their three-day trip. Debra felt a pang of envy. When had she had a weekend off? Not in months. It sounded so fun, a weekend camping and canoeing with a new love. Tom was a sculptor Sandy had met in the university art department during fall semester; later, at a party, they made a genuine connection which developed into a relationship after Christmas. During their first Christmas season here in this home, making ornaments and putting Mel's paper doll angel on top, he had come over to help with decorations. Ironically, he was a former Navy man like Dave had been, but the two men were totally different. A veteran taking art classes and running a canoe rental business he'd started up with another veteran, Tom smoked too much pot and ingested too many drugs for her taste, but Sandy had fallen for him slowly over a few months of his steady attention. Sandy had admired his sculpture and was pleasantly surprised that they had mutual friends. From there, he grew on her and now she declared herself in love.

After Sandy finished eating, Debra took the dishes from the table and filled the sink with warm, soapy water, enjoying the warmth on her hands, still thinking about these past few months and her sudden bout of envy. Debra had heard all about Tom's canoe rental business when he had come over for dinner back in January. He'd started it up with another veteran, a former helicopter pilot, more than a year before. *Deliverance*, the movie out a while back, had made wilderness treks by canoe a hit, despite the redneck dangers dramatized in the film. It had inspired Tom and his partner, she and Sandy had been told. He was poor, too poor for Debra's taste, a stoner, but Sandy had been smitten. After a string of brief affairs lasting no more than a few weeks, Sandy was ready for a loyal man. A real boyfriend. At first, Sandy hadn't been impressed by this tall, thin guy's look, his long nose and wire-rimmed glasses, combat boots and black bandana, but he'd quickly won her over with his attentiveness and her admiration for his artwork. They both loved the out of doors and art, so Debra couldn't begrudge her a little happiness. She felt a little small for even that moment of envy. It was just that her own life was confined to childcare and work, and she was really tired. She had rallied from the stupor of her depression after Thanksgiving and had found a waitress job before Christmas to supplement her income from the bookstore. Getting behind on rent, not able to save for a car, she'd finally realized the bookstore wasn't enough. Weekends at the steakhouse were big tip nights; the neighbor down the road worked those shifts, so she could ride with her once the rental car was returned.

Debra finished the dishes and put the kettle on for hot tea. How long could she keep this up? Church kindergarten had been a godsend, once she'd made the decision at Christmas to take Mel to the Methodist church nearby. Whether she still believed or not, or found religion too authoritarian for her taste, Debra thought Mel needed it. She could decide for herself later if Christianity didn't suit her, but Debra wanted that structure in her daughter's life. Even though she herself had taken to Sandy's calling the Holy Spirit "goddess," she had grown up in church and she wanted Mel to have that choice. Sandy had been around less once the relationship with Tom had taken off. Debra missed her. Thanksgiving and Christmas day at Sandy's mother's house had opened a longing for her own mother that she'd never acknowledged fully before. She and Sandy had shared some joyful moments over the holidays. Still, this was really, really hard and she was really, really tired.

She roused from her reverie when she heard Sandy opening the bathroom door after her shower. Sandy came into the kitchen, towel wrapped around her hair, bathrobe loosely tied.

"Hey, thanks for supper."

Debra, putting down her mug of chamomile tea, looked up as Sandy added water to the kettle and put it back on the stove. "You're welcome."

"I got distracted in the commotion of settling back in and getting a shower."

"Sandy, she's just a little girl."

"I know that. I was mad. But it's okay. I'm over it. She's a curious kid—"

"And willful," Debra added.

"That, too, but you gotta watch her every minute. The oil paints shouldn't be in my bedroom, but it's the only place…" she trailed off. "But she could make a real mess, or get it in her eyes or something…and those tubes are really expensive."

"I don't need a lecture," Debra said testily.

Sandy looked at her. Her expression was surprise. Sandy opened her mouth to say something, then closed it. The kettle began to sing. "Have we got any peppermint left?" Sandy asked, rifling through the tea bags in the basket.

"There in the box. I got a new one after work Saturday. I only worked 'til one at the bookstore, so I had time to get it before Mel and Tisha arrived."

"Ms. Williams' kid? From Sunday school? Good that y'all can swap babysitting…" Sandy said, seeming to be trying to find a friendlier topic.

While her tea steeped, Sandy put a record on the stereo her mother had given them when she got a new one. Peter, Paul and Mary, not too loud. They didn't want to wake the kid. Debra joined her on the sofa.

"I'm sorry I was cross," Sandy said. "I'm tired. My period's coming. I had cramps all day."

"Mine, too," Debra said. "No cramps, at least."

"Full moon women," Sandy said and smiled. "Blood sisters."

She was glad to see Sandy's features relax into the warmth of her friendly, expressive face; it felt like the sun coming out from behind a storm cloud, Debra reflected.

"I'm just so tired all the time," Debra sighed. "I don't spend enough time with Mel, either."

"It's hard working two jobs. I've done it myself. It won't get any easier when she starts grade school."

"My mama would say it's a hard row to hoe," Debra said, staring into her half empty mug.

"Have you talked to your mother lately?" Sandy asked.

"No, she sent the check with a card for my birthday, but she'll probably call Tuesday on the day."

"You know, Debra, I'm glad you'll finally have a car, but this is a struggle. You need more help than I can offer," Sandy said. Her expression had changed, darkened it seemed, like that cloud once more covering the sun, as she continued, "I've got the museum job, and art projects, and auditing that anthropology class.... By the way, I read something about the bay islands the other day. Columbus went there, and he encountered Mayans, about twenty-five of them; that was in 1502."

Debra, almost sidetracked from her thoughts about the situation she faced, continued with her worry. "I feel I'm neglecting Mel, with all this daycare while I work. My mom was home with me. I want to be home when Mel comes home from school, ask about her day. I guess I was spoiled living with Dave. Not the drinking or lying," she added quickly, "but the dinners out, the easy money, the nice clothes, the time with Mel."

"But y'all moved around a lot. That would have been hard to keep up," Sandy offered, "for having friends or Mel going to school."

She wasn't going to add that Dave was a jerk, but Debra could see the thought forming behind her eyes. The phone calls at Christmas she'd had to answer, since Debra wouldn't talk to him. They let Mel talk to him on the phone, but that only upset her. No money for the kid. Sandy tried to talk some sense into him during a couple of calls, his responsibility to his daughter and all that, but he'd hung up on her the third time she approached that topic; Debra had heard it all from the living room.

Tears were welling in Debra's eyes. They brimmed and quivered on the rim before she felt one slide down her cheek, as disloyal to her composure and dignity as a soldier going AWOL. She wiped it away, hoping Sandy didn't notice. But she did. Sandy reached over and gave her hand a squeeze. They heard the rattling of a trashcan outside, the metal clank. Sandy went to the back door, turned on the outside light. "Shoo! Shoo!" Debra heard her say, heard the can rattling more in a noisy scramble.

"Raccoons," Sandy said when she returned. "Two of 'em. At least they're cuter than the possums."

Back on the sofa, Sandy looked her in the eyes. Debra had wiped her eyes, but they were shiny moist, she knew. "It's just my period," she said.

"No," Sandy said. "It's a tough row to hoe. Your mom would say it, you said so yourself. Have you thought about going up there to live? You'd have more help."

The words were out and couldn't be taken back. How long had that been in the back of Sandy's mind?

"You don't want us anymore," Debra blurted.

"No, it's not that. You're welcome to stay, Debra, but I can't offer the financial stability, the support you need. I know you said your dad's a hard-ass. But could your mother talk to him? Mel needs a family."

Debra's tears didn't bother to brim; they followed the steady track of the ones before like a river after the dam has broken.

Leaning over, a strand of her still damp hair falling forward, Sandy hugged her, holding her close a moment. "Cry. Let it out. It's okay," she said. "I'm sorry if I've made it worse."

"We can't go home."

"You need to make peace with your family."

"This is too hard."

"Maybe your mom needs to stand up for you, just this once. You stood up to Dave. Your mom can stand up for you."

"And look where that landed me," Debra blurbled, laughing and crying at the same time.

"True," Sandy said, looking at the old furniture and India print bedspreads on her threadbare chairs. "It ain't no palace. But it's home."

They sat in silence a while. The music finished. Sandy put on another record, a used one Debra had brought home from the bookstore, and changed the subject. Anything to lighten the mood. Getting Debra's mind off her woes, Sandy told her about the research on Mayan culture she'd found. Twelve centuries of Maya lived in Central America where jade was more prized than gold, considered sacred. Debra listened to her detail her research discovery that in 1502, Columbus encountered twenty-five men, traders no doubt, and women with colorful shawls. These Mayans, reported to be gentle and polite, were in a canoe off the coast of Honduras. Among the bay islands.

"Right there in the bay where we snorkeled? Columbus?"

Sandy nodded and continued, "The Mayans traded along the coast. They mined jade in Guatemala, but I don't know where this group came from. They used jade for beads and they inlaid teeth with jade, I read somewhere—"

"Teeth," Debra murmured. "I remember...Dave had some teeth with—I guess jade I saw, I think, once—but there was so much going on, I didn't think too much about it at the time..."

"No telling what he found," Sandy said. Debra certainly didn't want to bring him into this conversation. "I even read there were burial caves. So much we didn't know when we were there."

Debra remembered Dave's stories about there being caves on Roatilla, but she didn't mention it. Talking about Dave only stirred things up. She was relieved the topic was moving away from her own situation.

They talked, or mostly Sandy talked, about how the Mayans mined jade in the hills of Guatemala, how they painstakingly carved it with primitive tools, how it was supposed to have healing properties and the natives had even buried it with some of the Maya; how Mayan traders, who met Columbus there in the bay islands making his fourth voyage, and those explorers might have perceived each other. Then Columbus, in his conquering attitude, was supposed to have forced one of the men to guide them throughout the region. The captive might have been a prince in his own land, but he was trapped into showing these explorers the Central American islands and land masses. Kidnapping natives had not been in the history books of public school, Debra contributed to Sandy's history discussion, when they had learned "in 1492 Columbus sailed the ocean blue."

Sandy found some of her notes about Gordon Ekholm, a leading American transpacific diffusionist, who had compiled a list of cultural similarities to support his contention several old world growth centers of early civilizations—Egypt, the Near East, China, India—were interrelated. Another colleague of Ekholm's speculated maritime expansion of Chinese dynasties could include voyages to the Americas in the 700's. Debra's mind wandered as Sandy rambled on about how significant root stalks and human figures could be found in both worlds, about similar representations in Uxmal in the Yucatan.

Through some of Sandy's details Debra spaced out, but she did see that Sandy was fascinated by the idea of the migration of cultures; she was always interested in a mystery and evidence to solve it or prove something. Debra understood how she loved the idea of a connection between Central American and Asian cultures. Flipping to another page in her notes, Sandy began to read aloud about how support for the theory of contact between the Americas and Chinese or related Asian cultures included pottery, particularly from the Han dynasty, that was similar to what had been found in Central America and the highlands of Guatemala at roughly the same time.

Finally pausing, she smiled at Debra. "Isn't that cool?"

She dragged out a sketch pad to show Debra some of the drawings she'd done. The lotus design in several, she said, came from pictures of carvings. She quoted from her notes about lotus friezes carved in the second century AD in India's Amaraviti region resembling water-lily friezes in Chichen Itza's Temple of the Jaguars in the Yucatan. Several drawings of gods and goddesses on the next page looked both Mayan and Oriental, some like a Buddha.

"Is there a Buddhess?" Debra joked. Sandy grinned.

"I drew these poses from pictures of figures done by the Mayans." She showed Debra more drawings, describing how Mayan clay figures having that same tranquil appearance of deities rising from lotuses were also found in Chinese images from the same century. She continued, pointing at her sketchpad, "I drew these from a picture of a Chinese Buddhist prince from the seventh century. He was representing divinity. Don't you think it's fascinating—that pensive expression is repeated in a Mayan figure dated about the same time?"

Debra looked at the drawings. She listened as Sandy talked on about these theories of the "diffusionists" and remembered her geology professor at Georgia, when she was a freshman, telling the class he was going to a conference, to present his theory of how the continents drifted apart, which had fascinated her. Debra had been intrigued at the time how a map of the world looked like puzzle pieces, how neatly South America fit into the curve of west Africa, and wondered aloud if they'd been connected.

"I think that would have been centuries before what these guys were talking about, but some even think the land bridge of the Bering Strait brought Asians into North America. Who knows who travelled where and when? And the Vikings were supposed to have moved around quite a bit at sea, too," Sandy said.

Sandy finally ran out of steam on the diffusionist theories. It was getting late. They both had a busy day ahead tomorrow. Sandy put up her sketch pad and notes, while Debra took their long-empty mugs to the sink. Wishing Sandy good-night and sweet dreams, Debra opened her bedroom door and entered as quietly as she could.

She had liked that geology class. She had liked learning. What had distracted her so, she wondered, that other dreams took precedence? That freedom from the confines of dorm life and the lure of Haight Ashbury could have pulled her so? Her mind drifted back towards the painful truths Sandy had brought up, her frankness both a blessing and a curse, but Debra felt that tug of loyalty toward her friend and the one to her family ties a bit uncomfortable. It wasn't meddling, since her life was so entwined in Sandy's, but somehow her comments had crossed some line.... Moonlight filtered through the curtains, so she could see her child's face in repose on her pillow, soft lips parted, curly hair tousled in shadow and silver light, before she let the blinds down and got into her own single bed.

How had her life come to this? Debra wondered. Her choice to go to California, run away from school, she thought she'd found the answer in Dave, the answer to her loneliness, filling the emptiness with the bigness of his personality. How could she have been so naïve? She wouldn't want life with Dave back; running away from that had been for the best. Still, she was glad she had gotten Melody as a result of their relationship, so she wouldn't change that. She'd do it again.

All she'd done with her life was run away. Except from Mel. If she left Tallahassee, would she be running from, or running to? Maybe it was time to face consequences. How long had Sandy been holding her thoughts back? These troubling questions she pushed out of her mind and thought instead of the Mayans and the great civilization that had crumbled somehow. How close they had been, down in those islands, their own personal histories in such proximity to a significant historical world event, and she hadn't even known it. Christopher Columbus, right out in those waters near Roatilla.

During the night, she had a strange dream. She was running the bamboo drill Sandy had told her about, twirling it in a piece of jade, her hands moving fast to rub the bamboo and grit, to carve a hole into a piece of hard green jade. In the morning, Debra lay half asleep and wondered about it. In her dream, she must have been a Mayan villager, a woman working with the design in a frieze, or was it a figurine, a jade figure like the one she'd dreamed about the night after she returned from Roatilla? That dream she had the night when she put Dave's packages, ones he'd mailed from the island and the one still at the apartment, into the storage unit in Ventura years ago, before she packed up and moved out, to their rough time ahead in Jacksonville with lawsuits and grievances piling up. That had been an odd dream, too. One so vivid she still remembered it years later.

Debra rose from this latest dream, and the memory it stirred of another dream of a goddess of green, to the smell of coffee and the sound of laughter. There in the kitchen, she saw morning light pouring in the east window, highlighting her little daughter's light brown curls backlit like a halo, Sandy's back to her at the table. Her daughter and her best friend were laughing over the scrambled eggs Sandy was spooning into the ceramic green and turquoise bowl Debra had made in her pottery class.

"Mel wanted to put cinnamon in them," Sandy said, spooning the last of the eggs out. "I have no idea what they'll taste like."

"G'morning," Debra announced. "This is a surprise."

Sandy smiled at her, looking both warm and sad at the same time. "You deserve it, almost birthday girl."

Mel wrapped her thin little arms around Debra's legs; she could feel the warm embrace, a circle of love like a wreath, as though those little hands and arms reached right up into her heart, filling it with warmth. "Mommy, Aunt Sandy and I made you breakfast."

"Thank you, sweetheart," Debra replied, running her fingers through her little one's hair and bending down to kiss her before the child danced off.

Sandy poured the coffee, hers black, Debra's with plenty of half and half she added from the carton. As toast popped out of the oven, Mel buttered each slice with firm and deliberate strokes.

"Toast and eggs, my specialty," Sandy said. "No time for grits. I've gotta get a move on. We all do. I got Mel to help me. She and the cat were up early."

The bowl that Debra made in the ten-week pottery class, which had mercifully ended in March, looked pretty on the wooden table with the yellow scrambled eggs, dotted with flecks of reddish gold. She scooped eggs onto two plates, and Mel's own bowl, one from her bisqued work when Sandy had brought Mel by Debra's night class to pick her up on glazing night; Mel had decorated it with her little childlike design of butterflies and cats all squiggly around the outside rim that Debra had helped her glaze. She felt poignancy coupled with a lightheartedness she hadn't felt in weeks, like sunlight and shadow streaming through the same window, when she looked into the morning faces at the table.

"I've made a decision," Debra said. "I'll tell you about it later, after we drop Mel off at kindergarten."

Mel looked up at her.

"Melody, did you feed the kitty?" Sandy interjected. "I think I hear her outside."

Mel got off her chair, headed for the screen door to call Snooky. She let the screen flap shut before calling the cat out in the yard. The cat mewed sweetly at the other door.

"She's at the front door, honey," Debra called.

"Mel asked me if I thought she was a devil. I told her she could be an angel today and help me with breakfast. I think it patched things up."

Debra nodded but didn't say anything. They both took a sip of coffee and watched Mel coming in the front door, her arms wrapped around the top half of the cat, its bottom half, legs, and tail dangling agreeably in the familiar hug-hold.

Chapter 19

Reluctantly, Debra and Sandy had agreed to join Mel over at Liz and Dave's house later that day after their snorkel trip. Leaving the inn to walk down to where the boats were docked, the two women were surprised to see Nelson talking with a young dark-haired woman at one of the snorkeling boats. He did not notice them, and neither of the women wanted to encounter him.

"Was that one of the—is that Nelson?"

"It looks just like him. What do you think they're arguing about?" Debra whispered, though the couple was too far away to hear.

"Let's go before they see us," Sandy said, turning away and looking towards the other boats. "I don't feel like chit-chatting with him this morning."

They turned toward one of the other tourist boats loading up for a trip out of harbor.

The two went snorkeling midday. Sandy declared the view to be somewhat disappointing, after her memories of diving off Roatilla, the reefs as colorful as the fish; here, washed-out patches of coral, few varieties of fish, too many novices' fins in her face left her feeling sad and annoyed. Was it time or place? Sandy wondered. She suspected the global changes to the marine environment, not an overactive imagination or memory, were to blame for the lack of vibrancy with the reefs. After snorkeling and rinsing off at the dock, the two women agreed that making margaritas in their room was too much work, too problematic, and too much margarita for one day.

"Let's just get one around here," Sandy said. "We know what too much tequila can do."

"Remember when you fell in the petunias?" Debra asked when they'd found a bar overlooking the water and ordered their drinks with extra limes.

"Me? That was you, sweetie. And those were zinnias. You broke the zinnias and smashed the nasturtiums, my first flower bed since I was a little girl gardening with my Mama…." She paused. "That was you who fell on your head."

Debra laughed. "Just checking. Seeing if your memory is as good as you think it is. At least I didn't break my neck."

"You were too drunk to break anything," Sandy replied, sipping her margarita with its rim of salt on the bar glass. "Your bones were rubber by then."

"Tipsy. I was tipsy," Debra corrected. "Ladies don't get drunk."

"All right, Miss Priss." Sandy smiled at her friend who stuck her nose in the air with mock dignity, her pinky lifted in ladylike genteel daintiness. Debra shifted in her seat, looked at Sandy.

"Tequila comes on all of a sudden," Debra warned, looking at Sandy's already half-empty glass. "I never was so sick as the next day after our first margaritas, that night we were coming up with how bad breakups felt."

"You mean our profound discovery of how lonesome lonesome was? We might have been stoned, too."

Debra took another sip of her own drink. "Not as good as yours were."

"Of course not."

Debra, looking invigorated by the day's swim and snorkel, time on the ocean, despite Sandy's complaints about the lack of color, smiled that sweet smile that endeared her to Sandy. Her cheeks a bit reddened by the sun despite the sunscreen, she looked healthy and vibrant, Sandy thought. Her warm brown eyes were bright in the afternoon light filtering into the bar. Light lipstick glossed her smile. The few signs of age were overcome by the vividness of that cheerful expression on her face.

Sandy, her hair already dry from their outing, ran her fingers through her short cut to push a lock from her forehead and licked the salt on her glass rim. "We had some good times in that old house in Tallahassee. Does Mel remember that?"

"Let's ask her," Debra said. "I know she has memories from your living with us that year after…"

"After Mama died," Sandy said softly. "Mama was way too young to go."

Debra reached over and touched Sandy's arm but said nothing.

"Odd I'm nearly the same age she was…"

They sipped their drinks, and finally Debra spoke. "We better check on Mel. It's already three."

They paid, and after the waitress never came back with their change, they made their way out of the bar. A hefty tip they decided after they had waited ten minutes; she must have thought two women wouldn't be generous, Sandy surmised, or bold enough to come after her, Debra guessed. They waded through the tropical-shirted tourists in shorts, grey-haired men with beer bellies, women in white slacks, young women in sleeveless dresses, college-aged buff young men in T-shirts with logos from all over. A people-watching mecca Sandy couldn't ignore. But they were all white, maybe tan, but white folks. Very few blacks. After so many years in Hawaii, the absence of Asian and Polynesian people seemed strange. The other half of the world, dark-haired, dark-eyed, in the Pacific…and those short rounded calves of the hula dancers she so loved to watch, dark hair down to their knees… She had become so used to being the outsider in a world of locals.

Debra interrupted her thoughts when Sandy almost stepped off the curb into the oncoming flow of sightseers. She felt the strong hand on her arm before she jerked back into the moment, faces of tourists moving, Debra saying, "I'm the one accused of being in La La Land all the time."

"Let's find a taxi," Sandy said. "It's hot out here and we've got to get to what—you've got the address, right?"

The two friends got out of their taxi in front of a palm-fronted house in what appeared to be a million dollar neighborhood. After a brief scuffle over who paid, both trying to put money in the cabbie's hand, laughing, they walked up the flagstone walkway to the door. Opening the door before they even knocked, Mel greeted them.

The two women followed Melody into the large, spacious home, both curious about the way Dave and Liz had lived, decorated. Artifacts and sea shells in wide glass cases lined one wall of the tile-floored room leading to the view of the ocean. Liz was sitting in a chair and when she stood up to greet them, nothing had prepared them for how sad she looked.

Liz had the face of a woman sunk in grief, trying to rally. Sandy knew that woman's face well. She'd stared her down in the mirror herself and she'd lived with a mother in mourning. Her widowed mother's sorrow had mellowed into Sunday sadness, but this was raw anguish. Like Sandy's mirror the year after her mother died. A face of pure grief.

She really loved Dave, was Sandy's first thought after recognizing that familiar look of grief and the memories it triggered. Liz had a cane, Sandy noticed, and didn't step far from the chair, using cane and chair back to steady her balance as she rose. She had forgotten Mel had said she had multiple sclerosis. Liz leaned the cane against the chair and took Debra's hands, then Sandy's. Her slender fine hands were warm, her long fingers manicured. Her gray and brown hair was pulled into an old-fashioned French twist. Her grey-blue eyes looked incredibly weary, but she brought a smile into them and asked the two if they wanted anything to drink. Sandy offered her arm, when she started to sit back down, but Liz shook her head and balanced herself with the chair instead. "Thank you, but this is easier for me."

Her short heels clicking on the tiles, Mel brought tea while they sat under the ceiling fan gently moving the air. Sandy noticed how familiar and comfortable Mel was in this house, with this woman. A stranger to Sandy, and yet, somehow she felt an ally. The small talk of snorkeling was short-lived before Liz got to the point. Dave had left some private messages in the event of his death, she told them, and she wanted to share these before the memorial service the next day or the reading of the will. She expected an uproar from that.

"Dave had changed, Debra, from the man you lived with. I got the husband you would have liked. Or at least I think you would have," Liz began. "He was fifteen years sober this year. And I know he was truly sorry for the pain he caused you. But I'll let his letter speak for itself."

She supported herself reaching into the cabinet next to her chair and taking two envelopes in her hand. Sandy took a quick look at Debra, who was looking a bit alarmed, her lip almost trembling, stunned. Mel had sat down and she, too, was looking at Debra. Then her eyes met Sandy's and Sandy saw both love and sadness in eyes that reminded her of a gentler Dave. The spell was broken as Liz continued.

"And, Sandy," she added. "He had one for you. I know it must surprise you, and you've probably wondered why…why he would want you here or why Mel would have relayed the message, that is, would have told you you had to come…"

She handed the envelopes to Debra and Sandy. Neither made a move to open them. Liz, speaking to Sandy, who thought she must have looked confused, said, "He really admired your spunk. And I think he eventually appreciated what you'd done for his family that first year when he was so out of control. He told me several times how sorry he was...for everything...but being in AA these last years, he was taking that twelve-step process, to make amends to those he hurt when he was drinking. That included you. I think he took a short cut," and here she smiled briefly, and continued, "instead of making amends with all the people out there he may have wronged besides his family, he let you represent the pack." Sandy just sat there holding the envelope, so Liz continued. "And Mel always had such good things to say about you..."

Debra was not crying, but she was clearly uncomfortable Sandy knew. She held herself stiffly and silently upright in the chair, her posture frozen. Sandy, for once, had no words. She sat back in her chair and looked at Liz who was sitting down again. Liz was trying to give Debra some space, not directing any comments her way, it seemed.

"There is one other thing," she said. "I've already given Melody the key. He had a storage unit. Actually he had a couple. That's where he was going when he died. As you may know, even after he stopped the treasure-hunting expeditions, got out of that business, he still sold items he'd collected. It was a bad business and eventually I got him to stop. It was black-market, but Nelson, one of the stepsons you met already, Mel says, Nelson was really engrossed with that. Dave and he had done some treasure hunting when he was a boy and Nelson caught fire. He loved it. Dave suspected him of breaking into one of the units, continuing to sell gold chains, artifacts from Honduras, Guatemala...even things he and the boys dredged up..."

Mel spoke then. "Barb is probably going to contest the will we think. She thinks Dave was worth more than just the salvage business. Her sons...she thinks they have a right to his fortune."

"But we don't even know what's in the will," Sandy pointed out. "Do we?"

She glanced over at Debra. Debra still sat quietly, holding her envelope in her lap. The tension in her posture had relaxed. Once she knew she would not be called on to speak, the relief showed in her face. But Sandy saw there more than a hint of sorrow. However, her own curiosity was piqued. They had a genuine mystery on their hands. Maybe Dave had turned into Mr. Nice Guy for Liz, but he'd still been a thief and a liar. The intrigue compelled her to ask this third wife, "So are you saying Dave did have a fortune worth..." *killing for*? she didn't say, but instead, "worth pursuing?"

"I've seen the will, of course, when Dave was making it. I think Barbara will be mad. "

"Can she go for more?"

"Well, this house is paid for. And it's in my name," Liz said. "They can't go for that. But how much he had in storage, I'm not sure. Or how much he knew Nelson had stolen..."

Mel interrupted. "You don't think Dan would have anything to do with this will business, do you? He liked us; he has a career in the salvage business. He wouldn't have any reason—"

"You don't have to defend him, Mel," Liz said with some hint of history between them unspoken. "Dave gave him the company. It's in the last will he authorized. He didn't put it in both names because he thought Nelson was..."

"A flake?" Mel interjected. "A rat?"

Liz smiled then. "Well, he was a bad boy. You could put it that way. I have no interest in the business and I'm set up for life. Unless..."

"Unless it all goes for lawyer and lawsuits," Mel said.

Debra looked like she wanted to correct Mel for interrupting, Sandy thought, remembering that look, but she still sat silent as a statue. This was definitely getting more interesting than she had expected, Sandy thought.

"What's this key?" she asked. "The one Mel has?"

Mel said, "Dad left me a couple things and a key. I've got directions to this storage site. We need to go before I leave. Y'all up for it?"

Sandy saw her eyes shift from her to her mother. Debra was sitting up straight, somewhat stiffly, Sandy thought, and she seemed to take a long time to respond, but she smiled at Mel, "Certainly, darling, whatever you want to do."

After Mel ordered and picked up Chinese takeout, they ate with Liz, who seemed to run out of steam after the envelopes and information had been delivered. It was an early supper and they left promptly after cleaning up.

As they were getting in the car, Sandy asked, "What's with these storage units? All this intrigue?"

"The man was a squirrel," Debra managed to joke.

"Why write these letters in the prime of life?" Sandy asked. She had read her letter already, surprised by its contents.

"Maybe he knew something was up," Mel said. She cranked the car. "Or maybe he was sick. I think there was something about his heart last year. They didn't talk about it. I didn't ask. Now I think maybe I should have."

"And you didn't ask Liz?" Sandy asked leaning forward from the back seat.

"Nope. But I will. It's just been so...so gut-wrenchingly sad."

"Heart condition? Or something up, like someone after him?"

"I can't believe you didn't talk to Liz about this," Debra said. "Or if he had a heart problem they said nothing to you. Surely not."

"When are we going to use that key?" Sandy asked. "And where is the unit or storage space?"

"I've got a map."

"Are we talking hidden treasure?" Sandy wondered aloud, keeping the rest of her thoughts to herself. The guy always has a trick up his sleeve. One more game. Even from Davey Jones' locker.

"We'll find out," Debra said, "but I'm getting a headache. Too much sun. Too much alcohol. Too much—"

"Too much of everything," Sandy said.

Chapter 20

After their early supper with Liz, Debra had claimed a headache, blaming the MSG along with too much sun. Sandy wanted to go hear music, do something to change the somber mood. "Maybe you'll feel better after a shower. See how you feel in a couple of hours? I need to clean up. Those showers at the dock just didn't do it for me."

"How about a nap? It's early yet, and you might feel up to it later," Mel suggested, but she looked skeptically at her mother. Debra had no intention of going out again, and she knew Mel recognized she had dug in her heels.

Two hours later, Sandy and Mel left her in her room before they went out to hear music in Key West. Girls' night out, bar-hopping. They let her off the hook. Sandy wanted to cheer them up, Debra knew, but she just wasn't up for it. She would read one of the books she had brought, go to bed early. But first, she had to deal with the letter.

Thoughts percolated up like one of those old time coffee pots of long ago, one her mother had when she was a child, thoughts bubbling up to the surface and bursting, one after another. Lying in bed, she was holding Dave's letter, still unopened. His handwriting on the page when she did open it a jolt she had not anticipated. The handwriting of a man she hadn't seen in twenty-five years.

Dearest Debra,

If you are reading this, you know I'm gone. I loved you, dear one, and I still do. I hope you are happy. I hope you have found someone to love you the way you deserved. The way I should have. I have found happiness and hope the same for you. I am grateful you let Melody back in my life. She is one good thing we did.

I cannot make up for the pain I caused you, the wrong I did you. I am leaving you some money, a portion of the money I owed you all those years you raised Melody on your own. It should be in my will, an account for you. Don't let anyone take it from you. You raised our daughter to be a decent woman. That's more than I could have done.

Remember those days in California, the sunsets on the water. You were the treasure I was always seeking and I threw it all away. Forgive me.

By the time she got to the last few lines, Debra was crying, crying for lost love, crying for regrets, crying for the vast gulf of years between then and now. She cried for the young woman she once was, and she cried for Dave, the man on the beach in Malibu, dancing barefoot on the sand at sunset with her. For Dave laughing out on the water in their boat. Even for the moments on Roatilla when he held her in his arms and kissed her, and all the cares of the world melted in one warm embrace. And then she realized she was crying for the lost years without him, the good man she'd seen in him at first and whom he had become without her there beside him.

All the years with him she'd lost. The life they could have had if only…. *If only* was a witch with long fangs who could suck the blood right out of you, Debra thought. This is why Debra had locked her heart up and thrown away the key. Pandora's Box. It was open, but she could shut it.

She finished having a good cry, blew her nose, and turned out the light. This was all the crying she was doing. Then those other thoughts bubbled to the surface of her consciousness. It had been a long and loaded day. Remembering being in boats with Dave when they were out snorkeling turned to memories of those days after she left him; days Sandy remembered as their having fun she had remembered mostly as a frightening and sometimes miserable existence for herself. If she hadn't been so scared and worried and tired, maybe there had been some good moments. Memories of Sandy and the Thanksgiving they shared. Sandy remembered it as one big lovefest, but Debra had remembered Sandy lighting into her soon-to-be stepsister when the girl got mad at Mel. Somehow, Sandy had forgotten that, but she had seen Sandy defend her daughter with the fierceness of a Mama bear. Funny, Melody had so many mothers, and even Liz, this woman she hardly knew, who had connections with Melody she could only guess. There had been unspoken connections, maybe even secrets hinted at there at the dinner table. Conversations swirling around her where she herself had remained a ghost, barely visible, she thought, hearing them where she herself had barely spoken, been polite, but overwhelmed by the flood of conflicting emotions that threatened to wash her out to sea, without a life boat, too many questions she couldn't ask. Too many feelings she didn't expect.

Sandy had read her own note from Dave there at the dinner table. "'The jade figure you found in Honduras is yours. I know you remember it. I took it from Hal Greenberg before he left Roatilla. It is in a storage locker on Sugar Loaf. My wife Liz has the key. If she is no longer around when you get this, the key is in a jewelry box Melody will inherit upon Liz's death. The map and address to the storage is enclosed. Thank you for standing up to me and taking care of Debra and Melody when I couldn't.'"

There was no map with the letter, but Mel had the information and key; evidently Dave had not expected the letter to be deployed so early, Sandy had speculated aloud at the table. Everyone was quiet after that. Sandy had tried to lighten the mood with, "Well, he's got us all on a treasure hunt once again!"

Debra had claimed a headache right after that, and Liz had seemed relieved. Maybe, Debra thought, being with them had been more trying for Liz than the other way around. Sandy would have stayed, enjoying getting to know Liz and learn more about all the complications of Dave's life, but she had enough sense to know it was time to go, too. Talking about the jade piece had taken any attention away from Debra and the letter she had tucked away in her bag with no intention of sharing at the table. And no one had asked her to.

Sandy had kept that secret about the jade goddess all those years. Even when she described the value Mayans place on jade back when she was doing research, when she was thinking about going to grad school in anthropology and took that course. She used to tell Debra about their carvings, lotus friezes and the theory of the Han dynasty and the migration of cultures.... All that time, she'd kept the figurine she'd once found a secret. Why? Didn't Sandy trust her? Debra had wondered then, at Liz's table, why Sandy didn't say anything to the dive crew about it. But she didn't ask; she was merely listening. It was Melody who'd asked, "What sort of jade figure?"

"A small goddess, sorta looked like a Buddha," Sandy said. She explained about her discovery. At the dinner table that night, she'd said she and Dave had been working on one of the sites, before that jerk Hal had come or maybe the day he came; she thought Dave knew about her discovery, but they hadn't said anything about it to one another, never announced it. Then he denied it the one time she tried to talk about it. Sandy said it disappeared while they were on Roatilla.

Maybe because that guy Hal was such a louse, such a conniving creep, maybe that was why Sandy had never brought up the figurine on the island. Later Hal stirred up some of the investors to a lawsuit and filed his own. All that litigation, that's when Dave did the heavy drinking every night…. And Sandy wasn't the only one with a secret. Debra had never told Sandy about her change of heart when she was living in Florida with her, back before that Thanksgiving, when she'd agreed to meet Dave for dinner and talk. She'd missed him so much; she'd agreed to go back to him.

He had always said he could control his drinking, it was under control, when she had finally spoken up about that being the problem she couldn't get over, the obstacle to their marriage success. She had zeroed in on that, not the lawsuits and shady dealings that disturbed her. And when she'd gone to the restaurant, sat down that night when they were going to talk about her terms for returning, she realized he was drunk. She sneaked out of the ladies' room and never came back. Locked her heart in a box. Threw away the key. She went to file the separation papers right after that but had not lived in Florida long enough. They had not actually divorced for a couple of years, when Dave finally filed. That must have been at Barb's urging, she realized now. She had been too afraid of a custody battle, willing to forego child support rather than risk dealing with him again. But there had been that time when she would have gone back.

This she had told nobody.

More thoughts rose and burst on the surface of her consciousness. That green goddess. She suddenly remembered, in the Mayan phase of Sandy's art work, remembered seeing several green goddess paintings stacked against the wall when she visited Sandy after she had gone down to the coast to work at Fort Fisher. That was in what, late '70s, early '80s? Sandy had lived in Carrboro, in North Carolina, with her and Mel for a year, after Debra had made the big decision to call her mother and say she wanted to come home, that day she got her car, her first set of wheels of her own. She and Mel had stayed until August in Tallahassee with

Sandy and had gone to North Carolina before school started. She had lived in the garage apartment her parents had in Chapel Hill until she found a place on Pine Street in Carrboro, and had worked at the Intimate Book Store for years, with its creaking stairs and rows of beautiful art books she could sometimes browse.

Her mother had cried when she called to say she wanted to come home. She was surprised when her mother called back the same day to say she'd talked with her father and they both wanted her and Melody to live with them. "Just never mention that draft dodger," her mother had warned. "Tread lightly. Both of you have too much pride for your own good."

So her parents had known all along about the draft dodger she went to California with, and maybe about the fellow from the Vietnam Vets for Peace who had urged her cousin's friend to dodge the draft, shoot himself in the foot, do anything to stay out of the war. They had known more than that the boy she went to California with was just a long-haired sort.

Debra lay on her hotel bed in Key West, remembering that year she had gone to live with her folks, her dad and Mel bonding over baseball, her mother happy as a clam to have her there, to fuss over Melody, to buy her little-girl clothes that Mel promptly got dirty playing with the neighborhood kids, all those girlie clothes, and then the call from Sandy when she and Melody were ready to get their own place and move from over her parents' garage. The night Sandy's mother died. The utter shock.

Debra's memories percolated to the surface of consciousness, like bubbles rising from the depths, dredging up details of that sad time when Debra flew down to Orlando before the funeral to join Sandy. Maureen's appendix had ruptured…peritonitis…botched operation…and she was gone, just like that. Sandy was too distraught to move. Debra had handled arrangements with Charles, Maureen's husband—

they were practically still newlyweds—moving Maureen's things that Sandy was keeping, paintings they split between Sandy and Charles. Maureen's sisters and brother had come down for the service from DC and Atlanta, but none could offer much help. Later, after Sandy had tried to go back to work, she broke up with Tom who had flaked out of the funeral, being in Maine getting canoes and saying he couldn't afford to leave to come down. By then she was so poorly functioning that she lost her job at the museum. Debra had driven down to pack her up and move her up to Chapel Hill, and the little duplex they shared in Carrboro. Sandy's small inheritance kept her afloat until she picked up work at the PTA thrift shop. She began to improve slowly, seeing a therapist and stopping her pot and alcohol abuse, joining Debra's yoga group.

So much history. So much water under the bridge.

Debra turned on the light to check the time, see how long she'd been lying there thinking, and saw Dave's letter on the night stand. She put it in her suitcase and got back in bed. It felt like Dave was there somehow, like the nights in her farmhouse when he had found her in the dark in her dreams before Mel called to say he was dead. That feeling he was there in her room, at that moment, comforted her and confused her that it was comforting.

That night Debra dreamed she and Dave were under a sea of green water, green water all around, and they were looking for a key, down below the surface. They were both young in this dream, not like the pictures of Dave in his house with the two grown boys and a big marlin hanging behind them or the one with Liz and Mel on the water. Not middle-aged, but young again. They were searching in the green depths for a key; then she was on the surface again, alone. And it was morning in Key West. Her grown daughter was in the single bed next to hers, softly snoring.

Mel would be horrified to know she snored, or would that be something Jeff had told her before? Debra wondered as she rose from her memories and dreams to face the morning light. She sat on the side of her bed, looking at her grown daughter sleeping in the other bed. Somehow the watery world of her dream had left her floating on the surface of what was past and what was before her, at that fine line between both. The here and now.

Chapter 21

"Your eyes are puffy," Sandy said.

"No good morning, sunshine?" Debra asked. "I'm wearing sunglasses."

"I am sitting down, Debra, and you're right above me. Besides, I guessed."

Debra took in the courtyard her friend had been drawing before she arrived. The tropical foliage created patterns in varying shades of green. Variegated philodendron climbed among the plants of the Westwind landscaping. Palms cast moving darker lines over the sunlit greenery that surrounded them. Sandy dropped her feet from the chair nearest her and Debra sat down.

"How late were you out?"

Sandy put her sketch pad and pencil she'd been drawing with into her bag. Her big white floppy hat Debra had encouraged her to purchase the day before nearly covered her eyes. Debra kept the shades on.

"We must have been back by eleven," Sandy said. "Way too loud, way too late for me."

"I didn't wake up when Mel came in," Debra said. She got back up to get breakfast. "You want some coffee?"

Sandy rose with her empty cup. Both women went to the back of the courtyard where a cheery young woman was putting a new canister of caffeine out. They selected fruit slices and Debra took a yogurt from the breakfast offerings. Debra squeezed a lemon slice into water, drank it, and put the glass on the tray for dirty dishes before she filled her coffee cup. Carrying coffee and plates back to their table, the two sat back down.

"I had a strange dream last night," Debra said.

"Me, too. You tell yours first."

"Dave and I were looking for a key. Maybe the one to the locker," Debra suggested, unwilling to speculate out loud about other symbolic values—like the key to her heart—which a key could represent.

"That's a good sign. Maybe we'll find the jade goddess. I can't believe it's turned up. When are we going to look for it?"

"We've got the memorial service today. Mel's staying through tomorrow. We'll keep the car after we take her to the airport. I know she'll want to look for the storage unit tomorrow. Why did you never tell me about finding a jade figurine when y'all were down on Roatilla?"

Sandy's jaw tightened. She shrugged. Then she sat up straighter. "I think I was always...conflicted. Maybe a little afraid of losing it, at first, when I was down with the expedition; that was before you got there, and then later...I was a little ashamed. I found it, so I felt it belonged...like I had a right to it...but it was wrong, sort of.... I took coral sea fans from down there. Now that's considered poaching. Back then, there was so much reef life, taking a souvenir seemed harmless..."

"Until fifty million people do it," Debra said.

"Who knows whatever finds supposed to belong to the expedition ended up being looted? Gold was what Oceanic's adventurers were after. It was really a beautiful little figure, translucent on the edges, and her face, so serene," Sandy said wistfully. "I remember that. But it's been so many years I sort of forget what she looked like."

"You had a painting—that green goddess showed up in some of your paintings. Do you still have those?"

"Only one. It's in my bedroom in Honolulu."

"Wouldn't Pele mind?" Debra teased. She knew Sandy's quest for goddesses had not ended with that Mayan artifact, if, in fact, it were the Maya who carved it. Sandy had regaled her with Aztec corn goddesses, too. Olmec Zapotec Aztec goddess of waters, rivers, moon goddess, that fertility goddess Tzzolteotl—it all ran together back then when Sandy would get on a roll.

Sandy smiled. "I've got a few of Pele, too, though I could never paint one as great as that one Herb Kane did. A fierce and beautiful Hawaiian woman with fiery lava coming out of her head for hair, smoldering in her eyes, glowing as she stares over her shoulder. When I saw that goddess, I knew that was the one for me. Nobody would mess with a goddess like that. In a book of goddesses I found her. I was taking some UU course on goddesses."

"I remember. You were also in that women's spirituality reading group and y'all went through all those books from women theologians to Starhawk and you started changing the words to hymns…"

"I still do," Sandy said, "but at Unity they call God 'creator' rather than 'father'."

"That suits you. But back to this jade piece," Debra resumed. "Do you want to go tomorrow?"

"Could we get back in time today?"

"The memorial service is at three. Let's don't push it."

"Want to catch the sunset afterwards? We missed it both nights so far."

Sandy hadn't told her dream yet, and they hadn't finished breakfast. What was that thing about telling dreams? If you told it before breakfast it would come true. Did eating a couple of pieces of fruit count? She spooned yogurt into her mouth.

"Did you read Dave's letter?" Sandy finally asked.

"Yes. It made me sad."

"I figured it would. You loved him so much."

Debra didn't say anything to that. They never talked about how much she'd loved Dave, or how hard it was to get over him. She still felt at sea after the dreams, the sorrow. Woozy. The safety of sunlight and palm trees and her friend all made things seem normal. She'd been in a time warp overnight and now she was back. Finally, for lack of anything better, she said, "Time heals all wounds."

"That's a cliché. But time sure takes the sting out of it. I thought I would never get over Paul, or Tom, at first. I think I finally got over Nick. It took a lot of distance. Funny, when we're young, the valleys are so deep, the mountains so high."

"I think you've got a country song there. Watch out; we'll be singing old love songs in a minute."

"What's a cliché for," Sandy said, "but to gloss over the truth with truisms?"

"Aren't we getting a little philosophical?" Debra asked. She took a sip of coffee. "What did you think of Liz?"

"I liked her. She seemed genuine. You sure were quiet last night."

"I know."

"We were worried about you."

"It was a lot to take in. Dave said he left me some money," Debra said.

"Really?"

"Really."

"Well, he ought to. You said he paid for Mel's college and wedding, but you never took child support, even after Dave offered. He owes you. He probably left some for Mel. He really did have some money, then."

"I guess so. That house was pretty snazzy…. I think Liz was good for him. I think he was happy."

"You're happy, too," Sandy insisted. "You've got a great house and it suits your personality. Farm life and nature all around. Your folks nearby. Your pottery. Grandkids."

"I do."

They lapsed into silence.

Listing some of Debra's blessings, Sandy felt she was trying too hard to be convincing. She'd wondered why Debra never found anyone after Dave, never remarried though she went with a couple of men, there in the late '70s, the '80s, even early '90s. A Chapel Hill sociology professor, a local carpenter, a few others scattered about. That professor she had gone with for a couple years before they broke up. Debra had admitted Dave had been the love of her life, but Sandy always thought she would remarry. She herself was one to talk. She'd never married at all...

"What are you thinking about?" Debra asked. "You've gotten so quiet. I can always tell when you're off somewhere. Those piercing green eyes of yours look so distant. Like a mist has settled over them. Mist shrouding still water..."

"You're getting mighty poetic. Maybe it's time I put on the shades," Sandy said, smiling at her, "so you can't read my mind."

"Ah, that genuine warm presence is back."

"I dreamed about Mama. Whenever she comes to me in dreams, whatever story is going on in the dream, it's my confusion, of wondering, 'so she's not dead after all', in the midst of it. It's somewhat like that lucid dreaming you used to talk about. It's like I'm aware she's gone, and supposed to be gone, but she hasn't died yet. And I'm aware, maybe when I'm waking up, that I'm wondering which it is, feeling sorta happy she isn't dead yet, but I know she's going to be. Until I wake up...and I'm still glad I saw her. Glad she visited."

"Do you believe in ghosts?" Debra asked.

"The Hawaiians believe we're walking around our ancestors in another dimension, here at the same time, here among us. We just can't see them," Sandy said.

"You mean all the generations or all the time periods at the same time?" Debra asked skeptically.

"Yeah, something like that. Spooky, huh?"

"Spooky or hard to wrap your head around that one. But you think all generations or all times at once? Which?"

"Both—all time and all people here on different planes or something like that...and I don't know what I think about ghosts. I think our spirits are more than our bodies, so why couldn't souls stick around?"

The early morning crowd was finishing; new visitors to the inn sat down at a table next to them. Light was shifting as the sun moved on. Sandy took her floppy hat off, fluffed out her hair.

"I felt like Dave was in the room with me last night. Both when I was reading his note, and later just this feeling I used to feel when he was around...warm and strong."

"My mother said she saw Daddy at the foot of her bed after he died," Sandy said. "I never felt Mama's presence anywhere, except sometimes that kitten I had—she loved cats so—I would just have this feeling when I was holding that kitty that she was there with us."

"I guess all the funeral dealings, talking about death, we're both getting a little..." Debra was at a loss for words.

"Spooked? Well. Let's get this service done today, and we can enjoy the outing to the key tomorrow. I wonder what else is in that locker?"

"No telling," Debra said, getting up for another cup of coffee. She offered to take Sandy's cup, but Sandy put her hand over the top and shook her head. When Debra sat back down, Sandy said, "Mel's certainly sleeping in. We didn't stay out that late."

"She's probably talking to Jeff if she's not still asleep. I want to say something before she gets here. You know when she first started coming down here to visit Dave and Liz, I think it was that second summer, she came back with a gold chain. I asked her about it. She said Dave gave it to her. But I heard her telling a friend she found it. I asked her about it, and she got mad. And defensive."

"Did you ever get to the bottom of it?"

"No. I didn't want to push her too hard. She was already pulling away." Debra sighed. "And maybe I just didn't want to know."

"You think she stole it?" Sandy asked, feeling a little unsettled at the thought.

"I don't know. She and Dave's stepsons were so interested in the treasure-hunting stories Dave told them. She came back talking about she and Dave's boys going out treasure hunting with him, and sometimes the three of them out searching when Dave was working. Probably she was up to no good with those boys."

"Is it too late to ask her?" Sandy asked, unwilling to spill Mel's secret about her stepbrother. It didn't quite relate to this story anyway. What good would telling Debra that do? And besides, she'd promised. She hated being in this position. Feeling unfaithful to her dearest friend, and conflicted about how it might hurt Debra if she ever found out she knew and didn't tell. Oh, damn. She was still reflecting on the ethics of keeping secrets when Debra turned and smiled.

"Speak of the devil," Debra said.

Mel, wearing a sundress and a big smile, headed for their table.

"G'morning," Sandy said.

"You look pretty today, sweetheart."

Mel acknowledged their greetings with a mock curtsy. "Glad to see y'all are both up already. I just got off the phone with Liz. I told her we'd come over for lunch before the service. Is that all right?"

The two women looked at her without saying anything.

"Is it a done deal?" Sandy finally asked. "Could I beg out?"

"No," Mel said firmly. "She needs the support right now."

"How 'bout you just go," Debra said.

Mel's face turned stern. "It won't hurt, Mom. I'd have to come pick you up if you don't go."

"What time? This lunch?" Sandy spoke up.

"One."

"That's two hours before the service," Debra complained. "What's there to talk about?"

"She'd like to get to know you. You weren't talking much last night." Mel's eyes that usually looked alert and bright hinted at irritation in the narrowing crinkle of the corners.

"Maybe we could drop you off and take the car?" Sandy offered.

"I have to pick her brother and his wife up at the airport first."

"You're just now mentioning that? We'd have to go to the airport, too? Well, wouldn't she rather be with her loved ones rather than strangers?" Debra asked. "Sit down; you're making me nervous standing there, honey."

Mel stood, debating. She seemed irritated, but trying to weigh her options. "Let me get some coffee."

As Mel walked away, Debra pulled her glasses down and looked at Sandy.

"Still puffy."

Debra made a face and pushed the glasses back up her nose.

"Does Dave have any family coming?" Sandy asked. "I hadn't even thought of him coming from...a family. Just sprung out on his own like Athena springing from Zeus' head or something."

"His aunt is in a nursing home Mel told me. She must be in her nineties by now. She raised him and his brother after his parents died in a plane crash."

"He had a brother?"

"Died in Vietnam," Debra said. "A couple of years older than Dave."

Sandy didn't know what to make of this information, so she said nothing. It wasn't as if Dave had been on her mind before this trip, and she hadn't thought of it all those decades ago. Probably she and Debra had talked about it sometime way back then, she couldn't remember, but thinking of a younger Dave in the context of family seemed strange. Somehow villains just dropped into life out of thin air. She wasn't sure why Mel wanted her mother to hang out with her stepmother, either; it seemed a bit strange, a tad selfish, but, giving her the benefit of the doubt, Sandy thought Mel probably needed moral support.

Mel came back with bacon and eggs, orange juice, coffee.

"You don't have to come, Mom," she said sitting down. "I guess I just thought…. I don't know what I was thinking. You're right. You don't need to be there."

Debra smiled. "Thanks, darling. We can catch a cab over there. Just give us the address before you go."

"I already did, remember? You guys got there yesterday."

"Right." Debra looked at Sandy, "Do you still have the address?"

Sandy said, "You kept the paper. You put it in your wallet."

"Did you read Daddy's letter?"

"I opened it."

"What'd he say?"

"He thanked me for taking care of such a fine daughter," Debra said, honey and vinegar dripping in her tone.

Ignoring the sarcasm or teasing irony, Mel asked, "What else?"

"I'll let you read it," Debra said.

Mel didn't ask more. Sandy watched the two women a moment, trying to appear not to be studying them. The air was fraught with layers of unspoken conflicting emotions. Clearly unwilling to discuss the letter, Debra looked irritated, still not over Mel's demand for more time with Liz, Sandy speculated. Why was she so unwilling to let Mel know how upset the letter had made her?

"Well, Aunt Sandy," Mel said. "Did you know you'd signed up for all this when you agreed to come?"

"I didn't know what to think, but I'm glad to get a good visit in with my two favorite gals—and to discover that jade piece wasn't lost."

"What are you going to do with it when we find it?"

"I don't know."

"Doesn't it belong in a museum?" Debra asked, then added, "Finders keepers, losers weepers? Which is it?"

Sandy watched Mel nibbling on her bacon and Debra moving a thin orange peel around on her plate before she asked, "Does Honduras have the same laws as Florida about antiquities? I know when I was working with the underwater archeology unit at Fort Fisher, we had a conference between treasure hunters and the government and archeologists—in Key West, as a matter of fact. But we artists went off partying while some of the archeologists attended those meetings. It gets murky, the role of treasure hunting and preservation of artifacts. I think the law lets the treasure hunters have some rights…"

Debra asked, "Don't they have artifacts from the Maya somewhere in Honduras? Seems like there would be an interest in it."

"I don't know. And I wonder if it would cause trouble to suddenly say we had it, or who would be best to give an artifact like that—the government? Mayans? Sell to a museum?"

"Maybe someone from that underwater archeology group you worked for at Fort Fisher would know or be able to advise you? Someone interested in cultural artifacts?"

"Like Nick?" Sandy knew Debra was baiting her, and did not want to appear interested in that direction.

"Like Nick. You said he was in touch with you not so long ago."

Sandy made a face, and she looked at Debra's smiling eyes, a hint of mischief dancing in them. She added, "Or maybe I deserve to keep it, not get tangled up in red tape."

A patch of sunlight crept across Sandy's head, over to Mel's arm. The palms' shade was shifting. Mel moved her arm back from the pool of sunshine before she said, "It's getting hot already."

"You'll have to change before the service," Debra pointed out.

"I'm taking a change of clothes to Liz's. I just couldn't wear a black dress all day."

Mother and daughter talked about clothes and outfits for Dave's afternoon memorial service. Sandy drifted off in thought and let their discussion swirl around her. Memories of the jade figurine and thoughts of what she might do with it if it became part of her life, if it returned to her, these contemplations occupied her mind. Memories of.... She emerged from her thoughts when she heard Debra speaking her name.

"By the way, Sandy and I wanted to ask you what you remember of living in Florida. That little house in Tallahassee."

"Oh, I remember y'all standing on your heads."

The two women looked at each other blankly. Then Debra nodded.

"I do recall that, come to think of it. Remember? We used to get on opposite sides of the door," Debra reminisced, "doing the headstand, and you wanted the wall for backup."

"Oh, yeah, I do remember now, and I remember one time when you, Melody, were lying upside down on the couch—

your head hanging down so you could see us right side up!" Sandy added.

"And the cat got on your chest, purring. You couldn't lift back up."

"We started laughing so hard—I fell over and cracked my knee on the chair."

"I couldn't stand on my head now," Debra said smiling. "I haven't done the headstand in years. I'd break my neck."

"I used to use those yoga moves you were teaching me with Tom, the canoe man," Sandy said mischievously. "I did the plow, but that was not a view you want to see making love without laughing…"

"Oh, Sandy," Debra covered her ears and made a face. "Enough already! That image is stuck in my head now. "

"Ewww," Mel looked at the two of them and shook her head. "Y'all are terrible. Dirty ole women. I remember y'all dancing. Y'all were always dancing. I remember the "My Girl" routine; you used to get me to pantomime that Motown tune with you. Y'all were so silly. I also remember my little friend—Tisha? We got in trouble. Every time I look at that painting in Mom's room, I remember how scared we were when Mom got mad. And Tisha, she thought she was gonna get a whooping…. Did she? I can't remember any more…. She was my first real friend, that little girl from the AME church."

"That was when I decided working two jobs was too hard," Debra said. "I didn't feel I could be a good parent any more. It took a while, but I got up the nerve to ask the folks to let me come home…"

"You'd just gotten that old Volkswagen then, hadn't you?" Sandy asked.

"Oh, what a clunker! But it made it to Chapel Hill."

"Was Gramps really that mean?"

"Pride," Debra said. "We both had too much pride. But he could be an ornery ass."

"Thus your calling him Grumps," Mel added.

"You called him that, too, 'til the stroke. He mellowed after that."

"Do you really remember all that dancing, Melody?" Sandy turned back to their Florida memories. "That must have been after Debra started bringing home discounted used records from the store."

"We had quite a collection of boogie woogie music by the time I left that August."

"I do," Melody said. "Looking up at y'all bouncing around and Snooky and I managing to not get stepped on. The cat used to get on the sofa, safe, or try to swat at one of you if she could. That was so fun."

"That had to be Florida, cause Snooky didn't end up in Chapel Hill when I came up," Sandy said. "She was such a great kitty."

"She got sick, didn't she?" Melody recalled.

"Distemper. I hadn't gotten the shots…"

The tension of a few minutes before had dissolved. The sun burned hot on Sandy's face. An angle between the palms was directing sunlight on Mel's head as well. "Time to get a move on. Tomorrow we'll use that key, right, Mel? You up for a little adventure?"

"Sure, why not?"

Chapter 22

Debra and her daughter had gone shopping for an appropriate dress for Debra to wear in the little time before Mel needed to leave for lunch with Liz and they went to Dave's memorial service. Sandy took her walk among the nearby neighborhoods of Old Town Key West before the day got any hotter. Some of the old houses and brick streets reminded her of Wilmington's river district, but more tropical. She had taken her camera, but mostly she was lost in thought, her vision in her mind's eye not of the present but the past. Her ramble through old neighborhoods became a stroll down memory lane and lost love.

That stroll down memory lane was full of potholes, Sandy reflected. They had spent Wednesday, between snorkeling and margaritas, reminiscing, and now Sandy was catapulted back to the North Carolina coast in the late '70s after her mother had died, to the time after she'd spent that year with Debra and Mel on Pine Street, when she had finally landed a job that used her artistic talents better than dressing window fronts for the PTA thrift shop and sorting through old clothes did.

The talk about Tallahassee had dredged up memories of lost love, of breaking up with Tom in the aftermath of her mother's funeral, when she'd done too much pot and alcohol to ease the pain, and he wasn't there for her the way she expected. How foolish she was to have later regretted leaving him. Her yearning and regret about him were inexorably mixed with the deep grief of losing her mother. She had finally worked through those losses, to a level at least where she could cope in the year after that. She remembered she had thought they made a better model for a man, and that she'd find it down the road. That road full of potholes and dead ends—wrong turns? Would she have ended up alone anyway? Just a few years delayed?

And maybe without Nick she would have found that better model, but after that deep love, as close to a soul mate as she had gotten, she hadn't given her heart so completely to anyone again. Maybe it was a matter of settling, choosing a path and then sticking to it, not second guessing. Her mother had said once you toss the rock down the hill, you just keep moving with it. The rolling stone gathers no moss.

So her mind rambled while she walked the uneven streets of Key West. Even Dave's note had brought up more potholes. The jade goddess, where did she belong? That figurine at the crossroads of ethical choices—Sandy had to decide whether taking something that she'd found which might have stayed lost if she hadn't discovered it, so it truly belonged to her, not some unscrupulous dealer, was better; or maybe she didn't have a right to it, and the preservation of history through having antiquities identified by proper experts, maybe that mattered more—which was better? She remembered those discussions with Nick, back in the Fort Fisher days, about the roles of treasure hunters and archeologists, and then the third group, the looters who just destroyed historical records with vandalism rather than preservation. The moral high ground, Nick would have said, was turning a treasure over for history to record, but who was Nick to talk about moral high ground?

She'd travelled five thousand miles to loosen her ties to Nick, bonds that held her heart captive, physical distance the only way to free herself from the hold he held on her. Only in the soft breezes of the trade winds and the multicolored waters of Hawaii, only with the fiery presence of Pele protecting those islands, and her, was she able to heal, to mend her broken heart and not think about him or miss him every day she breathed.

Over two decades had passed since she had met Nick in North Carolina, but those memories were buried inside the grey matter of that brain of hers and were still there to tug at her now. This digging around memory lane was bringing up some treasured memories, gold along with the dross, good times along with those hard times, and she kept wandering through those pathways to the past. But where was she going with this? Could she sort through the confusing and conflicting emotions and rationalizations to some sort of understanding? She could still recall their year together even if time had colored whatever truth was there in the kaleidoscope of sensory images, an ever-shifting prism of pieces refracting her past. She would never forget her strong impressions from that day she first laid eyes on him the summer of 1977, when she was almost thirty. She let memory carry her back to that June day on the Carolina coast.

Sandy walked out of the illustration and writing trailer into the strong morning sunshine to look for the new archeologist from Raleigh. She had been on site for a few months; she knew those broad shoulders on the tall man with his back to her belonged to someone she had not met at Fort Fisher. He was looking into a glass tube held up to the light.

John Anderson, the site supervisor, was saying something about analysis of water samples' residue and the turbidity of the river. His profile, with his wire rim glasses and hawk nose, was turned up towards a sample the stranger held to the light after shaking it. She knew what that muddy water sample meant. No visibility—not any place in the nearly twenty-foot deep river could she see more than half a foot in front of her face; it was no place she wanted to dive, except for that exhilarating feeling of flying underwater. Freedom from gravity. But even with that pleasure, diving here could mean hitting a snag—literally; water logged trees meant diving danger. Channel clearing up at the recovery site had already been completed, but that didn't make the diving anything she wanted to attempt.

Not wanting to interrupt, she waited. She heard the deep, distinctive voice of the state archeologist as he watched the water sample settle. "Lack of salinity and low light levels, like you say, with those bottom sediments, that Miocene clay, make an ideal location for preserving those materials."

"Ms. Perkins, you want something?" John asked, looking toward her.

The broad-shouldered, six-foot four man beside him turned around. Their eyes met. Sandy felt an electric buzz pass through her. She somehow recognized those greyish blue-green eyes as though from the past, as though she had known him before. He smiled. His eyes stayed on hers.

"Nick Wellman, this is one of our on-site illustrators, Sandy Perkins."

"Hi, nice to meet you," she said, her gaze still upon his eyes, her gaze steady. "You must be the state archeologist?"

"Yes, I'll be here through August."

"I'm supposed to ask you if you want to preserve the artifacts before we begin sketches or..."

"Which artifacts?"

Sandy had forgotten what she was supposed to be saying, looking up at the strong face, defined cheekbones, dark brown hair tumbling across his forehead. An odd tugging feeling of someone remembered. Yet this was someone she had never met before she was pretty sure.

"Sandy? Ms. Perkins?" She heard John's voice.

"Oh, we have a wood and iron wheel rim that was raised in the tree branches when they were clearing the channel in the project area. The underwater archeology team found the rim. Our staff will be completing the topographic survey of the site. Both of us—the illustrators—will be working on the survey maps and grids, eventually, so we didn't know whether first—"

"Can I see it?" Nick asked.

"It's outside the work trailer for preservation," John interjected.

The three turned toward the Underwater Archeology Unit's trailer. John and Nick talked technical mumbo-jumbo as Sandy managed to catch her footing, her balance, in the heat of that June morning. Unable to concentrate, she did think to suck in her stomach as she walked.

They passed under the heavy limbs of the oaks to the preservation site trailer surrounded by wax myrtle. Nick bent his lanky frame to pass under a low limb and he glanced at her as she, too, ducked under the oak closer to its trunk. In the clearing, artifacts found before they had begun the survey of the Civil War underwater site lay on a wooden pallet. Operations would begin at the location of the Confederate fort, once situated above the river's cliffs far north of this work site; a few fragments dredged up already when the Corps of Engineers helped clear the project area had been arranged near large empty metal tanks. These tanks would be transferred to the recovery site where guns or cannons could be cleaned, bathed in an electrolyte solution once they were brought up, she heard the two men saying. Pushed into the river one hundred-twelve years before, to prevent the Union Army being able to use them, these cannons were expected to be found rusting somewhere along the river bottom below the cliffs.

One of the summer field project managers called John over to where they were examining the survey tape that would be used to create grid lines across the river to the bluff. Sandy ran out of reasons to stand in the clearing in the steamy heat next to Nick after he examined the wheel rim. But then he spoke.

"The Confederate soldiers hacked the gun carriages up to prevent the Union using them if they retrieved them," he explained, his strong hands gently fingering a blunt edge of the broken rim. "See, here you can tell where it was chopped."

She looked where his hand touched the weathered wheel. Then he was watching students checking tags and measuring artifacts brought up in the channel clearing process. Her directives were clear. It was time to return to the art trailer. Still, she stood there.

"Show me what you do," Nick said.

She looked up at him. His comment had a provocative edge; the smile in his eyes confirmed a teasing note. He was flirting, she realized. Rather than feel flustered like she had when first surprised by the magnetism of his presence, she rose to the occasion. She smiled back.

"You mean the artists' lair?"

"Sure."

"We're not completely set up yet."

"I'm curious about the art team. And the division of archives and history will want me to cover everything. Might as well start at your station." Sandy just stood there until he made a sweeping gesture. "Lead the way."

Nick ambled along beside Sandy, who stretched her steps to keep up with his long ones, and she kept abreast of him.

"We're over here." She pointed. Walking beside him, she felt an inordinate pleasure in his closeness.

"I feel like I've met you before," she admitted. "Were you at the first meeting before the survey and recovery project began? Last spring?"

"No," he said slowly, leaning toward her as they reached the door to the trailer. She opened it. An art table and desk lamp were situated next to a couple of book cases. Lucille, the other artist, was taking paper from one of the shelves of supplies. She sat back down with the paper at the table.

"Hi," she said, pushing her glasses down and peering at him over them. "You must be the new archeologist. They said you were coming today."

"That's right. Nick Wellman. Pleased to meet you." He offered his hand. She took it.

"Oh, Nick, this is Lucille Young, our other illustrator. In the back is where the writers work," Sandy said, pointing to the open door to an office with desk and typewriter in view, adding, "Lucille, we do wait for the photographs to be printed. Nick here says we don't do sketches both before and after, except for some major pieces. We can do some sketches from before and after clean up but they'll tell us which, like with that wheel rim. I'll start those this afternoon. No telling how long it will take to complete the magnetometer survey."

"The barge is due by mid-July," Nick said, "as soon as the magnetic survey is completed. We can't bring it in until that's done. The iron on it would interfere with magnetism. It would create disturbance in the magnetic field."

"Oh," Sandy said. "Interesting. That's why they want to get a move on."

"Survey markers have to be laid on both sides of the river," Lucille said, "Once we get up there."

"John said the survey crew will extend the coordinates soon. Once we have the grids laid, you'll be able to start mapping."

Lucille, her blondish brown hair pulled on top of her head, a sheen of perspiration on her lip, was sweating just as much as the two who had been outside. The window unit barely cooled the trailer. She moved around them to put more paper on the table. They were squeezed closer in the small space between tables.

"Oh, one of the students came by. We're going to Bud and Joe's after we're done today."

"Bud and Joe's?" Nick asked.

"Oh, it's a local hangout. Down at Carolina Beach. A bunch of us go down for a beer, play pool, after work," Sandy explained. "You want to come?"

"Sure," he said.

They were still standing close together. Sandy could feel his warmth next to her. She hesitated before moving back.

"Come by around five, then," Lucille said. "We'll be ready then."

Sandy showed him their mylar film for later images to go into the report and the paper they used for preliminary sketches, explaining that they didn't have artifacts to show yet, except the ones from recent clearing.

"We'll be drawing the materials recovered. Perspective and side views. Until the surveying and cannons or artillery can be located according to the grid lines and be brought up, we will be using topographic maps located over here."

"Cool," he said, which didn't sound very administrative. Casual and interested was the way he came across, Sandy thought as she ran out of things to show him. After he left, Sandy fanned herself, mockingly wilting against the door he had just closed.

"He's a hunk," Lucille said. "Glad I'm already spoken for."

"Well, it hasn't stopped some people," Sandy said, for something to say.

"That's for sure," Lucille grinned. "John and Judy go at it like bunny rabbits. I hear them in the preservation room when I leave late."

"They never go home before eight," Sandy added, glad to change the subject, or at least the direction, from her too-obvious personal infatuation. "Do you think John's wife knows?"

Lucille shook her head. Sandy pulled out topographic maps of the fort from their bin and sat at the second art table.

She tried to concentrate on the lines in front of her, but they were just squiggles on a page. She rolled them back up. One thing was certain. She knew what love at first sight felt like. She went back out to start the sketch of the wheel rim, before the afternoon heat took its toll, and time flew by as she became absorbed in her work.

When Nick came by their trailer promptly at five, he offered to drive if they would show him the way. His easy smile, even in the shadow he cast in the trailer door, his brown hair backlit with afternoon light, brought a flutter to Sandy's heart despite the casual way she left her work on the table and gathered her belongings. Lucille and Sandy stepped out of the trailer, blinking in the afternoon sunlight, its rays shooting through the oaks into the clearing. Sandy pulled her large dark glasses from her bag, put them on, took off the band holding her hair in place, and shook her long dark hair loose to fall around her shoulders. She caught him glancing at her.

"I need to pick up sunglasses," he said. "Is there a drugstore down there?"

"There is," Sandy replied. Lucille was preoccupied with talking to a couple of young men in Seahawks T-shirts from the local university. Only Sandy was close enough to hear.

"Y'all go ahead," Lucille said. "I'll catch a ride with Richie and Adam."

Sandy did not protest. Nick led her to a well-worn Mercedes Benz and moved folders from the front seat to the back, carefully stacking them among books, a few clothes folded with a long sleeved shirt disarrayed on top, more files. Sandy slid into the space he'd made for her and he shut the door. John came up before Nick could move around to the driver's side. Through the window she could hear John.

"Do you have any literature on that new method of preserving waterlogged remains you were talking about?"

"You mean from the Pacific Northwest conference last year? You think you'd like to try it?" Nick asked, his voice smooth and resonant, a note of eagerness edging in. "The study of preservation of waterlogged archeological remains should be here some place." He opened the backdoor again and leafed through a couple of binders he had just moved. "Here it is. The guys in South Carolina said they tried it. Liked the results."

"Let me study it tonight. Can I keep this a few days?" John asked, taking the folder from Nick after he pulled his large frame out of the back of the car.

"Sure," Nick said, closing the door and moving around the car to the driver's side. "Let me know what you think."

"Will do."

John turned back to the project area. Nick opened the front door and slid gracefully behind the wheel. Sandy had taken the opportunity to comb her hair while the men talked. She put her comb back in her bag and placed it on the floor before Nick turned to smile at her and start the engine. Turning slightly to face him, she smiled back.

"Ready to go?" he asked, turning the car down the sandy drive. "You look happy."

"I am. Long day, glad to be off," she replied. "They're pretty loose about our hours, as long as we get our work done. What kind of preservation were you discussing?"

They talked archeology and techniques for cleaning and preserving artifacts as they headed down the winding coast road towards the beach town. He made it interesting and kept it simple. She plied him with questions to keep him talking. Before her head began to spin with details about the science, he began discussing the history behind the summer's field school recovery project and three cannons that had been found in the river by a salvage group. Although she knew some of the background of their project, Sandy listened while he explained that when the Confederacy had abandoned the fort and threw ordnance and equipment in the river, except for three guns the Union Navy had recovered in 1865, most of the artifacts remained under water until that salvage operation uncovered some of it in 1972. She almost mentioned her own diving experience with treasure hunters until she heard him saying, "The salvage was illegal; they got caught, had to go to court, and even though the court ruled in favor of the state of North Carolina, it brought a lot of publicity. The unwanted attention created problems. More looting. We're lucky we can recover the remaining material. Our Underwater Archeology Branch of the NC Division of Archives and History, the Department of Cultural Resources knew it was imperative we fund this recovery project as soon as possible." He looked over at her. "And here we are."

"That's a mouthful, all the departments and divisions," she joked. They came into the town full of beach supply stores, seafood restaurants, and rental offices. She pointed him towards the drugstore on a corner. "Along with that mouthful," she resumed, "then add the universities, the groups wanting to preserve history, all this has come together just in time. Right? The CETA grant Lucille and I are employed by—I was so lucky to get this job using my art skills. That's why I moved down. Plus winters up in Chapel Hill were too cold for me. Lots of kindred spirits, but it's too far from the ocean, and too much snow and ice."

"You lived up there?" he asked, pulling in a parking spot. "In the Triangle?"

She nodded, opening the car door and joining him on the street. After he had gotten sunscreen and sunglasses at the drugstore, with Sandy only too happy to be walking beside him, they drove over to the bar. Its dark interior was noisy with laughter and the crack of pool balls hitting and rolling. Cigarette smoke lifted and swirled when the door opened and closed. His hand on her back, guiding her in, felt natural. Right. Her pulse quickened.

"I'm buying," he said. "What's your pleasure?"

"My pleasure…," she said. "Rolling Rock is fine. Thanks."

He ordered Heineken, asked if she wanted to change her mind. She shook her head. Should she offer to buy the next round, or would that sound too feminist? Set the wrong tone? Offend him?

Students from the university and CETA employees mingled at the bar; Lucille and the students sitting in a booth beckoned. They joined the group. Sandy sipped her beer slowly, cold brew refreshing after a hot day, and she watched Nick interacting with the crew. He seemed easygoing enough, but as an administrator she estimated in his early thirties, he had a touch of officialdom that did not seem off-putting.

How had he risen in his division so fast, Sandy wondered, since most of those in the Department of Cultural Resources, if not clerks or secretaries, would be older, she thought. He was smart, she could tell, and liked that, but she also liked the way he put everyone at ease, even told a joke, had questions that showed he was interested in the young people at the table.

Eventually Lucille was ready to go, having a husband waiting at home. The students with her got ready to drive back to the project site. "You want a ride back to your car?" she asked Sandy.

"I can give you a ride, if you want to stay, finish your beer. I need to go before long, get some supper myself," Nick offered.

Sandy stayed. He headed to the restroom. She saw him stop by the jukebox on his way back. His features were lit by the machine; his arm rested on the clear top as he casually reviewed selections, chose a few, and put in coins. Fats Domino came on first, and then when the next selection began, "Unchained Melody," he asked her to dance.

At first, they kept a respectable space between themselves. But they moved closer when he turned her and she adjusted her steps to his. The aroma of his skin, sweet but manly, notes of the day's perspiration and pheromones and health mingled in her nose. She felt the warmth of his hand firm on her back, the other hand holding hers midair, strong, solid, gentle. She surrendered to his lead, the lyrical feeling of moving to music with this man, the rhythm of their movements synchronized. His warmth and nearness encompassed her. She felt her breasts against him and sighed. It had been a long time since she had been held this tenderly. When the song ended, they pulled apart reluctantly. Then he dipped her to relax any awkwardness and add a light touch of humor. It worked. She laughed.

Only two of the project members were left shooting pool, and outside the sun was starting to set. She got her bag and they left. Outside the bar he put his hand on her shoulder. "Want to get our feet wet before we go? I haven't stepped in the Atlantic yet."

She nodded.

They wandered past Art Deco buildings and the boardwalk where men with beards and tattoos, women in cutoffs and skimpy tops, families with little children in herds moved back and forth. They found steps down to the still warm sand. The cries of sea gulls, a line of pelicans passing overhead could not distract her from the awareness of his presence. She took off her sandals and he stooped to pull loafers and socks off, roll up his pants.

"How did you wear those hot pants all day?" she asked, to break the silence, the unexpected tension she felt wondering what if…

"Not easy," he admitted. "I didn't know quite what to expect. I've been in the Raleigh office too long." He laughed. "Good to be back in the field."

She noticed the pale skin of his hairy legs, his big feet next to her tanned ones in the sand. She was glad she had painted her toenails. He took her hand; his big man hand made hers feel small. They followed the line of foam at the edge of the sloping sand, where its wet, packed surface made easier walking than the ridged and rippled sandy beach.

They walked a way down the shore. He stopped. She looked up at him. He smiled and said, "You have the most incredible eyes."

Then he leaned down and kissed her. Tenderly at first, then with yearning. She felt wet with excitement, her pulse racing as their lips lingered together.

"Wow," he said.

She opened her eyes. Looking at her after their faces parted, he whispered, "I've been wanting to do that since the first moment I saw you."

"Really?" was all she could think to say. She looked up into his eyes, the color of the sea on a stormy day, and she knew there was no going back.

But Sandy remembered when he told her, during their first dinner together, that he had been married before, right out of college; he and his wife had separated. But she already knew. The day after their first kiss, she had gone to work after that momentous evening to find Lucille waiting for her in their trailer.

"Well," she had asked, "how did it go?"

"He's a great dancer," Sandy had answered. "He asked me out for dinner tonight."

"Hon, he's married," Lucille had said. "I asked."

Sandy looked so crestfallen, Lucille took mercy on her, "Well, separated."

"Separated is like divorced. They're not together, right?"

"You never know how those situations will turn out."

Sandy pulled out the preliminary drawing of the wheel and some photographs from a bin and sat at the second art table. She concentrated on the lines in front of her, hiding her face, which she knew revealed how disappointed she was. She never looked for rings on fingers. She never thought of a man flirting if he was married. She assumed the men she met when she and the gang went out were single if they paid her any attention. How naïve could she be?

Well, she had been warned, but it was too late.

The next two months had gone by in a whirl, Sandy remembered. She had been dazed by the intensity of her feelings for him, the deep feeling of connection in his company. Before, she had sometimes felt alone, even with a man she was seeing, but with Nick she always felt present, aware, communication passing easily between them, filling her up. It was inexplicable. How she felt with him, his intense awareness of her, their ability to be together whether talking or in silence created what always felt like a warm bond between them.

When they made love, sometimes with his hands holding hers over her head as he moved on top of her, she could not feel where his skin ended and hers began. Her heart sang. She knew he could feel it, the sweetness of her heartfelt love as she held on to him, held him close. He talked to her while making love, love talk that kept her fully engaged, so her mind never wandered off as it had sometimes done with other men. She was fully present, fully in the now whenever he was near.

Sandy remembered how delighted she was when she learned that John was taking a job with the University of South Carolina Institute of Archeology and Anthropology, and Nick was stepping in to take control of the underwater archeology branch at Fort Fisher as an interim director.

They had over a year of good, then several months not so good.

One of her fondest memories of those early days of their affair came when the team had gone north for six weeks to the river, East Carolina University field school students joining them for the survey and recovery project along its banks. The survey crew was working on laying lines across the river from the bluff. Because it would be Sandy's job to draw the teams

working down the embankment as they rappelled with a
controlled descent, she and Nick took the canoe out to watch.
Though she would have photographs to work with, she was
glad to "get out in the field" which sounded so much more
work-like than "have fun with her honey on the water."

In the hot air, large trees offered shade but little relief
from the high temperature in the nineties climbing steamily to
the hundreds as the afternoon progressed. One of the students
had a plumb bob on survey tape lowered to a team member
below who marked it with a stake. Sandy and Nick were
joking about the view from below, looking up at the young
man with the nylon survey tape, trying to wrangle it free of its
entanglement. Sandy had just turned back to Nick, bracing his
paddle across his knees while he took a swig of water, when
she saw a dark line, like a cord, drop from the tree branch
above.

The wriggling snake landed with a plop on the bottom of
their canoe.

"Snake!" Sandy managed to shout as the canoe tipped
side to side with Nick's sudden movement to whack at it with
his paddle.

The snake slithered toward her. She didn't know if it
would bite, but she wasn't taking a chance. Quickly slipping
her legs over the side, she lifted herself over the edge, scraping
her arm on the rim of the canoe as she dropped into the murky
water. Her response had been so instantaneous, she tipped the
canoe. Nick, trying to contain the snake with his paddle and
taking another whack at it, fell in, too, but he kept the canoe
from completely filling with water and sinking by quickly
grabbing the rim and steadying it. It all happened so fast—
where was the snake? Then she saw the ripple wiggling across
the surface, headed towards bushes and roots clinging to the
bank. Relief.

Treading water, she heard Adam call from the top of the
embankment, "Y'all all right?"

She nodded and shouted back, "We're okay."

Nick had the cord tied to the canoe and it floated down current behind him as he reached for Sandy. His hand below water brushed her breast, but didn't linger. Visibility was low, but no need to make a spectacle of their obvious attachment. She felt his thigh between her legs, his smile and twinkling eyes as he held her a moment before several young men on the north bank scrambled to help. The cool water on a hot day felt good, the momentary excitement and then relief that all was well energized her. Nick had taken it all in good humor, with a certain aplomb that impressed her.

"Here, bring it over here," one of the young men reached toward them. Nick pulled the canoe while Sandy steadied it in the current, then got out of the way until she reached the edge of the river where one of the boys gave her a hand climbing up the slippery yellow and bluish red clay bank.

Sandy sighed, remembering those sweet and enchanted days.

On those summer nights on location near the river, Nick, a Civil War buff, had detailed the history of the fort for her, and had explained the state's interest in getting the recovery project completed that summer. His enthusiasm charmed her. His knowledge impressed her. He was attentive, too, when she revealed her own background during evenings of long talks. He showed interest in what he called her "exotic" past, the treasure hunting, when she had finally told him, even the funny times when Disney World was first opening. They grew closer during the weeks on site. Then when they returned from the recovery site, their relationship deepened further.

He liked that she was artistic; it pleased her that he acted proud of her when he attended an exhibition in the fall that included two of her works, done before this job and he took so much of her time and interest. She learned that he had been married straight out of college, gotten a job with the state promptly; his former wife's family had connections with the governor and was influential in the state's cultural arts. She let him open up as he chose, not wanting to dwell on this other woman he had left a few months before he came down to the coast. Any natural curiosity was quelled by the notion that someone else had been with him that way, the way only she and he could be, as though the two of them had invented lovemaking. So, she learned the former wife had money and an influential family—that explained part of his quiet but quick rise in the Division of Archives and History, but the other part was his ambition, which had revealed itself before that summer's end.

His friendly questions of other team members in the recovery project, what appeared to be a random accumulation of facts from the field, the politics of the project, showed themselves to be a part of an orchestrated plan. When ordinance was found with one of the cannons, delaying its raising until the potentially explosive matter could be handled, he had been quite helpful in a hands-on way. Then when one of the cranes almost tipped over due to faulty rigging, handling, and placement, he and John argued. Behind the scenes he had led to John's ouster, who conveniently got another job. Their conflict had risen to the surface when John's position in the underwater branch came into question with the handling of the crane and in a short time, he was gone. Did Nick decide he wanted to stay, not leave her? She wondered. He said he was asked by the higher-ups to stay on. It was a little bit of both, she figured, afraid to ask. So by the beginning of that September, Nick took over.

Nick would be acting director for that year, and Sandy was head over heels with joy. They never discussed living together. Since she liked her little place on Dock Street, a find in the gentrifying historic district of Wilmington, and she had no room for his dog, an Airedale, she was happy to go to his place on nights he didn't stay with her. She was content with their arrangement, seeing him almost daily, one sleeping over at the other's most nights. Besides, she liked her quiet time alone with a good book or an art project. She also sensed that he had just gotten out of a strangling commitment and needed some space of his own. On weekends, they would take some time to themselves, getting back together in the evenings, sleeping in on those weekend mornings before one or the other went home after a leisurely breakfast, the strains of Billie Holiday or an old folk blues guitarist like Lead Belly singing in the background. She loved his blues collection; he would tell her about some of the old musicians, the difference between Chicago blues and New Orleans blues, and styles, instruments, and finally lose her interest with blues chord progressions and technical details. They enjoyed classical music both from his stereo and her public radio station on the nights after her aerobics class and his weight room workout, when they got back from the gym; they would fix dinner together. Other nights they ate out, took walks in the historic district or down at the beach with his dog. It was the happiest fifteen months of her life.

And she'd travelled five thousand miles to loosen those ties to Nick, unable to cut ties with him without physical distance to do it for her. And time. But here was time playing tricks on her. Memories came as vividly as though it had only been yesterday.

Chapter 23

Dave's memorial service was uneventful enough, but after the reading of the will, all hell broke loose. Sandy had thought the oldest stepson Dan did a marvelous job reading his eulogy; also, a few friends of Dave's had spoken. Even Liz had gotten up and shared a few words, between tears and wavering smiles, to convey how much he had meant to her.

Sandy recognized Gene Sherman in the small gathering. She vaguely remembered him as Dave's partner in crime, in those doomed ventures of the '70s, when Gene had flown back and forth from California to the outfit in Florida before she went down to Honduras. His hair had gone grey since then, and he had packed on a few pounds. Now that Sandy was aware of some of the relationships among Dave's relatives, she watched interactions more closely. She was pretty sure Dan's wife was oblivious to any youthful amorous affair between Mel and him, but she caught Mel studying him during the service and she caught Liz eyeing them both at the food during the reception afterward. Did she know? Mel held up well, dabbing her eyes from time to time. Debra seemed composed during the service.

Since Dave was to be cremated, there was no service at a cemetery, just a little ceremony on the lawn overlooking the water. The second wife and her entourage had sat quietly, somewhat remotely, during the memorial service. During the reception afterward, Gene spoke to Debra, who talked with him a few minutes before excusing herself to join Sandy, munching on chocolate-covered strawberries beside the punch bowl.

"I never liked that man," Debra whispered to Sandy.

"Here, fill your plate and keep your mouth full," Sandy recommended. "Maybe nobody will bother us."

She saw Nelson and Gene talking, saw them walk off to the edge of the lawn, where the water came towards the embankment. "What do you think they're talking about?"

Mel came up, overheard her, saw their line of vision. "I think they were in cahoots."

"I bet that's who put Nelson up to it," Debra said, "selling off those finds on the black market."

"You were paying attention last night," Mel said. "You were so quiet, I wasn't sure you were listening to Liz when she said he stole from the two storage units out on Marathon."

A third man, one whom Sandy hadn't seen at the service, approached the two men. Sandy studied the body language of the three at the edge of the water. They seemed to be arguing and Nelson looked agitated. Gene grabbed his arm, but Nelson jerked it away, flapping both arms as he walked off quickly. The two other men stood talking a few minutes. The encounter was brief enough others may not have noticed, but Sandy surveyed the scattering of people on the lawn to see who was watching. Dan excused himself from a couple of people and approached Nelson. Mel and Debra were now watching, too.

"What do you think that's about?" Debra asked.

"I'll ask Dan later," Mel said. "I'm not sure I could get an honest answer from Nelson."

"Why are these two so different?" Debra asked.

Sandy smiled and said, "I asked her the same question."

"Different fathers. And the daughter in Australia had yet another father," Mel answered.

Debra and Sandy made bemused faces at each other. "I think wife number two said something about Australia—a daughter in Australia not coming," Debra said.

"She went to live with her father after Barb married that third husband, Nelson's dad; I think there was something creepy about him, the one before Dave, so she left. That's about all I know about her. Except she's married."

Liz and her brother, his wife, were talking with a couple. Liz had had her back to the little scene the three women had witnessed.

"Do you know any of these people?" Debra asked Mel.

"Some of Dad's business cronies from salvage, a few of his fishing buddies Liz said were here. I didn't know them, but he and Liz had a few friends I've met a time or two. Her bridge friends were here; they may have left already."

"Well, Gene's no good. I'm sorry to see he was still in touch with Dave. When they got together they cooked up some sorry schemes. Hatched plans without remorse. I think Dave may have had a conscience, at least, but Gene? He thought the suckers deserved it, gamblers taking a chance on winning and losing, easy marks who got what they had coming," Debra said.

Sandy watched Mel's expression as her mother spoke, for perhaps the first time to her, about the unsavoriness of his treasure hunting business, or even anything remotely related to the expeditions he had launched. The thirty-year-old's forehead crinkled, her lips pursed as though she would speak, and then tightened, her eyes on her mother.

The gathering was winding down; people paid their respects and left. Those who were left were family staying for the reading of the will. When Sandy looked around, the stranger and Gene were gone. Dan and Nelson were collecting the folding chairs for the reading, setting them up inside.

The fireworks began as soon as Liz's brother Michael finished reading Dave's last will and testament. Debra's account was mentioned, Liz's property, Dave's life insurance. The business went to Dan, and mention of Nelson was limited to settled accounts, meaning what he had already stolen was all he would get. Melody, his daughter, inherited a substantial amount which was in an account set up for her. All materials in his storage units were the property of Melody, who would be in charge of distribution of particular items from the units to those so designated in his documents. As Michael finished, Barbara turned to look at Liz.

"You'll be hearing from our lawyer," Barbara hissed. Then her voice rose. "This is outrageous. Nelson's entitled to his share. He worked with Dave more than that girl ever did. By rights, he earned his share."

She rose and stood over Liz, still seated. Barbara's fists clenched, unclenched. Her face was red. Liz looked small, and sat motionless. The woman towering over her spoke. "You did this. You got your claws in him—"

"Mother—" Dan said.

"Don't you 'mother' me! You two boys invested the last twenty years of your lives in that man's business and you deserve more than just—"

Sandy calculated that would make Nelson eight when he started. Ha.

"Nelson will be taken care of, Mother," Dan continued, approaching his mother's side. "He can work with me if he wants. But he and Dave settled up last year."

"I contributed to his success, and I expect to be compensated," Barbara nearly spat. "I brought him contacts. I got him started again. And that gold from the wreck off North Carolina that he and Nelson found, that was *before* he married her."

Liz, lifting herself up from her chair, supporting herself with her cane, looking out from the netting of her black cloche, turned to her brother, who, somewhat red-faced and tired looking, spoke up. "The will is binding."

Nelson, looking nearer to tears than anger, said, "Let's get out of here."

Dan, whose wife and children had already left with all the other mourners, was picking up his mother's pocketbook and taking her arm.

"Can we talk?" Mel approached.

"Not now," Dan said. "I'm sorry, Melody. We'll sort this out—"

"Wait," Mel said as he tried to head his cursing mother towards the door.

"I'll call you," Dan said, "I promise."

"No, you won't," Barbara turned. "We're getting a damned lawyer. That crippled bitch can't get away with this."

An audible intake of breath, a gasp from someone, but no one moved.

"And you," Barbara said glaring at Debra. "You won't get anything. You wait and see. You left Dave when his Oceanic Expeditions went bankrupt. All he made on Ocean Ventures I helped with. That's mine."

Debra looked at her angry face. She stood up and spoke clearly. "Of that, you are mistaken. You have no right to talk to me like that. Or to make a scene in front of his wife, one who actually loved him, made him happy. Or my daughter."

Sandy was as shocked by Debra as other people in the room were by the whole scene. Debra had hardly said a word in this house in the two days they'd entered it, except to make a little small talk, and here she was having a face-off with this woman practically spitting fire from her eyes. But Sandy had seen that backbone straighten before, those usually sweet brown eyes turn determined before.

Dan tried to take his mother's arm again, but she shook him off and pointed her finger in Debra's face. "You. You can't claim anything. You just wait, damn you."

Liz's brother took three steps and handed Barbara a business card. "Your lawyer can contact me. We're done here."

Liz had not been surprised by Barbara's outburst, which she had expected, Sandy knew; but when she took Debra's hand and smiled, she seemed genuinely delighted as well as surprised.

"Thank you," Liz said. "Don't worry. Michael and his firm deal with estates in DC more contentious than this."

After Dan, Nelson, and Barbara finally made it out the front door, Liz sat down.

"Don't worry. But I would take care of the key business quickly, if I were you," Liz said to Sandy and Mel. "You might want to get an early start tomorrow."

Sandy thanked her, and then Mel asked Liz, "Are you all right?"

"I'm tired. This day has worn me out," Liz said, by way of ending the drama and the company.

Mel, her mother, and Sandy said their goodbyes.

"Well, that was the drama Liz promised yesterday," Sandy said as they headed for the car.

"And then some," Debra added. "That Barbara was madder than a wet hen."

"That's putting it mildly," Mel said.

"A rooster in a cockfight, then."

"Liz had an ace up her sleeve with her brother," Sandy added.

"Maybe Dan can talk some sense into her. Or maybe she'll back down when she finds out what all Nelson already took," Mel contributed.

Before they got settled in the car, Mel's phone rang.

"It's Dan," she whispered.

Chapter 24

After the memorial service, the three women went down to Mallory Square to watch the sunset, but the carnival atmosphere seemed a bit much after a draining afternoon. Still, the diversion of watching sunset provided a break from all the seriousness of the day. Mel had talked briefly with Dan on the phone. He told her Nelson had admitted to some of the thefts, but he would know more later. No one felt up for more speculation and the next morning they would have a few answers, maybe. They found a place to eat, went back to the inn, and Sandy was left with her thoughts after she returned to her room. The morning's reflections on her relationship with the last man she had truly loved was the first time in years she had spent that much time in the midst of those memories. This trip was dredging up more than stolen treasure and drama queens.

###

When Nick's year heading up the underwater branch at Fort Fisher was nearly up, Sandy prided herself on her independence. She wanted him to stay, figured he would find a way. She did not push; she had learned her lesson years ago with Paul, and she did not even question him about his trips back to Raleigh that second summer, sometimes staying the weekend, nor did she question his private conversations outside the apartment when she was fixing supper. When his phone rang at her place, a few times she heard the "Let me call you back later" and some mumbled excuse. Even then she should have known instead of dismissing her questions; even Debra, whom she confided in over the phone or on their visits when Debra and Melody came down to Topsail for a weekend, had suggested maybe there was more to it.

During the last few months, things seemed to change. After all their shared conversations about destiny and fate, what it meant to be a good person, whether God was personally involved in our lives or some life force we couldn't possibly understand, whether there was life after death—despite those philosophical discussions that so engrossed her, those last months she felt a slight distance creeping in between them. Why had she denied the truth she knew but refused to see? It had been right there in front of her love-bedazzled eyes.

Sandy recalled that evening, sixteen months into their relationship, when Nick had come back from a trip to Raleigh, stopping by while she was painting after work, her Georgia O'Keeffe phase slowing and her goddess phase revving up, influenced by books on the Feminine Divine she had been reading. Her hands were smudged with acrylic paint and she was immersed in her work, her easel and tubes scattered in her work space in the tiny apartment. He was at the screen door on her upstairs apartment porch with the limbs and leaves and ripening fruit of the pear trees stretching over the railing behind him. Her first reaction was a mix of delight, surprise, apprehension. He looked so wonderful, so welcome, standing there filling up the door frame, then moving towards her; she was wiping paint off her hands, her apartment a mess she usually cleaned up before he arrived. She'd expected to paint until nine, but here he was, a day earlier than she'd thought, no call ahead to let her know...

"Honey, I'm home," he joked, pulling her close.

"Hey, sweetheart, I wasn't expecting you.... Let me put away these paints. It won't take a minute.... I missed you."

She gave him a quick peck on his warm lips, pulled away and began grabbing tubes, cramming them into the fishing tackle box she used for them, reluctantly rinsing the mix of aquamarine blended with yellow, white, a touch of blue she had finally mixed to a shade she liked, from the palette at her kitchen sink. There was barely room to turn around in there. He was studying her canvas, waves behind a sea foam woman.

"I bought Chianti," he was saying. "How 'bout we go down to the beach? Have you eaten?"

He had come up behind her at the sink as he spoke, pressing against her. She pressed back, leaning into his hips. Moving her hair to the side, he leaned to kiss her neck and the same thrill of his being, his touch, spread through her that she always felt. She turned off the faucet, put the palette in the drainer. She reached behind, to put her hands on his behind and pull him closer. She felt his fullness. They stood like that a moment. Then he moved back.

"God, it's hot in here," he said. "Let's get out, let's get to the beach before the sun is gone—north end?"

"Let me get my suit," she said, thought better of it. Her cutoffs would do. They needed washing anyway. "On second thought, I don't need it. And to answer your question, I had a salad already."

"I ate a burger on my way down, but I've got cheese and bread and wine." He was already at the front door.

"I'll be right down." She grabbed plastic wine glasses, a corkscrew, put them in a bag, and headed for the bathroom to put in her diaphragm just in case. The springing form of the diaphragm and its icky goo finally worked into place, she washed her hands and grabbed her bag of picnic supplies.

Nick and his dog were waiting in the car, both smiling. She pulled her Mexican beach blanket from the trunk of her Datsun and joined him in the Mercedes. She petted Ace, his tail thumping against the back seat, his wet nose nudging her hand.

"I'd like to take him, but he had a good run before we left, didn't you, boy? So I'll drop him off…"

On the drive down to Wrightsville Beach from the riverfront historic district, he talked about endless meetings in Raleigh, but she felt a distractedness in his tone, language, something was off, but she was too glad to see him, three days gone, to bring it up. She chatted about work, how glad she was Lucille was willing to draw the boring straight lines of the cannons and leaving the interesting stuff to her, like an iron logging pin with a ring attached, a spoke fragment from a carriage wheel, the right side view of the carriage for a six-pounder gun with a brass sighting groove and its top view, artifacts she enjoyed detailing, then the clear mylar they would use for the topographic maps, how well it would take the black ink. She prattled on until they got to his apartment and he took his Airedale inside. While he was putting Ace up, she was lost in thought, which continued as they drove on towards the beach.

She was sorry he'd seen the mess she'd left behind in her apartment. His place was so tidy, her creative, wild, scattered side crashing into his need for ordered space. She admired the spareness of his apartment, the spaces empty except for an extensive record collection, but she treasured her inexpensive upstairs apartment, found through a serendipitous connection with a boutique owner moving out just as she needed a place last year, too good a deal to give up, a real find as rents went up in the gentrifying downtown. She needed her space, permission to paint, to leave scattered disorder in its wake, spilling into the little living room she cordoned off with a metal book case.

She'd had so little time for painting in this year of companionship, of belonging. The first year she had felt so in love, united in a way she'd never felt with a man before, not

Tom, certainly not Paul, so young, so long ago, yet into that utter contentment, so unfamiliar to her, had crept an uncertainty these last few months she couldn't identify, a slight feeling that he was pulling back. Sometimes she thought he was irritated by her independence, but then their lifestyles had been so different before they met. She was refreshing for him, he told her, a breath of fresh air; he loved her spirit, her spunk, he said, but still, her hand-to-mouth existence seemed to bother him. And sometimes he showed a conservative side that surprised her, like the time she wore an off the shoulder top, and he pulled the elastic edge of her blouse back up over her shoulder before they got to their restaurant...

He asked, "What you thinking about?" as they waited for the drawbridge, letting yachts and shrimp boats on the Intracoastal Waterway pass by. "You've gotten so quiet."

"Oh, nothing," she said, reaching over to rub his arm, finger his ear, a curl of hair. She put a hand on his leg. She was so aware of being a woman when she was with him. Mostly feeling like a person without regard to gender during her everyday life, when she was in his presence, the glory of femininity, of being a female in the midst of all his masculine energy, opened her romantic side. Like a rose, opening to the sunshine of his attention, her love was full-blown, open to the beauty of love.

"Watch out," he grinned, without taking his eyes off the line of cars starting up in front of them. "That monkey business may get something started we can't finish here."

He took her hand from his thigh, placed it between her own legs and gently patted her. "Soon."

Once parked, they trudged through thick sand at the undeveloped north end of the island, tall sand dunes towering fifteen to twenty feet into the sunset sky, sea oats waving in the breezes off the ocean, the occasional sandspur biting into an ankle, and followed along a path between smaller dunes onto the shell-scattered edge of the shore. They walked down beyond tidal pools towards the inlet. Like a gentleman, Nick carried the blanket, the bag with wine and other picnic fare. She held on to his bare arm, after offering to carry the blanket, her sandals dangling from her hand, allowing the luxury of his care to comfort her; the fierce independence she had held onto, paying for her half of meals when she could afford the restaurant, treating him to home-cooked meals to compensate when he paid for both, finally succumbed to his wanting to provide. His generosity, welcome with her meager budget, eventually won out—though her pride sometimes flared.

They passed a walker heading back from the end of the island. Farther up the shore, one fisherman and his Labrador Retriever were the only occupants of the deserted beach. She was glad Ace wasn't with them. It meant romance could flourish in the sand dunes without his inquiring behavior. His interest in participating in any hanky-panky embarrassed her. Obedient and well trained as he was, he sometimes got overly excited and his mere presence embarrassed Sandy at those moments of intimacy.

The full moon was rising beyond the ocean in the lingering pinks and rose of the gloaming. They settled in soft sand where dunes sheltered them from the breeze. Nick opened the wine. The fisherman and his dog were passing, the panting hot breath of the Lab suddenly on her face before the man called him back. A brief conversation about how many fish caught, and they were gone.

"What a great idea," Sandy said, lifting her wine glass. They toasted. "To the beauty of the moon and the sweetness of now."

He was leaning on an elbow, watching her face and the waves rolling in.

"You look so pretty in this light."

She heard a hint of wistfulness in his voice. "As opposed to daylight?" she teased.

"You know what I mean," he said. "You're a beautiful woman, Sandy."

Looking back over her shoulder, she thanked him and smiled. "A comely wench, eh?"

"Ei, ei, lass," he replied in an imitation of a sailor's accent.

They finished their glasses in silence, listening to the murmur of the ocean. They finished the bottle to the lulling sounds of tide rolling in.

"Wanna go for a swim?" she asked.

"I didn't bring a suit."

"Now it's darker, we can skinny dip. We don't need them."

She smiled slyly in the moonlight, pulling her top off, undoing her bra, her breasts exposed to the fresh salt breeze. He sat up. "Sure."

He was standing up, unbuckling his pants in the moonlight, while she wiggled out of her cutoffs and waited for him before they ran to the water. The ocean felt cold at first, waves splashing on bare flesh as she stood hip deep in the water, then she dove into the next wave coming at her and Nick plunged in after her. They swam just a few minutes beyond the breakers; then he was holding her and she wrapped her legs around him. They kissed, bobbing in the dark, lips salty.

Back on shore, the water feeling warmer than the air on their wet bodies, they made love on her blanket between the dunes, the waves coming in and out, in out, caressing the shore, receding and returning, until the crest of a wave arched, exploded with the ecstasy of froth and foam released on the moving sand and seashell lace. Waves of love washed over her, love for this man she held so close to her heart, while waves of pounding surf, cresting sounds of their lovemaking came together in the crescendo of a breaking wave.

There in the moonlight, in the afterglow of their lovemaking, the moon's silver white line along the edge of

Nick's body shone. She traced the rim of his body with her finger. The warm afterglow of their lovemaking filled her.

"I love you," she murmured.

"I love you too, Sandy."

She sat up. Something in his voice.

"You know I told you I was taking the position for a year. Til they got someone."

Her heart constricted in her chest. "Yeah, but…you could stay, you said. They told you it was up to you. What are you saying?"

"I'm going back to Raleigh, Sandy," he said.

She heard the words. She could see the moonlight on his face, his expression serious, sad? But she couldn't believe he was saying it.

"But what about us? I love you. Can't you stay down here, Nick?"

He didn't reply. He sat up. She watched his profile in the moonlight. "Sometimes love isn't enough."

He had said that before, a few weeks back. She had told him then, love is all there is. Nothing else matters. But she had known, too, she was being romantic. It took more than love to make a relationship work, for two people with two different backgrounds, different values, to find common ground and work through the obstacles. Their obstacles weren't insurmountable…but it had terrified her to hear those words, then. This time, this time she could only feel a white hot pain rising from the root of her being up the center of her body, exploding in her chest. From her womanness that had cupped him in her warmth, the jolt searing her center.

"You have a choice, Nick," she said, expecting no answer now. The anger, moving to replace the pain, spilled out in her words. "You can tell them you want to stay."

"Sandy, don't be angry," he finally said. "It's a done deal. I wanted to tell you; that's why I came back early. We can still see each other. I'll be down here all the time." He rubbed her back. She pulled away, stiff in her anger, her sense of betrayal, the world crashing before her. There was nothing to say. No way to get this pain off of her. No way not to sound like a pleading little girl begging him to stay. No way to get this lonely, empty feeling out, except through anger. The anger of the hurt. The anger of the broken-hearted, the betrayed.

He tried to tell her it wasn't over, he still loved her, but his words felt hollow to the left behind.

The next day, talking to Debra on the phone, she acknowledged that she had not heard him ask her to go with him—"He knows I think Raleigh sucks," she said, but there was something more to this move. What, she wasn't sure.

"How long have you known you were going?" she had asked him before she got out of the car that night. When he didn't answer, she had asked again.

"A month," he had said, his eyes in the light from the streetlight searching hers. "We were waiting for the candidate to say yes. He finally confirmed this week."

"Thanks for the heads up," she had said and got out of the car.

"Men are such blockheads," Debra said on the phone the next day, her soothing melodious voice like a balm for Sandy's wounded spirit. "Give him a break. There may be more to it than you know. Pressure from his bosses?"

"He's ambitious," Sandy replied. "But so am I. I have two pictures in that show at Front End gallery.... He's a Sagittarius. Shoots that arrow, sees the target, sees that goal, not the steps to reach the target, not the details. Big picture man."

"Can't see the forest for the trees, only reversed—can't see the trees for the forest, huh?"

"He could stay down here, direct the archeology division."

"It's a dead end, though, isn't it?" Debra said.

"If he's into underwater archeological research, it's a great position. I guess historical preservation is his true love...or..."

When Sandy wondered aloud if there was another woman, Debra, who had recently broken up with the university professor she had been going with a couple of years, after she realized he was cheating on her, was sensitive to the topic of infidelity, even if she had been somewhat relieved to have an excuse to break it off with him. She didn't really want to marry him, but it had been headed that way.

"You mean that other woman? The almost-ex-wife?"

"Ouch."

"Sandy," Debra said, "he never filed divorce papers, did he?"

"I don't know. I never asked.... I stayed clear of that topic."

"Are you burying your head in the sand, honey? That's not like you. You're usually pretty direct."

"He loves me. I can feel it. I thought my love could hold him. Nobody could love him like I do."

"I think there's a song along those lines, Sandy," Debra joked. Then she asked more seriously, "So are you going to see him tonight?"

"No. We had reservations at Mediterraneo, but I said I wanted to be alone."

"Cutting off your nose to spite your face. You draw more flies with honey than vinegar."

"I don't want flies."

A sigh on the other end of the phone. "I know."

"You sound like my mother."

"Don't give up. It might work out. It sounds like he still wants to try. He didn't break up with you, Sandy."

Debra's advice was as mixed as Sandy's heart and head, tugging her in different directions. But Sandy did cut off her nose to spite her face; in the days after, she picked fights, her own way of pulling back. Everyone at work knew that Monday a new guy was coming. She pretended a casual indifference. Lucille saw through it, though. Sandy and Nick had kept their relationship as private as they could, not wanting to be part of the gossip of the staff circulating stories to amuse themselves.

Looking back decades later, Sandy knew she had missed those last precious weeks with him, but then, she didn't believe it changed the outcome. He was going, going, gone. What she did next, however, she knew may have started the death spiral sooner, rather than later. A musician she had met at the Pine Street potlucks near Debra's house a year or so before and dated up in Chapel Hill had bought a sailboat when he came into an inheritance; it was moored at Masonboro Boatyard. She had gone sailing with him one afternoon; before the day ended, she had sex with him. Sex without love made her feel more empty and alone than ever. That communion, that union she had felt with Nick making love could not be replaced. She faced the desolation of the days ahead. She had sought to prove she could move on, be on her own, but all she felt was really sad, really despondent. But she told Nick about the musician anyway.

He was back in town for a few days, talking about the new female assistant in the Department of Cultural Resources in the Historic Sites section, when her jealousy welled over. Welled up and spilled over. She had seen him interacting with female staff before, like the time they had been trying to coordinate with the local university's chemistry department conducting tests on artifacts and he had been trying to wrangle test results sooner than the staff said they'd have them back; his charm had the two lab assistants melting under his attention. When she had felt confident of what they had, the love, she had been proud, if a little nonplussed, but now jealousy drove her and eventually jealousy consumed her. So she told him what she had done. His reaction was hurt and anger, which she watched him control with a clenching of his fists, a steely look in his eyes, before he asked why and left early.

Then after her jealousy-inspired revelation, there were marks on his neck she ignored, unsure, afraid to ask. The bruise on his neck when he came back in the fall, after he had moved back to Raleigh, she didn't have the nerve to question. A passion mark? Too close to passion marks to be anything else.... These decades later Sandy wondered why she couldn't see what was plain to see, denied her own eyes with doubt that's what it was, but hadn't she really known?

Then when he was at her door one Saturday morning, calling the night before to say he was coming down—he called now, didn't just show up at her door expecting to be loved and welcomed anytime, any way—she came out on the porch, since her apartment with fans going and open screens was still hot in the October air. She didn't want to take the time to close windows and turn on the air. He didn't sit down in one of the rocking chairs but stood instead. She remembered clearly his face, framed by pink petunias in the hanging basket behind him, when he told her.

"I'm going back with Leigh," he had said. "She's pregnant."

"How—" it started as a question but before she could get the one syllable out of her mouth, it became a statement. Jealousy flooded over her before the enormity of her loss could hit. The thought that he could do with another woman the things they did, the lovemaking they shared. That joy in their bodies, their passion.

His face wavered in front of her through her tears. He bent down, leaned towards her to kiss her. She turned her face away, a kiss planted on her cheek. Would it have changed anything if she'd kissed him on the lips, held him, clung to him? She did not. An invisible wall of glass separated them. Where once he had been inside her and she had felt one with him, now he was a separate entity with lines of demarcation separating his body from hers, his spirit from hers. The lines that formed the edges of his body, the edges of his face, his lips, these were the lines of separation, a person she did not know. He was gone.

"I'm sorry, Sandy. I didn't mean to hurt you."

"Go."

He started to speak, but her face was turned away. "Go. Now."

She watched him go down the steps to his car and then she went back inside to lie on her bed crying. She recognized the deep abyss of grief, the dark deep place where she was falling, the darkness where the pain of her father's death as a child had been buried, a grief too overpowering to face, so she had covered it up until her mother's death. Where that abyss had loomed, too deep to see an end to it, now this death carried her down. For Nick was dead to her now, his loyalty gone whether his love was or not.

Nick had wanted to be friends. Friends. How could she go back? Having been her own, she could not share him. Her love was too entwined with—ego? she speculated years later, too entangled in "mine" to be that sort of love that shares, love that wants his happiness above all. Agape love. Not for her. She wanted him happy, yes, but she didn't want to be tortured knowing he shared his body with another. She could not rise above it, though she succumbed in loneliness and longing to talk with him on the phone, even let him come over despite her best intentions not to let him near, but she was left hurting days after. The ties to her heart were too strong that his tugging her heart strings didn't feel like barbs constricting her life flow.

So she left. She had to get far enough away that the hold he had on her could not pull her back. After two and a half years with the CETA job before Reagan derailed it, and another year with the history museum where she worked with preservation, wearing white gloves to handle old costumes and materials too precious for finger oils to touch, she left North Carolina. When a friend who had moved to Hawaii with her husband told her about a part-time position at the Bishop Museum in Honolulu, after Sandy had learned the history museum was cutting her position to part-time due to funding, she went out to the Pacific islands, taking vacation time with what money she could scrape together, and interviewed for the position. If her resume checked out, the administrator told her, she had the job.

So Sandy had put her possessions in storage and moved. Five thousand miles from Nick. Five thousand miles from the friendships she had developed, from Debra and her daughter, to forge a new life in the islands. And slowly her heartache eased; the trade winds had blown the threads of entanglement loose and the multicolored waters had washed her heart clean. She was free.

She had finally had too much pain. The courage to go had come after Nick's message his daughter was born. Continuing to talk with him had brought too much heartache, though she had been unable to resist in the months that followed his initial news he would be a father. After the child was born, she wouldn't pick up the phone, return his messages, though he continued to call, to see how she was doing, if she was okay. Even a year apart did not stop her longing or her temptation to answer his calls, nor the anguish if he did catch her at home to talk a few minutes on the phone.

When Sandy told Debra she had been offered a job, Debra said, "You'll regret it if you don't go." A friend in her spiritual book reading group said, "I'd pick pineapples to live in

Hawaii!" Lucille, mother of two little ones by then, had said, "Go, girl, and don't look back!"

"I'm leaving, on a jet plane" and "Silver wings shining in the sunlight" played through her mind, but the songs of the islands soon lifted her spirits and soothed her soul.

Now, nearly two decades later, Sandy had images of her times with Nick flooding back. She remembered the time she had gotten him to let her sketch him nude, then when he saw the charcoal drawing, tasteful she thought, just his back side with those wonderful shoulders, strong neck, and his beautiful buttocks, powerful legs, he refused to model again, even as she teased him, "Your wang isn't showing, Nick. No ding-a-ling, no man parts. No weenie. No pecker."

He smiled, kissed her, and shook his head. "I'm not standing that still again. You've got your sketch. Enjoy it." She didn't ask him again.

She remembered the time in his apartment when she had put down her book and watched Nick reading, an eggshell white wall behind him, intent on his book. In the space between here and there, she softened her gaze, defocused her eyes to see the electric blue white light around his body glow. It was a trick she had learned in church, to stare into middle space and see what she later learned were auras. She thought about painting him that way, but it would look too much like Jesus or some saint. He was no saint, a lapsed Catholic, this lover of hers, but she had gotten him to Easter Mass in old Saint Mary's Cathedral that spring of their year together. He was fidgety and restless, but she enjoyed statues of the Virgin, the stained glass windows, even if the formality of the service did not appeal to her. She remembered they walked down to the Pilot House afterwards, with spring bursting at her seams all around them, bulbs glad to rise from the dark earth to the warm light, buds open in gardens; blooms of yellow and purple and pink crowded wrought iron fences in their joy to be alive. She had so loved that morning walk to the river rolling under the bridge, the wildness on the other side of the Cape Fear. Reservations already made ahead, Nick seating her near the window, the slanting floor of the old restaurant above the river's grey waters.

The statues of the Virgin Mary she had returned to on other days, alone, to stare at her pensive and kind face close up. The serene figure, hands spread in blessings, had caused her to recall the jade figurine that had disappeared, that small intricately curved woman, probably carved by a Mayan artisan. Where, she had wondered then, had it ended up? She'd never told Nick about it, though she had told him about Dave and the treasure-hunting expedition. The line between treasure hunters, looters and researchers somewhat blurred, Nick admitted, and some finds would never have been discovered if not for adventurers risking investments to search, with the incentive of wealth. In fact, she had accompanied their team of scientists and archeologists down to a conference in Key West where she and Lucille and others mostly drank and had fun while archeologists and treasure hunters met to talk over their differences. Back then, in the late '70s, treasure seekers were the ones mapping the territory of old lost cargo from gold laden ships, cataloguing finds, as state governments hammered out the property rights to sunken ships and gold doubloons. Nick gave the treasure finders some credit for their efforts, but the looting meant lost history to him, like that of their fort's Civil War relics sunk on the bottom of the river before Sherman marched through to burn a tragic swath across the South. Historic remains, never to be recovered and restored as relics of the past when pilfered by poachers, Nick believed were lost for posterity. With hunters and historians working together, however, some history could be salvaged, some order restored in tracing them back, identifying their past, their origins, a story attached, some clue to past life and war, chunks of military history that revealed strategy, the way people thought, the way they lived back then. The treasure of our past that so fascinated him he said could be restored through perseverance and preservation.

And now here she was facing that same crossroad between treasure hunters and historians. Without her, the jade goddess might have remained on the bottom of the bay. Without her, the figurine might have never seen the light of day. And without her, that artifact might be lost to history. But did it belong with a government in a country where the grinding poverty of the poor and the wealth of its upper classes were separated by tall walls topped with broken glass or barbed wire to keep those whose ancestors may have created this figurine from the lush lifestyles beyond those walls? Would she end up in some rich administrator's hands if Sandy let her go?

Chapter 25

Mel was gone when Debra got up. No note, no message, and she wasn't out at the Westwind's poolside breakfast bar. Sandy, however, was sitting in their usual spot sketching some of the palms. Debra watched while she finished a quick drawing of the friendly young gal who replaced the coffee so cheerfully and frequently.

"Have you seen Melody?" Debra asked.

"No," Sandy replied, putting the sketch pad aside, and turning to Debra. "She was already gone?"

"She left before I got up."

They talked a few minutes about the drama of the day before. Debra had been too tired of the afternoon's hornet's nest to want to discuss it that evening; the sunset diversion had helped take her mind off the drama. Sandy told her she had been surprised by Debra's reaction to the woman they'd dubbed Second Wife.

Debra shrugged it off with, "I never liked bullies. I put up with enough of it myself, though. Too much like watching a pit bull go after a little puppy."

Sandy replied, "I'm not sure Liz is a puppy, but I admired your standing up for her."

As pleasing as it was to have her friend's praise, Debra felt a little uncomfortable, like she was some ragdoll that finally got a backbone makeover. Had she seemed so spineless all along?

"Someone needed to shut her down. She was railing against us all," Debra pointed out.

She got up for her lemon and water, left Sandy sitting there. Debra was on her second cup of coffee when they saw Mel enter the courtyard. She looked serious, Debra thought, but she gave the two women a brief smile before she plunked into the third chair at their table with a sigh. Like a wounded baby bird, Debra thought suddenly, a feeling of sympathy and love moving her to take Mel's hand.

Before she could ask what was wrong, Mel said, "The coroner said it was a heart attack. Dad had a heart attack."

"So is that how he hit his head?" Sandy asked before Debra could think of anything comforting to say.

"Probably. But that's not all. I just met with Dan. Remember that man with Gene Sherman yesterday? The one who came after the service?"

"Yeah," Debra said slowly.

"Well, he was one of the investors who bought black market artifacts from Nelson. Apparently Nelson had cheated him, or refused to honor a deal they'd made. Nelson was still pilfering one of Dave's storage units."

"Oh, dear."

"The good news is the heart attack means Liz may not have to worry with the life insurance company anymore. But the bad news is Nelson was still stealing. We need to go out to that unit, too, today, and see what's left. I'll have to make arrangements to move it. And first we need to go to the one on Sugar Loaf. Liz said no one knew about that one but her and Dave. He'd just moved things there a couple of years ago when he did all this will stuff."

"Dan told you this?" Sandy asked. She put up her pencil and sketch pad in the big straw bag by her chair. She was leaning forward. Debra couldn't help but think that Sandy was enjoying all the drama. Sandy had certainly praised her enough for speaking up to Barbara the second wife, who deserved a good quick kick in the shins Debra wasn't about to deliver.

"Dan told me about Nelson. I think there's more to it, but Dan wouldn't say what. Liz had already called and left a message about the coroner. Then Dan and I talked—we met for breakfast—and he's a little shaken up about Nelson. He knew his brother was...was devious, but I guess he didn't know the extent of it."

"That conniving little crook. Apple doesn't fall far from the tree," Debra responded.

"Nelson thinks *he* deserves whatever's there, and not me. And I know he's been doing this for a long time, so he's probably going after the rest of it."

Sandy looked at her curiously but said nothing.

Mel pushed her chair back and stood up saying, "Well, let's go. We better get moving,"

The three women headed for the car "faster than butter could melt on a skillet," Debra announced as she found herself riding shotgun in the convertible with the top down. Though it was only nine, the sun was already hot and bright beating down on her arms and shoulders. They drove out of Key West with Sandy's hat blowing back in the wind, even with the windows raised. Not Key West cool, top down and windows up in a sporty convertible, Debra realized. From the back seat, holding her hat on with one hand, Sandy leaned forward shouting into the wind, "This is exciting. I can still remember what that jade goddess looked like and it's been nearly thirty years. I can't believe we're this close to finding her."

Despite having to shout, Sandy went on, sharing what she remembered of her research about the metamorphic rocks from which the goddess had been made, the pressure and heat transforming the material to stone so hard and beautiful the natives of Central America had treasured it centuries ago. She told them about the fault line in Guatemala where jadeite was mined, the jade pieces put into graves and carried to the afterlife, the jade valued for its translucent colors and its hardness.

"The quarried jadeite of Central America was believed to have spiritual value, healing properties," she continued. "I felt something holding that figure, like it did have some power..."

Debra remembered the enthusiasm for the mysteries of ancient cultures her friend had shared years ago. That figurine had never been discussed in all those times Sandy had talked about the Mayans or during their own time together in Honduras. Debra vaguely recalled her own dream of a green goddess floating somewhere in the past that had been disturbed when she saw Sandy's paintings years ago, but she had attributed her dream and Sandy's art to pictures they might have seen. She didn't believe it was coincidence anymore. She felt too unsettled to bring it up now. Mel would say she was being flakey. Sandy was still talking about Mayans and their jade, wisps of words broadcast on the wind from the back seat.

"Dave once said there were caves on Roatilla, both on the island and in the water," Debra contributed. "He thought the Indians might have buried things in those caves or used them for burial sites."

"Pirates may have looted those," Sandy said. "I'm guessing the jade I found, with the other stuff I didn't get to see, was being transported down the inlet to a pirate ship."

"Vivid imagination," Debra said smiling back at her. Her hair whipped in her mouth and she pulled what she could back with her hands, no scarf, no hat to hold it down.

The map Mel had handed to her led to a dirt road behind a fishing charter shop. Back in the palmettos and brush, two small key deer disappeared into the shadows of a thicket. Mel brought the car to a stop by a funky little storage shed, padlocked, behind the building. An old woman came out from the back door of the shop, standing beside rusty crab traps leaning against the wall.

"You looking for Ned?" she asked, shading her eyes with her hand. A long apron covering dirty dungarees and a well-worn plaid shirt gave an impression that matched the weathered woman's face, one of much use and much time in the sun.

Mel got out of the car, introduced herself, and explained why they were there for the storage unit.

"Dave is dead?" the old woman repeated. "That's too bad. And you his daughter? Ned used to take him fishing. Caught marlin and swordfish in their day. Hadn't seen him in a while. Ned will be sorry to hear that."

A couple of crab traps with weeds growing through them jumbled in front of the storage space indicated it had not been opened in some time. Mel moved the crab traps to the oyster shells piled along the side and tried the key. The padlock sprang open as she yanked down. Inside the darkness of the storage shed, musty boxes lined the back; rusty fishing tackle and spiders had made a home in the corners.

"Yuck," Debra said. Mel just stood there.

"Do you have a flashlight?" Sandy turned to the curious old woman.

"Sure do, honey. Lemme go get it."

"Not a glamorous setting for a hidden idol," Mel pointed out. She took the flashlight from the old woman and they entered.

In a few minutes they were gingerly rifling through the contents of a couple of old chests, checking for spiders and varmints before moving anything. There in old packaging, Debra recognized a cardboard box mailed from Roatilla, wrapped in torn brown paper still with old Honduran stamps, that she had once put in storage in California before they moved east permanently in '72.

"My goodness," was all she managed to say before Sandy took the package.

"That's it! I bet that's it."

Eagerly opening the box, Sandy pulled the contents out: a form wrapped in cloth, old newspaper stuffed along the edges. Sandy removed the paper. In the dark unit, the flashlight shown on the green goddess and reflected light off the tiny figure after Sandy pulled the cloth away.

"Oh my god—goddess," Sandy said, holding her once more in her hands. "She's more beautiful than I remembered…"

She cupped the six inch goddess in her hands and stared in wonder.

"She's so serene," Debra observed.

"She really is beautiful, Aunt Sandy," Mel said, pausing before she checked any of the other boxes in the chest.

"She looks like a Buddha," Debra added, touching the tiny carved face with a finger.

"More serene than my paintings I tried to do from memory…"

"It does look sort of…mysterious," Mel said when she moved closer to peer at the oval face. "Why would she look Oriental?"

"Well, I told your mom—you were too young to remember—back when I was researching this stuff, some anthropologists believed the Chinese in the Han dynasty may have made maritime voyages across the Pacific, all up and down Central America. The diffusionist theory was supported with lotus friezes, serpent-like creatures carved in jade similar to the shapes of dragons in Asia. The anthropologists pointed to all sorts of evidence of Asian influence. So there may have been a connection…"

"Let's take her out in the light for a better look," Debra suggested.

Stepping into the sunlight, Sandy marveled at the tiny woman in her hand. Debra, only too glad to get out of the musty dark interior, followed her out to look with her at the green figure.

"It's incredible, Sandy," Debra said. "What are you going to do with her?"

Sandy looked up from the small figure. "I don't know...look at her for the time being."

"It belongs in a museum or something," Mel said from inside the dim shed. "It must be worth a small fortune."

Debra looked at her friend's face, mesmerized by the light on the goddess.

"Ironic, coming from you," Sandy mumbled. Debra gave her a stern look.

Mel, exiting the door, squinted at her. "What'd you say?"

"Nothing, sugar," Debra interjected, "Is there anything else in there?"

"You never call me sugar."

Mel gave both of them a penetrating look, then turned back into the dark unit where they heard her rummaging around.

The knowledge of the long-ago gold chain and Mel's probable involvement with Nelson's early pilfering hung in the air like a shimmering soap bubble, one she would not poke a finger to burst by saying a thing. And Sandy better not. That unspoken awareness none of the three would burst by mentioning.

"Wonder how old it is. You reckon some Mayan carved it hundreds of years ago?" Debra mused aloud. "I wonder if there's any way to trace it back to a time period or something.... Do you think an expert would consider it a big find?"

"I don't know how valuable it would be; it's hard to tell." Sandy hesitated. "I felt bad all those years, knowing we disturbed all those artifacts, with hardly a system for cataloguing them. The archeology community considered it looting, the way treasure hunters—even if they were sort of pioneers in underwater archeology in the early days making the rules as they went along—the way some of the treasure hunters plundered like the pirates...but nobody would have found those without...without an incentive and we did discover those relics; no one in the government down there was investigating..."

"But...," Debra's voice trailed off before Sandy spoke again.

"I want to enjoy her a few days."

Debra looked at her. She looked like a kid with her hand in the cookie jar.

Sandy added, "I'll figure out what to do with her. But for now..."

The old woman had come back out. "Why, she's a purdy piece. Was that in there?"

"Sure was," Sandy said smiling.

From inside the unit, Mel said, "Y'all help me get these chests. There's only two. We can fit them in the trunk of the car."

Cobwebs and dirt scraped off, the two chests stood in the light of day. Nothing but fishing gear remained in the unit. Mel pulled out a couple of wooden gun pieces, part of a musket from one trunk she opened, put them back in the chest on top of a few folded faded newspapers.

"Not much of value in one, a few gold chains and silver coins in the other, but there seems to be a false bottom or something," Mel said in a low voice to Debra, while the old woman looked inside the dark storage space.

"Really?"

"Why didn't he keep this at the house?" Sandy asked, holding the figurine. "Liz had those shelves full of seashells and a few artifacts. The jade goddess could have been on display. But that would have brought unwanted attention, I suppose. But at least keep something like this at the house."

"Thieves?" Debra guessed. "No gold was on display as much as he would have liked to show it off. I think he would have distrusted some of the people he knew, or friends of theirs. They were a bunch of crooks."

Mel shot her a look. "Are you gonna help or just stand there badmouthing Dad?"

"Eww. Testy," Sandy observed.

"It is getting hot out here," Debra said, her hands on her hips, her face as inexpressive as possible.

"We still have the other unit to find. I chartered a boat for two o'clock this afternoon."

"You did?" Debra asked, leaning down to grab the handle of the chest Mel was standing beside. They lifted it into the trunk of the car, and Sandy and Mel lugged the second one over.

"It's not that heavy," Sandy said as they hoisted it up and then leaned it against the car bumper, "but I don't know if they'll both fit."

Tugging and pushing, they repositioned the first chest. The trunk of the car wouldn't close, and Mel said, "We need a bungee cord. To tie the trunk down."

Debra, still wiping dust off her hands and top, spoke to the woman who had watched their efforts without offering to help, and closed the storage door. Once they had the trunk secured with twine the fishing store owner provided, they said their goodbyes and headed back down the dirt drive and onto the main highway.

Sandy, still holding the goddess, said from the back seat, "That part of a musket you pulled out of that trunk reminded me of ones we used to draw when I was working at Fort Fisher. I wonder what that was doing in there."

"More mysteries," Debra said. "And maybe more to come."

"We could find out about this goddess…You want to go down there with me? Go to Tegucigalpa or someplace when I find out where she belongs? That might solve one mystery."

"Well, I don't know. What about that archeology expert back when you were working at Fort Fisher? Would he know where to start?"

There was no answer from the back seat.

It was going to be a long day, Debra thought; good thing they had gone to bed early the night before.

Chapter 26

"Why do you think Dave wanted me to have the jade goddess?"

"Who knows why he did anything, Sandy? My best guess is that AA tells people to make restitution. Go around making amends. Maybe he 'got it,' " Debra speculated. "Even if that's a far cry from the man I knew…"

"But why this way?"

"Maybe he felt guilty. The guy had a conscience, I guess, even if he drowned it for years in booze. I guess he felt bad taking it from you, or not telling you he had it, at least. And remember, Liz said he was cutting corners on making amends to all the people he ever wronged by picking you to stand for them all."

"It's a double-edged sword."

"What do you mean?" Debra asked, forking a chunk of chicken salad into her mouth and looking at Sandy while she chewed.

Sandy swirled the tea in her glass, watched half melted ice cubes moving around.

"Well, I have to decide what to do with it."

"I thought you were keeping it."

"I didn't say that. I said a few days."

"Hmmm," was all Debra contributed.

"I don't know if I'd be in trouble for having it in the first place. So how could I give it back? And to whom? A third

world government that went to war over a soccer match with
El Salvador?"

"That was decades ago."

"And the contra rebels Reagan and the CIA were
supporting. It's a mess down there…"

"Well, Mel has to decide what to do with whatever loot is
left in her unit, too, those relics."

"If Nelson knows about it, I doubt there's much left by
now."

"It's not that one," Debra said, looking at Sandy with clear
mischief and delight.

"What do you mean?"

"That one's a decoy."

"Who says?"

Sandy stopped swirling ice cubes and looked at her
friend, twinkly-eyed and enjoying stringing her along,
chewing her salad too many times. She took another bite
before answering, chewed that slowly, too.

"Come on, Debra, out with it."

"Mel told me there's another unit or location that's never
been bothered. She found a map in that first trunk. When she
unloaded it, there was a false bottom. That's where we're
going."

"Really? Cool. The adventure never ends."

"When Mel gets back, we'll head out there."

"Fun!"

"You are enjoying this, aren't you?"

"Of course. It's an adventure. It beats wandering through
boutiques or bars. If I'm going to come all this way to see you,
we might as well have some intrigue. I love Hawaii, but I am
working pretty hard out there. Nose to the grindstone and all
that. I do take time to hike and swim, but it's pretty tame.
Sailing with the wahine sailors sometimes, in those cobalt and
teal waters, can get the adrenaline pumping, the blood going.
Otherwise, my life is pretty mild, mostly work, and more

work. And this has been an interesting stroll down memory lane, some good, some bad. I love being with you. I miss y'all."

"Why don't you come back home?"

"Home? Hawaii is home."

"Home is where the heart is."

"There's lots to love out there. My business is out there."

"We miss you. You could find something in Chapel Hill or Raleigh. It's growing, changing."

"Living in Paradise. It's good right now. Maybe someday I may feel different."

"But the economy is good now, with the Clintons in office. It has stabilized things. No telling what the next election may bring. The job market is good now. You could start a business in North Carolina. "

"Too close for comfort."

"What do you mean?

"Oh, Nick pulling at my heartstrings. It took five thousand miles to get some distance. So I couldn't feel him. So there was no tug on the heart."

"Still? That's been years, Sandy."

"I've realized I'm not as safe as I thought. Memories can jump on you any time. Take you right back where you thought you'd never go again," Sandy said. "Remember I told you he called me almost three years ago? On my birthday. Got my number from Lucille."

"You mean when he told you you were the love of his life?"

"Yeah, I think he'd been drinking. He dreamed about me. Even said Leigh had asked about me when he woke up a few times. Apparently he was talking in his sleep."

"I think he really did love you. Marriage. Separation. Divorce. It gets complicated."

"He was pretty convincing, about still loving me. Said he thought about me every day. Still fantasized about me." At that, Debra rolled her eyes. "It was flattering to my ego. But...sad for him. Well, if he was married, and I was the love of his life, then he couldn't have been that happy. I did want him to be happy. Once I got far enough away from him, the strong feelings that possessed me, and time passed, I did want...I did let go.... His daughters, when he called, were teenagers. I left before I found out he had another daughter. I think he would have kept the affair going, family one place, me the other.... I had to get away from him and his hold on me. Once I learned his first child was born, it was too much. Hearing from him just wrenched me."

"He wanted to have his cake and eat it too. The jerk."

"I'm healed. He's the one who stayed torn up. Said he had panic attacks. That was one of the reasons he'd left her in the first place.... He worried about me, he said, and regretted not getting a divorce. But he did have his kids."

"You didn't compromise yourself. It would have been messy."

"It *was* messy. I may have missed out on love.... Maybe I missed my chance. Didn't want to settle for someone else when I knew I had more love to give. I wanted a soulmate. I know in my heart I have more love to give."

"You're an idealist. Me, I almost settled. That college professor, remember him? I wanted more babies and I think I would have married Andrew for that. He offered stability. I was still working at the Intimate, finishing my degree, not making much. He saved me the trouble, though, of having to settle. Maybe he knew my heart wasn't really in it. I'm glad it didn't work out. Now I've got the grandkids. They are fun, and I can spoil 'em. And send them home when I'm tired."

"Mel did figure it out. Got a man who'd treat her good."

"Relationships take a lot of work. I think they both put a lot of effort into it. Not marrying Andrew saved me a lot of compromising. Besides, I would have lost my independence if I'd married him, and I think I enjoy it too much now. Not having to tell where I'm going, take care of someone else's feelings, priorities, cater to their whims…"

"I think you were more idealistic than you realize, about settling for less than true love. You would have stuck it out with Dave if it hadn't been so bad. Some of our '60s generation, we just kept moving on. If a relationship lost its shine…. The bad boy, left over from the James Dean era, always seemed so exciting. Mel's generation, on the other hand, seems more practical. Or at least better at taking care of their own needs—or realizing what they are! But that could have been just me…"

"James Dean doesn't look like such a bad boy compared to what's out there now. Nick seemed straight enough, especially after some of the men you got involved with," Debra said.

"Oh, he could be a bad boy," Sandy said. "We had some wild times in the sack. Couldn't keep our hands off each other; nobody turned me on like he did. And I liked that he was so responsible. Of course, that's why he stuck it out once he found out Leigh was pregnant."

"You seemed so happy that year. I wish…"

"We were happy. I really loved him. But sometimes it takes more than love. He said that. I didn't really get it then. My views have changed with age. I like being stable, economically, even if it's a challenge. And emotionally, I've mellowed…"

"Y'all were so happy for a while, I was so glad for you…"

About that time the cell phone rang. Sandy was glad Mel called. The conversation stirred too many memories she didn't want to discuss. Too many regrets. Too much sadness. Too much water over the dam as Debra would say.

"She has the charter confirmed," Debra told Sandy, even though the phone conversation from one side had revealed this.

"What's she doing about the trunks? I thought she was leaving tonight?"

"She delayed her return flight. She opened the bottom of that one, like I told you, and found the extra map. Surprised Liz. She didn't know about the extra map. Liz will store the trunks for her."

"Apparently Dave had a few more tricks up his sleeve," Sandy said, feeling somewhat justified thinking he couldn't have changed completely from the devil she'd known, even with AA. That AA angle couldn't explain why he had given her back the goddess.

"That he did," Debra said, pursing her lips and frowning. "I wonder how much Liz had to do with...with his change of heart or whatever made him settle his accounts...write those letters. You. Giving you back that goddess instead of selling it. Guess the black market for jade didn't pan out..."

"Can you ask her?" Sandy queried.

"Think I should? Would she know? Or would we be probing too far..."

"Let's see what's in this new locker or whatever. If it's just stuff for Mel."

"Mel said 'SS Central America' was written on the map."

"Do you know what that means?"

Debra shook her head. "Well, it said '1857' on it, too. Would that be a year?"

Sandy shrugged. "Guess we'll find out."

Chapter 27

"What do you know about the SS *Central America*?" Mel asked Liz. She pressed the yellowed map flatter on the table.

Liz looked puzzled. "I know he'd explored the Southeast coast. The islands and keys around Florida. Long ago he'd been down in Central America. Is it a boat?"

"It says 1857."

"Well, it wouldn't be the Spanish fleets. He had some interest in the Civil War, the East Coast, too. Dave and Nelson took a trip up the Atlantic, as far as Charleston, I think, maybe to Wilmington? That was back in...what? '87? '88? They used to dive off wrecks. Maybe it was one of those."

"That was after I started visiting y'all. Would Dan know?"

"Maybe. I know Dave would have liked to continue getting venture capital and outfitting another expedition...but I made him stop going after investors. I didn't want him selling pipe dreams. He could be very persuasive. You know how his eyes could light up when he was describing finds. Sometimes his imagination got away with him. He had a lot of charm, your father. It wasn't fair, I didn't think it served him well, when...well, he embellished some of those stories; let's leave it at that. I made him promise he wouldn't start another treasure-hunting expedition. I didn't want to move around and we had a good life here," Liz said. Her eyes looked troubled. Since the funeral, she looked drawn. Lines around her eyes seemed to have deepened, Mel thought. She was talking to herself as much as to Mel, it seemed. And she was speaking of her dad in ways she had not heard Liz do before.

"But he still liked to explore."

"I never heard him talk about this one, or if he did, I can't remember," she said. "Maybe you should ask Dan. Do you trust him?"

Liz looked at her, searched her eyes.

"I think so. He and Nelson went their separate ways on treasure hunting, I know that."

"Would he remember if they searched for that boat? Dave had some newspaper clippings in his office. Do you want to try to find those? There are a lot of papers I haven't gone through. It might take a while…"

"Well, we've got the charter set for two. I'll look later. The map's the best place to start. So you don't remember anything about this one?"

Liz shook her head.

"Do you want to go with us?" Mel asked.

"Darling, I just want to take a nap. Michael and his wife just took a taxi to the airport, and I was relieved. If I had more energy, it might be fun to get out on the water. Or at least a diversion. But I'm tired. Call me when you get back. Let me know what you find."

Relief. Mel glanced at the clock. She was meeting her mother and Aunt Sandy at the docks. Adding Liz would have slowed things down. Did she even have time to call Dan?

She gave Liz a peck on the forehead. Liz squeezed her hand. "Go. You'll be late. I'll be fine."

Folding the map and putting it in her bag, Mel picked up her keys and left. The words on the map "Use caution" written in small script on the side near their destination had left her feeling a little rattled. She wasn't sure whether it applied to the trip itself, where they were heading, or what they might find. She tried calling Dan before she pulled out of her parking spot but he didn't answer. She left a message.

Mel was a few minutes late arriving at the charter boat. Both her mother and Sandy were standing on the sidewalk outside. They looked hot in their shorts. Aging hippies, she thought, her mother's conversion to earth mother a done deal and Aunt Sandy, who had called herself "artsy fartsy" from time to time, always the artist, stood there with a scarf tied through her hair, geckos on her shorts, a loose tank top covering her bathing suit. Mel did not apologize for the time it had taken to park and walk to this location, even if her mom looked exasperated. Besides, Dan had called her back when she was on her way to the docks; he remembered a steamer found in 1988 that Nelson and Dave might have been pilfering. Talking to Dan had slowed her down, too. She did not mention this as they boarded.

The slightly freckled woman with dark hair, their captain, looked somewhat familiar, but Mel couldn't place her. Probably someone she'd met with the guys years ago. She looked to be maybe twenty-six or twenty-seven? Certainly not in her thirties, Mel decided. Mel took in the young captain's dark tan and her almond eyes, her appearance somewhat Asiatic looking, but then those freckles. A distinctive mix, but Mel just couldn't place her. Mel gave general directions to the young woman.

The captain, introducing herself as Lydia Morrison, was attentive to the older women, cordial to Mel. The older women were excited about having a female captain, making small talk as they left the harbor and Old Town behind. "I just got my license for one hundred gross tons," she told them. "I'm working for this outfit until I can get a position piloting one of the large yachts, or go commercial up in Miami."

"Young pretty woman captain for a private yacht owner—that could be fun," Sandy said. She spoke everyone's thoughts. Good ole Aunt Sandy. "Don't see many female captains. Does anyone give you a hard time?"

"You can thank Gloria Steinem and Betty Friedan," Debra piped in before their captain could answer. "All the feminists who paved the way. Back when we were your age, it was a man's world."

"It still is in many ways," the young woman said. Sandy stood up front with her watching the boat cut through the water. "I've been on the water over ten years, crewing, being a first mate, and, yes, some mariners gave me a hard time. Not so much anymore. If you're good at what you do, you earn respect. And I am."

"You're confident. I like that," Sandy said.

"You're talking to a couple of women's libbers," Mel said. "They pushed books on me when I could barely read. Mom dragged me to an Equal Rights Amendment rally in Raleigh when I was what? Twelve?"

"You loved it," her mom made a face. "Admit it."

"Even dragged Grams to that rally for the Equal Rights Amendment."

Debra beamed. "We marched together. I was so pleased my mother went. The three of us."

"It was defeated, anyway," Mel said, realizing a hint of cynicism had crept into her voice, and added, "But you made a convert of your mother."

"She even read one of Gloria Steinem's books," Debra directed at Sandy. "That one you gave me, *Outrageous Acts and Everyday Rebellions*. Remember swapping those back then?"

Sandy nodded. The captain made a turn that made them all hold on. Slowing to bump over a wake from another boat, they again picked up speed, well away from the harbor now. After Mel got a bottle of water, she joined her mother who had just sat down at the back of the boat, both of them watching the wake of the boat, the white waves forming a V blending into a moving sea and the wakes of other boats. Debra whispered, "We think we saw her with Nelson a couple of days ago…and today we thought we saw Gene at the harbor."

If her mother did see Gene, what would that mean? Mel paused at the reference to Nelson. Maybe that's why Lydia Morrison seemed familiar. Had they picked the wrong boat?

When they were well underway, along what was still the Intracoastal Waterway, headed somewhat northeast in a big arc, Debra asked where they were going precisely. Mel replied, "To a little island, or key, I guess they're all called, near Marathon."

The boat bumped over the waves of another boat.

"Couldn't we have taken the highway, gotten a boat up there?"

"No," Mel replied. "Dan gave me this charter's name, said they were reliable. Enjoy the ride, Mama."

She gestured toward the big open sky, a few puffy white clouds, the expanse of water. Actually, she had not paid attention herself to the smell of fresh salt air, the sultry smell of primal energy, nor the angle of light, intense, so far south. She was reminded of her younger days, more carefree times, time that seemed to stretch out before her forever then.

"It is relaxing," Debra admitted.

Mel was a bit worried about the connection between the captain and Nelson, now, but it was natural that if Dan knew her, Nelson would, too. She decided not to keep thinking about it. Nothing she could do about it now except stay alert. With the folded map, Mel made her way to the front of the boat. After an hour on the water, the captain slowed the boat and Mel showed her where, off Marathon, the island with its few homes was located on the map. "We need to get to the other side, the west side," Mel said.

Lydia looked down quickly at the map and back at the water ahead of her. "I know those islands."

"You do?"

"I've been up here before."

"With Dan?"

"No, Nelson, his brother. I took him up here a few weeks ago."

"Doesn't he have a boat?" Mel asked, studying the captain's profile.

Sandy, still up front, was paying close attention to their conversation.

Their captain Lydia, looking at her directly with what appeared to be an honest and open gaze, said, "He didn't want to use it. He thought he would be followed."

Sandy, across from the captain, raised her eyebrows and looked back at Mel. Mel wondered why this woman would be telling them about another client, even if they did know him. She and Jeff kept their boarders', their horse trainers', their riders' business to themselves, even when it involved the same horse. They remained tight-lipped.

"I think Nelson was in over his head," Lydia volunteered.

"How so?" Sandy spoke up. She was ever the direct one, Mel thought, for better or worse.

The boat was moving slowly now, under bridges and into the afternoon sun glaring down into their faces.

"I don't know what was on the key, Nelson wouldn't tell me, but he was scared. That man Gene. The one worked with their stepdad. Black market dealings."

"Gene Sherman?"

"The one. He brought some unsavory characters with him to talk to Nelson another day. I saw them."

"How do you know Gene Sherman?" Mel asked.

"You don't remember me, do you?" Lydia said. "Remember those beach parties? With the boys? I was a kid, fifteen, maybe; y'all were older. I used to hang around. My brother was friends with them. Never liked me tagging along, hanging around—but there were several of us, and I just got lost in the crowd. You and Dan used to go off. My brother had a crush on you. That's why I remember. You were down for the summer."

"Oh," was all Mel said. Now she sounded like her mother. One syllable. About all she'd spoken the past two days around the others. Until yesterday. She looked back to see if her mother was listening. She wasn't. She was looking back, hair whipping around her head, no hat, glints of gold and copper waving in the wind. Watching the waves or something behind them.

"Gene?" Sandy asked.

"Dave, Gene, the boys, we'd see them out in the boat. Or Gene over at Nelson's house. He was friends with their mother, I thought," Lydia said.

"Well, what happened when you and Nelson came out?" Sandy asked.

"We turned around."

No one spoke, so the young captain added, "He thought someone was following him, and I don't think he knew for sure which of the three little keys was the one he wanted."

"Why do you think it was something to do with the black market?"

"Nelson used to brag. He used to tell us he could make money any time he wanted with one phone call. He had contacts; he could sell stuff he'd found diving or wherever," Lydia said. "And sometimes he had a lot of money to throw around."

As if reading her mind, the captain said to Mel, "I'm telling you this because Dan recommended me to you. I know you lost your father. I'm sorry about that. And even if you don't remember me. I agreed to offer my services. I want to help. Nelson was in over his head."

They were heading northeast and Debra was facing forward. She beckoned to Sandy. Mel watched as Sandy made her way back; then she went herself.

"There's a boat back there following us. Even if it's only a speck, it's been sticking to us like white on rice."

Mel heard the words, squinted into the distance, sunlight sparkling off moving waves. She went forward, got the binoculars and returned, to point them in the direction her mother had motioned towards.

Once she had the distant motorboat in the dark circle of her telescoped view and she focused the lens, she saw two men, one with binoculars directed their way, and then quickly removed. Maybe he had seen her. But she recognized Gene Sherman, with his grey hair, hardened face, at the wheel, steering. The other, was he a man she'd seen at the funeral?

"What are we gonna do?" Mel heard her mother ask, but she didn't reply. She had to think. All that came to mind was, "How did I get in this mess?" Her husband and children were all waiting on her to return, Jeff needing her at the barn—he'd sounded stressed when they spoke after the road trip to Sugarloaf that morning—and she was headed towards who knew what. Leslie cried when she'd said she wasn't coming back today. To be back home where she belonged. That's what she wanted. Not all this confusion. A break in routine certainly put things in perspective, even if it offered a respite from the daily demands of home life, but she had had enough of emotion. Sadness. Grief. Confusion. Now fear.

"Is there any way to lose them?" Sandy asked.

"Do they know we're even looking for Dave's storage? How would they know?" Debra looked from Sandy to Mel.

Sandy replied, "Gene is shrewd. No telling about that other man. If Nelson said something…. What else would we be doing out here?"

"Wasn't Bahia Honda State Park about twelve miles from Marathon, by road anyway, when we were looking at the map? We could act like we're going there," Debra suggested.

"I could take you there," the captain offered. "Sightseeing."

"Too far back," Sandy said.

"That's near where they found Dad."

"How about Marathon itself? We act like tourists?" Debra added.

"I could drop you off, circle back. How many need to go to this place, anyway?" Captain Lydia spoke over the engine's roar.

Sandy and Debra looked at Mel. Suddenly, it was on her. Finding the map, her father's last adventure-joke-whatever-it-was, had reminded her of the fun he had invented for her, back when she visited as a teen, hiding things in shallow water they could snorkel to. That had led later to their own searches, hers and her stepbrothers', and to surprises and even to a few moral dilemmas. But this was no longer a lark. Four women tackling two men—none of them were prepared for confrontation with these guys, not capable of it if it turned physical, nor even sure what they would find. But if these men were following them, whatever they were seeking must be something valuable.

"Who is a strong swimmer? Any of y'all?" Lydia asked. "I could let a couple of you out. Could we pretend we still have four on board if we did it fast?"

"I've got a hat we could tie on that seat, prop it up, sit there myself awhile, slumped down. Slide out the far side? They wouldn't be able to see anything but the hat above the edge of the boat," Sandy offered.

Debra smiled at her. "That's quick thinking, you spunky gal. You are very good at this connivin' game."

"That only accounts for one."

"Maybe we just need to see what's in there first," Mel said, hesitated. "But I should be the one to go. It's my responsibility. I've got the map. And the key."

"Does it matter?" Sandy asked

"I've got several of those dry bags in that locker over there," Captain Lydia motioned with her head.

Debra took the binoculars from Mel. Lifting them to her eyes, she started to wave at the men idling their skiff, and thought better of it. Mel grabbed the glasses back. She gave her mother a stern look. "Not funny."

"They're on to us," Debra pointed out.

"Well, I'm willing to swim, if it helps. I swim every day, almost, year-round in Hawaii."

No one could think of a better plan, except to give up and try again later. The captain sped up the boat and curved around one small island, then slowed close by one with a bridge before heading for a third, the one marked on Mel's map. The hat was tied to a shirt stuffed in a chair, and Sandy stripped to her bathing suit beneath the outfit she had worn.

Debra looked at Melody. "Do you want to go? We'll have to find a getup for you, too, stuff something near the captain?"

Mel hesitated. Only one person would cause less suspicion, but who knew what might be on the island, or in the building indicated on the map, a small cottage beyond what appeared to be bushes or trees and a big house? She didn't want to go, but she didn't want the guilt trip her mother would lay on her if she let Sandy go alone. She wanted, instead, to go home and braid her daughter's hair. She would never be too busy to fix Leslie's hair again, or follow Jack looking for crawdads in muddy patches by the creek. And Jeff, if she could love on her man one more time, instead of put her life at risk following some ridiculous game her father had set up for her, she would never complain about mucking stalls again when one of the teens bailed out. Never. Maybe her father had been a con artist and this was another strange scheme of his, but she had to follow through, get this over. Maybe Dan was right. He had called her dad a control freak once, and she had gotten mad at him.

"Honey, you look a million miles away. We have to hurry if we're going to do anything," her mother told her softly.

The boat had passed by the key and continued moving before circling around two of the small islands. Could she hold her breath long enough to reach the dock, where Sandy had suggested they could hide under the boards, make their way to the shoreline rimmed in bushes?

"Better hurry; they'll be around here soon—" Sandy pointed out.

In water no more than fifteen feet deep, the captain slowed the boat. Sandy slipped over the edge and was immediately underwater swimming towards the dock. Mel rolled over the side, slipped into the surprisingly chilly water, and followed Sandy. Opening her eyes in the salty water, she was able to see her ahead. Surprising herself, Mel reached the first piling before she had to gasp for breath, her lungs burning. Sandy was bobbing under the shadows of the short dock toward its land end. Melody took a quick look back. Her mother and Lydia were already gone, following the game plan to dock at Marathon, ostensibly to get gas, Debra to go get four cokes and act like nothing had happened. If anything went wrong, Sandy had suggested a backup plan, but Mel hadn't been listening by that point. All her mind had done was spew images of her children in front of her; then once the plan was set, all she could focus on was getting out of the boat and making it to the tiny island without getting caught.

The small motorboat carrying Gene and that other man puttered into view. Sandy had already reached the shallow end of the dock and was crouching under its dark shadows, only her eyes and nose above water, lapping at her face. Mel joined her, staying underwater until it was too shallow and she felt hidden in the dark. Looking back from their dark hiding space to see the boat move east to follow the others, they waited, but the boat did not return.

Sandy, in an abundance of caution, whispered, "Let's stay under water 'til we can get to that bunch of branches over the water. Make sure we're safe."

Sandy adjusted the dry bag hanging from her neck, ducked back under water, so Mel had no time to offer an opinion. She, too, ducked under the planking, salt water stinging her nose. Her earlier dread had now been replaced by excitement, perhaps adrenalin fueled by fear. If a fifty-year-old could do this, she could, too.

Under some bushes hanging over the water, she stopped. Climbing out of the water, scratched by branches between the waxy leaves, she followed Sandy. Once they could stand hidden in the shrubs and trees, they could see the pool and house of an estate beyond a clearing.

"Let's be careful, Sandy," Mel whispered. "Even if the boat can't see us, we don't know what the setup is here. Dad's note on the map said 'use caution'."

Nodding, Sandy pulled a plastic zip-lock holding the folded map out of the dry bag. They studied the map closely. Unlike storage units Dave had used for his finds, this one seemed to be part of a little house. Sandy got their bearings and crept toward a cottage through the bushes. Mel followed, her tender bare feet finding every stick or rock it seemed. Still hidden in bushes, Sandy stood close to the front of the cottage, which seemed very exposed. She turned towards Mel.

"Do you think there's a back door?"

Mel thought Sandy didn't look as confident as she had on the boat, her bravado drained in the reality of trespassing and the possibility of getting caught.

"I think this must be the yacht manufacturer's property. He was a close friend of Dad's and had a place up here," Mel offered, hoping to get that look off Sandy's face. "I remember the guy coming to the house a few times when I was there. I remember he and Dad talking about a vacation house up near Marathon."

"I hope so. Not one mad investor."

"Of course not. Dad couldn't put his loot in an enemy's property. It would have to be a friend. If we get caught, I'll just explain."

"Okay, but I don't wanna get shot."

They scraped along the edge of yaupon bushes and trees, but there was no back door. Looking in a few windows, they thought the cottage looked empty. It appeared to be only a two-room cabin, a guest house. Sandy tried the bathroom window. After hitting the wood frame a few times, she got the window to budge, got her fingers under the window frame and pushed up.

"Hoist me up," Mel said. "I'll go first."

Partway in, she felt the stifling hot, musty air of the little cottage. She braced on the window ledge with one hand and put the other atop a porcelain toilet tank. She wiggled her butt halfway through, her torso like a caterpillar lifting up for a leaf or an inchworm lifting its front half, waving for a leaf, the kind her mother had said when Mel was a child was measuring her for clothes, whatever part it landed on: hands, gloves; her chest, a shirt—what a silly thought.

She heard Sandy laughing behind her. "What a view."

"I'm stuck. I'll land on my head if I keep going." She worked her way back out backwards. "Should I try feet first?"

They jimmied another window open, this one opening to a bed below, and Mel tried the same wiggling and worming way to work her upper body into the room.

"Push," she managed to mumble back at Sandy, who obliged with a mighty heave of Mel's feet and suddenly she was plopped face down on a bedspread. She had hit her knees on the sill and winced with the pain.

"I'll get something you can use to get up," she said, turning to see Sandy's face peering at her from the bottom of the window.

Crawling over to the edge of the bed, she sat up and looked around. Small bedroom, closet door, a door to the living room and kitchenette open. After looking around inside the cottage, she found a kitchen chair narrow enough to get through the window. Sandy climbed up and in, as glamorous a spectacle as she had been.

"You look like one of those inchworms, you know the green ones, or a caterpillar wiggling through that window."

Elbowing herself across the bed, Sandy gasped, "Yeah, right, except unlike a caterpillar, I won't sprout wings."

Sandy sat on the bed and pulled the map back out of the bag where she had returned it. She examined it a moment. Mel stood there waiting.

"Okay. I think," she said, looking out at the front door, and back into their room, "that closet is what we want."

Mel turned the knob. The door was locked.

"Try the key," Sandy said, pulling it out of the wet bag.

It worked. Mel found the light switch. It didn't work. She could see the closet had a small safe with a dial lock. "That must be what these numbers mean," Mel said, pointing at the numbers on the map Sandy was holding.

"Are you good with combination locks?" Sandy asked.

"Yeah, let me try. Dad always had those on storage units, places he didn't want us to explore," she said and paused. "I got pretty good. Nelson and I used to check what Dad had hidden. Dan was a fuddy-duddy. Refused to go with us. But I always liked to explore."

"You got that from your father," Sandy smiled. Mel thought she was trying to make it sound okay, not judgmental, but she caught the flicker behind those eyes. Just like her mother. Neither one had liked him.

"Well, let's get this over with," Mel said. "Can you read me the numbers? There's enough light out there."

She followed the numbers as Sandy read them out to her from the doorway, using the light coming through the windows. When the door opened they were both shocked. Six gold bars sat in the safe.

"Is that—gold?" Sandy asked, incredulous. She was peering over Mel's shoulder.

Mel picked up one of the ingots. Heavy. Solid. Stamped on it was "1857." An envelope sat in the back of the vault.

"It's Dad's," she said, opening one note folded inside. "It reads 'From the SS *Central America* California shipment. Found off Cape Hatteras, sunken side wheel steam freighter, debris scattered sixty miles from discovery site.' He's got the longitude and latitude right on this note."

"What should we do? If it's his...."

"Here, it says, on this second note, 'Hayman safe and contents stored on the property of Alberto Romero with permission'. See both their names on it."

She showed the paper to Sandy, as though that dispelled any wrong doing, being on a stranger's property, trespassing. Sandy looked at Dave's scrawl, and the signature of another, with a notary stamped on it.

"He was being careful," Sandy said, "I'll give him that."

"How much are those worth?" Mel asked, and before Sandy could answer, "Can we carry it back; will all those fit in our bags?"

"I don't have any idea about the price of gold; it's not something I run into every day," she replied with a smile in her voice, and in a more serious tone, wondered aloud, "Why didn't he mention it in the will? Or that map?"

Mel frowned. "Liz didn't know about this."

She looked up from the safe and into Sandy's eyes. "It was a secret. From her."

"So that explains why he didn't put it some place safe and simple—like a bank vault," Sandy said. "Well, let's see if we can carry this."

Heaving one of the bars in her hand, she said, "This is way too heavy to carry it all swimming. We could carry one each? We've got the extra dry bag stuffed in this one."

Under the gold was a rental contract for the cottage, held for the last twelve years, dated 1988. "This cottage is rented by Dad; it says so here."

Behind the bars in the very back was a small box; she opened it to find gold coins. Mel handed Sandy a couple of coins. Lady Liberty was on one side, an eagle on the other, and all were dated 1857.

"Not golden doubloons. These were minted in California," Sandy said.

"During the gold rush?" Mel asked. "I'm starting to remember Dad talking about a lot of gold minted in California and a ship full of gold minted out there coming up from Havana; it sank in a hurricane in the Atlantic. He was always telling such good stories about shipwrecks and such. I never knew which stories were real, and which were legends. He even searched for gold along the west coast of Florida. Said treasure was buried by pirates all along those islands. He could certainly spin a yarn."

Mel continued, "I talked to Dan about this before I got up with y'all today. He knew Dad and Nelson were trying to find treasure off the Outer Banks, a ship loaded with gold that sank. Some other outfit laid claim to the discovery, technology for deep water Dad didn't have, but he and Nelson claimed they found something along the Gulf Stream. I had a vague recollection of one of their tales, Nelson's story he told me one time. I'd never thought much about it. I'd forgotten that, so long ago. In fact, Dad's story about some golf course workers finding treasure caught my fancy more; these guys were working on building a new course, and then three of 'em disappeared and a hole the size of a small chest, with wooden fragments in the hole, was found the next day—that story sounded more intriguing to me at the time. Pirates captured my imagination more than deep water technology and all that."

Sandy hefted the metal box. She was focused more on the logistics than the memories. "We need to get a move on. The captain said they'd come back in an hour."

"What about those men? If we try to carry some of this off…"

"We'll have to come back with another boat, get permission from the owner first. There may be someone staying on the island here. They'll see us if we walk out on the dock, or if the boat is out there waiting."

"Well, I'll just explain I'm Dave's daughter."

"Take the contract for the rental, at least. That's got both names."

The two women chose a few gold coins, a bar of gold, stuffed those in the dry bag, and then the contract and map into the plastic zip-lock. Mel put the zip-lock in the bag. She closed the safe, locked the closet, and put the key in the bag.

"This is heavy," Mel said.

"Want me to carry it?"

"Nah. I lift bales of hay. Bags of grain. I'm strong."

"Can you swim with it?"

Mel made a fist and pumped her arm up to show muscle. The comic relief allayed their jitters. She was glad Sandy was smiling. Her anxiety about getting back to the boat was making her stomach queasy. After Sandy climbed back out the window, feet first, feeling her way towards the chair below, she lifted the chair up. Mel pulled it through the window. She didn't waste time taking it back to the kitchen and exited feet first, Sandy guiding her towards the ground, steadying her. Both windows closed, they crept back through the brush.

Back near the landing, they waited in the bushes but saw no boat. More than an hour had passed by now. Still no boat. Mel, who had felt nervous throughout this ordeal, thought it was a bit too much adventure for her taste, now that she had children to consider; now it seemed like pure danger. Had her own father really anticipated this? Expected them to do this? Have strange men pursuing them and have them being stuck on a stranger's property, an island, no less?

Sandy was squinting into the distance, trying to manufacture a boat out of thin air it seemed.

"Sandy, do you think Dad expected us to follow his map like this? I mean, out here on an island with Gene and that other man looking for us? Surely he couldn't..."

"No telling what he was thinking. His mind worked differently from mine, I know that. I don't think he expected to die, at least not so soon, so this was probably not the final plans he expected to make," Sandy said, still looking out over the blue green waters.

"You didn't like him, did you?"

Sandy turned, shadows and sunlight dappling her face, to look at Mel. "The truth? No."

"Mom never talked about him. Neither did you, but I minded not hearing about their life together, what it was like when we were a family. What he was like when I was little."

"Your father put your mother through the wringer," Sandy replied. "He was a self-styled adventurer, and that part was interesting, even fun. He could make things happen. I think Debra liked that. But he was an alcoholic, Mel, and he bilked a number of people, investors, all that. I think it was a scary time for your mother, with him.... And without him, well, she was a single mom raising a kid. That's hard, you know. My mother did it. Being poor is not fun. Even with your grandparents helping, she had a struggle. I know she felt overwhelmed at times, trying to do right by you."

"But why did Mama never talk about him? She always changed the subject when I brought him up."

"You need to ask her that yourself. I'd say she didn't know what to tell you, or didn't want to deal with the pain, probably, at first.... Later, I think she didn't want to ruin him for you, let bitterness or anger poison any memories or ideas you formed. Instead, let you make your own decisions about him or not get your hopes up."

"She let me go visit him. Let me go down to Florida.... Still she wouldn't talk about him."

"Only after she had cleared it with Liz, had some understanding he was sober and had changed. Or so we thought."

Mel looked out over the water beyond the bushes. "I think this is Nelson's doing, this pursuit from those men, having to hide. I don't think Dad would have wanted this."

"Well, if the gold's from a boat Nelson helped search or something, maybe he thinks he has a legitimate claim. I don't really know." Sandy had turned back towards the water. "Golly, I wish they'd show up. They should have been here already."

"It won't get dark for a few hours. What do you suppose happened?"

"I don't know. If they don't come in another hour, we need to make another plan. I saw a sailboat, a small sunfish. I learned to sail with the Wahine Sailors in Hawaii. Maybe I could get us over to Marathon?"

"That really would be stealing."

"Got a better plan?" Sandy sounded a little testy.

"Maybe we could see if anyone is at the big house? Explain ourselves? I'm tired of standing around here in my bathing suit."

Mel realized she sounded a little whiny. "Guess we can wait a while longer here."

Sandy turned back to her. "Mel, when I was talking about your dad...he did love you, you know. When you were just a toddler, I remember him holding you, and he always cared about you."

"I felt that, somehow, even if my memories are few," she was saying when she saw Sandy's face change.

A man's voice from behind her shocked them both. "Who are you? What are you doing here?"

Chapter 28

The charter boat bumped across the wake of another boat, plopped into a trough and then bounced across waters choppy from the cross winds picking up. Debra wasn't one to get seasick, but her stomach was churning and her chest felt tight. They had circled several islands after they had dropped Mel and Sandy off, and still she could see the other boat following from a safe distance. Once they reached the marine fueling station, Debra felt enormous relief. Only on dry land could they get some help. Do something besides bounce around the water with those sharks following, like a Jimmy Buffet song come to life. *Fins to the left, fins to the right.* The lyrics in her head made her smile, but she didn't like being bait.

The captain had slowed down a few times, like she had done letting the two women slip overboard, to try to keep the guys from knowing what they were up to or where the others might be if they figured it out. Debra thought they had done a good job fooling them. Her job now was to go get four Cokes as though they were all there. She'd make a phone call from a pay phone if Melody's cell phone wouldn't work. She looked back, and Gene's boat was closing in. They were like sitting ducks. The captain was pumping gas. She, too, saw the men approaching. Her face was as non-expressive as a good poker player, Debra thought. And her own? Well, her hands were shaking and when she stood up, her legs felt weak. The small motorboat pulled up beside them. Idling. Exhaust fumes hit her nose.

Debra put a smile on her face, as fake as a dime store ring. "Hello, Gene."

"Where are they?"

"No 'hello, how are you'?" Debra stalled. "No gentlemanly how-de-do?"

How dumb and Southern could she sound without sarcasm dripping off her voice?

"You boys been following us awhile," the young captain said from the pier.

"We're just out for a joy ride," Debra said. She had learned how to flirt once upon a time. Maybe it was a fallback position for stalling until she could think of something to say or do. What would Marilyn do? she wondered, then considered that Marilyn Monroe could have flirted with a chair, not Debra. Somehow, Debra hadn't expected them to come up, hadn't talked with Captain Lydia about what to do. Gene grabbed the side of their boat. The other man was scowling from the cockpit. Gene's sweaty face reminded her of —

"Cut the crap. Where are they?"

"What's it to you?" popped out of her mouth before she could clamp it shut on the words.

"Look, lady. We had a deal with Nelson, and we plan to see it through," the stranger said.

"What kind of deal? Nelson is my daughter's stepbrother, of sorts, but I don't know him personally very well, and whatever deal you made doesn't involve us."

Gene cleared his throat. His sunglasses shaded his eyes, but she knew they'd be beady ones on her, like in some cheap paper back thriller. Oh, hell, why couldn't she think of anything to do instead of seeing this like some story she didn't belong in?

"This man here had a deal with Nelson. Nelson backed out. Nelson owes him bigtime."

"For what?" she asked, feeling a little steadier as she looked down on him. She stood taller than the man holding on to their boat.

Neither man spoke.

Finally the stranger spoke gruffly, "Just tell us where they are. Where the gold is."

The captain had not paid for the gas yet. She stood on the deck.

"Gold?" Debra said, knowing she looked genuinely surprised. Because she was. "You need to take that up with Nelson. I don't know about any gold."

The sun was hot. The breeze over the water did not cool the boat, collecting heat in the afternoon light.

"Just tell us where they are, Debra," Gene said. "You've got to get them eventually, and we can wait you out."

"This isn't legal, is it? You holding us hostage? Stalking us?"

She knew they were in a public place, safe unless the men did something foolish in front of the marina staff and customers coming and going. She looked at the stranger. The stubble on his face was peppered with grey. His scowl and his grizzled face made him look like a jailbird. His shirt, unbuttoned and open, revealed a weapon, a pistol, in a holster slung on his hips like a bad guy in a cheesy Western when he pulled back the shirt a few inches. Uh-oh.

"Are you trying to intimidate us?" Captain Lydia spoke loudly.

A man hosing off his boat looked over. He stared a moment, then resumed hosing. Another boat pulled up to refuel.

"I've got to pay," the captain said, pulling out her wallet. She turned and walked away.

Debra looked back at Gene, then the man driving the boat, without saying a word. Finally she spoke. "Gene, you've managed to stay one step ahead of the law all this time. You want to risk it now?"

Gene's eyes were covered, but she knew him well enough from years back to know she got to him.

"Show us where he stashed it, and nobody gets hurt," the driver growled low. Now it really was a bad movie.

Debra realized she had to pee. She had been holding it so long, it dawned on her, that if she didn't go now, she'd lose it.

"I gotta go tinkle," she said. "Can we discuss it when I get back?"

"You wait until that other woman gets back. One of you stays here."

"I gotta go," Debra said. She clambered over the side of the boat onto the dock.

The captain was returning. "I'll move the boat over there," she said in passing, pointing to a free space where mariners could dock temporarily. She said it louder to the two men. Debra kept walking fast, cellphone in her bag, and made it to the "gulls" door in time, no waiting.

After relieving herself, she tried the phone. No luck. Maybe she could duck into the little store and ask to use their phone. Opening the bathroom door, she was confronted with Gene, standing outside in the hot sunshine. She heard the roar of the boat before she saw it. Her captain was zooming out of the marina, making a wake that rocked boats on both sides, the other boat following, bouncing over waves.

"Shit," Gene said, staring out at the speeding boats.

"Shit's right. Up shit creek without a paddle," Debra said, also staring in the direction her ride had gone. What was Lydia doing? Would she come back? Was she going to give the girls up?

The two of them stood on the dock of the marina, saying nothing. Gene clenched and unclenched his fists.

"Well, there's nothing for us to do but wait," Debra said as nonchalantly as she could. "Want a Coke?"

Gene took his glasses off and rubbed the bridge of his nose. Put the glasses back on. "I'm sorry about all this."

Gene's words surprised her. He continued, "I didn't want to get involved. I put Monroe up with Nelson two years ago. They had some sort of deal worked out. Nelson asked him for an investment, after he sold Monroe some gold coins, then some bars. He said he could bring up gold if Monroe would front him the money. He said he'd trade bars of gold. I only hook up dealers with sellers. That black market trade. I didn't know what this guy was really like. Nelson sold his share of gold to Monroe back then. Said there was more."

"His share?" Debra asked. She walked over to the drink machine, fished around for change.

"About a quarter million."

The can clunked on the bottom of the machine.

"Dollars?" she said incredulously. She pushed the lid down and took the cold drink from the dispenser. "Here, you want one?"

Gene, looking hot and rattled, took the can. "I don't even have my wallet on me."

"I've got more change," she said, picking more quarters out of her bag before she spoke again. "Dave and Nelson had what? Over a half million?"

"About that," Gene replied. "Or more. Nelson said Dave may have been holding out on him about how much was brought up and how much it was worth. Nelson told Monroe he and Dave had brought up bars of gold off an Atlantic coast wreck over several months."

"I thought he got out of all that."

"You knew Dave. He couldn't let it go."

"Seriously? He told his wife he was out of treasure hunting."

"He was for a while. After Hurricane Andrew he was too busy with salvage. Before that. Big find off the Outer Banks. He couldn't resist."

She put the second can of Coke to her forehead before she opened it. The chill of the wet can cooled her hot head. "Let's sit down. We may be in for a wait. I could call Dan to come get us. I've got the number."

"No. Don't do that." Gene, who was spilling the story, seemed relieved. "Maybe Monroe will come back. I'm tired of this. I'm too old for this."

She sat on a bench outside the store. Gene sat down beside her, gulped down the drink. "Thanks. I needed that."

"This man, this Monroe fellow. Would he use that gun?" she finally asked.

"Shoot one of them? I don't think so. He's pretty irate, but from what I can tell the gun was for show. He just bought that holster; I was with him right after he got it. I told him not to bring a gun."

"Still, men with guns..." her voice trailed off.

"He's full of bluster."

Debra wasn't so sure, but there was nothing she could do about it unless there was some sort of marine patrol that could find them. She didn't think Gene would go for her calling them. She was pretty sure she could identify the island. She would wait and see if their boats came back. If the captain could lose him. Or had Lydia abandoned them? She decided to change the subject.

"So...Dave was still treasure hunting?"

"Just that one find. A big one. Some outfit out of Ohio he got wind of in the mid-to-late '80s, using advanced technology in deep water. He and Nelson were sniffing around. Nelson was just a boy. Teenager. They found gold outside the debris field. A hurricane had sunk the ship before the Civil War, a steamer loaded with gold. You know what a fool for those stories Dave was. I was down in Panama at the time. He'd researched this ship with a bellyful of gold sinking off the Carolinas. He felt that Ohio group stole his idea. But he didn't have the resources for exploring so deep. And he was trying to go clean for Liz."

She gave Gene a sidelong glance. He was older than Dave had been by several years. That put him, what—maybe in his early sixties or so? He did look tired.

"So, just that one last haul?" Debra prodded.

"Yeah. Nelson was so young, he hadn't figured out what it was all worth. They found several bars of gold. Neither one would tell me how many. Also, coins from the California gold rush. The two of 'em sold coins on the black market. That's how he financed some of his projects. Nelson, that is."

"What about the…" She hesitated. Maybe Gene didn't know about the old rifles or muzzleloaders or whatever that stuff was in the trunk they had found that Sandy claimed looked like Civil War relics she used to draw.

"The what?" Gene asked absently. He looked at his watch.

"What about this gold? Why did he keep it so long? That was more than a decade ago."

Gene shrugged. "Saving for a rainy day? Who knows. Besides he couldn't let too much go at one time or Liz would find out."

"Up to his old tricks." She tried not to sound bitter, but Gene picked up her tone.

"He really loved you, you know."

She said nothing.

"He thought he could…could make things right. If he had something for his daughter someday. That's probably what he intended. He always felt he got cheated. Short-changed. Cut off from you two like that. But he did mention making it up to Mel more than a time or two."

"Well, his will was pretty explicit," Debra said. "Gene, what really happened to him? They said it was a heart attack, but I wondered."

"You'll have to ask Nelson about that."

"Nelson? I thought the Coast Guard found him."

"Ask Nelson."

Gene stood up. He walked to the edge of the dock, peered out, turned and sat back down. "Maybe we should call somebody. I don't know if that girl—"

"Captain Morrison," Debra said primly. "Our lady captain seems to have taken off and she's not coming back."

"Can't blame her. Think she'll give you your money back?" Gene made a feeble attempt at humor.

Debra got up and checked the clock. "It's nearly five o'clock. Everyone will wonder where we are. My daughter's out there somewhere. And Sandy."

"Where exactly?"

Debra shrugged. "I have no sense of direction. We turned around sight-seeing. You know me. You remember how turned around I used to get."

Gene took his glasses off and rubbed the bridge of his nose, again, squinted at her with bloodshot eyes. "I know you're shrewder than you let on. Dave had to give you credit for that. When you took off without a word." He chuckled. "Dave was so pissed you got off the island. He couldn't figure how you pulled that off. Until the money was missing."

"He was drunk all the time. How would he know?"

"Well, that sobered him up."

"Tell me how he died. The bump on his head."

"No. Don't ask again. It was a heart attack. He had a heart attack. Ask Liz; she'll tell you that."

"Well, what did Nelson have to do with it?"

Gene stood up. He looked irritated. He moved to the edge of the dock and peered out.

"Well, why did y'all follow us today? Why did you think we would lead you to something?"

A small skiff was coming into the marina. On board were her daughter and her best friend. The tight knot in her chest untied itself as she took her first deep breath since this all had started with sighting the men behind them. A young man with a pony tail, maybe early twenties, steered the skiff to the dock. Mel was waving happily and Sandy was grinning.

"What's he doing here?" Sandy was asking as soon as she reached for the cleat to pull the boat to the planking.

"We got a ride with the caretaker. He and his girlfriend live on the island. He found us hiding in the bushes," Mel said, giving her mother a big hug.

Her exuberance surprised Debra.

Sandy climbed out of the boat after the caretaker tied up and she stepped onto the dock. She introduced the caretaker, Todd, to Debra and pointedly ignored Gene. Debra saw that the dry bag they had taken with them seemed empty. She said nothing except, "I'm so glad to see y'all. I was getting worried. We lost our captain."

"We saw them go by," Sandy said. "Our boat with just the captain. Then only that one guy in the other boat. Like a Tom and Jerry cartoon. They passed again going the other way. That was before we ever left the island. I gave her our sign. Then she did the thumbs up."

What sign? What thumbs up? Debra wanted to ask, but Gene interrupted her thoughts before she could speak.

"Where were you? Which island?" Gene quizzed.

"Does it matter? We were just sight-seeing," Sandy said. "What happened to you? Get tired of boat riding?"

"She took off without us," Debra said, "When our chaperone here decided to follow me to the ladies' room."

"Did you call Dan? Or Liz?" Mel asked.

"I never got a chance. Gene and I've been reminiscing about old times."

"Let me call," Mel said, giving her mother a severe look. "Someone can come get us."

"Your phone doesn't get reception here," Debra said to Mel's already retreating back as she opened the door to the store.

"I'll use their phone."

The young custodian reached up from the skiff and shook hands with Sandy. "See y'all."

"Thanks for the ride. We really appreciated it."

With Gene standing there, Debra did not ask if they found anything, but Sandy looked pretty smug, like the cat who caught the canary. Mel, coming back out, said, "He's on his way. Captain radioed in."

"To Dan?"

Debra knew she looked surprised.

"She radioed her charter company. One of the guys called Dan for her."

"So Dan can take us all?"

"Unless you wanna let him walk," Sandy said, glaring at Gene.

"Nelson, when he heard Dan got those messages from me, he told Dan what these guys were up to," Mel said. She gave Gene a withering look.

Gene, watching her pace back and forth in front of them, put up his hands. "I just made the connection. I wasn't part of this."

"Then what are you doing out here?" Sandy snapped. "It looks like you're in it to me."

"The guy's mad. Monroe feels he got swindled. I owed it to him to help...but he's a hothead. I didn't want—I wanted to keep an eye on him."

"That's mighty decent of you," Debra said sarcastically. "Now you tell me. A hothead with a gun."

Chapter 29

"So Dave was still in the black market? Still involved..." Liz was saying. She sat at her patio table, early evening falling over the water, the darkened lawn, shadows flickering among them in the light of tiki torches.

"He had been. I don't think he was getting investors, or anything like that, for wreck sites, but what he already had, he was holding on to these last years. Maybe not dealing anymore. The boat we were talking about today, that search was in the late '80s, and Nelson...." Melody was looking at Liz carefully.

"I found clippings," Liz said. She had a couple of yellowed newspaper articles. She placed them on the table.

Sandy watched the exchange closely. They had decided to tell Liz all they had learned from Dan that afternoon. Mel wasn't mincing her words; she flat-out told her. It had been a long day and Sandy was tired, but Melody had insisted they come over after they cleaned up. So here she was with this scene playing out before her, the boat adventure and discovery of the day already discussed during supper. Sandy, following the emotional dialogue, found her thoughts were straying back to her room and a phone call she'd received after they returned from Marathon that afternoon.

When she had reached her room, she had needed to recharge her batteries, calm down. She had wanted to get centered, grounded, after a too eventful day. Her chanting and meditating had always been sporadic, yoga breathing while moving had engaged her more fully in the moment than meditation, but there wasn't time for much yoga. Sandy had had a few minutes to meditate in her room, do her deep breathing and *"om"*s, even *"nom myoho renge kyo"* from an intermittent practice she had followed in Hawaii, after first being introduced to it in Wilmington long ago, when her phone had rung.

Nick's voice was on the other end. She was enveloped suddenly in this warm and heady sound of a voice once so dear to her heart. It was not quite the same feeling she had had the time he called her in Hawaii three years earlier on her birthday. Suddenly time and space disappeared. She was somewhere between here and there, the present she was no longer anchored to and the past she couldn't quite bring forward, suspended midair. His voice out of the blue back then had unmoored her, but today when he called, it was not the shock it had been then, since she had left a message at his office, but still...

Sandy snapped back to the present with three women sitting at a table in front of her, torchlight flickering in the breeze, her jade figurine standing serenely on the table. She had grabbed the goddess at the last minute, wrapped her in her old, soft cotton shawl she'd bought decades before in a Guatemalan market on the trip through Central America with Carrie and Stan to Honduras. Warm light danced on the green jade goddess. Debra was examining one of the newspaper clippings. The other two women were still talking.

"When Dave was found past Bahia Honda Park," she heard Melody saying, "he was headed to the island, they think, and this man, Frank Monroe, Gene's contact, this man who got involved, the one pursuing us today, had tracked him down. Nelson had some sort of deal with him, but Nelson couldn't follow through. The guy thought that if he followed Dave, he could locate the gold Nelson had promised. Dave was going out there to check on it. Nelson had looted another storage unit, so Dave was checking. He didn't know he was being followed at first. Nelson did and had gone out after them. Then Dave must have realized something was up, confronted the man on the water. They scuffled. Nelson said he saw Dave double over and clutch his chest, he thought, before he fell back when the boat rocked with that man getting off."

"Nelson was there?" Liz stared at Mel.

Mel nodded and continued, "He had gone after this Monroe fellow and that's when he saw them fighting. He got there just after the guy took off."

Mel hesitated. Would she tell Liz all they heard today? Sandy wondered.

"Nelson was there. Yes. He got to the boat; Dave was still alive. Barely. Nelson didn't know CPR. He panicked, he said. He said he called the Coast Guard. But he didn't stick around. He didn't want to be implicated. But Liz, Dad was already gone, Nelson said, when he left. It was massive. His heart attack. You said the coroner told you..."

Melody let all this sink in. Sandy and Debra looked at each other, unwilling to look at Liz. Finally Liz spoke, "The little coward. He was following this man? And Dave? And he saw Dave die?"

"Apparently so."

"Poor Dave."

Mel continued, "Dan said Nelson confessed when he found out we were going out there. He saw Dan's messages. Nelson had followed Dave months before and knew the general whereabouts of this stash, but not its exact location. But he was following Monroe, to stop him, he said, when he caught up to Dave. It wasn't the blow to the head, falling back on the boat, he'd thought it was at first. Now we know Dave had had that massive heart attack."

After a moment, Liz said, "Well, there's no point in telling the police. I don't want to drag this out any more than we have to."

Debra was looking down again at the clippings of the *SS Central America* discovery, fingering them. She looked sad, pensive, tired. She looked up and spoke.

"Well, that explains Gene going out there with him today. He didn't want a murder on his hands if that guy was crazy enough to—" Debra began and stopped. "He was being his most charming, his version of it, when we were sitting there waiting. I've seen him be cut-throat and nasty, but that explains why he said he was sorry. He didn't mean for today. He meant for getting Dave dead; I think he thought his getting that man and Nelson together contributed."

"Nelson freaked out after that. When Dan came today, he said Nelson kept saying how sorry he was. He did not mean for that man to attack Dave..."

"And Nelson was there when he died. He wasn't alone," Liz murmured, her voice sounding wistful.

"Liz," Debra spoke softly. "He died where he loved to be. On the water. He always loved the water. Blue sky above, blue water, white sand below."

Maybe, Sandy thought, Debra was saying this as much for herself as for Liz.

"I didn't know him as well as I thought I did," Liz said. "Still enthralled with gold. Chasing dreams 'til the end. I got him to go as clear of it as I could. Even asked him to return this figurine to you. He told me about it, how he'd taken it from that man leaving the island where you all were diving, the man who sued him later, and he told me you had found it originally," she said, looking at the goddess, then Sandy, "but somehow I didn't feel it was right to keep her, and I kept telling him he needed to make things right with Mel. And with you, Debra."

Sandy knew it. The scumbag didn't come up with all this good-hearted change by himself.

"He must have resented me," Liz exhaled in a whisper, "Keeping him from something he loved…"

"No, Liz," Mel said firmly. "You must remember he was happy with you. Why, I remember seeing you together, laughing and joking, every time I came down. Y'all were a good team. I think being sober was too important to him, and he had the salvage business, plenty of action there, and he was good at it. He built a good business. And it was still on the water, and with boats."

"But…searching for treasure…"

"I don't think Dad was still treasure—I think Dad did give up treasure-hunting expeditions for you, Liz, and he did try to go clean of it. The Atocha thing—Mel Fisher's big find—got him all riled up, but really, he didn't put any more ventures together, investors, after the mid-'80s. But diving on wrecks, it was in his blood. So salvage kept him solving problems, going down in the water…"

Mel was starting to ramble. Sandy guessed she was as nervous telling Liz as she had been upset hearing the story herself from Dan. Mel seemed to be floundering, so Sandy spoke up. "Liz, Dave didn't do anything he really didn't want to. I knew that much about him. Those gold pieces and those gold bars, those were from over a decade ago, and it was something he saved for Mel, apparently. Or mostly for her."

"He always loved the water. Diving, salvaging. And he was still doing that," Mel insisted, trying to reassure Liz.

"And he didn't have to worry about lawsuits," Debra added. "Those weighed heavy on him, keeping him wound up and mad when he was harassed by angry investors."

"And he was not dealing with Gene's contacts; that was Nelson," Mel stated firmly.

"Dan told you all this today?"

"Yes, when he came to get us."

"The captain had radioed in and one of the guys at the charter company reached Dan on the first try. He was already on his way when Mel called him from Marathon," Sandy explained.

"That's why the captain never came back," Debra was saying. "She had to get the boat back by six. She and Sandy here—" at that point she patted Sandy's hand and smiled— "had cooked up a plan. You tell it."

Sandy, glad to move off the subject of Dave, and of Liz's reconciling of facts, a confrontation with the image of the man she thought she'd lived with and the one he now appeared to be, said, "We were hoping to lose the guys, but if things went awry, which they did, we had signals. The divers' okay, the thumbs up or down if we could or couldn't talk. If we got on land, or some of us did, we knew we could get back, even by taxi. Thumbs up meant she was free. So when she was passing by our little key, right before we got in the skiff with the caretaker, I popped out at the side of the boat shed and gave her the okay sign; she saw me and signaled a thumbs up before I ducked back behind the trees. That creep didn't see us. We were too fast for him."

"And too smart," Debra added. "I wasn't paying attention when they were talking, something about Channel 16, I could barely hear from the back, and all that hand signal jive I missed entirely. So I was flummoxed a while."

"So where did Monroe go?" Liz asked.

Debra shrugged.

Mel spoke up then. "Dan said he followed the captain partway back to Key West, then realized he was bamboozled. Gene was long gone by the time he came back. If he came back. We dropped Gene off at his motel. He and Nelson will try to work something out with him. It could cost Nelson years to pay it all back. Or sell the real estate he bought to pay it off. The boat captain called Dan after she got to Key West to make sure everything was okay."

"So you reached Alberto Romero? The number worked?" Liz asked Mel. "I forgot to ask about that."

"Yes, and he was getting in touch with the groundskeeper—that's the guy who gave us a ride to Marathon—to let him know it's okay. Mom and I are going back out in the morning," Mel said. "But we're taking Dan's boat. He's already got it hitched up and we'll take off from Marathon."

"And I'm going to sleep in," Sandy added. "Let these two ladies collect their loot."

"We've got some decisions to make," Debra said, looking at Mel. "What to do about the authorities and the gold, or if we even have to deal with them."

And now Sandy had the goddess and a decision to make herself. A few of them, actually. She had talked to Nick when he returned her call; he was excited about the relics she thought were from the Civil War era. He wanted to come down to see them. Down here in the Keys. When she had asked if that was a good idea, he told her he'd been divorced nearly three years. That meant when he had called her that time in Hawaii and she only talked to him long enough to hear him say she was the love of his life...that meant he was leaving that other woman, the mother of his children, the girls raised; he'd fulfilled his obligations.... Her thoughts were interrupted.

"Mom's taking the car back to Westwinds tonight. I'm staying here with you," Mel said to Liz. "We'll get an early start, and if you feel up to getting out, you can come, too; I'd like that. Enough of staying here, among all these memories. It will do you good."

Sandy was impressed with how tender Mel could be, how sweetly she'd hugged her mother earlier at the landing and a couple of times since.

"I've never been to Alberto's island," Liz said. "I'd heard about it from Dave. "

Liz looked weary. Her hair, down from the twist she'd put it in for the service, was loose around her face and made her look softer, more vulnerable somehow. She kept patting her chest as they talked. Sandy watched her hand move back and forth from her throat back down below her collar bones.

"It's time we go," Sandy spoke up. "You have a big day ahead of you. And I'm bone-tired from this one."

Sandy and Debra made motions to leave, clearing the plates and glasses from the table, Sandy wrapping the figurine back in the folds of her multicolored shawl, the two gathering their things, saying their goodbyes. Leaving Liz and Mel behind, they headed to the car and back to the inn. They were walking in the evening shadows and Debra headed towards the courtyard.

"Let's sit out by the pool a while," Debra said. "Tired as I am, I'm not ready to go to bed. It's only nine. Besides, you haven't told me about that phone call, and I want to hear."

Sandy sighed. Debra picked up one of the glass covers around a candle on a poolside table, struck a match, and lit the candle. She blew out the match. The smell of sulfur wafted on the night air momentarily. Sandy watched her sit down and joined her.

"You seemed off in another world tonight," Debra mused. "You looked like you were in LaLa Land for part of this evening."

"I was. Nick returned my call. I called the Raleigh office. I suppose the coastal underwater division at Fort Fisher could have answered my questions...but..." She looked at Debra, the glow of the candle warming her face and eyes. "You look pretty in that light, by the way. A little tan looks good on you."

"Thank you, darlin', now go on. What did he say when he called back? This the first time y'all have spoken in nearly three years, right?"

Sandy nodded. "Well, he wants to come down here to see the guns."

"And you."

"And me."

Sandy looked Debra in the eyes, those brown eyes that took in her own, those warm eyes that through the years looked on her good days and her bad days and were still here for her after all these years, and looking at her now.

"Well?"

"I told him I wasn't sure it was a good idea. But, Debra, he said he's been divorced nearly three years."

"Really? Meaning when he called back in '97..."

"Really. The divorce was final in '98. He didn't say the mushy stuff he did that other time. When I told him I was seeing someone and not to call anymore. Back then, he called four or five times, left messages on my machine...but I never called him back."

"All these years."

"He must have been thinking about it, but he didn't say he was separated when he called me in Hawaii. Lucille had finally given him my number. And now he says he might be retiring; golly, he's been at that department more than twenty-five years. He was so ambitious, I would have thought.... Anyway, he can take a few days off to check those artifacts out. I told him we'd be here through next week. I haven't decided what to tell him about coming down..."

"You want to see him, don't you?"

"I started to ask him about the goddess, but I guess I could call down in Honduras or Guatemala about jade pieces."

Sandy ducked the question and Debra didn't pursue the answer to that question which had been distracting her throughout the evening. She was grateful.

"You thinking about returning her?"

Sandy leaned over, pulled the shawl-wrapped goddess out of her bag, put her on the table, fingered the features of her face. Debra picked her up, stared at the little figure in the candlelight, the distant night light of the pool area faintly adding to the candle's flame dancing with the night breezes stirring the palms.

"She truly is beautiful," Debra said. She put the jade goddess on the table where light played on the translucent edges of the carving.

"I feel comforted by her presence," Sandy said, "like I did all those years ago.... But would you go to Honduras with me if I found a museum or appropriate place for her? You've got money, now."

"Yes, I've got money from the will."

"What'll you do with all that moola?"

"I won't quit the library, that's for sure. They let me have these two weeks off. Part-time hours all covered. But I may set up my pottery studio, buy a new kiln. Build a good space—one with heat. If I get enough done before Christmas, I might join the studio tour, local artists in Chatham who open their studios and sell artwork. People tell me they love my work. Not just a hobby, I could make it a small business." At this, Debra smiled. "Mel told me she doesn't think I'm too flakey to run a business."

"Of course not. You kept your little family afloat on low-paying jobs and lots of grit all those years."

"But my parents helped—the farmhouse they gave me when they moved into retirement. That was a boon. I think Mel resented our living on the edge so long."

"Mel may give you a hard time, but she sure loves you," Sandy said.

"I've learned a lot watching her grow up, learned a lot about myself. That's one of the things our children are good for—checking on our priorities."

"Today had to be tough on her. This whole week. Facing up to...well, the whole ordeal."

"She has that warrior spirit," Debra said. "She really gave Gene a piece of her mind on the way home."

"That she did. What will she do with all that gold?"

"I hope the right thing. We need to find out the legalities, the ins and outs of it all. "

"Dan's been a big help. He's taking time off to help y'all tomorrow?"

"Perks of running your own business. It's all his now. Mel said he and his wife will be checking on Liz, including her when they can. She was a second mom to him. More reliable than his own mother. Did you know Barb and Gene had an affair? Learned that after we got back."

"Gene? Really?" Sandy couldn't imagine. "Gross."

"It takes all kinds. She knew a little about the *SS Central America*; that's why she felt her sons were entitled to more. But I don't think she knew what Nelson was really up to." Debra looked at Sandy. "Mel and I were talking a little while you were resting in your room. I told her her father was the love of my life; I never admitted that to her before. She told me her first love was Dan. I had suspected...but there are some secrets you just don't want to know. I'm glad she told me. I'm glad she didn't tell me when she was seventeen. Now I know it all would work out okay—back then I would have been crazy worried. But she says her big love is her man. And Jeff's a sweetheart. Good with her. Good with horses. Good with his children. A really good father. She chose well…. And me? I'm glad Dave gave me Mel. I wouldn't trade that for the world. He gave me a run for my money. But I never would have seen Honduras, or met you, if I hadn't been with him. Now I'm happy on my own, free of all those worries, the compromises a relationship entails. I felt I was swallowed, my own personality buried. I love the peace and quiet of my own life. And you, your big love was Nick, right?"

Sandy nodded. She looked at the green jade in the candle glow. "I never loved anyone like I did him."

"Then you should let him come down, Sandy."

"We're braver in our youth, leaping into love, risking..." Sandy began, then added, "I've finally found my footing in Hawaii. Cartography is my bread and butter. My art..."

"You keep dodging the question here. You've put a wall around your heart. Even if the spark is gone, you have a connection with this man. Our friends can be hard to find, the ones who get us, ones we really can love. Who love us. You know whatever way it goes, you'll survive. You're strong."

Sandy nodded. "Maybe you're right. And yes, I have kept myself apart. Maybe the childhood upbringing, maybe my idealism, maybe fear of closeness. Always searching.... I used to be looking for the next adventure, the next interesting thing up the road, the next party. When I was with Nick, I realized I didn't have to go find a party; wherever I was, that's where the party was. And before I was always moving to find that still point where love resides."

Always in motion to find that still point where love resides. Always in motion to find a place of refuge from the storms in her heart.... She picked up the jade goddess, rubbed her thumb across the smooth stone, then set her down again. "And it's been here all along. In me."

"You just have to be still enough to find it," Debra said.

"That's the big secret we each have to discover. It's in us, the love, the contentment. We're not really alone. It's not all out there, in externals to make us happy..."

"But they help," Debra said.

They lapsed into silence. Debra stared at the candle encased in the glass. Sandy, watching the light moving on the little goddess, finally spoke.

"I'll call him in the morning. Is it all right with you, if he comes down for a couple of days? Our vacation..."

"Of course, Sandy, it's okay," Debra said. "I've got books I haven't opened since we got here. I brought Maya Angelou and Barbara Kingsolver along. Reading at the pool would be relaxing."

"Well, you'd be with us, too, I'll be glad for your help...it might be awkward."

"We'll see. I'd say I'd visit Liz, but I don't want to talk about Dave anymore."

"The trunks are there."

"A short visit, then. The gold will be put in a bank vault until Mel figures out what to do."

"I've had lots of time to think on this trip, reconsidering my choices, whether they were good ones, all the memories this trip has stirred up…. But we wouldn't be where we are if we hadn't made mistakes, and maybe they weren't. They all led us to who we are now. It works out for the good in the end. Life's lessons, like you've said, some we keep circling back around to learn again and again in a different form. Mine, I think, has been to learn I can make my own way; I'm strong enough. And I can love, and I can exist without love. I won't flip out the way I did back then. I've mellowed, I think."

"We're both waxing philosophical," Debra said.

"Profound. Very profound."

They both burst out laughing. Then Sandy spoke again.

"Yeah, all these discoveries. Like this goddess, sitting here. We don't even know who made her, how she got to the bottom of that bay off of Honduras. I thought I'd keep her. But I don't want bad karma taking a goddess to the islands. Hawaii has washed my soul clean, all those island breezes, my spiritual quest to pay homage to the goddess, when she's inside us all the time. We have our own goddess within, to honor—our own divine selves."

"What a lot today has revealed, Sandy," Debra said. "Lots of secrets came out. I think Liz will recover from learning about secrets Dave was keeping. Mel kept her secrets. I kept my secret, that Dave was the real love of my life, even from myself. I think I was afraid to face it. And Dave kept his own secrets."

"Do you think keeping secrets is the same as lying?" Sandy asked.

"I don't know. I don't know if not telling a truth is the same as telling a falsehood. Secrets everybody keeps.... We don't have to share everything to be loyal to a friend or partner."

"I think we are entitled to a little privacy. Not share everything. Do you think Dave lied to Liz? Or do you think he just didn't tell her?"

"Either way, she felt deceived."

"When Liz may not be feeling so sad or vulnerable, she may be glad she stood her ground, and realize Dave respected her for it," Sandy said.

"Despite Dave keeping secrets, she will remember the love. I'm content with the memory of a great love, but you — you deserve to have another shot."

"I don't know what will happen with Nick. The future is that great mystery, keeping its secrets. Only to be revealed with time."

"But we create the future, Sandy," Debra said. "The choices we make, the causes and effects we set in motion. We've both learned we're strong, in whatever form that takes. Strong enough to face whatever comes. And love lights the way. We can see the way ahead; love will be there.

"You're a romantic at heart." Sandy smiled at her friend.

"Well, so are you, honey," Debra replied. "Let that love light shine."

Sandy and Debra fell silent, the conversation having reached its end. While they sat in quiet reverie, staring into the candlelight, the two friends both grew peaceful watching the blue and gold flame of the candle flickering beside the jade figure. The goddess sat serenely on the table between them, keeping her own secrets.

Acknowledgements

Thanks go to Bonnie Ferguson for her enthusiastic encouragement with this project, though she did not get to see it in print, and to Shelia Rudesill for her support throughout the endeavor. To my copy editors Hatsy Nittoli and Nancy Donny, and my design team Bud and Shelia Rudesill, I offer my grateful appreciation. My thanks go to Molly Luby for reading the first few chapters of the first draft and offering her opinions; to Sherry King for her information on her artistic career and an underwater archeology project; and to the Writers Potlucks where creativity was shared and ideas about writing were swapped. I offer my appreciation to those who provided feedback along the way. My thanks go to friends through the years who shared their lives, their stories, their laughter, both those dear friends who have gone to start the party on the other side of the river and those still here to enjoy. Thanks go to all the friends who encouraged and supported this novel's creation and publication; you were a blessing. I am thankful for family who shared childhood memories with me. I am grateful to all the writers whose works opened worlds for me to explore, kept me company, and sparked my imagination. I am also thankful for my years as an English instructor and the opportunity to teach literature which allowed me to share many authors' works in great detail.

I would like to acknowledge *Mysteries of the Ancient Americas*, with Joseph Gardner as project editor; and *Fort*

Branch Survey and Recovery Project, from NC Cultural Resources, from which I drew ideas and details to enhance parts of the story and background. I am indebted to the internet for providing portals to the past and to the greater world at large without leaving my living room. Many websites, including ones on treasure hunting, Spanish Galleons, charter boats, and even custody laws, were searched and webpages on numerous topics provided additional details to lend authenticity to this fictional story. This story is not intended as historical fiction so events that may have occurred, like a ship sinking in 1857 or a fleet of Spanish ships traveling the Caribbean, are not to be construed as accurate historical records, but merely triggering points for imaginative creation.

The font is Palatino Linotype, designed by Hermann Zapf. First punchcut in metal in 1950, it was then adapted for Linotype machine composition. It is a highly legible typeface based on classical Italian Renaissance forms and the font was named for Giamattista Palatino, a master of calligraphy from the time of Leonardo da Vinci.